The Mountain: Book One of the Jomsskari Report

Ike Barnett

DEDICATION

To Zach

Chapter One

Humbridge, West Banks, the 1156th Year

The rain fell steadily. It fell in big, tepid drops, pattering off the looming boughs of the forest. There was a flash of lightning in the distance, and a while later the overcast sky growled in reply. It had been raining all day, and the darkness of night closed in. It was almost entirely black.

The boy was only about seventeen. He crouched in a shallow hole he had dug for himself in the mud, his eyes peeking out from beneath his steel helmet and cloak. He was soaked to the bone, his feet blistered and his eyes bloodshot from fatigue. The moisture penetrated everything—the top of his head, his shoulders, his socks. His boots sank into the mire beneath him, borne down by the weight of his equipment. Beneath his cloak, he had strapped just over two hundred rounds of ammunition, several grenades, water, entrenching tools, bayonet, a few tins of potted meat, and his last two packs of dry cigarettes wrapped meticulously in a leather pouch. He held his rifle carefully, nervously stroking the wooden fore-grip and running his thumb over the fire selector, flipping between semi- and fully automatic. The rain ran over the weapon and beaded on the underside.

His name was Erik. He had been born in a dusty corner of a poor convent outside the Industrial District. Erik had never traveled further than thirty miles from his home in Havenstead, until his enlistment. He had secrets he didn't dare speak of, he liked books, he thought too much, and had dreams unattainable for his station. Sometimes he laughed at jokes he didn't get, just because everyone else was laughing, and he had never loved a woman.

None of that mattered now. His past and his future were irrelevant. Now, in this singular moment, every particle of his being was focused on the woodline before him. Something was wrong, but he didn't know what.

The boy moved suddenly, wiping his nose and leaning back against the wall of his foxhole. He blinked a droplet from his eyelash and huddled deeper into the mud. Despite his discomfort, he was alert, listening intently, his gaze darting fruitlessly from black to black.

Behind him, over a hundred men, four to a tent, slept their share of the night. Some were awake, writing or reading letters, while others studiously cleaned their weapons. It was the first watch, and the boy was not alone. Spread out along the perimeter, his comrades lay quietly in their holes, watching the dark shadows of the night sway back and forth in the rain. The steady noise made everything sound silent.

The boy suddenly raised his weapon, lining up on a lumpy shadow in the miry brush thirty yards out. With his supporting hand he waved, then indicated his eyes. His comrades glanced over and began searching their fronts. It was too dark to see anything.

Finally, one of his buddies crawled out of his hole and ran, crouching to him. "What is it?"

"I smell something."

His friend wrinkled his nose. "You smell something. Like what? What do you smell?"

Erik scanned the underbrush and didn't reply at first. Then, "Like an…old broom. You know, really musty, not like rain."

His buddy remained crouched above him, and shook his head. "Man, I don't see—"

A single shot rang out. There was a sickening *splat* and his buddy staggered as though he'd been struck. Slowly, almost in slow motion, his weapon fell from his grip, and he gurgled softly. Around the perimeter, trumpets began to blast. The forest erupted into tiny pricks of light, and then the boy saw a dark figure rising from the shadows, moving forward—a muzzle-flash appeared and the boy heard a loud *snap* and felt wind by his ear. He felt a strange—he squeezed the trigger, his gun barked and the burst caught the figure in the chest—it toppled, began to scream, and writhe—*snap, snap,* two more rounds passed close by—the boy stood up slightly and fired another shot at it, and it lay still.

The snaps were coming faster now, and he heard the punchy staccato of goblin machine-guns nearby. Around the perimeter, dust and fire rose up together as grenades flew from the dense tree-line into their positions. Mud leapt up as heated lead ricocheted around. But it seemed quieter, somehow. At first the gunfire was deafening, but it suddenly seemed almost tranquil. Erik picked another figure, running, and fired a few shots. He didn't see if he'd hit it. The trumpets sounded again, and an unearthly wail filled the air to the north. The gunfire crescendoed. The goblins were charging.

Erik could hear the men scrambling into position from the camp, amid shouts and commands. His buddy was still upright, kneeling on both knees, held in position by the weight of his gear, as though praying. He was gurgling, blood bubbles burst at his lips, drooling a thick, steady stream of viscera onto his lap. Erik fired another burst and turned to pull him down in the hole. Then a sound like a loud cymbal crashed in his ears, earth shaking, and a bright light—*no sound*—illuminated behind his friend like a horrific halo. The force of the blast threw the corpse into his face, and his head struck the wall; a sanguine stench filled his nostrils and, an instant before it was all dark, he wondered why he felt no pain.

*   *   *

It was almost 0300. Kolskegg sen Gunnar was tired and sore from the day's march, but it seemed that rest was not an option. After four hours of sleep, he had been called to the command tent. He shuffled across the camp, belt undone and shirt unbuttoned, tucking in his undershirt and muttering curses as he went. To the north-east, the storm-clouds were heavy, but here, his path was lit by the half-moon. As he began to button his shirt he noticed a bleeding cut on his hand. *Where did that come from?* he wondered. It was weird what details he would miss when he was in the field.

Tightening his belt, he arrived at the command tent and saw that there was fresh tea brewing. S*mall blessings, at least.* He grabbed a tin cup from the table and helped himself. The command tent was made from a thick, heavy canvas that was supposed to be waterproof, but leaked like a colander. Fortunately, it was not raining, not yet, at least. There was an improvised table in the middle, made from a few planks and a barrel, with a map of the surrounding territory set upon it. Kolskegg drew closer and, nursing his tea, began to inspect it.

They had been in the Belvade River Delta for nearly seven weeks now, and in that time, he had become very accustomed to the maps of the area. The nomadic goblin tribes in the foothills of A'kaylii had banded together against Humbridge, rushed into the halfling's rich farmland, and were making a royal nuisance of themselves. They were killing cattle, burning villages, pillaging, looting, and generally making a mess of things. Goblin raids were nothing new, but this time the goblins bit off more than they could chew. When they seized the Belvade River Delta, and all the lush grain fields that the rivers and sublets of the delta nourished, they had ruined the year's wheat crop. There was an immediate uproar. The Alliance existed to ensure trade security between the four nations. So when the goblins attacked Humbridge, they attacked not only halflings, but the elves of Iaelia, the dwarves of White Mountain, and the men of Haelhan. The goblins were in over their heads, and were paying dearly.

From the map, it looked as if the Iaelians had finally gotten into the fight. The north end of the delta had small icons representing Elven clunker companies swarming south-east across the Belvade. They looked like they were headed to begin their assault on Cyddustead itself, the only real municipality in the country.

Meanwhile, the Haellic forces were consolidating south and pushing east, presumably to cut off the goblin's access to the sea by boat and force their retreat. But there was one infantry company that was a few miles north of the rest, uncharacteristically isolated. The terrain looked like heavy forest, and there was a goblin tribal element directly to the east, at the first crossing. Kolskegg's company was only two miles south, and two more clunker companies were coming in to reinforce his current position.

I bet we're going north to reinforce that infantry, he thought, and breathed the tea vapor into his lungs. It was cheap tea, weak and pale, like everything they got in the field, but it was welcome so early in the morning. He wrapped his hands around the tin mug and turned as several men entered, talking quietly among themselves. He stood back in deference, but did not salute. Their commander, Sir Harold Knight of the Northern Foothills, was among them, but they had learned quickly that to salute an officer was to mark him for snipers. It had become such a problem that many officers had traded in their fancier clothes to wear the common uniform of their subordinates. It didn't stop officers from getting hit, but it did stop the goblins from choosing them above others.

Sir Harold waved his captains in and they gathered around the map table. Among them was Kolskegg's captain, a lean half-elf named Thjostolf sen Skarp-Hedin. Thjostolf was, at first glance, an unimpressive man, wiry and just under six feet tall, but Kolskegg knew him well enough to know better than judge this wine by its bottle. Thjostolf could carry his scout load of three stone at a fair clip and fight with it, never asking for a break and never wavering. He looked like he'd gotten only a few hours of sleep as well, but he didn't go for the tea. He looked over the map and pursed his lips, running a hand over his braided head. It was dirty and tangled, but he didn't seem to mind.

Sir Harold waited until everyone had gathered before beginning.

"All right, friends," he said quietly; there was a somber lilt to

12

his tone. "The 107ᵗʰ Fusilliers, about one-hundred-twenty men commanded by Sir Lief, sent its last runner to us fourteen hours ago at this location. They reported heavy rain and were holding their position until 2200 hours, at which time they had planned to pack up and head south to this location," he pointed to the map, "On the west bank, where we would join them in two hours. However, they have not sent a runner yet, and our runner, who I sent to check their condition, has not returned. Our scouts have reported that they are not at the rendezvous site, either. I believe Sir Lief may have come under attack and may need reinforcements. We are moving to assist them. If they are not in position there, we will attempt to follow them and conduct a link up at their current location, wherever that may be.

"Thjostolf Captain, prepare your company to reconnoiter their last known position and track them. We will follow at seven hundred yards. If there's an ambush, I want plenty of time to assess the situation before engaging the enemy. Clunker commanders," he went on, addressing the other officers in the room, "Be flexible and set your formations accordingly. We may be assaulting a fixed position, or we may be assuming a defensive position. Make sure your crews are clear on the situation, your signalmen have their pipes tuned and flags set, and be ready to maneuver into whatever formation is required. Jorgi Captain will divide his company and provide flank security for my clunkers. If there are no questions, all of you may go. I want to move out in twenty minutes."

That's not good, thought Kolskegg as he drained the last of his tea. Seven hundred yards was particularly cautious; that meant that Sir Harold suspected a superior force out there.

As the officers began to leave, Sir Harold called Thjostolf back. Kolskegg lingered, and the knight waved him over as well. "This concerns you, too," he said.

Sir Harold pulled a pipe from his pocket and started to fill it. "Thjostolf Captain," he said, and then paused. "I received a runner earlier today with a packet of orders for you. Your bravery and competence have not gone unnoticed these past months. I assume you know that I've commended you both by name to the King?"

Thjostolf nodded. "Yes, sir."

Kolskegg glanced over and thought, *I didn't.*

Sir Harold continued. "It seems the Alliance is preparing a special unit. Njal General has ordered you two to report back to Brandstead Castle as soon as the new scouts arrive tomorrow. They want you to join them."

Thjostolf nodded again. "I hear and obey, sir." He didn't say much, and Kolskegg didn't blame him. Royal commendations were one thing, but these Alliance units were usually feck-ups for cross-training purposes, meant to give some administrative pencil-pusher a job. They had been to several already, training with the Elves for ambushing and the Dwarves for alpine fighting. Kolskegg didn't mind the idea, at least during peace-time, but it seemed wasteful to trade out a skilled captain in a combat area just to cross-train him. It was insulting to be pulled off the line, hardly befitting the honor Sir Harold implied. *I wonder who we're with this time*, Kolskegg wondered.

Sir Harold dismissed them and as Kolskegg loped off to gather his gear, Thjostolf caught him. "Get our boys together and meet me at the north nests," he said. "Feckin', we have fifteen minutes."

"I hear and obey, cap," muttered Kolskegg. "I'm going to lose a canteen and get more ammo, okay?"

"Yeah, this sounds like a fecking ambush. It is what is it, yeah?" Thjostolf said over his shoulder. Outside, Kolskegg could hear the clunkers gearing up, their engines rumbling like steel monsters, and the tell-tale squeaking of their suspensions as round after round of cannon ammunition was loaded into their turrets. Clunkers were rolling fortresses. Constructed of thick armor, driven by rumbling diesel engines that drove heavy treads and spewed acrid smoke in their wake, they each carried an artillery piece, and machine guns. The Haellics had learned how to use very few to spearhead an assault and overrun the goblin positions with speed and ferocity. But they were slow, vulnerable without infantry, and until someone figured out how to communicate out of their direct line of sight, they needed someone to screen their flanks, lest they be caught by surprise.

That was where Kolskegg and Thjostolf came in. They were scouts, Kolskegg a sergeant and Thjostolf, his captain. In a company of fourteen men, it was their task to run ahead of the clunker company and sweep back and forth, looking for signs of an ambush. It was a dangerous job, because if they found an ambush, they were usually outnumbered and out-gunned. As a result of this sobering fact, scouts tended to be silent and invisible. They moved in the shadows habitually and painted their faces with coal. Most wore black or dark green, and carried so much ammunition and explosives that even if they got pinned down without the comforting clunkers, they could fight their way to safety against a much larger force.

There was a certain amount of pride that came with the job, but everyone knew that the scouts were expendable. If the attacking force was too big for the clunker company, they would probably leave or hole up and try to wait for reinforcements. The scouts would be on their own, and five hundred yards is a long way to run under fire. Sir Harold's cautious addition of another two hundred yards was disconcerting.

*   *   *

When they moved out, the stars had only just begun to fade. It was the time of night when the sky had not yet begun to turn gray, but the moon had set. Sunrise was in two and a half hours, so the scouts moved quickly. Behind them, the clunkers rolled slowly, the infantry following behind like ducklings, using the clunkers armor for cover. The storm ahead loomed like a canopy, and in the distance

Thjostolf could hear the rain falling.

They reached the forest about the same time they reached the rain. There was almost no wind, but the worst of the storm had passed and now there was only a constant trickle of small droplets, almost a mist. Thjostolf waved his men forward. The clunkers made a lot of noise, so he wanted to get ahead. It made no sense to alert the enemy before the attack.

He crouched in the darkness and moved forward cautiously. Scouts used simple staggered line formations so that a single grenade couldn't take out the whole unit. Divided into two groups of six and led by Kolskegg and Thjostolf, they had spread the two formations out so they could flank an ambush. Practicality was paramount.

Thjostolf had put one of the more experienced scouts in front as the vanguard, and he was behind him. His vanguard stopped every few seconds to listen and look, and Thjostolf watched the right side. To the left, Kolskegg kept his men abreast with the captain's, and his vanguard moved so low that Thjostolf couldn't keep track of him. One moment he was a shadow against a tree, and the next he had simply vanished.

They were less than five hundred yards from the company's last known position when his vanguard raised his hand in warning. Thjostolf went down to one knee, watching the soaked forest carefully. A moment passed, and then a full twenty seconds. Suddenly the vanguard waved him forward. Thjostolf scuttled over to him and looked at him expectantly.

The vanguard indicated his eyes. *I see bad guys.*

Then he pointed straight ahead; then showed five fingers, then a fist, then an upwards chopping motion. *Fifty or more.*

Then he mimed touching a wall and rubbed back and forth. *Look fortified.*

Thjostolf glanced around. He couldn't hear the engines of the clunkers because of the rain, but they'd be too close soon. He waved the men in, and as they gathered he whispered, "Enemy, seven-hundred-twenty yards ahead of clunkers. Fifty to seventy-five, maybe fortified. Wait for daylight and better vision. Runner, go."

The designated runner, one of the younger bucks, nodded and slipped away.

By now Kolskegg had joined them. "Flanking position to the north?" he asked simply.

Thjostolf nodded. "Take your team left flank. My team will feckin' hold here and get set to mark the lines. When we pop the flares, lay down some feckin' fire discipline and take out their heavy weapons crews. Go!"

Kolskegg nodded and they vanished into the darkness. Thjostolf waved at his men to form on him and he crept forward, moving so quietly that his breathing rang in his ears. Ahead, he could see goblins moving back and forth among tents. It looked like Haellic positions. The tents were set up in orderly rows, and the goblins were wandering around calling at each other in the soft, guttural moans that characterized their native tongue. Thjostolf found a position a few yards into the tree line around the clearing, and his team spread out. Behind him, he could hear the ever so faint sound of the clunkers' engines idling. It blended into the rainfall perfectly.

Bastards; a company of clunkers are at your doorstep, and you're still patting yourselves on the back. He lay flat, behind a gnarled tree root, and slipped a flare out of his vest. His men had vanished into the murk, and the goblins continued talking amongst themselves. Thjostolf glanced back and forth. They were about thirty-five yards from the closest enemy position—almost close enough to make out facial features. He looked at the sky. They had about half an hour before daylight.

He had positioned his men oblique to Kolskegg's, so that the clunkers could hit the center without risking rolling over them over. Thjostolf was positioned at the south-west corner, and Kolskegg had the north flank covered. There was a slight ridge to the north, which improved their firing position immensely, while the forest provided good cover from return fire. They had the flanks covered; the only way for the goblins to escape was back east. It looked like the goblins had attacked mostly from the south, judging from the mortar holes and shredded vegetation. Thjostolf's position was in some low ground, but it was suitable. His team could put heavy fire on any attempts to flank the clunkers once they got close.

The sky was turning gray. A bird began to sing, and then another. As the world awoke, the clouds began to break, and a brief spot of dark blue, with the last of the stars, appeared above the foliage before it was covered again. Thjostolf could make out his targets now. Glancing to the sides, he spotted a few of his comrades and nodded, indicating the flares. They had theirs out, too, and nodded in return.

Behind them, there was a sudden roar of engines, and the crashing of vegetation. A few of the goblin sentries looked up, confused by the sounds, and then began calling out to each other. Thjostolf armed the flare and threw it into the first line of defenses. It popped and burned bright white, sending showers of phosphorous sparks into the sky. An instant later, the clunkers opened fire. With them, the eerie wailing of the bagpipes began to pierce the dense atmosphere, and the company drums pounded the assault. It was a terrifying sound, almost as terrifying as the sound of the 12-pound guns that had begun their relentless throbbing.

The goblins began to panic. Scattered bursts of fire issued forth from the first line, but the main camp seemed dazed. Thjostolf lined up on a sentry and methodically pressed the trigger. His target twitched, a red mist, effervescent and transient, appeared for the briefest instant behind his chest, hanging for a second in the moist air before dissipating. The goblin slumped down in the foxhole, and Thjostolf glanced back to see the first three clunkers, rolling in a line abreast, crashing through the thin trees. Their cannons roared, and the shell whistled for a moment before they struck the ground with a loud *thump*. That was what the explosions sounded like—deep, like heavy stones smashing the earth. The world trembled.

A goblin, wearing a Haellic helmet, leapt from his foxhole and began to run. Thjostolf heard his vanguard, stationed to his right, fire a burst just as he did. The goblin staggered, and then Thjostolf fired another burst. The goblin's helmet flew off comically, and he went down. Thjostolf rose to his feet. "Move up!" he shouted. "Cover the clunkers, right flank!"

In the chaos, his men echoed the command and began to move. "Right flank, right flank!"

The Haellic infantry were swarming over the positions, and the first of the clunkers had hit the first line of foxholes. To Thjostolf's right, another four clunkers were performing a flanking maneuver, trying to cut off the goblin's retreat to the east. Thjostolf ran; the clunkers had only a handful of infantrymen with them. Sir Harold had probably expected Thjostolf to position the scouts further south. One of the clunker commanders was out of the turret hatch, firing a machine-gun mounted on a swivel and shouting to his piper, drummer, and flagmen. He couldn't see his scouts and Thjostolf could tell he was worried about being overrun by goblins with satchel charges and grenades. His bagpipes began sounding to hold and the clunkers slowed to form a half circle.

Thjostolf's team reached the clunkers and as the rest of the scouts fanned out among the clunkers, picking off targets. Thjostolf ran up and waved to the commander. The commander waved back and grinned in relief. Rich or poor, it's always nice to have friends.

The southern side of the encampment was poorly defended, and Thjostolf could see many of the goblins trying to escape to the east. Thjostolf knew he was in Kolskegg's sector of fire. Stray bullets from the scouts on the ridge could take some of his own men out. He shouted for the team to move back, out of the fire, but the clunkers didn't get the message. They were taking a station on the south side, and looked content.

Up on the ridge, Kolskegg had seen Thjostolf's men crossing into their sector of fire, and. he wasted no time. He called out, "Cease fire! Cease fire!"

His men stopped shooting immediately and scanned their zones. A moment later, Kolskegg heard the pipes and drums changed to "Hold." The assault was over. It had lasted less than five minutes. The sun had not yet risen. Its head was just beginning to peak over the horizon, and the clouds had barely broken. The forest was still dim.

To the east, a few goblins ran for their lives, leaving their weapons in the mud behind them. Kolskegg lined one up and squeezed off a shot, but the bullet fell short. *No matter*. That unit was broken. Dozens of dead goblins lay where they had fallen, their gaunt, sallow faces twisted in expressions of surprise and pain, and the infantrymen were binding the hands and feet for any that lived. He turned to his team and called, "Face out, set a perimeter. Check your weapons and ammunition."

*   *   *

Dark. There was a swirling sickness, inside, deep in the stomach. Head. Hurting. Wet.

"Lift him up, careful…"

Dim lights. Throbbing. Mother? Tingling. Shoulders, ears hurt. Neck. I can't feel my neck.

"Is that his…are those…?"

So quiet.

"No, there's two guys."

"Who? Oh…feck."

"Gently now..."

Mother?

"Watch it! Careful now."

"Get an NPT in him?"

"No, he's breathing. Looks like he set a tourniquet..."

"Got it; maybe a brachial bleed."

"Get an IV started and find his blood type."

Mother? Mother, I can't feel my neck. Where's the light?

"His tags say Erik...Erik? Can you hear me?"

"Lock's in. Where's that IV?"

"IV's going."

"This is why you write your fecking blood type on your boots!"

"Take it easy, buddy. What's your blood type?"

My head...I can't feel my neck very much. My head hurts.

"It's O positive."

"Just lay back. Get a couple units of O pos!"

Can I see it?

"Ok, get him on the litter...One, two, three!"

Where's my gun?

* * *

The goblins had done their work well. Thjostolf looked over the encampment grimly and shook his head. They had attacked late in the night, probably before the second watch, and had systematically shot every survivor they found. Two bullets—*bastards*—right in the head. *Death is too good for them.*

There was one survivor. He was a young soldier, lying in a foxhole at the south-east corner. The goblins must have thought he was dead because a grenade had detonated right beside one of his comrades. He was shielded from most of the blast, but knocked senseless, and among the dozens of shrapnel splinters that pierced him was a large piece of steel that had dug deeply into his arm. He was so covered in entrails that he looked blown apart. He must have had the presence of mind, at some point, to fashion a tourniquet out of a strip of leather. It had saved his life. As it was, his prognosis was good, but he'd be out of the fight for a few weeks. The effects of the concussion alone were enough to get him some time in a rear-area hospital.

Poor kid, Thjostolf thought. He looked less than twenty. It was bad enough to be half-deaf from the blast, much less have suffered such a blow. It was remarkable that he'd survived.

The rain had stopped. Through the clouds, the sun burst forth and bathed the clearing in light. Thjostolf raised his head skywards and breathed deeply. It felt so good to be in the light. The mist was clearing, but there was still enough to cast a rainbow across the sky. The rain had fallen, and was taken up again as a vapor.

Thjostolf took another cleansing breath. *I fall to the earth, and I am taken up again.*

He breathed again, and opened his eyes. Around him, the company swirled in activity. Sir Harold was calling for the commanders to convene; they'd be moving out soon. The doctors were putting the boy on a stretcher and talking amongst themselves. Kolskegg had taken up a defensive position. Everybody was busy. Thjostolf picked up his rifle and started towards Sir Harold. They had work to do.

*   *   *

When the new scouts arrived around mid-morning, Thjostolf and Kolskegg were put on a truck and sent off. They sat in silence as they rode mile after bumpy mile on the wooden benches in the back of the transport. It was almost one hundred miles to Brandstead, and they were tired. Kolskegg knew Thjostolf was disappointed, but the half-elf wasn't showing it. Complaints only went up, after all. Thjostolf wouldn't say a word to question his officers so long as Kolskegg was around, and Kolskegg did the same for the foot-soldiers. Doubt was a luxury the lowly could not afford.

Brandstead was an old city on the border of Haelhan and Humbridge, and was the staging point of the Haellic liberation. Situated on a low hill in the sprawling Haellic lowlands, surrounded by orchards, farms and oil derricks, Brandstead had outgrown its own walls centuries ago, transforming into a bustling trade center at the intersection of a dozen highways running from the South Seas, north to the Ahaern River and Iaelia, and the many roads from Humbridge in the east to the highlands and fjords of western Haelhan. When Cyddustead called for aid, Haelhan had been the first to respond. They were followed by the Iaelian elves, and the Dionysian dwarves from White Mountain, across the sea to the west. Despite its failings, the Alliance was the best system devised so far to keep wars like this from happening. Granted, there was inevitable, political bickering within the system, but the Four Monarchs had taken the reins of the known world. Peace and prosperity flourished so long as the power to enforce that peace was available. And while the Elves of Iaelia designed some of the best equipment for war, it was the men of Haelhan who had the iron reserves and manufacturing power to make weapons, as well as a population of young men willing to give their lives in service.

Brandstead was evidence of all of this. The city was bustling when they arrived, with military convoys and industrial machinery running back and forth on the main roads leading up the gates. It was about noon when they reached the outer wall. The closer they got to the keeps, the more frequently the convoys were stopped for checkpoints. Each one was manned by an assortment of grisly old militia men and sheriff's guards. At long last, they arrived at the castle. From their position in the back of the truck, they couldn't see the walls. As they rolled through the gatehouse, Kolskegg saw the massive drawbridge being lifted behind them, and the steel portcullis lowering onto the cobbled road. The castle was obsolete from a military standpoint, but it provided a great spotting position and HQ. They came to a stop in the center of the courtyard and Thjostolf and Kolskegg jumped out.

They were out of place. The courtyard was filled with intelligence officers and military aristocrats with their families. Everyone was pretty and clean. There were a few ladies in fine gowns, apparently walking to lunch with their preened escorts in fine suits and uniforms. One of the girls looked over at Kolskegg and their eyes locked for a moment. She was about seventeen, with a fine figure and dark brown hair braided and tied in a bun behind her head. She smiled at him as though he surprised her. Then she dropped her gaze and, picking up her skirts slightly, hurried on. Kolskegg reflected on himself. The scouts were filthy, with mud and camouflage caked on their clothes and faces. They still had their weapons and ammo, and Kolskegg's scoped rifle made him look like some kind of primitive hunter. Neither looked very professional by the spit-and-polish standards that surrounded them.

Thjostolf looked around and, seeing Kolskegg's preoccupation, poked him in the side and murmured, "She's too good for you, buddy. Feckin', that's Sir Harold's niece."

Kolskegg smiled and turned. "Doesn't hurt to window shop, cap'. Where're we going, anyway?"

Thjostolf didn't answer. A young and slightly plump sergeant in a fresh uniform jogged up, huffing and puffing, and asked why there were there. Thjostolf showed him his orders and the sergeant nodded. "Njal General awaits you in the council room," he said. "I'll show you the way. Have you eaten?"

"Not today," said Thjostolf.

The sergeant looked horrified, but didn't say anything in reply.

They were escorted in the main doors, and Kolskegg saw the Great Hall ahead. The smell of the midday meal crept through the stale castle air. The torches that lit the path flickered, but there were so many that the entire front corridor was well lit. They were taken to a room to the left, and led up a winding staircase. Kolskegg had been in castles before, and was used to the great stone slabs and the stained glass. He remembered gawking at the majesty of the building only a few years earlier, when he first enlisted as a young man. At twenty-one, he was now used to the show and splendor of the fortress. He had learned how to sneak close enough to count the men in the barracks, how to analyze the defenses, and how to relay signals to the spotters to correct an artillery battery's aim. The castle no longer represented invincibility to him, it was just a particularly annoying obstacle in the way of a determined warrior.

Kolskegg liked the castles, though. They were pleasant to be in and fun to look at. He could certainly understand why they would make a nice house for a Lord and Lady. He wouldn't mind owning one himself, if he could get a good gardener and perhaps a small fortune.

Someday I'll discovered a way to make light without fire, he thought to himself. *Or make an engine light enough to put on a glider and fly. Then I'll buy a castle and all kinds of knight's nieces will come running.* He chuckled to himself and Thjostolf glanced back.

"The feck you laughing about?" asked the captain.

Kolskegg shrugged. "Just thinking."

They reached the top of the staircase and found themselves in a small room about twenty feet square. There was a small window, and around an oak table were several small packets of paper. The plump sergeant told them to read over the papers and await their audience with Njal General. "I'll bring some soup up," he offered, and Kolskegg thanked him.

When he had gone, Kolskegg picked up one of the packets and looked over it. It was a letter, and it bore the seal of the King of Haelhan. Thjostolf opened his and began reading out loud. Kolskegg followed suit.

"Njal Skull-Splitter sen Jenner, Lord of the Central Highlands of Haelhan, General of the Armies of Hrapp King sen Hrut, Ruler of Haelhan and the Guardian of the Southern Isles.

"To the scouts recommended by their Lords and Military Overseers for the virtues of Courage, Loyalty, Wisdom, and Brutality. May you forever be blessed with such virtues, and may the light of the One Unsayable illuminate your understanding. Peace be with you and your families.

"The Four Monarchs have convened in council and have decided that a new breed of soldier must be raised and trained. Membership in this unit will be based on virtue, not heritage, since the Philosopher writes, 'A man's virtue is in his own blood, and not his father's.' You, who have been recommended on account of your virtues, will form the cornerstone of this unit and will develop a list of equipment and facilities necessary to achieve the objectives set out by the Four Monarchs.

"In the highest tradition of Haelhan, the unit shall henceforth be known as the Jomsskari. The Jomsskari shall be tasked with infiltrating enemy controlled territory, identifying installations and persons, and gathering other useful information as you are directed. In this capacity, the Jomsskari will be a scouting unit. The Jomsskari will also be tasked with conducting raids behind enemy lines and returning to friendly territory without being destroyed, as well as performing high-risk raids on enemy rear-areas.

"The Jomsskari will be composed of all races, and no consideration will be made on the basis of origin. Instead, there shall be a unified effort to produce the single most versatile fighting force in the known world. The Jomsskari will maintain the peace among the Alliance and from the dangers of the uncivilized world.

"You are honored, above all, to be a part of this great project that will serve the world and will testify to the blessing and favor that the One Unsayable has bestowed upon the Alliance of the Four Monarchs. May you ride on the wings of the wind, and may the One Unsayable remember your prayers in life and death."

Chapter Two

The Cave, 6 September, 1159

In the absence of light there is darkness.

Only reasonable - until the lights go out.

Then the magnitude of it sets in.

He wondered if the priests ever asked, "Where are you?"

Regardless, the answer was silence.

Silence.

Silence.

It was absolutely silent.

He crouched in the darkness. There was a persistent stench in the air, the foul odor of insect droppings and decaying flesh. The twisted figure of a goblin, its body shriveled and bounded tightly in white, silky webbing, lay close enough to touch. Two punctures were visible just above the shoulder blades. The goblin's face was blue and contorted, with none of the usual jaundiced coloration remaining. It looked like it had been eaten more than a week ago. Ahead, he could see the web open up, and in the darkness, he could see a looming form. It was barely visible, still as a stone, more a shadow within the shadows than anything else, but he knew better.

The goblins feared the cave spiders. Goblins were small creatures, only about five-feet tall standing. They were spindly and green, and had long, gaunt arms that they scratched their backs with. Their nomadic culture led them to hunt in bands of two or three in the mountains south of A'kaylii. When one of them had fallen prey to the spiders, the others left him and fled. They had no sense of honor.

The orcs had a different approach. Orcs were much larger, standing about six-foot six-inches on average, and weighing at least two-hundred and fifty pounds. The cave spiders were slightly smaller than they were, and much lighter. The orcs hunted them; they had for thousands of years. Now it was a rite of passage — to become a warrior, a young orc had to complete of a series of tests, the last of which was to hunt down and kill a spider in her lair with nothing but a knife and a live rabbit for bait.

Erik sen Bergthora was not an orc. He was a human, averagely built and unremarkable but immensely strong. If he played this right, he would make history as the first foreigner accepted into the Clan A'kaylii as a warrior. This was not all. He had decided to pursue another orcish honor as well, to be trained as an orcish combat surgeon. To be honored as such, he would have to make the traditional orcish pain killer from the spider's venom. "Khem-khat," they called it; the pain killer was a grayish liquid that numbed intense pain in a few seconds and was a powerful sedative. Erik had made it before, in a laboratory at the university, but this final test of his mettle required that he harvest the poison sacs from the spider in view of the councilors, waiting outside the cave.

It meant that he couldn't kill the spider the easy way, by slashing the brains from her head. Her central nervous system was too close to the poison sacs. He would have to go for her abdomen, which meant risking getting pinned down in the spider's own game. Nobody, not even the strongest orc, could out-wrestle a full-grown cave spider.

He took a breath, and let it out slowly as he gathered his nerves. The thought of even a small spider was enough to make his heart pound. A cave spider was the stuff of nightmares. It was no use dwelling on it, he told himself. He would have to make a diversion to lure the spider away from the sticky part of the web. So long as she remained there, he couldn't reach her.

He reached into his pouch and pulled the rabbit out. It was bound on all four legs, and struggled a little. Carefully, Erik cut the bonds and then, in a deft movement, tossed the rabbit into the thin lines of web before him. The rabbit stuck to the silk and began to thrash, tangling itself in its bid for freedom.

Just a few moments. Erik slipped up the side of the rock and crouched low, preparing to spring. Behind him, some twenty yards, his friend Khalan stood, shotgun in hand. Khalan was large, even by orcish standards. He weighed at least fifteen stone, stood over six feet tall, and his arms, etched long ago with the runic tattoos of the orcish clans, were as thick as Erik's thighs. He was also an experienced hunter. If anything went wrong, he would be there to kill the spider. But Erik almost wished Khalan had stayed behind. Better to die at this point then to fail. He wasn't sure he'd be able to gather the nerve to try this twice, and he wasn't sure he could bear of the shame of fleeing the field.

There was a faint scuffle, and then the silence returned. The dark shadow loomed still, unmoving. *Come on, you.* Erik readjusted his grip on the knife, one finger at a time.

The rabbit stopped struggling for a moment, and lay panting. Then it jerked its hind legs and struggled against the adhesive bonds around it. The web quivered and shook. The shadow didn't move. Then, ever so faintly, a gentle hiss floated across the murky air. She was curious.

Sweat had beaded on Erik's forehead. His orcish headband, fashioned from woven goat-wool, soaked up most of the perspiration. Still, he was worried about being blinded. In the dark, he relied on his peripheral vision so much that to lose it would mean total incapacitation. He didn't move.

Something changed. It was like the shadow gleamed, as if a black light had suddenly turned on around it. The rabbit collapsed again, and lay still, panting.

The shadow moved forward.

The first thing Erik saw was the striped legs—first one, then two. Long and thin, they protruded from the darkest part of the shadow and exposed themselves ever so slightly in the wavering light. Then Erik saw the eyes. They were green. He could only see two of them, but he knew that the other six were smaller and to the sides. They were her peripherals and he would have to make sure they weren't pointed at him.

The thing about spiders, he reminded himself, was that they had fixed eyes resulting in tunnel vision. This meant that so long as Erik remained motionless and attacked only when the spider was close to the rabbit, he could get in a mortal wound before the beast had a chance to see him. But those legs were tipped with the most sensitive of feet, and the spider would know if he budged prior to the attack. She could feel the vibrations of movement through the stone, as clearly as one might see ripples in water. If she figured he was there, he wouldn't stand a chance trying to take her down. He might even have to run.

At first the spider moved slowly. She inched forward, and then pulled back slightly. There was activity on her web, but she could not see anything big. Erik knew that she was curious but wary. If something worth eating was trying to get out, she would have to assess if she could take it down. She didn't stand much of a chance against a mountain lion, for instance. But a goat was good food and a goblin was better.

She saw the rabbit, Erik could tell. She rose up on her legs and clacked her fangs together. They were big fangs, just underneath the two eyes. He didn't see the abdomen yet, but the shape of the head and four of the legs were evident.

Wait for it. Wait for—

She leapt forward, skittering across the web with a ghastly puffing noise. Her abdomen shone in the dim light and she reached the rabbit so fast that Erik was stunned. He had expected the spider to charge like that, all spiders did. But he hadn't expected the charge to

31

be so fast. This spider was not small, either. Her legs spanned eight feet, and she looked to weigh about two-hundred pounds.

She stopped abruptly, mere feet from Erik's hide, and the rabbit began to scream. Erik sank a little lower in his crouch, coiling to leap. Her abdomen rose in the air as she thrust one leg down, pinning her prey to the ground. Erik pounced, knife upraised as he made a down stroke. His feet landed at the base of her left, back leg and he brought the knife down hard into the tough exoskeleton— suddenly the world pitched—Erik saw the roof of the cave descending, then ascending. She jumped and Erik's legs slipped and he swung out. The knife held fast, then tore – *Eshé*! – The earth rattled as he held with both hands on the grip, a spider leg struck him in the face and he lost his grip with his left hand, and the spider rolled over and squealed, and Erik's foot struck the earth—he dug his heel down hard and tore the knife from the wound.

He scurried back, regaining his balance and readjusting his grip on the now-slick knife handle. The spider fell over itself and tried to flee, but her legs became tangled in her web and she stumbled. Erik looked for an opening. Black blood dripped out of her gaping belly, and she made an odd wheezing noise. He could see her open circulatory system; the blood ordinarily flowed freely over the organs, but with the deep wound, it poured right out of the body. Erik stepped forward, to the very edge of the web. She was within arm's reach, but she didn't try to defend herself. She had gone very still.

He picked up the dead goblin by the tattered shirt and threw him over the web, weighing it down and making a narrow path close to her flank. The spider twitched and one leg began to curl beneath it. He carefully stepped onto the corpse and stood beside her. She was dying, and didn't fight back.

Raising his knife into the air once more, he struck down on her bleeding back and cut a hole large enough to put his arm into her. She shook again, but offered no resistance. Gradually, her legs all slipped beneath her. Her fangs struck the stone, and clear liquid drizzled into a shallow pool.

Erik stood back a few paces and tried to catch his breath. His heart was pounding so hard that he felt his throat closing, like he had swallowed a whole apple. His hands were trembling and his clothing was soaked in sweat. They had spent five hours finding a spider, twenty minutes sneaking up on it, and only a few seconds fighting it. Yet despite his throbbing nerves, he felt a distinct pride welling up in him. This was his fear, he had pounced on it and killed her. It was exhilarating.

Khalan knew it, too. He stood behind, shotgun hanging in its sling, smiling his toothy grin and nodding. Erik had passed the tests. He was an orcish warrior now, a voting member of the clan; an initiate of an ancient order that very few outsiders had ever come into.

The less pleasant part was yet to come. Wasting no time, Erik seized the beast's foreleg and began hauling her out. Khalan came to help. That was permitted.

As they dragged her, Khalan glanced at Erik and said, "She is a big girl, a good fight. Are you ready to cut her up?"

Erik smiled through his sweat and tried not to think about that. His hands were less than a foot from her jaws, but it was better just to not think about that either. The hard skeleton crackled as they dragged her, and he could hear her blood squeaking against the cool stones beneath. Every so often the leg he was holding would twitch, and he was start, reaching for his knife. Her jaws opened and closed slowly.

He looked back at her, then looked away quickly, swearing with a raspy orcish expletive, "Eshé-ma, I hate feckin' spiders."

Khalan laughed. "You have mentioned this frequently."

* * *

The orcish councilors were seated in a semi-circle on a stony patch of hill outside the caves. Among them was Thassed, Khalan's father. He stood a bit apart from the rest, his hand rested on his falchion, a wry grin on his face. They had been skeptical at first, all of them. Erik was a youth even among men, and no human had ever so much as attempted to gain warriorship in the clans. Erik sen Bergthora had set out to cross a chasm between the worlds of men and orcs that had never been crossed before.

And yet here he was, his orcish clothing stained in the slick blood of the beast, his long hair tied back with an orcish topknot, and his orcish knife dripping. He strained up the slope, dropped the dead animal before Thassed, and stood up with a triumphant grin smeared across his sweaty face. "Welcome me into the ranks of A'kaylii," he said softly. "For I am a warrior of the tribe, and have proven myself."

There was a brief pause, and a gentle wind blew over them, sending a few loose strands of hair into Erik's face. Erik had scars on his face, his arms, and his chest from the training. He looked tired and in pain, but his face was set in determination. Thassed smiled, and nodded. Behind him, the councilors, smoking their black, acrid pipes, murmured to each other. Thassed turned to them and, bowing in reverence, said, "Council, with your approval, Erik sen Bergthora takes his stand among our ancestors." The elders rose, and then spoke together. "We welcome you, Erik sen Bergthora, into the tribe of A'kaylii, as a warrior."

They sat down again, and resumed puffing at their pipes. Thassed turned and asked, "You have also trained to be a doctor, have you not?"

"I have."

"Then proceed." Thassed stepped aside once more, taking his seat, and Erik pulled out his knife.

He climbed onto the back of his quarry and carefully cut open the beast's head, starting between its two largest eyes and ending at the joint between the head and the abdomen. The first cut only passed halfway through the thick, hairy outer bone, and he began cutting again, this time far less cautiously.

There was silence on the mountaintop, except for the soft, steady squeaking of steel on bone, and the occasional gust of wind. Erik toiled for a few moments, and then, sheathing his knife, gripped the outer shell of the spider and cracked it open. There was a crunching sound, like someone biting celery, and the skull tore open. Erik wrinkled his nose at the smell, and pulled out his knife again.

Inside, there were several sacs, and the spider's blood flowed freely between them. Each sac contained an organ, and tubules connected the organs by nerves. Erik's first move was to sever the optic nerves. They were thin tubes, leading from the brain right to the eyes, and they got in the way. One of the tubules got caught on the serrations of his knife, and he wiped it off on his pants.

Erik saw two gray bulges that appeared to be filled with fluid on either side of the brain stem, just below the main mass. The rest were covered in blood. He couldn't tell if they were the venom sacs or not. He needed to get rid of some the excess blood.

Climbing off the spider's back, he gripped a foreleg and pulled back, tilting the whole animal on its side. Blood spilled out of the head wound and flowed onto the rocks below. Erik kept pulling, until the tide ebbed to a steady dripping. Then, gently, he lowered the spider back.

Returning to his position on her back, he examined the contents of the now bloodless head. The two gray sacs had tubes running down to the fangs, which he could barely make out by the tell-tale muscles that surrounded them. The poison sacs themselves had muscles on either side to squeeze the venom through the tubes.

Carefully, he pinched the tube of the right and tried to get his knife in. The brain was too big and both of his hands couldn't fit. He tried again, rearranging his position on the spider's back and shifting his knife grip to his left hand. *There*—his right hand gripped the tube and pinched it off, and with a deft movement he cut the tube about

35

four inches below. The venom below his pinch slipped out and found a crevice in the skull to trickle into.

Carefully, he sheathed his knife. His right hand was getting slick from the remaining fluids inside the head, and he had to work fast. He wrapped the dangling tube around his index and middle fingers. Then, using his thumb, Erik pushed the end into the loop they formed. Carefully, he tugged on the end of the tube, until the knot was tight.

Moment of truth, he thought, and stopped pinching. The venom slid down and stopped at the knot. He waited a moment, and carefully tugged on the knot a little bit more to make sure it held fast.

Once satisfied, he took out his knife again. Supporting the venom sac carefully with his left hand, he began to cut away at the thin, soft tissues that secured the sac to the sides of the skull. As he cut, he felt the weight push down on his hand, until the sac fell from the skull and lay, detached, in his hand.

He lifted it out, and placed it in a handkerchief before the elders. Khalan glanced at the council to gauge their reactions. They looked satisfied, but he wasn't done yet. Erik returned and performed the same operation on the other side. This one went well, but at the last moment, his fingers slipped and the sac fell into the bottom of the skull, resting on her throat. Erik had to reach in with one hand and grip it, lifting it out. For a moment, he feared it would burst, but he soon laid it beside the other.

The council rose, and Erik picked up the poison sacs carefully, and bowed to them.

"Come," Thassed said. "Return with us to camp, and make khem-khat. Then the warrior shall be the surgeon, and your honor shall be great."

As they left, the shattered spider lay still, her legs curled beneath her. A vulture called out from the heights, but kept his distance. The orcs, trudging down a mountain path, vanished into the gathering fog, and only the wind remained.

*   *   *

Njal General Skull-Splitter sen Jenner was hunched over his desk and seemed completely preoccupied when Thjostolf entered his office. Njal had an air about him that made anyone nearby feel somewhat less masculine. He was a bear of a man, with thin, white hair that was balding on top, hanging in longs wispy strands about his ears. His once-thick beard was also now succumbing to emaciating age. Thjostolf had no idea how old the general was—he knew that his father had fought under Njal some forty years ago, and Njal was at least forty at the time. And while it was not so uncommon to hear of a man reaching one-hundred and fifty years of age, hearing of a warrior still potent beyond fifty was indeed rare. Njal was a legend in his own time; certain goblin tribes were said to keep their children in line by telling them that the "Skull-Splitter" would come. Thjostolf wasn't sure where the nickname had come from either. He did know the wars of that era were fought when single-shot rifles and swords were still prevalent, so it wasn't so hard to guess. Wherever the stories had originated, whether they were real, imagined, or a mix, they made Njal General sen Jenner seemed far greater than any man alive. Others had written of their exploits and made decent money at it, but Njal remained a soldier, and so the tales were embellished and retold without his input.

Thjostolf stood awkwardly for a moment while Njal finished whatever he was so absorbed in. Finally, the old warrior looked up, smiled, and indicated the chair on the opposite side of the desk.

"Hello, Thjostolf sen Skarp-Hedin."

"Hello, Njal General sen Jenner."

Njal put his quill down and leaned back as Thjostolf took his seat. He looked tired. "Last week, the orcish council of Kaꝗi ratified a Republican constitution that had been previously approved by the Four Monarchs. That means the orcs have gained entry in the Alliance. It is now the Alliance of Five, not Four." He paused briefly, and smiled stiffly. "Our personal feelings on the matter are no longer important. For better or worse, the orcs have become both economic and military allies to Haelhan and the rest of the Alliance. Hrapp King wants to begin cross-training, as a show of faith to them, and would like us to consider a few candidates from the A'kayliian ranks for the Jomsskari. I don't think more than a few candidates will come, but orcs are…well, they've a reputation for being tough, and I'd be surprised if we didn't have some new and somewhat uglier faces. I believe it will be quite beneficial to learn their tactics and capabilities.

"Now I know you're one of my best educated officers, and you have excellent combat records. I see here," Njal indicated a report on his desk, "That your peers consider you one of the best officers in the Jomsskari. I also understand you lost your support man the other day?"

Thjostolf nodded. "Yes, sir."

Thjostolf's company had been drilling for alpine scouting, and they were moving along a ridge, staying hidden on the slope. The support gunner, a young Haellic buck named Olaf, had slipped on an exposed root and had fallen. Olaf was carrying almost ninety pounds of weapons and ammo, and he had reacted too slowly to twist the weight of his gear away from him. His heavy rucksack had flown right into the back of his head, jamming his face onto the hard steel of his weapon. He was alive, and swore a lot initially, and he'd be okay in the long run, but with a broken jaw, a dislocated shoulder, and a gash the length of a man's hand across his right eyebrow that swelled his eye closed, he would be in the hospital for some time recovering. Until then, 2nd Jomsskari was short by a great deal of firepower.

Njal nodded. "I'm sure you will find one or two that you feel are qualified. In any case, I want you to take charge of the orcs for now, until they find their feet in an Alliance unit. Are you up to that?"

Thjostolf knew the question was rhetorical. He took a deep breath and said, "Yes, sir."

Njal saw his disquiet. "Captain," he said, more gently now, "The world is changing. We must change with it. I am entrusting you with this task because I believe you can set aside your reservations and be objective in your assessment of the candidates. You were among the first of the Jomsskari. You were successful in integrating Haellic, Iaelian, Halfling, and Dionysian efforts, despite the difficulties. You have succeeded in the past, and I need you to succeed now as well."

Thjostolf nodded. "I understand, sir."

"Good," said Njal, and picked up his quill again. "I'll see to it you receive further information as it arrives. Dismissed."

*   *   *

As Thjostolf mounted his horse outside and began the ride back to the Jomsskari compound, he thought about the orders he had received. There was no good way to treat an orc – they always felt threatened. They had good reason, the world of Elves and Men was as different from the world of Orcs as the day was from the night. This was not merely a poetic comparison. The orcs preferred the night. For a long time it was thought that their skin was like the goblins, and easily blistered in the sun. But when the orcs began sending envoys to the Haellic universities, and the Elves began sending their merchants into the A'kayliian mountaintops, it was found that the orcish pension for the dark was a practical one. They could see well in the dark, as well as any elf, and many of the animals they preferred to eat only came out with the moon. Besides which, the goblins usually raided at night. It made sense for their culture to exist in the starlight. But in the past few decades, since their efforts to join the Alliance first began, the orcs had tried to live during the day, to improve their trading and, when they were in Haelhan or Iaelia, to coexist with the culture around them. As the world shrank, the orcish nocturnes became semi-nocturnes, and their primitive clan-based social structure began to collide violently with the Republican constitution they themselves had ratified by consensus. Their lives, in every respect, were torn between their ancient traditions and the new, intimidating developments from the Alliance.

Surely, if anyone had reason to be on edge, it was the orcs. The past prejudices against the barbarian tribes were hard to overcome, and many Haellics were still wary of them. Thjostolf knew this attitude wasn't entirely justified. The orcs had quietly kept their borders, proving by their actions that they were putting aside the old aggression; but nobody could easily forget the stories their fathers told them of orcs ravaging the countryside and sneaking into camps to kill every other man while they slept. It didn't help that the orcs always looked angry. It was just their physique. Their faces were twisted into permanent grimaces.

And so the thought of several orcs in his unit bothered Thjostolf. The company's efficiency was entirely based on teamwork; the orcs, for all he knew, might still be used to a purely individual effort. Even if they did operate as a team, he didn't know what that looked like. The company needed unwavering discipline; the orcs might try to prove themselves and end up getting killed or injured unnecessarily. That had been a problem with the Dionysians when they were first brought on board – though after several months, the dwarves had stopped their needless bravado.

And then there was the problem with unit integrity. Thjostolf had worked with a bastard once, and if anyone lost anything, someone suggested that the bastard had stolen it. There needn't be any foundation for such claims to eat away at the soul of the unit, and the last thing Thjostolf needed was an easy scapegoat for the men. The worry of the scapegoat getting mad, losing his temper, shooting someone . . . well, that didn't help either.

Orcs. He was breaking new ground, that was for sure. But there was always some ground best left unbroken, and Thjostolf couldn't help but wonder if perhaps it was too soon to bring Elves, Dwarves, Men, and Orcs together in one company. As much as the Jomsskari had benefitted from this alloy of allies, Thjostolf was acutely aware of how fast it could break down. This experiment was either a recipe for astonishing success, or catastrophe – there could be no other conclusion. The latter, unfortunately, seemed more probable.

Chapter Three

The Orcish Steppes, 2 October, 1159

Nothing. Nothing. Nothing, nothing, no thing, no one, no where, no why.

No one but himself. Nowhere but himself. It all seems too silly.

No more, never again, cast the Holy Book aside.

Where it fell—no where. Pick it up—no why.

Tear stained pages, no one, no thing, nothing, nothing.

Nothing.

"Erik! Wake up!"

He opened his eyes, squinting at the light. Khalan peered at him, silhouetted against the window behind him. There was the smell of steamed rolls on the air, and tea, but neither of them seemed like sufficient cause to leave the comforts of his bed. Erik grunted and tried to imagine that Khalan was just a dream and would go away.

He wasn't, and he didn't. Khalan thumped his heavy fist on Erik's head, as if checking a melon to see if it were ripe. "Wake up, jai-khu," he repeated, more rudely this time.

"Your mother is a jai-khu," Erik snapped, and groaned, flopping his arm over his eyes. "What time is it?"

"Almost day break, and the fields need tending."

Khalan turned away, and Erik sighed deeply before kicking his blanket off. It had been a month since his induction as an orcish warrior, and the two of them had gone to the A'kayliian steppe to work Thassed's farm. In time of peace, even Khalan's unit, the Kaħi Royal Guards, were permitted to live civilian lives. This arrangement kept the warriors, who had legal authority in the councils, in touch with the peasants, and kept the society from splitting along class lines as the Elves and the Haellics had. It was typical orcish politics: pragmatic, earthy, and simple.

He put on his boots and pulled his tunic over his head. His gun belt hung by his head on a thick nail in the wall, and he wrapped it around his waist. In the leather holster was a .46 caliber revolver. In the Old Order, when a young orc became a warrior, he gained three things: the right to vote, the right to own land, and a thick, chopping sword called a "falchion" that warriors wore to distinguish themselves. These things remained under the New Order, but the sword was replaced with a powerful handgun. Erik's revolver had etchings of the same pattern as the tattoos on his arms—intricate, winding runes in old orcish.

Khalan wore one, too. His father, Thassed, was from the Old Order, and carried his falchion with pride. Erik suspected that Thassed resented his son's affinity for firearms, but knew better than to incline an orc to an argument, especially in his own home.

Thassed had made breakfast, and they ate quickly. It had been hard for Erik to eat enough at first. There was a time when he could only stomach two steamed rolls in a morning, but he soon found that the hard field labor left him faint from hunger by noon. Now he gobbled down seven or eight, and stashed another two in his trouser pockets. He still wasn't eating as much as Khalan, who cleaned his bowl three times before belching loudly and rising.

They spent the morning toiling in the fields. Erik liked the work; it was brutal but satisfying. In fact, he could describe most of his experiences living with the orcs in that way. When the sun was directly overhead they stopped for lunch. Thassed always brought a pound or so of salted pork, and they ate it with the rolls leftover from breakfast, along with some small, crunchy apples that grew bordering the field. In the rocky, mountain soil, there wasn't much that grew big. Thassed's potato crop would mostly serve to supplement the pigs and goats he kept on the other half of the land.

They were just finishing their meal and getting up to finish their labor when they heard beating hoofs approaching over the hills. A rider was coming, his horse was adorned with the black banner of the A'kayliian Royal Council. Erik nudged Khalan with his elbow as the rider approached.

"You just stay in trouble, don't you?" he joked.

As the rider halted before them, Thassed stepped forward and opened his hands. It was how the orcs showed they were unarmed, a traditional greeting in this part of the world. The rider swung down from his mount and, spreading his palms in a like manner, spoke quickly in orcish, and presented a scroll. Thassed took it and read it while the rider mounted and turned, riding off.

Erik spoke orcish quite well, although he couldn't pronounce some words very well at all. The language of the Clan A'kaylii relied on the underbitten jaw of its people, and whenever Erik tried to imitate those sounds, he elicited laughter from whatever company he was in.

Roughly translated, he thought as he read the scroll for himself, the orcs had formally joined the Alliance, and were sending volunteers to join some new Haellic military brainchild. The rider had come to ask for volunteers. At first he was skeptical, and even disgusted. There was nothing about Haelhan he wanted to remember, and yet they seemed to pursue him even to A'kaylii. But as he read the list of required qualifications, he grew intrigued. It didn't sound like any unit he had ever heard of. The physical requirements were at least as high as a Royal Guardian could be expected to maintain, and the last line, printed almost amateurishly, caught his attention.

We guarantee a medal, a body bag, or both.

As the rider departed, Thassed spoke. "My sons, were I younger, I would greatly desire such an honor as this."

Khalan grinned, and Erik couldn't help but smile a little, too. The Old Order didn't like to say things directly, any more than they liked being out in the daytime. Both knew what Thassed wanted.

"Erik, are you intrigued, as I am?" asked Khalan. Even the New Order didn't say things outright.

Erik shook his head. "I left Haelhan for a reason, brother," he said factually, "They didn't want me, and I didn't want them either. Besides, we just started here. Father cannot tend the fields alone." He turned to get his tools.

"You have earned honor now," replied Thassed, "and there are many young orcs seeking to work in the fields."

Erik didn't reply.

Khalan seemed to know what he was thinking. "I'll go if you go," he offered quietly.

"I'll give it a think," Erik said. "Let's finish this field. Ask me later."

One of the things Erik liked best about field work was the introspection. As the sweat dripped off his nose, he thought about Haelhan, the mighty factories and the Castle Havenstead. He wondered how it had changed in the last three years and if he'd recognize the streets.

He was different now. He had a new identity. The tattoos on his arms were proof of that. He could vote in the assembly and start a new life here. It seemed ridiculous to return to Haelhan, just to face the society that had cast him out in the first place.

But there was something in him that wanted to go back. He didn't know how to describe it, but he felt pulled. There was a part of him, he knew, that would never be orcish. No matter how much he bled, Haelhan flowed in his veins, and he knew that if he let himself admit it, he missed the Haellic highlands.

If he went, he reasoned, he wouldn't risk losing anything in orcish society. Even if the Haellics rejected him, he could come back here. He just didn't want to face that humiliation again, especially after working so hard to earn the respect of his new family. Family had a nice sound to it. Khalan had started calling him "Brother" and Thassed called him "Son" shortly after he had made it through the first phase of his training. He wasn't sure what they would do if they saw him as a pariah.

All day long, he worked silently, thinking it over. Khalan and Thassed didn't interrupt him, and as nightfall came close, Erik felt increasingly split. The memory of Haelhan brought with it the deepest pangs of regret and isolation. But it also brought his childhood, his life, and the recollection of the quiet joys that he had missed since his departure. The challenge offered by this new unit was too tempting to cast aside.

Finally, he came to a decision. As they were returning that evening, he said, "I'll go. Just to feck with 'em."

They left the farm a few days later, and traveled to Kaɦi. They wore their military uniforms of black tunics, black trousers, and stubby black boots perfect for scrambling over mountains. On their hips they carried their revolvers, and over their heads they donned wool shemaugs. They wrapped their bodies in thick cloaks, banishing the cold as best they could. Erik carried his medical kit, including the khem-khat he had made from the spider's venom. If the Haellics were hesitant to respect him as a warrior, maybe they would respect him as a field surgeon.

There were trucks waiting for them. About four dozen orcs

had gathered, and several Haellic trucks were parked in a cherry grove outside the city. When Erik and Khalan arrived, they found some familiar faces and traded small talk. It was early morning, and everyone was bleary and stood shuffling from one foot to the other. There was frost on the grass, but even as high up as Kaḥi the weather hadn't turned to full-on winter yet.

One of the drivers, a Haellic sergeant with too much belly and an absurd handlebar moustache, spotted Erik and stared rudely before shuffling off. Erik ignored him. He was sure it was the first of many rude stares he would receive in the coming days.

Finally, they were told to mount up. Erik followed Khalan and a couple of Khalan's buddies into the truck, and they chatted while the drivers struggled to start the engines. The trucks ran on a diesel fuel, which burned by compression in a cylinder. To start the cycle, they needed to light it first. To this end, they used a crank-and-steel mechanism that generated sparks, creatively called a "sparkler," in a laborious process. While they waited, everybody wanted to meet Erik. He had become something of a legend—the only human in history to gain status as a Clan Warrior. Khalan introduced him with some pride.

The engines roared to life, first one, then the other. Once they were aboard, it was difficult to hear one another, and the orcs settled into their seats and tried to sleep. They rode on long wooden benches, the furniture of the typical troop-truck. The truck beds were covered by canvas, like old covered wagons, so there was nothing to rest their backs on. As the trucks began to move. they bounced uncomfortably about. Erik, for his part, fell asleep before the convoy had reached the main highway leading back to Haelhan. He had spent enough time in the back of these dirty behemoths to know how to sleep sitting upright.

He awoke a couple of hours later, and saw they were in the lowlands. He fell asleep again after a while, dozing in and out, and awoke as the trucks stopped at a checkpoint on the border to Iaelia. He heard the elven guards talking to the drivers, and smiled a little when one poked his head into the back, wrinkled his nose at the overwhelming smell of pepperweed, and then vanished. They pressed on, crossing over the Ahaen River before dusk. That night, they slept on the side of the road. He lay still under his cloak, listening to the sound of the orcs snoring around him. These were the moments he hated, when there was nothing to listen to besides the persistent, troubling thoughts...

The next morning, they started early and Erik found it more difficult to sleep. He was frightfully bored and the view wasn't great from where he sat. All he could see was the truck behind, and the vast plains of the Haellic lowlands obscured by a haze of dust from the black smoke of the engines. They stopped at a Haellic military outpost for their midday meal. While the truck refueled, the orcs filed into a mess hall and got a bite to eat. It was odd to taste Haellic cuisine again. It didn't have any pepperweed in it, and Erik was startled to realize how much he missed a good Haellic loaf of bread. Wheat was scarce in the mountains – everything in A'kaylii was made from potatoes.

They mounted up again, and Erik fell asleep again and woke up with Khalan snoring on his shoulder. He spent the next half hour trying to figure out if it was endearing or not. He saw tractors in the fields, harvesting the last crops. They must be getting close to Havenstead; the industrialized farms were mostly in the foothills around the highlands. Sure enough, the road began to climb, and he began to see more pedestrians and horse-back merchants on the road. Khalan had woken up, too, and nudged him. "Are you ready for this, brother?" he shouted above the engine.

Erik laughed. "Too late to back out now!" he shouted back.

*   *   *

Rhys ap Bledri was listening to his friend, Wendyll, attempt to defend a bad line of reasoning, and it amused him. The elves were sitting together at a small café in the suburban part of Havenstead, sharing a delicious meal of roasted goat, aged cheese, a salad made from cabbage, mushrooms, and tomatoes, and lightly toasted, dark sourdough bread upon which was spread a thin film of honey and butter. Rhys had a small glass of wine in his hand, and rolled the sample he had just taken around in his mouth. It was a little too dry to be paired with goat, but not unenjoyable. It had the distinct taste of Iaelian oak casts, a thick, viscous body and the sweet, lingering smell that only comes from the vineyards of Northern Iaelia. It paired well enough with the meal, and paired quite well for a conversation with a good friend. The sun was still in the sky, and had begun its long descent into the west. Now it sank towards the waiting horizon. It would be nightfall soon.

They had been discussing a problem for the Elven philosophers of late—the definition of art. "My father is finishing the revisions for his paper on 'True Excellence'. He's been working on it for many years now." Wendyll's father was a doctor at the University of El Commulbalbro. "I think you would find his dissertation on the 'quantity over quality' argument particularly interesting."

"I assume he rejects such a utilitarian stance."

"Of course, but his reasoning is unique," Wendyll said, lifting a cherry tomato to his mouth. After a brief moment of savoring, he grinned wryly and said, "He holds that art cannot be created in a factory because art necessarily includes the slightest errors, that is, the unintentional imperfection. A machine may make errors, but it is mechanical error, replicated in each piece. But an artist's hand slips. It is the touch of the craftsman, you see. The beauty rests in the imperfection."

Rhys considered it. "Well, certainly I'm inclined to agree. But for the sake of argument," Rhys continued, "Gems and diamonds are valued according to their perfections. While it may be true to claim that perfection cannot be created en masse now, there is no reason to think that it is impossible in the future, is there?"

"You're speaking of an excellence in objects, even excellence of utility," countered Wendyll. "I am speaking of art."

"But what is art but the creative production of excellent objects?" Rhys said. "Of course, I am not an artist myself, and an artist might disagree."

"I think most artists would disagree," replied Wendyll. "Art must be something higher, or anyone who produces anything must be an artist in some capacity."

"That's true," Rhys conceded. "But it leads us back to the foundational issue: what is art?"

"How is everything?" The waitress had returned and smiled pleasantly.

"Very well, thank you," said Rhys.

"Anything more I can get you?"

"No, thank you."

She smiled again and walked off. Wendyll was still pondering, and Rhys took the interim to reflect briefly on his friend. Wendyll rarely had conversations, except when they were about philosophy. He was just over six-feet tall, and was as wiry as a young fox. His long black hair was carefully braided and held back out of his dark brown eyes, which were always slightly closed as if he was bored with the world around him. It was a deceptive impression. Wendyll ap Cadfael was one of the best snipers in Rhys' acquaintance, and constantly alert. He had told Rhys once whether or not each man who had passed by in the last half-hour was carrying a pocket-watch.

Wendyll spoke suddenly. "I believe our time here is up."

Rhys looked behind him and saw two military orderlies approaching them. As they came to a stop in front of him, Rhys rose politely.

"Message from Thjostolf Captain sen Skarp-Hedin," said the first orderly, after saluting. "You're to report to the compound within the hour."

"Thank you," said Wendyll. His face was impassive, but Rhys detected a weary annoyance in his eye. As the orderlies left, Wendyll mumbled something under his breath and glanced at Rhys, shaking his head. "Our lovely captain has precise timing, don't you think?"

"There must be a reason," said Rhys reassuringly. "Thjostolf doesn't end passes without a good reason."

Wendyll looked skeptical but didn't disagree. Thjostolf occasionally played head-games with his men by cutting their free time short and rushing them off to a well-constructed emergency scenario. The idea was to teach them to be prepared to move out at any time, and to make sure that each man had properly cleaned and maintained his equipment before leaving for town. Those who didn't were easily spotted by their peers just prior to moving out. While there was no drastic disciplinary action taken, everyone was aware that Thjostolf kept notes on them. He wanted to know for sure who was reliable and who wasn't. Occasionally he would induce a jam or malfunction in the weapons, call everybody back, and see if anyone spotted it when they were inspecting each other. So far, he had been pleased; his men took such good care of their gear that even he could find nothing functionally wrong with it, unless he had put it there himself.

But Rhys was confident that no such games would be played today. He was the company's lieutenant and second-in-command to Thjostolf, and usually got wind of training exercises before they happened. And since the objective of such games were to prepare for an emergency, it was only fair to assume that an emergency was on hand.

They left a fair tip and mounted their horses, riding down the cobbled streets of Havenstead at a placid trot. The Jomsskari compound was a large part of the Havenstead Castle, secluded by a forty-foot bridge, twenty-five feet of elevation, and a gatehouse. Havenstead Castle was built with three keeps—the Central Keep housed the Great Hall, the chapel, and currently served as the King's quarters. It was cut directly into the stone behind it. On either side, set some fifty-feet up, two smaller keeps were set into the mountainside. In the old times, these two keeps could fire on any enemy forces that had breached the three outer courts, each of which was fifty-feet below the next. From ground level, the west and east keeps towered nearly four hundred feet above, and while no arrow could fire accurately that far up, the arrows traveling down had every benefit of gravity. The keeps each had at least two layers of tunnels below the surface, which permitted them to store enough food for each keep to be self-sufficient and supply its garrison for at least two years. The Central Keep could survive on its own for nearly five, when fully stocked.

Now the Jomsskari had taken over the West Keep. It was a good spot. From their position above the city, they were virtually invisible, and their underground offices allowed them to hold meetings and interviews without risk of spies. To reach the inner courtyard outside the keeps was a feat in itself. The final gatehouses leading into each keep were heavily guarded, and the walls were one hundred feet tall from the bridge. All around it, the ground dropped another fifty feet; a climb from the inner courtyard over the keep walls would amount to one-hundred-fifty feet, with no significant handholds and no cover. That would be incredible even in broad daylight and without interruption. An intruder would have the benefit of neither.

It gave a Rhys a feeling of comfort. It was nice to be given such a secure location, although they spent most of their time far from it. As they rode up the castle's first drawbridge, he looked up at the West Keep. As the crow flew, it was only a mere one-hundred yards. But the walls, and the terrain the castle was built on, demanded that one zigzag through the narrow streets, through two more gatehouses, and finally across a bridge to face the final gatehouse. It always gave Rhys chills to imagine attacking such a fortress with nothing but bows, spears, catapults, and swords. In the year 421, it had withstood its most vicious, and one of the last, attacks that left the outer curtain breached. The attacking orcs had stopped at the second gatehouse because the bodies had piled so high they could not climb over them. When the dead were counted, the Haellics had lost only forty-nine men dead. They had killed almost nine-thousand orcs.

The castle echoed with the sounds of that battle. Rhys could almost hear the cries of the orcs as they fell, and the shouts of the Haellic officers. It was as though he had been there yesterday although he had not seen the battle. An elf only lives eight-hundred years, nine-hundred if he had the strength. Rhys and Wendyll had been born nearly two-hundred years ago, and did not remember the Battle of Havenstead. But his father, Bledri, had been there. Bledri had fought against the orcs in many campaigns. Rhys had often wondered what the world was coming to; it was said the orcs were becoming civilized. Thjostolf had even mentioned that the Jomsskari may accept orcish candidates. *I'll believe that when I see it.*

They rode through the second gatehouse and were stopped by the Haellic guards on the other side. Security in the castle was tight most of the time; occasionally, it slackened off a bit around the first and second gatehouses, but the third gatehouse was always watched by snipers and a pair of machine-gun nests. The gatehouses leading to the keeps were maximum security. When Rhys and Wendyll arrived at the bridge leading to the West Keep, Rhys saw the distant figures on the walls take aim. He was in the cross-hairs of at least five of the most experienced snipers in the country, and there were observers inspecting his baggage from afar. They all knew him by name, but in the West Keep, there were no exceptions to security. Only Hrapp King was exempt from arbitrary search, and occasionally he was asked to turn out his pockets, too.

Rhys drew his horse to a halt at the final checkpoint and glanced up. It always made him feel a little nervous. He was on a bridge about fifteen-feet-wide, with short guardrails on each side. Almost fifty feet below, the inner moat gurgled softly, and he could see prying eyes peering at him from the murder-holes. The two portcullis' were shut, and the heavy wooden door leading into the courtyard was shut behind the furthest of them, denying Rhys any view of the inside. Above him, the sunlight glinted briefly off the scopes of the sharpshooters as they kept their vigil. The first portcullis opened, and the two elves entered. As the heavy bars lowered behind them, an old sergeant peeked out of a murder-hole on their left and beckoned them over. The hole was too small for anyone, even a halfling, to crawl through, and offered excellent cover if the bullets began to fly. Rhys produced his identification papers, and Wendyll his. They wordlessly handed the small booklets through the hole and waited.

After a few moments, the booklets were handed back. The second portcullis rose, creaking ominously as the chains ground against the gears behind the stone walls. Rhys saluted and the sergeant saluted in return. As the wooden doors opened, Rhys saw something he had never expected to see.

In the failing evening sun, a Haellic truck stood in the center of the compound, its rough canvas back glowed ethereally from the bloody red light that poured over it. A shadow crept slowly towards its hood. Gathered around the back of the truck were a dozen or so orcs, each one bearing gear and rudimentary supplies. Their black skin gleamed, and they looked around nervously with their piggy, dark red eyes. They were like devils, and if Rhys had been on foot, he would have stopped dead in his tracks. It was best, he decided as his horse cantered placidly on, that he did not stare.

Truly, Thjostolf had not canceled their leave without good cause. It seemed they were, all too soon, meeting their new allies. Rhys tried to look unflustered, but the sight of orcs in the compound threw him immeasurably off balance. Beside him, Wendyll seemed shocked as well.

Then, suddenly, the master sniper grinned, leaned over, and said softly, "It is something that is produced by the labors of an artist."

Rhys glanced at him incredulously. "Orcs?" he asked.

"No," said Wendyll, and winked. "Art."

Rhys stared at him, not comprehending. His friend smiled, and chuckled lightly. "Of course, that begs the question, 'what is an artist?' But I haven't got an answer to that, either."

Rhys looked back at the orcs, and noticed a single human standing among them. He looked up at Rhys and as their eyes met, he gave a small nod in greeting. There was an odd flavor to the man. Rhys looked at him again, then back at Wendyll. Wendyll had already dismounted, and was leading his horse to the stable. Rhys hesitated, then hurriedly followed suit and felt the earth touch the bottoms of his boots. He felt better on the ground. He heard a call from behind him, in the raspy, orcish tongue, and glanced back. They were falling into an administrative formation, and the human fell in with them.

This is incredible. There was no other term that came to mind. Rhys knew he couldn't change the course of history, or the paths of civilization, but somehow, he had never thought this day would come. He wasn't sure if he was upset or not. For now, the feeling of shock was too great to permit any other feelings to register. The orcs were in Havenstead by invitation, on the same ground they had once lost nine-thousand lives trying to destroy. And orcs didn't forget spilled blood any more easily than elves did.

But allies? Rhys handed his reins to a servant, who began to take the horse away. The two elves went inside one of the buildings and entered a staircase leading down to the lower levels. Rhys felt angry, but he didn't know exactly why. He was a good stoic, and didn't ordinarily let his feelings get the best of him. It just didn't make sense. Or else it made perfect sense…he didn't know for sure.

This is just incredible.

*   *   *

Thjostolf knew the elves were rattled the moment they walked into his office. They were both smiling with that peculiar half-smirk that Elves wore whenever they were trying to politely express their consternation. Rhys raised his eyebrows quizzically upon catching sight of his superior but held his tongue. Wendyll, however, said, "Failed to mention a little something to us, didn't you, Captain?"

Thjostolf waved him off. "I guess you saw the feckin' orcs, huh? I didn't want to ruin your pass. Feckin', we probably won't have another one for a little while. How was it, by the way?"

Wendyll grinned and glanced at Rhys. "Well, our friend here has discovered a wonderful young lady he thinks he's in love with, so we visited her."

"Oh yeah? Is she in town?"

"Northern Foothills," corrected Rhys, somewhat self-consciously. "She's a nurse for a, ah...decrepit old aristocrat." For some reason he could not explain, he chuckled shortly at his own remark.

"Well, don't give her the key to your bank box. She'll clean you out and feckin' run off with someone less interesting. That's what happened to my cousin, Torgyll."

"Tell me about the orcs," said Wendyll. "I'm curious. Are we going to recruit them, or is this some elaborate prank?"

Thjostolf laughed. "We need more men. Feckin', we lack a machine gunner and the other companies lack mortar crews and snipers. Feckin', need a good surgeon or two if they have 'em."

Rhys nodded, but he still looked troubled. Thjostolf sighed and sat down on the edge of his desk. "Okay, look, guys," he said slowly, "I know you're not happy about this, and, feckin', I wish I could've given you more time to prepare yourselves, but the Alliance has accepted the orcs and I think we'll benefit from their experience. Even if I didn't, we haven't much choice but to let 'em feckin' have a go at it. What I need is for you guys, especially you, Rhys, is to hang in there and not let your emotions cloud your judgment. Team integrity is vital. You know that. And we can't let it fall apart, whether we get orcs or not. Do you understand?"

Rhys nodded again. Thjostolf could see his approach had worked. Most good leadership was understanding how and why his men thought, and approaching each of them as necessary. The elves were stoics; so, tell them that nothing would change except their attitude about the situation, and they could live with it. He trusted elves for that reason, they were consistent. They could deal with uncertainty. It was harder to find a Haellic, a Dionysian, or a halfling who would adjust so easily.

Wendyll asked, "Do the others know?"

"I told Kolskegg and he said he'd talk to Brutus and Peter. They should be here soon."

As if on cue, the sound of short legs scurrying became evident, and the door opened to reveal Kolskegg, accompanied by a fierce, stubby dwarf carrying a bottle of mead and several tankards. They were joined by the company's recent acquisition, a halfling veteran named Peter Stills, who had a loaf of bread under one arm and a large wedge of cheese under the other.

"Hello, cap," said Kolskegg jovially, shutting the door behind him and brushing past Wendyll with a little smile. "I reckon we need another couple of mugs."

Thjostolf jerked his thumb towards the cabinet and looked at the dwarf. "Brutus of Gath, Peter Stills, Kolskegg sen Gunnar. What's all this about?"

"We've got new guys, yeah?" said Peter, setting his food

down. "Short people have always been hospitable; didn't you know that?"

"New guys, I don't care if they're orcs or angels, we should have a drink together, right?" said Brutus. "Of course, right. It's unit integrity, yes? Are you thirsty?" He pointed at the elves and grinned widely, leaning in as though conspiring. "Did you see our new friends? You could sink a dreadnaught with such ugly faces!"

"Mama," chimed Kolskegg in a falsetto child's voice, rooting around in the cabinet, "Dey follow'ded me home, can I keep 'em, oh please mama?"

"Truth be told, I am excited," returned Brutus, setting the bottle down with a loud thud. "Anyone so ugly must be skilled at killing and after all, what are Jomsskari for? Peter! Let's have some bread and goat-cheese." Brutus coughed into his sleeve and grabbed a stool from the corner, placing it at the base of the desk and standing on it. From his new vantage point, he began to line up the mugs, and looked up at Rhys with his beady, glimmering eyes. "And how was your weekend off, my friend?"

"Short, really, by about a day," Rhys said. The dwarf's cheerful ease was contagious.

"Ah, but I heard you have found a fancy dame to distract you from your philosophy," said Brutus, and began pouring the mead. Kolskegg came by and put the tankards he had found in the cabinet down, and Brutus made a low grunt of acknowledgment before continuing. "Still, it's worth drinking about, right? Of course, right! Orcs in Haelhan, and nobody shooting at them, and now you even have the attention of a fair lady. The times are changing, yes?" He put his mead down and looked around. "So where are they? I want to start drinking; why not?"

Thjostolf smiled and shook his head. Of the six men in the room, Brutus was undoubtedly the most gregarious. All of his men were easy-going, but Brutus of Gath, the company's demolitions engineer, was always energetic, and always loved to laugh and tussle.

He loved his work, and Thjostolf supposed that anyone who enjoyed blowing things up, and got to every day, tended to spread good cheer everywhere they went. He was good at demolitions, too. He had all ten fingers to prove it.

The sound of tramping feet down the corridor broke them of their good mood. Rhys glanced at Thjostolf and asked, "Are they coming here?"

"Well, yes, of course they are," said Thjostolf. "We're responsible to try out about thirty-four of them. I've heard rumors that we may be deploying soon. No, I've no details, so we need to train up whoever we choose quickly. We could be out and about for a while."

The men nodded, and Brutus hopped down off his stool. Peter was leaning against the desk, rolling a sliver of cheese into a sphere between his thumb and forefinger. Everyone was watching the door. The tramping stopped just outside. There was a pause, and Thjostolf felt himself hold his breath. The silence was agonizing, though it last only for an instant. Then, a knock came at the door.

The orcs filed into the room looking remarkably self-conscious. Some of them glanced back and forth cautiously, while others folded their arms almost defiantly. Thjostolf noted his men's reactions, too. Most of them simply stood slightly apart, but didn't seem particularly distraught, while others, especially the elves, seemed highly agitated. They kept their hands folded in front of them and forced smiles, but their tension was pervasive. He felt it in the air.

Peter and Brutus were apprehensive at first, but quickly broke the ice. "Mead!" cried the dwarf, and offered a pair of mugs to the closest two orcs. Kolskegg grabbed another pair and began handing them out. The orcs examined the mead distrustfully, but as Thjostolf took a mug and began to drink, they relaxed.

And then Thjostolf saw the kid.

He looked to be in his early twenties, wiry and strong, with a trimmed beard and long, brown hair in an orcish topknot. He had bushy eyebrows that seemed to point downwards, and he stood a little awkwardly, as though he didn't appreciate having some many people around him. Kolskegg gave him a mug of mead, and the kid smiled with half his mouth, mumbled his thanks, and gave everyone in the room the once-over. His black orcish uniform was slightly big on him, but he carried himself as though he owned the room.

Then Thjostolf noticed the kid's tattoos, and his revolver. This kid was something more. Thjostolf couldn't remember much about the markings, but he was sure it put him in a position of authority. The kid must have gone through hell to earn those etchings; even some of the orcs didn't have them. In fact, he realized, those without the tattoos kept looking towards the kid for cues, and imitated whatever he was doing.

The last of the orcs shut the door gently behind him, and Thjostolf wiped the mead-foam from his mustache before speaking. "Welcome, friends. My name is Thjostolf sen Skarp-Hedin, and this unit is the Jomsskari. For those of you who do not know, that's old Haellic. It means 'wolfpack.'"

He rose from his position, setting his mug down and moving to the center of the room. "You're here to attend Selection for my unit. I did not say the Alliance's unit. I said my feckin' unit. Now, this unit is not regular infantry. We're not even regular scouts. We are the greatest feckin' warriors in the known world. I don't say that to brag, I just want you to understand what we're up to here. Feckin', I don't expect many of you to be selected, and that's not an indictment on you. Our standards are exceptionally high for a reason.

"We are not single entities in a group; we are the group. Should you enter this company, your very identity will become one with your compatriots. If a comrade falls, a part of you will fall with him. If there is discord among us, we are nothing. We are to be as a tortoise: our shields locked, our eyes looking together in a single direction, moving as a single organism. Feckin', as the Philosopher says, 'Be of one mind; a rope of many threads does not break.'"

He paused, and looked around. Some of the orcs looked a little nervous, and the elves looked even more upset than before. Thjostolf glanced at the kid. He was smiling.

Thjostolf turned to face him. "The selection process will consist of a series of exercises designed to test you in all of the warrior virtues. For those of you who haven't read the Philosopher, these virtues are humility, loyalty, discernment, benevolence, brutality, courage and honor." He glanced around, picked up his mead, and took a long sip before continuing. "We are humble in our respect for the enemy and our recognition of our place as warriors. We kill for the good of all, as servants to our kings and to the One Unsayable."

The orcs raised their eyebrows, and the kid glanced at the orc by his side and murmured something in orcish. Thjostolf made a mental note of it and went on.

"We are loyal to each other and our superiors, discerning in the best course of action, benevolent in peace, which sustains peace, and in war, which upholds our humanity. We are brutal in speaking truth, brutal in our physical bodies, and brutal in our capacity to exact violence on the enemy. We are courageous in the face of danger, and in the face of moral conflict. And Honor is the greatest of these, because Honor holds all of this together."

Thjostolf leaned against his desk again, musing for a brief moment. The room was entirely silent. Kolskegg looked around, watching each of the newcomers and gauging their reactions. Thjostolf looked at Peter. The halfling was rubbing the rim of his mug pensively, and Thjostolf smiled slightly. If anyone had the right to despise the orcs, it was Peter, but the halfling didn't show it. He glanced at the kid, who nursed his mead and stared dejectedly into the floor.

He cleared his throat. "Now, feckin', everybody probably has the same question, which is how the feck do we choose objectively?

Now, I'm not going to feckin' reveal our process or anything, but we have found that our selection process only brings in folks that can hack it. Feckin', if you're the right man for the job, we want you with us. So, here's what we're going to do, tomorrow morning at 0600, we will meet in formation in the courtyard. Uniform is boots, trousers, and tunic, and make sure you have a canteen."

One of the orcs growled, "What will we be doing?"

Thjostolf smiled and shook his head. "Could be anything. There's a lot of uncertainty in our line of work. We'll give you information as you need it. Just be sure to do as we say and you'll be fine. And don't worry, nothing we do in Selection is specialized."

The room was silent again, and Thjostolf let them stew over the information he'd given them before speaking. "Kolskegg, Rhys, show our friends to their quarters. You—" He pointed to the kid. "May I speak with you for a moment?"

The kid seemed stunned to have been singled out, but he caught himself quickly, bowed slightly, and said, "I hear and obey, sir."

"Good," Thjostolf smiled and glanced around. "If there are no questions, I'll let you all go. If you want to mingle about and finish your mead, that's fine with me, but you've had a long trip and I imagine you're tired. You've got some hard weeks ahead, so get a good meal at the chow hall and a good night's rest. Dismissed."

As the room emptied, Thjostolf circled around the back of his desk and took a seat. There was a small painting of Thorhalla on the desk, and he admired it for a moment. He hoped she would still be awake when he got back. Aud was wearing her out, and she liked to get to sleep as early as she could. He wanted to spend a few moments with her, just a few moments would be enough. It was lonely otherwise.

The kid waited until Kolskegg had gone, and as the door shut softly behind him, he snapped his heels together and stood at attention. Thjostolf looked him over. "Relax. Take a seat. I just wanted to ask you a few questions."

The kid sat down, looking somewhat nervous. He bit his lip, and Thjostolf saw him scratching his fingers together; perhaps it was a nervous tick. The kid looked somewhat larger now. Maybe it was because the orcs were no longer standing on either side of him. Thjostolf offered the kid some more mead, but he turned it down politely.

"What did you want to know?" he asked.

Thjostolf took a sip and leaned back. "Well, feckin', I wondered who you are and where you're from. I've never seen a man bear the markings of A'kaylii."

The kid hesitated for a moment, and then said, "Well, my name is Erik, sir. I'm from Havenstead."

Thjostolf raised his eyebrow. "What, here?"

"Yes, sir."

"You're feckin' me."

The boy shook his head and smiled. "No, sir."

"You're what, twenty?" Thjostolf asked.

"That's correct, sir."

"So, did you serve in the Belvade? You'd have been old enough, I think."

"I did, sir," replied Erik.

"And you returned to your father's house after the war, did you?"

Erik's smile faltered. "Well, no, not exactly, sir."

Erik shifted uncomfortably in his chair, and Thjostolf cocked his head. "What, then?"

"Well..." Erik wasn't making eye-contact. Suddenly he heaved an exasperated sigh, looked up, and locked Thjostolf with a tight-lipped stare. "It's...I'm a bastard, sir." He looked almost irritated.

Thjostolf looked at him. "Are you now?" *This is going to be interesting.*

"Yes." Erik smiled slightly as if bracing himself. "I'm not overly eager to tell you about it, but I suppose you want to know where your candidates come from."

Thjostolf thought for a moment, then leaned back and pulled his pipe out of the desk, stuffing it with tobacco. "I do have a vested interested. Feck it," he said. "I've got a few minutes, go ahead."

Erik breathed deeply and dropped his eyes. Then, with his eyes fixed on the desk, he began.

Chapter Four

The History, 10 October 1159

"I was born in 1139 in a small convent about seven miles from here, in the Industrial District. My mother was the daughter of a mechanical engineer. That's all I know about my extended family.

"When she got pregnant, she moved to the city to begin working in a factory. I think her family must have disowned her because she never spoke of them. She worked all through my childhood, and I grew up on the street. I had very little education but my mother encouraged me to read and bought me a few books that she couldn't possibly have had the money for.

"I began to work in a textiles mill when I was nine, but then they passed the Fair Labor Law that kept me from working until I was fifteen, so I had to leave. Instead, I found a job with a bookkeeper named Svend, who paid me a little and let me borrow books in exchange for odd jobs. My mother died when I was twelve, so Svend gave me a corner of the bookshop to sleep in. I ended up reading every book in the shop: philosophy, history, medicine, and the epics and tales of great warriors. That's heady stuff for a kid, you know. I was pretty sure I wanted to be a surgeon, but being a bastard, I knew I had no hope of entering the university. So, I put my hope of studying medicine behind me and tried to accept my role as a bookkeeper's assistant. I couldn't do it, though. I thought I was being unfaithful to the One Unsayable because I didn't like where I was, but I couldn't help but hope I could find a loophole.

"I had always been street-wise, but after my mother died I began intentionally exercising and getting into scraps with the kids in the schoolyards. I'd get beaten one day and come back and win the next. The fighting gave me an outlet and the exercising helped me stay still while I was in the shop. All of it kept my mind from dwelling on the past. Svend was a nice enough man, but he got angry when I fidgeted too much behind the counter or when I didn't pay attention to the customers. He was very particular about how things were done, and I learned to get all of my energy out in the mornings and evenings, when the shop was closed, so that I would be docile during the work day. Around that time I developed an affection for the physically demanding—climbing, running, anything that would push me to new heights.

"I had a few friends in the streets, but I was mostly a loner. See, I couldn't trust anyone for anything, even Svend, who intended the best. He was senile and forgot about me when I wasn't right in front of him, and so I often had to find my own food. I also learned to balance books and manage the store. Honestly, I kept the place running long after Svend's mind was all but gone.

"By the time I was sixteen I had learned enough from my reading to discuss theology and philosophy with the doctors at the monastery. They liked me, I think. I remember them asking me where I lived and whose son I was. I lied and said I was from El Commulbalbro and my father was a businessman who managed a warehouse in the town. I saved enough money to buy new books for myself. I chose books on anatomy, botany, and alchemy. Then one day I was discussing history with one of the doctors, who had become a sort of mentor to me. His name was Thorvald sen Arinbjorn, a historian, and he told me about a book he was sending to the printer's called *Modern A'kaylii*. He asked if I'd like a copy, and I told him I would. The things I learned from that book stayed with me."

Erik paused, and Thjostolf asked, "What did you learn?"

"Just about orcs," he replied. "How they think and why. Their history is one long tragedy. Did you know that?"

"How do you mean?"

Erik laughed a little, and said, "That's a very long story, sir. We'd be up all night on that topic."

"Fair enough," Thjostolf replied.

Erik nodded and paused, collecting his thoughts. "I suppose it was shortly after that Svend died. His younger brother Jan came to take over the business. Jan was ill-tempered to say the least, and when he discovered my...illegitimate birth he threw me out into the street without any of my belongings, shouting about how he wasn't going to have me stealing his money and sullying his good name and all kinds of eshé. Later that night I returned, gathered my things, and left. In his haste to get me out," Erik smiled wryly, "He forgot to relieve me of my key to the shop. And nobody knew that I no longer worked there, so I had no need to hide my actions.

"Mostly I had books, and I sold them, one by one, to buy food. Soon all I had left was *Modern A'kaylii* and a copy of the *Holy Words*. With nowhere else to go, I went back to the monastery and took Thorvald aside. I told him everything about my birth, my life, and my current situation, and then I asked for help. He was surprised, of course, but Thorvald was not unkind. He told me that he could help me get a job because the army was rarely concerned with parentage. And while I was unlikely to become an officer, I could easily become a sergeant before long. I had never thought about joining the army, but for whatever reason, it appealed to me and I accepted his offer. He took me to the barracks and pretended I was an orphan he had adopted. 'He doesn't care for the monastery,' he explained. 'He'd like to be a warrior.' They took me, of course. They had just recently heard that the goblin tribes were moving on Humbridge, and they expected a memorandum from Hrapp King calling for the army to prepare for war. They knew they would need me soon.

"I left that same day for training. I liked the army at once; I liked the rigorous discipline and the pride that each man had. They all knew that they were a part of something much bigger than themselves. It centered me when I was scattered and gave me a purpose. Our training cadre was rough and punished us often, but at the end of our first three months we were welcomed as brothers. I'd never had a family like the army."

"Where were you assigned?" Thjostolf asked.

"I was assigned to the Third Army, First Cohort, First Company, under the command of Sir Lief. I only had the simplest training as a rifleman. When I arrived at my new home, I saw that I was just one among many new recruits who had come in as replacements. Sir Lief had recently returned from the Belvade, and his company had taken heavy casualties. I think it affected him badly. I saw Sir Lief three times in the two months I was with him. He was not particularly interested in mingling with his inferiors, and he expected his sergeants to motivate us." Erik laughed, and shrugged. "If only there had been someone to motivate them."

Thjostolf was looking at him wonderingly. "I know that unit."

"Yes, sir, it earned some infamy. We were massacred, but...I'm getting there. When Haelhan attacked goblin-occupied Humbridge, we were placed on the northern edge of the Belvade river delta, which was thick forest territory. The goblins knew we were there and sent small raiding parties constantly. We repelled an attack every few hours. I now know what they were doing. They were wearing down our morale by killing one or two of us. They always carried away their dead, so we didn't know if we'd hit anyone, and when we advanced and found nothing, it looked like they had escaped unharmed. They were also testing us to see how much firepower we had. When they realized we were a relatively inexperienced infantry company, they let us advance in bad weather, waited for several hours for the climate to demoralize us, and then attacked with a full-strength infantry company reinforced with a small heavy weapons company."

Thjostolf gazed at him. "I was one of the scouts that came to investigate that raid. Sir Lief had been silent for hours, and we were afraid something had happened."

Erik cocked his head. "Really? I suppose you know that I was the only survivor."

Thjostolf nodded respectfully. "I'm surprised I didn't recognize you, to be honest. Now that you tell me, I do remember you. You had twisted a bit of leather around your wound and stopped the bleeding, yeah?"

"So I'm told. I'm afraid I don't remember much myself," Erik said. "I was taken to an aid station and patched up. But by the time my wounds had healed, three things had happened. First, the doctors tried to contact my family and found out I was a bastard. Someone then recommended that I be discharged. Secondly, the war ended, and the troops returned victorious. I was not permitted to take part in any of the ceremonies, partially because of my wounds, but partially because of my parentage. Finally, I got a letter informing me that my time of service was over, probably because of something one of the doctors had said. In any case, I was out of the army. It seems that my origins always find me.

"I was furious. I took my back pay and spent three days in Brandstead, on the border of Humbridge and Haelhan, trying to think of where to go next. I didn't want to resort to crime, but I had no legitimate prospects. I was afraid I'd have to steal bread to live. It was a long way from my dream of becoming a surgeon. Then one morning I awoke and remembered about the things I'd read about the A'kaylii warrior traditions and their code of honor. See, the A'kayliians believe that if you can prove yourself in their trials, then the One Unsayable has blessed you, and that'd be good enough for them. And I figured that, if it came to it, I'd just say I was an orphan.

"It sounded like a place I had a chance to fit into, so I spent the last of my money on a few supplies, a rifle, and some ammunition, and set out. I lived off poached game for months while hiking and sleeping in the open. By the time I reached A'kaylii, I was confident and skilled in stalking and foraging, and I was many times stronger than I had ever been in the Army."

"And the orcs took you in?" asked Thjostolf.

Erik hesitated, and smiled. "Well, sir...not exactly."

Thjostolf waited for elucidation.

"When I reached A'kaylii," Erik continued, "I had been traveling cross-country for about three months, and I really looked the part. I was...I was filthy, my hair was long and all tangled up and I had this scruffy beard. You know, face all scratched up and bloodshot eyes, I looked feral. After hiking up the mountains, I came to a plateau with a mud-shack and a small herd of goats in a pen. It was dusk, I remember...the sun was behind me, so I was silhouetted as I came up over the edge. The orcs were stirring, you know, how they're nocturnes by necessity. I saw a fire burning in the window of the mud-shack. Now I knew enough about orcs to know they didn't like surprises, so I kept my distance and hollered a greeting. Three orcs came out, real quick, with shotguns and kukris. We stood facing each other, about twenty yards apart, and just watched each other. I didn't know quite what to do, but I knew that they needed to know that I wasn't, you know, hostile. I had my rifle slung over my shoulder already, so I unslung it and set it down on the ground, stood with my hands facing palms up, and called out the greeting again. That seemed to relax them a little, and we traded pleasantries for a few moments. Finally, I asked if I could pass through their land, and they asked where I was going. 'To Kaḥji,' I answered, 'To enter the trails and become a warrior in the Clan A'kaylii.'

"The orcs looked at me for a moment, and I didn't know if they would laugh or get angry or what. It hadn't occurred to me that it might be an affront to them to suggest that I would participate in the trials. As I watched them, I suddenly wondered if I'd have to run. But then one of them sheathed his kukri, stepped forward, and offered to bring me before the council. His name was Khalan. He's one of the candidates with us now, a good friend of mine. He immediately took me to Kaḥji, and as we went he told me about the trials and asked me why I wanted to go through them.

"When I stood before the council, they told me I was too small to complete the trials. They told me to go back home. I looked at them and I said, 'I have no home. I will pass the trials and become A'kaylii, or I will die trying. But I will not leave these mountains until then.' In fact, everybody was curious if a little human could do it, and I understand there were a lot of bets riding on my performance. I got ridiculed a lot, especially at first. And so, the trials began."

Thjostolf nodded. "What was that like?"

Erik laughed. "Just over two years of unrelenting brutality," he said, "Once I spent four days with no food or sleep, in solitary confinement, and then was told to run ten miles up a peak and back. It was five miles up and five miles down. It actually felt really good to get out of the cage, but when I was finishing, three orcs leaped from the bushes and beat me senseless with their fists. When I regained consciousness, my trainer, an ancient orc named Mhal, was standing over me. He told me factually that I had to get up. I was so stiff and weak from starvation, the confinement, the run, and the beating, that I couldn't move at all for several minutes. I just started to struggle against myself. I remember thinking I was going to bleed out, though I wasn't sure if I was even bleeding. When I finally struggled to my feet and stood wavering before him, he put his arm around me and led me back to the training camp. And he told me something. He said, 'Death is an animal that preys on the hopeless. Hope is the food of hunger, fatigue, and pain, and where these dwell, hope is in danger. Therefore, be the master of yourself.'

"The physical conditioning was difficult, to be sure, but the training wasn't about that. The training was designed to break the mind, and remold it into something unbreakable."

He sat back, and sighed. "Two years of that," he said. "Two years of medical training, two years of being an orc with no such thing as a day off..." He shrugged and laughed. "I gotta say, after all that, I feel pretty good about any test."

They sat in silence for a few minutes, and Thjostolf looked pensively at him. "You'd better get some rest," he said. "You've got a long day ahead of you."

Erik left, and Thjostolf sat at his desk, silent. For several minutes he did not move. Then, he lit another bowl of tobacco, and puffed away, watching the smoke curl and dance before him.

I am entrusting you with this task because I believe you can set aside your reservations and be objective...

A bastard...it wasn't enough that he was a member of the orcish clans, but a bastard as well. But what had he himself said? A man is judged by his own blood, yeah?

The proof, he knew, was in Selection itself. Erik had a good story, and a good heart, perhaps – but he would have to prove both in the coming days. Thjostolf, for his part, was just excited to see how it turned out.

Chapter Five

The Regime, 11 October 1159

Erik and Khalan got up early and were in formation in the courtyard at 0550, just to be sure. All the other orcs were also ready, and there was a distinct sense of excitement in the air. They stood in a loose formation, ready to snap to attention when the situation called for it.

0600 came and went, and then 0615. There was no sign of the training cadre, and Erik was getting worried. Was it this courtyard, or another? Had they all just simply misunderstood?

By 0630, the orcs were grumbling among themselves, and a few had wandered off to sit down. Erik was considering joining them when the door at the far end of the courtyard creaked open. In a few frantic seconds, the orcs formed up, and stood rigidly at attention. *About time, too,* Erik thought.

He heard the footsteps coming across the courtyard, unhurried, and light. The elf, Rhys, the unit's second-in-command, was coming. Erik couldn't help but stare. Rhys was in a bathrobe and slippers, his hair disheveled and a cup of steaming tea in his hand. He spotted the formation, and, stopping in front of it, grinned at them as if confused.

"What are you doing out here?" he asked.

One of the orcs barked, "In formation as ordered, sir!"

Rhys looked taken aback. "What, now? Who ordered that?"

The orcs glanced at each other. The dwarf came out of the door, in half a uniform, chatting with the halfling. Rhys turned to them. "Hey, Brutus! Did you call formation?"

"No," he said, and then he addressed the formation. "Who put you knuckleheads out here, eh?"

The three gathered in a small circle and chatted idly for a few minutes. Erik could feel the tension tangibly in the air, and felt a little heat under his collar. *Who the feck do these people think they are?*

The dwarf finally took notice of them, and called out, "Hey, you guys can go get some breakfast or something."

"Yeah, fall out or whatever," said Rhys, taking a sip of tea. "The cafeteria's back there."

The orcs broke formation and headed out. Several of them griped quietly, but Erik decided to keep his mouth shut. Still, he felt abused somehow.

Khalan caught up with him. "That was strange, was it not?"

Erik shook his head, but didn't respond.

"I think I have a theory," the orc went on, in a conspiratorially low voice. "Either this unit is the most disorganized bunch of morons on the continent, or they are geniuses."

Erik glanced at him, confused. "How do you mean?"

Khalan smiled, but didn't reply. *Fine*, thought Erik, *Be mysterious*. But he considered it. Looking behind, he saw that the three were watching, and he thought he saw the halfling scribble something on a pad.

Breakfast was decent, no more or less, just a typical military meal of eggs and bread, with cheap tea. They emerged to find the training cadre assembled, and as they formed up, Erik noticed that the captain was absent. Rhys was in charge.

They started off with a physical fitness test of pull-ups, sit-ups, and push-ups. Then they loaded up in trucks and went out of the city, onto a plateau. There they ran three miles and navigated an obstacle course. The cadre really had their act together, Erik had barely enough time to catch his breath before he was doing the next event. It felt good, though. He hadn't been able to move much the day before.

The run was especially nice. Erik was a good runner, but not a great runner, and had learned to pace himself carefully. While some of the others surged ahead, he found himself a niche in the middle of the pack, and finished in nineteen minutes flat. Khalan was already stretching at the finish line when Erik arrived. Three miles was just a warm-up for Khalan.

The obstacle course consisted of jumping and hurdling several low walls, crawling through a tunnel, and carrying a sack weighing eight stone across a series of quick sprints before doing it all backwards. A perfect time was supposed to be forty-five seconds, but Erik managed forty-two seconds without too much trouble. He was used to these tests, they were the standard tests the Haellic army used to evaluate their troops. He was surprised, though, to see several of the orcs fail outright. Some of them couldn't do the run. Others couldn't finish the obstacle course, gasping for breath by the time they reached the halfway point.

They returned to the castle, and got some lunch. As they left the cafeteria, Khalan punched Erik lightly in the arm, and pointed. "Look at that," he said, "Out-processing."

Six or seven orcs stood in a queue, giving information to a staff sergeant before boarding a truck. Erik shook his head. The advertisement had clearly stated the physical requirements. This was an awfully long way to travel to flunk a fitness test.

That afternoon, they did a road march carrying forty-five pound loads. It was twelve miles long, and took Erik just under two and a half hours. He was in prime condition after the trials, and the march was a good stretch. By the end, he was sweaty, dusty, and his legs hurt, but it was a good feeling. He had paced himself off of Khalan, and as they finished, Erik commented, "Can you imagine having to work a desk job?"

Khalan just laughed. But when they got back to the Castle, they saw another three orcs throw in the towel. Ten orcs were already gone and it was just the first day.

*   *   *

Thjostolf had hoped to be present for the first day of the selection process, but a runner from General Njal found him at home as he woke. He quickly ate a wedge of bread and cheese, kissed Thorhalla, and mounted his horse with a brew in hand. Now he stood, a little bedraggled and with crumbs in his beard, in the Royal Council Chamber.

He was more than a little intimidated. General Njal stood nearby, his hands folded in front of him, looking at Thjostolf with a strangely troubled expression on his face. Seated at the head of the table was none other than Hrapp King himself. He wore a crown and his white beard and silver locks flowing perfectly from his head. He stared at Thjostolf almost manically, and said suddenly, "Thjostolf Captain?"

"Your Majesty." Thjostolf knelt in deference, and Hrapp coughed.

"Oh, get up, get up." The King stood and stalked around the council chamber as Thjostolf rose, looking him over. "You're a fine soldier, I'm told. I've heard your name mentioned many a time in my day."

"Your Majesty, I do what I can to honor your name."

"And you do well." He stopped in front of him, and nodded in satisfaction. "General Njal himself has personally recommended you on several occasions. You are in command of a detachment of

Jomsskari, am I correct?"

"You are, Your Majesty."

"And you are even now integrating the A'kalyiians into your ranks?"

Thjostolf nodded. "Your Majesty, they are here and beginning Selection as we speak."

"Fine, fine. Now listen, Thjostolf my boy, I've talked to the other monarchs and we think that once the training is complete we may have a job for you. How soon will these orcs be ready?"

"From this moment," Thjostolf said, trying to remember, "It will be eight months at least, I believe."

King Hrapp grunted harshly. "Then you will have them ready in four, am I right?"

Thjostolf blinked. "Yes, Your Majesty." *Four months?*

Hrapp clapped his shoulder and smiled knowingly. "Yes, you will."

He turned and stalked back to his seat, and flopped down. "You will be accompanied by our friend, Gabryl. He cannot be held to the same physical standards, but you will accommodate him."

Thjostolf took a deep breath. "Your Majesty, if I may be so bold –"

"Speak freely, captain."

"Why the rush, Your Majesty? Is there war?"

The King looked at him for a few moments, and his countenance darkened visibly, "I will let Gabryl explain."

Thjostolf glanced to the right and saw an old man sitting in a chair. Thjostolf wasn't sure how he had missed the man before. He was dressed in a simple brown robe and had a cane in his hand. He had been sitting so still that Thjostolf hadn't even noticed that he was there. The man looked up, and smiled vaguely. At his feet, a large wolf lay, silent and watchful. This shocked him more than the man had – the wolf was so out of place, once he saw him, that Thjostolf could not imagine how the creature had gone unnoticed until now. Yet as he looked at them, he was suddenly aware that they both knew – somehow, they *knew* – that they would be unnoticed until they chose to be seen. It was a disconcerting revelation, but he had not time to dwell on it.

"Have a seat, captain," invited the King. "Come, Njal, you too. Gabryl?"

The old man stood, slowly and a little painfully, and cleared his throat. "Thjostolf Captain sen Skarp-Hedin, your reputation precedes you. I am Gabryl, and this is my dear friend, Edwin Grey." He indicated the wolf, which whimpered softly. Thjostolf blinked, and tried not to smile. *Old guy really likes his dog.*

"I bring news from the north," he went on. "But if you will permit me, I will begin with history."

Thjostolf took his seat, and listened.

"Four thousand years ago," Gabryl began, pacing slowly the way old men often do, "The world was a different place. The Haellics were but wild fishermen, and the land above the Ahaern River was a kingdom in turmoil. Two rulers claimed two deities, and each demanded that the other bow the knee. One of these, led by an elf named Lord Matsu, served the Demons. His people where called the Alnethar, and they numbered 533,000 men-at-arms. The Iaelian king Delwyn ap Padrig served the One Unsayable, and his army numbered only 50,000. They were called the Iaelians.

"They met on the field of El Commulbalbro, land that had been named by Lord Matsu in anticipation of certain victory. But the One Unsayable blessed his servants, and Lord Matsu was killed, and his army routed. On that day, the Alnethar lost 400,000 elves. The remnant fled north, taking their women and children, and the Iaelians established a new kingdom and built their capital on the field of victory.

"The Alnethar wandered the wilderness for three thousand years, living as nomads. As the generations passed away, only a few remembered the Battle of El Commulbalbro. But there was one who remembered well: Lord Matsu's son, Lord Mushi. He passed his hatred on to his son, Lord Mouri, who passed it on to his son, Lord Mashutsu, who now rules the Alnethar.

"They have traveled a thousand miles to the north, and found the land of the griffins. It is a lush land, ripe with iron mines in the far north, and filled with oil beneath its eastern deserts. The griffins live in the lowlands, and have established a civilization in accord with the Alnethar. Under their alliance, the Alnethar have built factories, and have made weapons and equipment equal to your own. Moreover, they have learned to ride the griffins. The two species are allied, dominating both air and land. Everything north of the Wilderness now belongs to them.

"Lord Mashutsu has sworn to conquer the land north of the Ahaern, and destroy the allies of the Iaelians. They mean war, but they are not yet strong enough. Their war machine grows, but it is young. The time to strike is now.

"The land I speak of is El Ornahar," he said, "And you will know it better shortly."

He sat down again, and Thjostolf glanced at King Hrapp. The King looked grim. "What he says is true. The Monarchs have agreed to field an expeditionary force," he said, "To establish a line of defense along the southern border of El Ornahar and the Wilderness. We will learn their capabilities, tactics, and their resolve. The Jomsskari are the principles means by which this shall be accomplished."

Thjostolf looked back and forth at them, and nodded. "I hear and obey, Your Majesty," he said.

"Gabryl shall accompany your detachment," Njal said. "Take him to the training and teach him what he needs to know. He will be an advisor."

Thjostolf blinked again, and spoke as respectfully as he could. "General, if I may object, we are an elite unit. We march quickly and without delay, and we must fight without sleep or food. If he is to come with us, he must be able to keep up on his own strength."

Gabryl stood suddenly, and a brilliant light flashed through the room. It was as if the sun itself had descended on them—a wind, strong a gale, swept over him, and Thjostolf gripped the sides of his chair in terror.

The old man was transformed, and his voice thundered as if it came not from his throat but from the entire room. "I was there when Lord Matsu came onto the field!" he shouted. "I was there when his chariots shattered at our speartips, when his men fled in fear of us, when he himself fell, pierced a dozen times by our arrows! I struck down ninety men that day, and pursued them far into the desert!"

The light faded, and his form seemed to shrivel and shrink to its previous shape. His face glowed ever so slightly, but he smiled. "I can keep up," he promised.

Thjostolf stared at him, and when his voice came back he could only ask, "Who are you?"

*　　*　　*

The next morning, Erik and the orcs loaded their packs to weigh two and a quarter stone, drew their lunch rations from the quartermaster, and assembled in the courtyard. This time the cadre arrived in time, and Thjostolf addressed them.

"I was sorry I missed the start yesterday," he said, "But Rhys tells me you all passed the feckin' fitness tests, so let's get to the actual challenges." There was no mention of the morning's confusion, or those who failed.

Interesting.

"For the next week or so, we'll be doing feckin' long distance ruck marches over the mountains," Thjostolf went on, "You'll be carrying a rucksack weighing what we tell you. Today is two and quarter stone, plus water, a compass, a flare, and a map. You will be given a number and letter designating your lane, and will board the truck with your letter on the tailgate. Once you reach your starting point, you will be given your current coordinates, and the coordinates of your first waypoint. You will then navigate to your waypoint, receive your next coordinates, and so forth. This is not a self-correcting course. At each waypoint you will simply be given your next coordinates, not your current coordinates. That means if you end up at the wrong waypoint, assigned to another lane, then you will not receive your correct position and all subsequent navigation will be incorrect.

"Let me remind you that this is a feckin' personal effort. If you are spotted assisting another candidate, you and that candidate will be removed from the program. If you run into trouble, remember that you have been issued an emergency flare. Stay put and fire your flare. Our medical teams will locate you. Any questions?"

One of the orcs raised his hand. "Sir, how much time do we have to complete the course?"

"There is a time standard, but it is not yours to know," said Thjostolf. "Just do your best."

*   *   *

And so, it began. For the next few days, they trekked back and forth across the mountain. For the majority of the time, Erik was alone. When he did see another candidate, they would only briefly cross paths. They would greet each other, but neither would stop. At each waypoint, there was a member of the cadre, who would weight his rucksack and tell him to get his new coordinates from a reference sheet. Erik would write it down, find his heading, and be off. Luckily, he was quite skilled in land navigation. It came naturally to him, and he had practiced a lot traveling to A'kaylii.

The system was simple. As Thjostolf had explained, they needed only to navigate from one place to another. At the first station, they were told the current time and the time when they were overdue. If they were overdue, they got cut from the program, but of course, they didn't know for sure how far they'd be going that day. The objective was fairly obvious; the candidates had to push themselves, but they had to be smart, too. Each candidate had to know how to use the land to their favor and how to pace themselves. They didn't get much sleep, either. Most days they were up before dawn and kept going until well after dark. After a few days of this, sleep deprivation began to affect Erik's judgment. Even simple tasks now took his undivided attention.

These things didn't bother Erik much. What bothered him the most was the silence of the cadre. They spoke very little, and never gave any indication that Erik was doing well or poorly. At one point, he was so exhausted from the lack of sleep and so frustrated by the lack of input that he forgot to watch where he was going, and almost slipped into a ravine.

Shortly after that incident, Erik had an epiphany. The unit was looking for people who could endure not only the physical stress of the work, but the mental stress of constant uncertainty. They gave the impression of being unprofessional, but it was just because of the kind of work they had to do. He could see it now in the unpredictable schedules and the surprises—the first morning, for instance, and the fact that nobody knew much about anything that was going on.

Armed with this revelation, Erik found the tests much easier. Even when the coordinates called for him to cross the same territory four or five times in a day, and even after a twenty-five-mile hike, he kept reminding himself that the unit was looking for something more than a great warrior. They were looking for long-range scouts, men who were made of a different mettle. At the end of every day he basked in the satisfaction of making it through the last march, and every morning he found himself more and more driven to prove himself.

One day, when they returned to the barracks, Erik saw that an acquaintance, Mukhmed, was already there. His feet were propped up and wrapped in bloody bandages. The stick of a lollipop stuck comically from the corner of his mouth, and he waved cheerfully at Erik when he saw him.

"Eshé, what happened to you?" Erik asked.

Mukhmed shook his head and smiled the way someone does when they are making light of an extremely painful condition. "Good doctor, I walked my feet off."

"You what?"

"I used to march a lot with the Royal Guards, but then I was given a job as a clerk," Mukhmed explained. "I retained my calluses, but they were not rooted to my feet, so when I started marching last week I got blisters underneath them. I took off my boots yesterday and the bottoms of my feet stayed in the boot."

"Eshé-ma." Erik shook his head. "Are you going to be okay?"

"Yeah, it'll all heal. I'm going to try this again next year, but I think I should work up to it." Mukhmed laughed. "How about you? Are you still in the game?"

"So far. We'll see."

All week long, the candidates crisscrossed the terrain, now

carrying three stone, and Erik ended each day sore, soaked in sweat, and more determined than ever not to cave. The routes were getting harder, too. The terrain was rough, and the waypoints were in such a position that Erik couldn't use the land to his advantage. He frequently found himself having to wage war on the mountain, and as exhaustion set in, he found it harder and harder to make intelligent choices about the routes. He suspected that this was one of the primary skills the Jomsskari were looking for.

Going back to the barracks everyday was always welcome. Then, on the twelfth day, they got a nasty surprise. They had just finished a twenty-six-miler, and everybody was worn out. The lights went out and Erik fell asleep in a matter of seconds. Then, shaking, lights, and shouts erupted. They were called to formation, no more than an hour after going to sleep. As they stood, bleary-eyed and irritated, Thjostolf came out.

"Sorry to wake you, guys," he said, "But we need you to write an autobiography for tomorrow morning, six to eight pages. Try to be specific. Brutus has paper and pens. Thanks!" He went back inside.

Erik finished his and got about a half an hour of sleep before they were roused. That day was the hardest. They only went about twenty miles, but it was a dozen shorter runs, and through the rockiest and thorniest territory on the mountain. When they got back to the barracks that night, Erik was totally exhausted, and many of the orcs had vanished into the out-processing lines. For the first time, he realized that there were only six orcs left, including himself and Khalan. The numbers were dropping rapidly.

The next day was a comparatively easy day. Erik finished by midafternoon, and as he sat by the last waypoint, he calculated that he had only traveled about eighteen miles. That afternoon he took a nice long shower, found Khalan, and played cards with him for a couple hours. He was glad that Khalan had made it so far. Even though they couldn't help each other on the field, having a close friend nearby was comforting. It made the whole experience a little less surreal. That evening, Thjostolf convened them. "Try to get some good sleep tonight," he advised them. "Tomorrow is the forty-mile. And make sure your rucks weigh three and a quarter stone."

Erik woke up the next morning with a splitting headache, and knew the day was off to a bad start. The sun had barely risen when they arrived at the starting points, and each of the remaining candidates was sent off according to the roster number they had been given, just as they had the days before. Erik's had been 3-B, and when the 3's were called forward, he shouldered his rucksack. The dwarf, Brutus, was there, and impassively pointed to the map on the tailgate of the truck. Erik took down his coordinates and the coordinates of his destination, and began plotting his course. He had to choose a path that would give him the best time while holding a pace that he could keep up.

It wasn't easy with the beast on his back. Carrying the rucksack was like giving a ten-year-old child a piggy-back ride mile after mile, and the mountainous terrain made a simple misstep downright dangerous. Erik had lost his footing a couple of times in the last week, but had managed to twist his body so that the rucksack didn't drive into the back of his head. He wasn't at all sure he could recover from that kind of blow. It could easily lead to a concussion or fractured skull.

He started off. The first leg was about a mile and a quarter, and when he got there he felt okay. The sun was up, and the earth was beginning to warm. It was mid-October, and the trees were brilliant with color. His headache was starting to go away, too. As he started the second leg, he was beginning to feel pretty confident.

He was moving up a draw—a stream had cut through the mountain, and his course dragged him right across it. He spent several minutes navigating a patch of wait-a-bit vines, and when he emerged, cursing and bloody, he had to stop and find his bearings.

By his calculations, he was about a mile from the next way point. He checked his azimuth and took a drink from his canteen. As he started off, his foot slipped on a wet stone. He flew forward, the weight of the ruck rising on his back. He twisted, throwing his hands out. *Crack!* He cried out as he landed on his side.

He had averted the broken skull, but had twisted his ankle. Now swearing profusely, he took off his boot and inspected it. It wasn't broken, but it was swelling and bright purple— a bad sprain. The pain was intense. He could barely put any weight on it.

The thought crossed his mind, *Maybe this is it. Maybe I need to be sensible and fire my flare.* He thought about it for a few seconds, and shook his head. That wouldn't do. It wasn't broken, he could continue.

He rolled onto his chest, pushing himself up to his knees before standing. The pain in his ankle was excruciating, but it wasn't immobilizing. Gingerly, he pulled his bootlaces tight and winced at the pain. Then, steeling himself, he got his heading, and with one last expletive, started up the mountain.

The next mile was agonizing, and as he limped up to the waypoint, he saw the cadre member, the halfling Peter Stills, watching him. When he reached the spot, Peter asked, "Do you need medical attention?"

Erik knew it would mean removal from the course, but as tempted as he was to throw in the towel, he shook his head. "I'm fine – it's just a twist," he said. "My number is 3-B."

"Get your next coordinates and move out when you're ready." Peter scribbled something on his pad, and turned away.

The next leg was even worse, and by midday Erik was muttering an oath with every footstep. His rucksack was merciless, too. As the day wore on, the shoulder straps dug deeper and deeper into his shoulders, leaving his hands tingling and his neck sore. It wasn't extraordinary, it was just how it felt to march. But it felt worse now because of his ankle. At each waypoint, the cadre offered him medical attention, and took a note when he refused.

In the late afternoon, he did the calculations, and felt crestfallen. He was lagging behind the pace he'd set, and had only gone about thirty-two miles. That meant at least eight more to go, and not much more daylight left. He would be overdue at 2100, which only gave him two and a half hours to make the last way points. What if it was ten more miles, or twelve? He couldn't cover twelve miles in that time, not with a busted joint.

He was so tired, his head so filled with confusing fog that he had to talk himself through it out loud. He decided to do his best anyway. If he was late, then he was late. At least nobody could say he'd quit.

He made the next waypoint. It was Thjostolf at the truck, and the captain seemed vaguely amused. He was playing with his pencil, and as Erik came up to him, he waved. "How you holdin' up, trooper?" he asked, as if they had just met in the street.

It was the first time in two weeks that any of the cadre had talked like that during the day, and it took Erik off guard. "I'm good, captain," he said, a little suspiciously.

"Get your next coordinates," Thjostolf instructed. "You sure you don't want some medical attention? You can come back and try later, you know. And if you need a break, this is the time and place to do it. Nobody's around, and I promise I won't tell."

"I'm good," Erik snapped. Actually, he felt terrible. He was exhausted, and the change in his stride had given him a large blister on the side of his good foot. His feet were already chewed up from the constant marching. For days, they had felt like someone had been hitting them with a sledge hammer. Now he was limping off both sides and the best he could do for it was to tighten his boot laces and drive on.

Thjostolf shrugged. "Whatever floats your boat," he said, and returned his attention to the pencil.

Erik started the next leg gritting his teeth, and kept gritting the whole way through. Night fell, and he almost twisted both his ankles again as he stumbled through the darkness. He was so tired that his eyes wouldn't quite focus. Ironically, the pain in his feet kept him alert. He could feel his ankle swollen inside his boot.

What if this isn't the last march? he thought suddenly. *Can I do this again tomorrow?*

He decided to deal with one problem at a time. It was fifteen minutes until he was overdue, and he was just under a mile from the next point. He was heading into a mountain, too, with a steep hillside. He had tried his best, but there was no way to get around this one. He had to face the mountain.

The foliage wasn't too bad, he was thankful for that. Every step up the slope was a battle, and everything in him demanded that he stop. Erik found himself crawling up the hill at moments, and he knew from the wetness in his boot that his blister had burst, and the raw skin beneath was bleeding. His chest heaved, his tunic was soaked in sweat, and the droplets dripped in his eyes, burning and stinging at the same time. His breath burst from his chest in ragged gasps. He spotted the truck up ahead, and as he limped up to it, he glanced at his watch. It was 2058 and he had only two minutes to spare.

The quiet elf was there, Wendyll. Erik gave him his number and letter. Wendyll nodded, wrote something down, and said, "Get your next coordinates and move out when you're ready."

Erik shook his head in disbelief. He splashed some water on his face and took a long drink. Then, setting his face grimly, he got his coordinates and began plotting his course. He didn't know how he could have gone any faster. He realized that even with the ankle, he had made decent time. He knew he couldn't make it to the next point in time, especially when he saw that it was almost four miles away.

He swore softly to himself, shouldered his rucksack, and started walking. Overdue or not, he was going to finish this march.

"Wait!" Wendyll called. Erik glanced back, and Wendyll beckoned him back. "Sit here, by the side of the truck," he ordered. "You're done for tonight."

Erik wasn't sure how to take it. Had he been cut from the program? Had Wendyll called him back so he wouldn't waste anyone's time? He decided, as he flopped down by the big tires, that he really didn't care. There was nothing to do now but hope that he had made it. If he didn't make it this time, he knew he had to come back and try again. He couldn't look at himself in the mirror knowing he had come so close and failed for a twisted ankle.

He waited for a few minutes and then an orc staggered in. Wendyll got his information and ordered them both on the truck. They were the only ones in the back of the truck, and Erik felt distinctly alone. The orc fell asleep immediately. Erik considered taking his boots off, but really didn't want to have to put them back on. He decided to wait, and spent the rest of the ride trying to think of something besides the pain.

When they got back to the castle, they were the last truck to pull up, and Erik gingerly climbed from the truck. His feet were so tender that he could hardly move them. As he pulled his rucksack after him, Wendyll told him to follow him, and instructed the orc to return to the barracks.

Erik rested his rucksack and followed Wendyll back down to Thjostolf's office. Wendyll went in and closed the door behind him. A few seconds later he came back out, "Come on," he said.

Erik stepped into the room and saw Khalan was there, too. There was another orc that he knew, a tough demolitions technician named Khlannad. They were both seated, and looked at Erik with languor. The rest of the team was there, too, and Thjostolf stood, leaning on his desk. "Take a seat," he offered.

Erik sat down next to Khalan. Thjostolf looked them over. He had a curious expression on his face. Finally, he spoke.

"Gentlemen," he said softly, "Welcome to the Jomsskari."

Chapter Six

The Jomsskari, November 2, 1160

They were given a few days to heal, just the three of them. Khalan and Khlannad weren't in much better shape than Erik, although their ankles were okay. Khlannad had a stress fracture in his shin, and all three of them spent much of their free time soaking their feet.

Out of the original thirty-four candidates, they were the only three that had passed. It turned out that the other Jomsskari units had taken similar numbers: First Jomsskari processed two, and Third Jomsskari didn't get any. Since Third Jomsskari were still a man short, they asked Thjostolf for one of his. Naturally, Erik and Khalan wanted to stick together, and conspired to convince Khlannad into transferring to Third Jomsskari. But it was unnecessary. Third needed a demolitions technician, and Thjostolf wanted a medic and a machinegunner. "Ordinarily we would let you have some say in the matter," said Thjostolf, "But you happen to be exactly what we need already, and we're pressed for time."

It was the first week of November when Erik and Khalan began training with the rest of the unit. The first day, they were issued their new gear and Erik knew that the hellish ordeal of sleep deprivation and exhaustion had been worth it. The Jomsskari were privy to the best of Alliance equipment. They had cloaks made by the Elves with ancient magic woven into the very fabric. When Erik first put his on, he was startled by how soft it was, and as he watched, he felt his eyes deceiving him. It was as if no matter how hard he tried, he couldn't look directly at it. The cloaks, and anything beneath them, seemed to vanish before his eyes. The Iaelian mages, he learned, made them specially for the Jomsskari. He was so enthralled by the magical properties that he tried it out on every surface like a schoolboy with a new toy. Of course, the other Jomsskari laughed at him, but Brutus told him that they'd all done the same thing when they'd first gotten theirs.

The Dionysians mages had forged their own contribution of chainmail tunics, made from a pearly grey stone mined from the heart of White Mountain. Erik couldn't fathom the cost of the armor. He had heard of Dwarven armor before, but only in legend. To hold it in his hand left him spellbound. It was extraordinarily light, and nearly indestructible. Thjostolf took them out to the shooting range, put a piece of the Dionysian mail on a dead goat, and invited them to shoot it. Erik and Khalan tried everything from knives to sniper rifles, all to no avail. They even tried their revolvers. Erik found out that the goat's meat was badly bruised from the ordeal, but otherwise unharmed. Khalan, being practical in that way, reasoned that it would suffice for dinner. That night the unit was introduced to A'kayliian cuisine, and everybody was pleasantly surprised when even the Elves declared it exotically delicious.

They were also issued vests with pouches sewn in various positions. It was a vast improvement on the thick canvas belt and bandoleers that Erik had been issued in the Haellic infantry. The vests allowed Erik to carry eight hand grenades, twelve spare magazines for his carbine, and enough food and water to survive for several days. They also had pouches for maps, loops to attach more items to, and a butt pack that Erik stowed his medical gear in. In this way, every one of the company could fight and survive off of nothing but the contents of their vests, and these essentials were soon dubbed the "oh shit kit."

There was a downside, though. Altogether, without the rucksack, his gear weighed about thirty-five pounds. With his ruck, he carried nearly eighty-five pounds. By the New Year, he remembered the days of carrying only fifty pounds with some fondness.

Their weapons were beautiful, too. Most of the Jomsskari

were given a Haellic Mark 7 rifle, about a yard long and eight pounds in weight. They were made simply, and Rhys showed them that they could be dragged through mud, snow, and water, and still fire accurately. Erik was issued a M27, a short carbine version of the same rifle, using the same magazine and the same ammunition. It weighed less and was a little more compact; it helped to offset the extra weight he carried in his medical kit.

For Khalan, they had a GP-10 machine gun. For an elf or a human, the weapon was bulky, but Khalan hefted it easily. It fired from an ammunition belt, and Khalan carried eight hundred rounds in his kit. Peter, who had been the assistant gunner for the injured Olaf, volunteered to assist him, and carry an addition twelve hundred rounds. His immense pack was somewhat lessened by Khalan's capacity to carry his own tripod.

As November drew closer, they prepared to go into the field for extended training. Erik was in the unit barracks, checking all his gear as he packed it into his rucksack, when Thjostolf came in and called for their attention. "Gentlemen, I'd like to introduce Gabryl and his companion, Edwin Grey," he said. "They are going to accompany us in the coming months."

Erik and the rest of the team looked him over. Gabryl was unimpressive and slouched a little. He looked about sixty, and was beginning to bald. His eyes were hidden behind a pair of thick glasses, and his white hair and beard were a little unkempt, hanging lazily from his head as if it had already resigned itself to falling out entirely. He was dressed in Haellic fatigues, a little too big for him, and carried a stripped-down kit over his shoulder. When he noticed that Thjostolf had stopped talking, he waved casually and said, "Good morning, gentlemen."

Edwin panted, looking at his master. Erik thought the wolf looked concerned, and smiled to himself.

"Gabryl is not a soldier," Thjostolf reminded the team, "He won't be carrying spare ammunition or explosives or the like, just the essentials. Edwin will do his part, too, but make sure they understand what we're doing and their role in it."

"Where'd you get the wolf?" asked Kolskegg, coming over and running his hand over the animal's head.

"It's a long story," replied Edwin, wagging his tail. "I'll tell you when we have time to discuss matters of leisure."

Kolskegg jerked his hand back as though he had been touched by lightening. Brutus fell off his bunk. Rhys and Wendyll leapt to their feet, and Peter, in his typical unabashed manner, exclaimed, "Whoa, hey, talking wolf, the feck!"

Edwin panted, and looked to Gabryl for direction. The old man smiled. "Go on," he said softly.

"In brief," said Edwin, "I am sworn to my master, Gabryl, from when I was a pup. He gave me a mind worthy of my station, and a long life to serve him. Please don't be alarmed. I know it is a bit surprising at first."

Erik laughed uncertainly. "Well…I'm sure we're all happy to meet you, but…it doesn't answer the question of how exactly the feck is this happening?"

"Who cares?" declared Peter exuberantly. "This is the best!"

From that moment on, Edwin Grey was a favorite.

*   *   *

They started their training by marching out into the wilderness and spending a fortnight or so in the field. While they were out, they practiced their combat drills – reacting to an ambush, breaking contact, react to contact – the basics of infantry warfighting. Erik learned to communicate with his team members amid the deafening roar of combat: exploding grenades, chattering gunfire, everybody shouting. He learned how to turn an ambush around on the attackers, and how to escape from a pursuing force. All this was standard to scouts from every nation, and it didn't surprise Erik much. The ferocity and realism of the training, however, was unique.

Then they started learning more complex skills like how to raid a fortified position, and how to wire a bridge or some other structure with explosives. Like Selection, the training was intense, Erik got used to fighting with very little sleep and not enough food or water. Unlike Selection, however, he was working in a team, and while he was still responsible for his own kit, he felt a sense of group identity that he felt he could get attached to. He was really beginning to enjoy himself.

After they had spent almost two months honing their basic infantry drills, the Jomsskari began to ply their new recruits for skills and insights. Erik taught the Jomsskari how to treat various wounds, and how to improvise not only extremity tourniquets but junctional tourniquets, to stop arterial bleeding in difficult spots such as the pelvic girdle and the shoulder. Khalan and Brutus traded knowledge on explosives. They trained with pack horses, learning how to protect them without losing the initiative, and move the steeds through forests and mountains without leaving a trail. Throughout all of it, Erik found himself amazed by the professional and dedicated sense of duty the Jomsskari displayed on a daily basis. Everything they did, they treated as essentially important, from digging a slit latrine to handling high explosives to feeding the horses.

December came, and then the New Year. They camped in the snow, living in the frightful cold of the Haellic highlands. Erik was getting to the point where responding to enemy contact was reflexive; he could shoot moving targets at two hundred yards. Every day they fired hundreds of rounds, and Khalan got so good with his GP-10 that he could cut a tree in half without wasting a bullet. It was impressive to watch, if not a little disconcerting.

The snipers were incredible to watch, too. Wendyll and

Kolskegg were so good they could put bullet after bullet into the same hole at five hundred yards, and they had competitions to see which of them would have the tighter shot pattern at distances as far as nine hundred yards. Whoever lost the most in the course of their time in the field had to buy the entire company a round of ales when they got back to Havenstead. Twice in a row, Kolskegg won by one eighth of an inch, and he took every opportunity to remind Wendyll of the fact. Indeed, it was the first time he had ever beaten the elf.

They only returned to civilization to refit, get more ammunition, and targets before heading out again, but they finally came back for good in early January. Now their training became focused on map making, and Erik learned the techniques of cartography. They went out to the coast and learned how to use boats, and how to land on a beach and mark a landing zone. They learned how to control a beachhead and how to withdraw with casualties. Erik became very concerned about some parts of the Jomsskari's established procedures, and they worked on new methods to move wounded. The old system would only work to move ambulatory casualties, that is, wounded who could move themselves. After they discussed it, the unit designed and build compact stretchers to move immobilized casualties.

Through it all, they spent at least a couple hours a day shooting at the ranges, and Erik's marksmanship just kept getting better. Even Gabryl, who didn't seem like he had ever handled a rifle at the beginning, had mastered his fundamentals and was becoming a crack shot. In fact, any lingering doubts the Jomsskari had about Gabryl were quickly dispelled. Edwin proved himself invaluable in short order, using his exquisite sense of smell to navigate and scout around their positions. Gabryl, for his part, proved stronger and faster than he looked, and while he spoke very little, the Jomsskari soon respected him as a member of their team, rather than an impostor.

In mid-February, Thjostolf called them together. When they were all assembled in his office, he shut the door and leaned against his desk.

"Well, gentlemen," he said, smiling proudly, "I talked to King Hrapp today, and informed him of our progress. We both agree that this company is ready to go."

Ready or not, they weren't going anywhere yet. For the next several weeks, they sharpened their skills, keeping their ears open for news of the coming campaign. It was early March before Erik began hearing whispers of a build-up, and shortly afterwards the Jomsskari were relocated to the fjords on the western coast, where the vast bays formed natural ports. Erik had never been to the fjords, and was awestruck at the sight. They stretched out majestically, the waves crashing against the rocks and the smell of brine filling the air. He had read about the fjords as a child, but had not imagined that they could be so beautiful.

Fjordstead was their new home for the next several weeks. It was the primary naval base on the channel between Haelhan and White Mountain. Already, Dionysian warships from White Mountain, trawlers and troop carriers from Haelhan, and tankers and cargo ships from Iaelia had begun to assemble. While the Jomsskari spent their time marching to remote corners of the fjords and practicing their tactics, Dionysian engineers and weapons companies began to arrive. When they got back from the field, they found Elves, Dwarves, Haellics, a handful of halflings, and even a couple of A'kayliian weapons companies had arrived. Each time they returned, they discovered more.

In all, there were seven warships and twenty transports in the bay, and as they watched over the next week they saw ton after ton of materials loaded aboard: steel girders, lumber, food, potable water. Clunkers, piglets, small armored gun trucks that squealed when they drove, and millions of rounds of ammunition were all loaded. Every day brought with it more activity, until Fjordstead was a veritable beehive. Thjostolf went to a lot of meetings, and so Rhys was largely in charge of training, but by now everybody was getting the hang of it. Erik was aware that he was going to have to learn much of the trade as he went, but he didn't mind. If nothing else, his experience in A'kaylii had prepared him well. The only orcs that passed Selection had already passed the Trials, and while some Orcish Warriors didn't make it through, Erik was sure that the intense training had given him a leg up.

They received orders to board their transport on the twenty-first of March. It was the first time Erik had been on a real ship, and he wasn't impressed. The warships were new dreadnaughts, with enormous guns that fired hundred-pound shells across miles of open sea. They were made from steel and powered by big diesel screws. But the Jomsskari weren't quartered on the nice new vessels. The troop transports they were on were somewhat more archaic, made from wood and originally designed to run off steam-engines. The big diesel propellers that moved them now had been retrofitted in the last five or six years, and the guts in the engine room were so suspect that Erik made it a point to be near a lifeboat when they finally started their engines.

Of course, they didn't get under way until the twenty-third, and the constant bobbing had given Erik a nicely queasy stomach over the last week. He was eager to get going despite the nausea – although, at that point, he still didn't know where exactly they were off to.

All that changed when they finally chugged out of the fjords and turned north. Thjostolf gathered the Second Jomsskari together on the forecastle and, shouting over the churning engines, he told them about their mission. Erik had never heard of griffins, and was a little startled to learn about them. When it was time to ask questions, everybody had several.

*   *   *

They steamed towards El-Ornahar for six weeks. In order to maintain their calluses, Thjostolf had the Jomsskari doing calisthenics in their vests and boots every day, and they used the open deck to learn hand-to-hand fighting. It was illuminating for Erik. He had learned a little from his time in the Haellic army, but most of his knowledge came from the A'kayliian arts. The Iaelian martial arts were completely different than anything Erik had done before, and the Dionysians had developed an entire method around their low center of balance. They spent an hour or two a day sparring for a couple weeks, until Thjostolf got worried that they were going to break each other's necks and asked them to focus on wiring inert explosive systems instead. While he was asleep, though, they still organized their own matches, and Erik found himself crushed by Brutus, who mercilessly pinned him to the deck every time they fought.

They talked a lot, too. The debates started only a few days out of Fjordstead, when Erik had found himself sitting with Rhys and Wendyll during chow. They were arguing about something that had cropped up in a philosophy forum the week before they set sail. Soon the range of topics had spread to include everything from politics, to theology, to philosophy, and even physics. Erik loved it. One of the things he had missed in the regular army was talking to highly educated men. The Jomsskari was the best of every world.

For the most part, Gabryl stayed out of the arguments, sitting off to the side with his wolf and smiling slightly to himself. In fact, he didn't talk much in general, and when he did, it was to exchange soft words with Thjostolf or Edwin. Though the Jomsskari would not be so rude as to discuss him within earshot, his presence was also a consistent topic of conversation. Nobody really knew what he did or why he was with them.

The hardest part of sea life, Erik quickly discovered, was not the food, or the motion sickness. It was finding a moment of solitude. A few days out of Fjordstead, he discovered a small shelf near the stern of the ship, just large enough for him to sit on. It was out of the way and quiet, and afforded a good view of the stars. As crowded as it was below decks, he found himself retiring to the shelf for an hour or so every night. Letting his mind wander, smelling the fresh air, calming himself until he began to be tired enough to sleep, though he could not.

There was something he had left out. He hadn't told the whole to Thjostolf—there was one central impression that was missing. Perhaps it was because he had hardly spoken of it to anyone, even to himself—the dawn of it was slow, more like the emerging of a faint star through a cloudscape than a sunrise. Or perhaps it was more like a sunset—a gradual descent into the deep.

He had first realized it when he received his discharge papers, after the massacre, after his so-called "healing" was over. He remembered the shock of it quite well. Standing outside the hospital, facing the town, he had been hit by a sudden sense of futility. No, not futility. He had felt as though he stood on air, plummeting in total darkness, and seeing himself as though he were another, he gazed.

It was not merely his actions that felt futile. In the coming days, he became increasingly aware of the extent of the futility. He was more than just a "who," he was a "how" as well, and neither of his two pieces had a place. It was like a miss-matched jigsaw puzzle.

He fell, deeper into the dark, and his grasping at the darkness only spun him around. He gave it a name. He called the feeling the Absurd. It was not merely absurd in its consequences or its causes. The cycle was not merely absurd, nor was the conditions that made the cycle possible. All of these were absurd, but the Absurd was more, it was the wholly terrifying blackness that crept closer and closer around him. It was his state of being, not merely an act or condition, but a characteristic.

He fought it. He thought perhaps he was missing a home, and so set off to find one. All he needed was a welcoming community, and so the orcs became family. Once he had thought the same about knowledge, and studied hard. He had thought the same of the military, as well. There was something more than having a place, he had to approach that place in a certain way. That was what it was to have no "how." But with no "who," he had no chance of acquiring the "how."

Long nights crying out to God Almighty, to lay still and hear the wind whistle coldly through the rocks. Long marches, long runs, long days without food, and long weeks wishing for a hot meal or enough water for a bath. And leaving a shattered spider for the sport of crows had earned him his tattoos, and not one drop of understanding. The sun rose and set, and the trees bloomed and died. Harvest and spring ran by, and the tides sashayed every night.

The hard work distracted him from the Absurd, but only for a moment. As he lay awake at night, he would remember the dead, and remember the living with even more horror. Cry out to God— whistling wind. As regular as the day.

So, God was silent. The One Unsayable said nothing. Perhaps only for a while, perhaps for a good reason, perhaps this, perhaps that. The problem was not for the future, nor for the past. The problem was for the present, the immediate "now," and with every passing day it became more urgent. For with the silence of the Divine, the only question left was not of abstract theology or high philosophy, but simply the question of suicide.

*　　*　　*

Four weeks into the voyage, Erik was getting the hang of sea life. The sickness was gone now, and the food, though still rancid to the taste, no longer made him ill. To pass the time, he and Khalan had started taking pointers from the Dionysian Marines on how to fight aboard a ship. It was intense, and excellent training. All told it was not so different from the inside of a cave, claustrophobic and very dynamic. Clearing tight corners became paramount.

It was late afternoon. The sun was setting to the west, and the amber orb lit up the ocean like a match touched to pitch. Erik was barefoot, his boots set aside. As he stood, leaning on the port rails and watching the daystar sink, he thought about the last couple of months. Jomsskari was an incredible unit to be with, he'd have to thank Thassed when they met again. They'd received a few letters from him, and sent their own, but Erik missed his orcish father. It would be a while before Thassed even learned they had departed.

Peter joined him, a bag of walnuts in his hand. The halfling was only about three feet tall, and he had to climb up on the first rail to see over the top. "Hey, mermaid," he said suddenly, and pointed.

Sure enough, a woman's body slid up through the waves, and Erik heard a melody, low and haunting, sail through the air to him. She disappeared after a moment, and Peter shook his head, grinning and tossing a walnut shell into the sea. "Don't see that every day."

Erik nodded dumbly. "I thought they were mythological," he said, after a few seconds.

"No, they're real enough. Oh, see, she brought a friend."

There were two of them now, and then three. Some sailors whistled affectionately at them, and they cooed in response. Erik watched the exchange with wonderment, reaching distractedly into the bag. Peter grinned again, and rested his chin on the rail, chewing slowly. "You ever seen a lady like that?" he asked.

Erik shook his head, cracking the nut. "Unmarried," he reminded him.

Peter nodded. For a moment they didn't say anything, and then the halfling laughed, "Well, that didn't stop me."

Erik laughed.

"Yeah, well..." Peter shrugged. "Young and impertinent, that was me. The girls from the finishing school down the road used to bathe in the creek, so of course some of the guys would try to sneak around and have a look-see. The first time I went it was with some of the older guys. They said they wanted to show me something, didn't specify what. Well, I can't say they never did anything for me." Peter laughed again, and Erik chuckled, shaking his head. "Well, that was a long time ago," finished Peter, and cracked another shell. "But, man...talk about some fine women. They're just not the same with cloth in the way."

They watched the mermaids swim around for a while, trading small talk. Finally, Erik glanced at him and said, "So how are you doing with orcs? I know A'kaylii and Belvade have had a history."

Peter's smile faltered a little, and he hesitated before answering. Then, "Eh, better than I expected, to be honest. I mean...never got along with 'em on a personal level, I guess."

"How do you mean?"

Peter didn't answer for a moment. Then, delicately, he said, "When I was about twelve, a couple of orcish bandits ambushed my family on the road. They killed my ma and brother, and crippled my da. I escaped because I was small, and hid in the brush before they knew I was there." He crunched a nut, and shrugged again, "I know that not all orcs are bandits, and we're on the same team now. Jomsskari are Jomsskari, am I right?"

Erik looked at him. "I'm sorry about that."

"Ancient history," Peter returned, tossing the empty shell into the ocean and rooting in the nearly-empty bag for another treat. "I had to work through it, but...I don't know, working with Khalan has been really good. He's a good guy. Best thing for a soul is to learn to forgive, anyhow."

Erik nodded his assent. "Yeah, I reckon," he murmured.

"What about you?" asked Peter, a little mischievously. "Mr. Orc? How'd you fit in?"

"Oh, that didn't go so well for a long time," Erik laughed. "I spent half a year thinking 'Jai-khu' was my orcish name."

"Ouch."

"Yeah, I caught on eventually, but not before I had introduced myself to a fair number of strangers by that name." Erik thought for a few seconds, and added, "They're a rough crowd, but they're all right."

Peter mused for a moment, and rubbed his eyes wearily. "Yeah, they're all right," he said. "Hey, I'm going to hit the sack."

Erik waved vaguely as he left, and stood watching the horizon.

*   *   *

The world was shaking.

For a moment, Erik thought it was an earthquake. Gradually, his senses clearing, he could make out the shape of a face, and a fierce beard, short—

"Wake up, Erik!"

Brutus was shaking him, and Erik growled something in orcish. Brutus didn't seem perturbed. "Come on, you milk sop, we've sighted land. We're leaving in half an hour, we are, so get your gear together!"

It took Erik several moments to understand what he was saying, but as the word sunk in he felt the sleepy fog dissipate. He blinked several times, and swung his feet unsteadily out of the canvas hammock. "What time is it?" he said.

"Nearly midnight," Brutus replied. "There can be no sleep for us tonight, orc-child."

They gathered in the cramped interior of the ship. Thjostolf looked as if he'd been awakened only a short time before, and had a small piece of paper in his hand. "Good morning, boys," he said, grinning. "The lookouts sighted land last night, and we received a warning order to scout out a disembarkation site about half an hour ago. I just got the feckin' confirmation as you were forming up. We leave in half an hour. We'll be inspecting a feckin' bay. Third Jomsskari will scout out the land to the south, and First Jomsskari has the beach to the north, that leaves us holding the center. Rhys, what do you have as far as intelligence?"

Rhys was in a hammock, looking down on the narrow corridor from above. "It doesn't look populated," he said slowly, "And the lookouts said that the nearest forest is almost a mile off. We are working on the theory that the griffins will not nest in this area, but of course we have no way of verifying that without looking for ourselves."

"We'll trade food for ammunition," said Thjostolf. "Dionysian Marines will be our Immediate Reaction Team, so if we get in trouble, we'll fire a red flare and they'll feckin' beat feet to snatch our happy arses out of the fire. However, the minimum time before they can respond is about twenty minutes, so we need to have enough feckin' ammunition to make ourselves look like a battalion. Otherwise, they'll overrun us. Any questions?"

"How many longboats?" asked Khalan.

"We'll have two per company," Thjostolf said. "It's a forty-five-minute trip to shore paddling, so we need to arrive before 0200 in order to do a quick scout out and be on our way before first light at 0520."

"0520?" someone asked.

"That's when they say first light is," Thjostolf said, and shrugged. "Feckin', the sea isn't too choppy, so we should make good time, but our silhouettes will stand out against the flat sea. We need to move fast. Okay, get your gear. Draw extra ammo—Peter, make sure you have a thousand extra rounds for Khalan. No questions? Okay, break!"

It was a long ride strained against the oars, with the Jomsskari hardly breathing, afraid to breathe, hunched low in their helmets. Gliding through the water, sweaty from exertion and nerves, the thought of having to fight for their lives was in all their minds. Erik looked out into the darkness. *Twenty minutes before help arrived, at best. A long time to have someone trying to kill you. A long time for something to go wrong.*

They struck sand, and waded ashore. They crouched together, dispersed, and headed inland across the grassy plains around the bay. *No sounds. Deathly silent.*

Crickets, cicadas, night birds hooting. A firefly flashed and their hearts stopped for a moment. *Rough sketches. Check the watch—ten minutes ashore.*

The continued silence became comforting.

They lay still a while, listening intently, scanning the dark horizon. Erik added detail to the sketch. *Looking for paths and trails in the grass—found deer droppings, and saw a rabbit scamper away in fright.*

Quietly, they moved forward, the ocean was almost a thousand yards behind.

Nothing.

Look—then, the rush of wings, and— only an owl, no threat, no worries.

They gathered up with silent hand-signaling to circle around and head back. Looking everywhere, they found nothing.

Feeling better. Careful—not home yet.

On the beach again, the security detail stood against the sea-wall, peering over the top, watching the rustling grass. The rest began to push off.

Security is falling back, climbing aboard.

It was another long ride, but this time with sighs of relief.

Good intelligence, good information, good location. And it looked safe.

The sun rose as they reached the transports. They hoisted the boats aboard and briefed Lord Hoskuld on their findings.

The Jomsskari stowed their gear before breakfast. Then they brushed their teeth, went below deck, and caught a nap. They would do it all over again when they woke.

Chapter Seven

The Coast of El-Ornahar, June 11, 1160

It was very quiet on the beach. The regular lapping of the tides was little more than white-noise; the seagulls slept, and the wind was low tonight. There were a few clouds in the sky, partially obscuring the light of the moon and the stars as they shone down on the glassy sea. The sand sparkled as the waves withdrew, and then the rich sea foam billowed up again as the next came in. The tide was lower and getting lower. From the heavens, the moon seemed to watch the world with a disinterested languor. It was about 0100 hours, and everything was still.

Above the beach, the sand broke in lush, grassy fields, with cool green vegetation standing knee-high. Crickets chirped to their mates. To the south, the coast swung back to the west, forming a bay, with a river leading east at its head. On the side of the waters, the coast was rocky, with a cliff only a few feet inland that towered over a hundred feet. A dark forest loomed over it, gazing over the ocean like a watchman on his rounds. An owl hooted warily from the boughs. The bay below shone brightly up at the sky, the rippled reflections of the stars gleaming up like a million tiny gems cast haphazardly over a blanket.

At the helm of his longboat, Thjostolf took it all in and couldn't help but smile. It looked beautiful, and peaceful. It would be a wonderful place to spend a few days fishing, relaxing, and watching the waves come and go. If they were to be here long, it wouldn't be a bad place to move the family, after, of course, he had finished his job tonight.

To his left and his right, five more longboats slipped through the deep, cutting though the water to the regular and tireless *plops* of the oars dipping in, pulling back, and lifting out. They were almost silent. The wooden crafts, each about thirty feet long, contained half a company of Jomsskari, various members of either a Haellic or a Iaelian weapons company reinforced by orcs, and a squad of Dwarfish engineers. The longboats had been stripped of their sails and mast to keep their profile down. Now they held only the bare necessities of a mariner's life—nothing like the longboats that had sailed to White Mountain in previous years. These were not built to survive long months at sea, or even a week. Their purpose was singular; to transport twenty men over four miles, to a lonely beach on the coast of El-Ornahar, the fabled Land of the Griffins.

Now they were about a mile from the coast, and had left the fleet behind them. If they came into contact, they were supposed to fire red flares, and the dreadnaughts would swing forward and deploy the Dwarfish Marines. Thjostolf felt true comfort from that kind of power behind him.

He was glad that they had checked out the beach the night before. When they had first landed, they weren't sure if they'd be met by hostile fire. It had been a long ride, but far too short for every man on board. Nobody like the idea of being cut off without retreat against a superior enemy. Now, he figured, things were looking up. The scouts had an escape, seven warships full of some of the toughest dwarves White Mountain could muster standing by to steam into the assault. Three hundred dwarves didn't always sound like a great idea, especially at parties and weddings, but they were always welcome in a fight. They had more spirit than a distillery, more guts than a butcher, and were always, without exception, armed to the teeth. They lived to use all three.

The coast was now only half a mile away, and closing quickly. He consulted his map and turned around to face the ten rowers, who sweated and strained on either side of the ships narrow hull. The other nine men aboard checked their weapons and each other's gear for the dozenth time. They had taken the first two miles rowing, as had Thjostolf, and would be the first on the beach. The young captain looked back towards the landing zone. They would be there in less than twenty minutes.

Thjostolf's company had been tasked with securing the center of the mile-wide landing area. First Company Jomsskari would take the north edge, and Third would take the south, as they had the night before. As they pushed inland, they would provide a security screen for the subsequent landing parties.

As confident as he was from the previous night, Thjostolf still suspected that the enemy might be nearby. The Alnethar must have recognized the strategic value of the bay, and there must be some reason they hadn't built their own base there, unless there were significantly superior positions further north. And there was still the possibility that the Alnethar had seen them the night before, or that a high-flying griffin had spotted the convoy during the day. In either case, it was plausible that the beach deemed unoccupied the night before, was actually home to a sizable enemy force. The thought was troubling.

Thjostolf planned to beach his shallow-drafted longboats and leave the weapons company to disembark while the Jomsskari raced to the seawall at the edge of the fields. From there, the Jomsskari could provide security while the weapons company unloaded their machine-guns and mortars. Meanwhile, the engineers would unload their surveying gear. They had weapons, but they weren't expected to fight. Thjostolf thought that was stupid. He felt they should have sent another weapons company instead, and sent in the engineers with the second wave. But the powers that be wanted to set up an expedient dry-dock as quickly as possible to start landing the clunkers and tractors so they could build a fort. These guys were supposed to know where they wanted it by the time the equipment they needed arrived with the second wave. Thjostolf just hoped, for their sakes, that the beach was really and truly uninhabited. Engineers didn't grow on trees.

As they closed within two hundred yards of the beach, and then one hundred, the scouts lined up by the edge of the forward gunwales. Each one carried a full scout load of five stone, nearly four hundred rounds of ammunition, with extra bullets for Khalan's GP-10. Kolskegg stood behind Thjostolf, running his hand contemplatively over the scope and barrel of his sniper rifle. A M27 carbine, like the ones Peter, Erik, and Brutus carried, was slung across his back.

Twenty yards, then ten. Thjostolf gave a quiet order and the oarsmen lifted their oars from the water. There was a growing, guttural growl that boiled up from beneath the boat, and then a loud, raspy hiss as the keel struck sand. Thjostolf swung his legs over the edge of the gunwale and felt the extreme weight of his rucksack pulling him over the edge. Briefly, he had the sensation of flight, and the vision of the withdrawing surf flashed in his eyes. His boots touched the water, cutting down, and then the rucksack drove downwards and back. He felt nothing beneath his feet, only more water, rising up to his legs. He began to fall, his torso and shoulders fully submerged. As the water closed over his head, the sound of the world dimmed to a quiet pulse.

Thjostolf struggled upwards, his feet slipped in the soft mass beneath. A force pushed into his back, like someone shoving him forward, and then the lapping of the surf sounded once more on his ears and he heard splashes behind him. He shook the water from his eyes and cursed quietly to himself, wading forward and straightening his lanky body. There was less than three feet of water below him, but the weight of his gear had forced him down to his knees. The worst part about disembarkation was wondering, for that split second, if he would ever breathe again. The feeling only lasted an instant, but it was memorable. If the water was deeper than they thought, or someone jumped out too soon, they could get pinned to the ocean floor by the weight of their equipment.

No harm done, though. Behind him, Peter floundered forward with Kolskegg right behind, water streaming from their clothing as they held their rifles above their heads. It was harder for Peter because he was short. Thjostolf stopped his advance long enough to grab his outreaching arms and pull him towards the shore. Khalan and Erik, who had landed in the second longboat a few second earlier, had already moved up the beach towards Thjostolf's left. Khalan had dropped to one knee and was scanning the field ahead for motion, while Erik cleared some obstruction from the breach of his carbine.

Gabryl and Edwin had come ashore, too. Gabryl moved serenely, looking around as though he had come home and found everything the way he had left it. In fact, he had stayed behind the night before. The mission had been too dangerous in too many ways. They would not risk losing him to a sudden gale or a skirmish. Edwin sniffed the air and wagged his tail curiously, looking up at the grass and back to the longboats suspiciously. Taking off at a canter and panting lightly, he disappeared into the grass, heading inland to take a quick look around. Thjostolf knew he would be back in a few minutes.

Rhys ran up beside Khalan and squatted, peering into the darkness. For a brief moment, the elf and the orc exchanged soft words, and then Rhys, apparently satisfied with Khalan's assessment, turned and gave Thjostolf the thumbs-up. So far, so good.

Thjostolf, Kolskegg, and Peter moved up the beach and Brutus, lingering a few feet behind, waved in the infantry who were still on the longboats. They were already piling over the side, followed by the diminutive engineers and the bundles of weapons. As the infantry began to move east to take up a position between Second and Third Jomsskari, Thjostolf ran towards a small hump at the beginning of the grass, some thirty yards from the waterline. When he arrived, he dropped, looked back and forth, and waved his arm in a rapid, circular motion. The others gathered around in a few seconds.

Looking out over the fields, Thjostolf asked, "Clear?"

"Well, it appears to be," said Rhys.

Thjostolf nodded. "Okay, we're going to feckin' clover-leaf the field another hundred yards or so and set up an OP. Rhys, Brutus, Kolskegg, Gabryl, and Erik, stay here to provide overwatch. Wendyll, Peter, and Khalan, you're coming with me. We move as soon as Edwin gets back, okay?"

Everyone nodded. This would be the first of many such runs. The "cloverleaf", as they called it, was a method of reconnoitering an area by walking in a series of circular patterns. It was shorter then walking a grid, but thorough enough to detect any threats hidden in the foliage. The Jomsskari would continue to establish a wider perimeter as more soldiers arrived, until they had secured the entire twelve-hundred-acre area the Alliance planned to build the fortress and its defenses on. All they had to do now was make sure the next few landing parties had enough protection to land their heavy equipment and materials.

Edwin came bounding through the grass and lay down at the edge of the ridge, looking over the edge and panting happily. "I can't smell anything that I'd be afraid to eat, masters," he announced quietly. "The spores are mostly deer and elk, with a few rabbits, but I'd be willing to bet my life—for what it's worth—that no Alnethar and no griffins have been here for at least two weeks."

Gabryl smiled and ran his wrinkled hand through the wolf's shaggy neck fur. "Good work, Edwin."

"Feckin', we're setting up an observation site about a hundred yards out," Thjostolf said. "Are there any bumps or ridges we can use?"

"There's a kind of lip about a hundred-twenty yards from here, master," replied Edwin. "Not quite a hill, but it would give you some cover, and a slightly higher aspect. I'd be glad to take you there."

"All right, lead on." Thjostolf nodded to his team and then to Rhys. "We'll give you a light; when you see it, flash the fleet." He glanced at his watch. It was 0140.

They followed Edwin to the lip and settled in. Khalan set his machine-gun down on the left and Peter took a position next to him with a spare box of ammunition. Wendyll sat upright and looked slowly from the east to the north, and then on to the west. "I don't see anything," he said. "Looks clear."

Thjostolf rolled over and reached into his shirt pocket, producing a wallet of matches. Shielding it from view to the north, he lit one carefully. It flared, and he let it burn for a few seconds before blowing it out. Beside him, Edwin smiled as best a wolf could and said softly, "That smells nice."

On the beach, Rhys saw the signal and nodded to Brutus, who had set up a kerosene lantern with a shield and a mirror to project the beam in one direction. It also had a shutter, which allowed him to cut off the beam entirely if the need arose. Brutus lit a match and touched it to the wick, which began to burn brightly. He adjusted it to a steady flame, opened the shutter towards the sea, and closed it again. He repeated this for a few seconds. Then, one light in the darkness flashed back. To either side, the other teams were doing likewise, and their respective ships flashed in reply. Brutus blew out the fire and nodded to Rhys. "The landing ships are on their way now, lieutenant. They will arrive at," He glanced at his watch, "maybe 0230. As good a time as we can hope for, I think."

Rhys nodded and glanced back up towards Thjostolf. "Yes," he murmured, and smiled to himself. *Don't get too confident. It's early yet.*

The first rafts arrived nearly half an hour late, but the interim was uneventful. They were loaded with men, tractors, and materials, and their first task was to make a dock. The weapons company and the scouts moved inland to provide additional security while the infantry from the rafts grabbed ropes, waded ashore, and beached the monsters. Each raft was forty feet wide and sixty feet long. Made of steel pontoons and a sort of wooden box with a gate at one end and a motor on the other, they were possibly the ugliest vessels in the history of boating. But they were easy to tow, and could hold all the materials they needed safely aboard during the trip. Another wave of rafts was inbound, filled almost entirely with more men, and so the beached whales opened their doors quickly and the engineers began hauling out their equipment and driving out their tractors. A team of dwarves ran ahead of each tractor, unrolling strips of perforated steel to keep them from sinking into the sand. As the last of the material was unloaded, the rafts were pushed back, and the heavy diesel motors growled into reverse. The next wave, only a few hundred yards behind, slowed to let the first wave maneuver out before they, too, disgorged their men and material onto the beach. The tide was at its lowest now, and they had to get an operational dock built before sunrise, as well as a rudimentary perimeter defense established.

The fusilliers that landed in the second wave brought with it coils of barbed wire, thousands of empty sandbags and entrenchment tools, as well as several weapons companies including one from the A'kayliian Royal Guard. They ran up the beach and found the perimeter marked out about two hundred yards inland. That was as far as one-hundred-twenty men could secure, but the reinforcements swelled their numbers to over six hundred. Thjostolf and Rhys took their teams forward, and First and Third Jomsskari moved northwest and northeast respectively, taking the newcomers with them. They mapped out their permanent perimeter about eight hundred yards from their landing site, and began to dig. In the next several hours, they would have to have basic trenches established, and positions for future bunkers. Thjostolf took his company another hundred yards out and took a look around, carefully inspecting every shadow. As they settled in, Edwin loped off on his own and returned a few minutes later, wagging his tail. "I see nothing, master," he reported. "It's all quiet."

Chapter Eight

Feldhall, June 11, 1160

By high noon, Feldhall was a buzz of activity, and fully operational. Crammed with soldiers and materials, it sprawled across the twelve hundred acres the perimeter had allowed it. It was defended by concrete pillboxes, most of which were still being poured over their steel skeletons, and by trenches reinforced with barbed wire and clunker barriers. Two batteries of howitzers had been set up on the northeast and the northwest corners, with heavily reinforced bunkers nearby to house their spotters. Near the North Gate, they had erected a clunker pen, housing over sixty clunkers and a hundred piglets, and some distance south of that was a motor pool fielding Feldhall's fleet of trucks and ambulances. There were stables as well, and two large stockpiles of ammunition—literally millions of rounds for the rifles, the howitzers, and the mortars, let alone the clunker's twelve-pound and the piglet's rapid-firing one-inch cannons. There were thousands of gallons of diesel fuel close to the dry docks to the south, and this was just a fraction of the supply aboard the oil tankers in the bay.

But much of Feldhall was filled with longhouses. They were simple buildings made of timber and corrugated steel, measuring about seventy feet long and thirty feet wide, and were used either as warehouses or as barracks. Four of them built in a tight cluster served as a hospital, and another two side by side served as the kitchen and the cafeteria. There were dozens of them, set in rows, squeezed between other structures, strewn around the docks, and lining the main road.

Those that did not contain men, food, or ammunition, contained building materials for the next fortress. Once Feldhall was established, about half of the soldiers would leave to build and garrison the next emplacement, and there were those who believed that the families of the scouts would be brought to live in them. Thjostolf wasn't so sure. Feldhall was, as far as he was concerned, unready for civilians. In two different locations, heavy machine-guns had been rigged to fire skyward at attacking griffins, but nobody knew for sure how their new foes would fight. Until they knew for sure, Thjostolf had determined to write Thorhalla and forbid her to come to Feldhall. He refused to expose her to such danger; she could come when another fort had been built to the north, and a third to the east.

He was walking down the main road now, tired and hungry from the last twelve hours. Lord Hoskuld, who had Thjostolf's allegiance during the War for Humbridge, had put up his residence in a longhouse near the center of the encampment. Thjostolf had been called there to receive a new mission. He hoped he would have time to catch a few hours of sleep and perhaps a meal before they left, but he could only hope. Hoskuld drove his men hard, especially the Jomsskari. Well, that was what he had signed up for.

Rhys and Gabryl were with him. It was their duty, as much as his, to understand the task at hand. Besides, Thjostolf wanted their opinions of any briefing. Gabryl was no soldier, but Thjostolf was quickly come to appreciate his insight. Gabryl understood the grand scheme of things better than anyone else in Feldhall. Rhys, on the other hand, was just simply experienced. He had fought in more than eleven wars. He had fought against barbarians, goblins, and pirates, and in each war, he had seen a progression in the tactics and roles of the scouts. Thjostolf knew that kind of knowledge was invaluable.

They reached the Lord's Quarters and passed from the blazing sunlight to the dark and cool interior. Hoskuld was inside, with several armed guards who stood at attention as Gabryl entered. Thjostolf wasn't used to foot soldiers giving him that kind of recognition, and glanced at them curiously until he realized they were paying respect to the wizard. *Well feck me, I guess.*

Hoskuld looked up and waved. He was used to the Jomsskari' relaxed manners and didn't take offense. To be saluted by a member of the Jomsskari would be odd at best, and suspicious at worst. Hoskuld was leaning on a table, examining a sketchy map of the surrounding area and pursing his lips. Nodding in greeting, he said, "Thjostolf Captain, Gabryl, Rhys ap Bledri, welcome."

"Hoskuld Lord sen Ogmund," replied Thjostolf, removing his cap. "What are your orders, m'Lord?"

Hoskuld indicated an area about thirty miles north of Feldhall. "I need eyes to our north. I want to know if there's anything alive within sixty miles of Feldhall. I've already sent First Jomsskari to examine an area to the northwest; they'll be leaving in about two hours. Third has already set out to investigate the river to the east. They plan to move about twenty-five miles and mark an area for another fortress. I want you to make maps of this area to the north and find out for me if the enemy has established fortifications or cities."

Rhys glanced at Thjostolf. "That should take us four or five days, don't you think?"

"At least," said Thjostolf, and sighed. The area that Hoskuld was showing them was nearly a hundred square miles. There was no way they could do a thorough search in less than a week, but he knew that wouldn't be fast enough for Hoskuld. "If First Jomsskari is already scheduled then I'd like to stagger our departures. M'Lord, if it pleases you."

Lord Hoskuld nodded his assent.

"Okay then, let's move out in four hours. That would be...1700." *So much for getting some sleep.*

Lord Hoskuld nodded again and dismissed them. Thjostolf turned and they walked out, past the impassive guards. He rubbed his eyes, gathering his thoughts. "Rhys, have the men meet me in our longhouse."

"I hear and obey, cap'," replied Rhys, and loped off.

Gabryl was walking slowly, his eyes glazed and pensive. Thjostolf looked at him. "How do you feel?"

"Well, I'm not a young as I think I am," Gabryl said wanly. "But I am concerned that Hoskuld..." He trailed off, and suddenly glanced up and smiled. "I'll take a nap before we go, if that's all right."

Thjostolf grinned, but Gabryl's condition made him more than a little nervous. He slowed them down, and Thjostolf worried that Erik's skills would be used trying to keep an old man alive after a heart attack instead of treating the wounded. With Gabryl's pace, they could be too slow to escape their enemy, or to slow to reach a battle before it was over. Thjostolf didn't know which was worse. He suspected the first was, but he had come to fight. All the work they had put into the Jomsskari project would mean nothing without the test of combat.

Thjostolf found his men gathered in a circle in their corner of their longhouse. They were chatting softly among themselves, and eating some stew from the cafeteria that someone had brought over in a pair of helmets. Wendyll offered him a plate and Thjostolf gratefully dug in.

Gabryl sat down on a cot and began scratching Edwin's ears. Edwin whined softly and thumped his tail appreciatively.

"All right, guys," said Thjostolf, speaking through his lunch. "We're going out on a feckin' patrol of the northern flank. The area we're covering is pretty big and from what we can tell, there's not a whole lot of feckin' cover. Is there anything extra you guys think we need to carry? I'm thinking we'll need a lot of smoke grenades if we want to break contact out in the feckin' open." He swallowed a hot piece of potato and glanced around.

There was a pause, and then Erik said, "Well, I know I always say this, but any extra drugs or IVs can always be useful. Like you said, no cover or concealment could mean a sustained fight," He shrugged, "If anyone has any extra room in their packs..."

118

"Additional bullets would be useful," said Khalan, "but we are unlikely to need much demolitions, am I correct?"

Thjostolf glanced at Brutus. "What do you think?"

Brutus nodded. "I would like to have a few pounds at least, why not, but we can replace a few pounds of demolitions with drugs and ammunition."

Rhys thought for a moment. "We can trade eight pounds of explosives each for something extra...that should suffice, should it not?"

Peter asked, "Will we need a mortar crew?"

Brutus shrugged. "I don't think we do. If we are attacked we will only break contact; we will not be defending a static position, correct?"

Thjostolf blew on a spoonful of stew and said, "All right, we'll spread the load so if one guy gets blown the feck up we don't lose all our assets. Peter, Brutus, Erik, and Wendyll, take extra rounds. Rhys, Khalan, Kolskegg, and I will take the IVs and khem-khat. Gabryl, you and Edwin just take your usual loads. We'll leave at 1700, so get your stuff ready and meet by the North Gate at 1645 to check each other's equipment. Okay?"

Everyone nodded. By now, the team did their meetings quickly and each man knew his role; there was no need to go in depth. Thjostolf preferred it that way. He liked working with the Jomsskari. As they went back to eating, and Gabryl rolled over on the cot to take his nap, he felt a profound sense of satisfaction to be their captain. He could not have asked for a better group of men. He was even getting fond of Khalan and Erik.

*　　*　　*

Second Jomsskari left Feldhall at 1640, ahead of their schedule. The sun was well on its path to the horizon, and as the Jomsskari began their long walk through the grassy plain, they cast long, dark shadows. Pressing northward, they moved in two widely dispersed wedges, with Thjostolf and Gabryl in the center on the formation. Edwin ran ahead, sniffing the air and inspecting the ground. They looked like a flock of walking geese.

As the sun sank below the grass and the clouds turned first pink, then red, Thjostolf checked his compass and raised his hand, signaling the company to stop. They came to a halt, and Thjostolf and Rhys huddled, scratching on a large piece of paper. There wasn't much to report. The grassland stretched for miles in a series of shallow crests and troughs that formed a sort of lazy, rolling piedmont. At about 2100, they discovered a long, narrow pond some two hundred yards in length, which they recorded as a landmark after refilling their canteens.

By midnight they had progressed only about fifteen miles, and found another water hole, with some low shrubs around it. Thjostolf ordered them to form a perimeter and while four of them slept, the other four stayed awake, watching the darkness. Thjostolf took the first watch. He always did. At about 0300 they switched watch, and Thjostolf took his first moments of shut-eye in twenty-seven hours.

They roused themselves at 0500, as the sun was beginning to gray the sky. Bleary-eyed and a little cranky, Thjostolf reached into his rucksack and got some rations. It was Elven bread, tasteless and bland, but it filled a man's belly in a few bites. Its tasteless quality was ironic, he thought, considering the Elves' pension for beauty and perfection. He guessed they didn't care much for their own food in that respect. But they had a way with magic, they weaved it into their clothes, baked it in their bread, and Wendyll seemed to have it in his gun. He could shoot a bird out of the air at several hundred yards, but that may have been several hundred years of practice.

And of course, the Elven girls were reputed to put it in their hair. Thjostolf wasn't sure how magic could be like that…or, for that matter, what exactly magic was, since the Elves seemed to treat it like an element but talked about it like a discipline. But he wasn't about to dispute the assertion about the hair. His mother had been an Elf, and his own wife was from El Commulbalbro in Iaelia. Thjostolf loved Thorhalla's hair and it did seem to have some kind of remarkable nature.

Although she was fully Elven, Thorhalla wasn't an Iaelian name. She had been given a Haellic name because her father thought Haellic names were pretty. It wasn't uncommon on the border regions. *Whatever floated his boat*, Thjostolf thought, and munched on the dry bread, washing the crumbs away with a mouthful of water. Khalan and Erik were filling their skins in the pond, and dropping small purifying tablets into them. The rest of the company followed suit. At 0520, as the sun began to peek the top of its head over the distant hills to the east, Second Jomsskari started again.

The day was typical of a scouting operation. They moved at a moderate pace, mapping as they went, maintaining a state of constant readiness. Staying watchful was more exhausting then the pace. Everyone watched the sky, but the vanguard and flankers kept their eyes peeled continually. Around midday, as they stopped to eat another few bites, they switched up the formation and gave their leading scouts a break.

At 1430, Rhys, who was out in front, held up a fist and sank into the grass. The company dropped too, and Thjostolf wiggled forward on his hands and knees. Rhys glanced back and began hand-signaling. *Visual, in the sky. Three contacts.*

Here we go. First contact.

Thjostolf squinted. His half-elven eyes could make out cluster of distant specks several miles away, soaring in the clouds. He mouthed, "Let's get closer."

Rising to his feet, he signaled. *Move forward.* Despite the heat, he wrapped the cloak around him and drew the hood over him.

The fabric faded into green stripes, like the grass below it, and he crept forward, moving at a walk. They couldn't afford to crawl, but the camouflage worked to keep them hidden. The company followed, putting their cloaks over their heads as their captain had done. Gabryl, leaning on his staff, peered out of his hood with a glower on his face. It was warm enough without the garments, and the sweat dripped from his nose. Only Gabryl looked natural in a cloak. Everyone else looked slightly awkward, like a group of hunchbacks as the folds rose over their rucksacks beneath.

They advanced another mile or so in this state. The ground sloped upwards, forming a hill that they could not see over. The cluster in the sky seemed to be moving southwest, and as Wendyll reached the top of the hill he turned suddenly and whispered, "Cap!"

Thjostolf moved up followed Wendyll's gaze towards the west. The ground was beginning to slope downwards, and in the shallow valley he could see a small encampment about a thousand yards away. The griffins seemed to be moving towards it.

The Jomsskari knelt and walked in a low stoop just below the opposite edge of the crest. Edwin ran along, sniffing as he went. Wendyll watched the birds. They were circling a few miles off. Thjostolf peered over the hill and took another look at the camp, which was now about eight-hundred yards away. There was something odd about it.

He got out his binoculars and, checking to ensure the lenses wouldn't reflect the sun and give them up, looked closer. In a circle about two-hundred yards around the camp, pale elves stood with notepads, wearing khaki uniforms and carrying rifles slung on their backs. They seemed to be watching the camp carefully. Inside the camp, more pale elves, dressed in rustic clothing, moved about as though they were working. There were women in the camp as well. It looked like a village, and yet, almost more like a stage.

Then, over the opposite ridge, Thjostolf spotted a group of elves in the same khaki uniforms crawling towards the camp. They had machine guns, bolt-action rifles, and carried very little gear besides small pouches that he guessed were filled with ammunition.

Kolskegg was watching through his scope. "What're they doing?" he asked softly.

Thjostolf looked around. "Perimeter up! Go on then!" He laid the binoculars down and glanced at Wendyll, who was watching impassively. "I think they're training for something. This is pure feckin' gold! They're going to demonstrate their tactics for us!"

As they watched, the griffins swooped down from the northeast, and the company of elves rose about three hundred yards away from the camp, one half sprinting while the other half covered them, leapfrogging towards their target. The people in the village didn't seem to notice. Then, the first griffin, diving at an incredible speed, let out a cry.

Thjostolf couldn't help but stare. The griffins were beautiful creatures, with long, golden, slender bodies like those of lions, a great head like that of an eagle, and a pair of massive white wings. They let out long screeches, sailing through the air like the giant birds of prey they were. Thjostolf was astounded, even eight hundred yards away, at the grace they possessed. They were like angels of death.

They soared over the village and each of the three dropped a pair of objects, each about the size of an ale keg, from their talons. The objects spun through the air, and exploded in a bright flash of white and a shower of sparks over the heads of the villagers, who began screaming. Some of the men grabbed the women and began hurrying them into the huts, but by then the ground troops had arrived. Shouting, they flooded into the village, striking the men to the ground and quickly rounding the women into a group. The griffins began to land in the center of the village, and the elves burst into each and every hut, bringing out the inhabitants. They had secured the village in a matter of minutes.

It was overwhelming, but Thjostolf was already asking

questions. *What was it they just dropped? Was that some kind of flash bomb? They aren't shooting any of the men. Why?* Most importantly, he thought, *Why didn't they bother to set up a perimeter?*

One by one, each of the women was forced into one of the huts with an officer and came out less than a minute later, crying. *Rape?* No, they were too quick, too clinical, and they forced every woman into the hut as though they were checking them systematically. What were they doing?

"Irkalla," murmured Gabryl.

Thjostolf glanced at him. The wizard had abandoned his security post with Erik and Brutus and was looking down the camp grimly.

"What's that?" asked Wendyll softly.

"They are practicing raiding to find suitable sacrifices for their god," murmured Gabryl. "They call him Irkalla. He demands virgins."

*   *   *

Second Jomsskari watched the elves in the valley as they rehearsed the attack again and again, approaching from different avenues. Sometimes the men in the village resisted violently, other times they seemed passive and almost indifferent. Once, some of the women attempted to escape through the tall grass, but were quickly rounded up. Different scenarios were introduced. One of the griffins pretended to get shot, and the assault force practiced protecting and evacuating the fallen griffin without relinquishing the girls they had come for. Thjostolf scribbled down notes furious, while Rhys and his team slipped off through the grass to the east to examine the rest of the valley. It was almost nightfall when the Elves finally packed up and left. The griffins flew off, and Thjostolf and his team stayed still, watching the darkened village below. Khalan and Wendyll were both with Rhys. Gabryl was laying low in the grass, and seemed a little preoccupied. Thjostolf was dying to ask him more questions, but silence was most important at night. He had taken three pages of notes, front and back, on the enemy's capabilities and weapons, but the whole "god" idea still grated on him, and he didn't know quite what to think about it.

As the moon rose at about 2100, Edwin slipped back into the perimeter and whispered, "We've inspected the rest of the area, master. We have discovered four more such villages, each on different terrain and with different types of buildings involved. We also discovered a road going from northwest to south, which turns east about two miles from here and then swings almost due north after a few miles, maybe five. Rhys also claims he can see a large, built-up area about twelve miles north of the road, and he thinks the road leads to it. He says this entire area appears to be a training complex, and suggests that the built-up area is either a military settlement or a fortified city. He asked that we assemble..." He placed his paw on Thjostolf's open map. "...about here, at the saddle near grid 3556-4227. They're mapping the area as we speak, master."

Thjostolf nodded and waved to his men. "Let's go," he whispered. "But feckin', keep an eye out for anything needing a second look."

His team slipped away, and Gabryl followed Thjostolf closely. The wizard looked troubled, and let his weapon dangle dejectedly from its sling. All of the Jomsskari had learned to sling their weapons with the butt against their shoulder and the grip in their hands, so they had only to move their finger from the guard to the trigger in the event of an ambush. Gabryl had adopted the same kind of sling, but it was clear to Thjostolf that he was not minding his surroundings. He reached back and tapped the old man's forearm. Gabryl looked up, startled, and Thjostolf indicated his eyes. "Focus," he whispered. "Think later."

Brutus led the team, with Thjostolf navigating off of a compass and the map they had assembled, moving slowly. In a couple of hours, they found Rhys' team in the saddle Edwin had described and quickly formed a complete perimeter.

For a few moments, Rhys and Thjostolf discussed their options, looking at their maps and the surrounding area in the pale moonlight. The saddle was about four hundred yards from the road, which did indeed bank northwards, just as Edwin had said. Thjostolf apprehensively imagined griffins flying high in the night, watching for intruders. But he and Rhys agreed that they had to find out what kind of traffic travelled on this road. As they whispered together, Wendyll watched the west, from whence they had come, while Khalan and Peter kept an eye of the east. The team had taken up a position on the western hillside of the saddle, and had an excellent view of the surrounding countryside without presenting a silhouette on the ridgeline.

Rhys and Thjostolf murmured together for about a minute. Finally, Thjostolf glanced around and waved the company in. As they gathered around, Thjostolf did a quick headcount. Satisfied, he whispered, "We're going to set up an observation site right here, with three security holes facing east, west, and south. Wendyll, Peter, and Khalan will be facing east, Kolskegg and Erik will face west, Rhys and Brutus will face south, and Gabryl, Edwin, and I will take the observation post. Fifty percent security."

The men nodded and slipped off. Thjostolf didn't have to tell them where or how to dig and conceal their holes. They knew their weapons, their fields of fire, and how to position themselves. They mumbled briefly among themselves, and then got to work. Thjostolf started digging, saving the topsoil and filling small sandbags as he went. Gabryl and Edwin watched the road cautiously, and the sound of quiet shovels striking the soft earth rang all too loudly in his ears. He grimaced and looked around. This was his least favorite part of scouting—hunkering down a few feet from the enemy and watching. There were so many ways for a scout to be discovered, and so few ways to prevent it. But they had work to do, and the night wouldn't last forever.

When the sun rose red, and the clouds rose up from the north, the holes were ready. They were just barely wide enough for three men each, about three feet deep, with the sandbags piled on each side like battlements, and they had carefully placed the topsoil on the sandbags. The men inside the holes had laid their heavy rucksacks on the ground and wore their cloaks pulled around them, concealing the holes completely.

The clouds gathered, dark and ominous. As the storm rose higher, Thjostolf peered down on the road from his hole and turned to Edwin. "Keep watch," he murmured. "I'm going to get a few minutes sleep."

Edwin nodded and Gabryl sat down on the edge of the parapet, covering the wolf with a piece of his cloak. Thjostolf sat down and curled up against his rucksack, shutting his eyes wearily. Outside the bare shelter, the storm came closer, and raindrops began to fall. First they came slowly, with small drops, and then the rush of water sounded as the sky opened up. Thjostolf didn't notice. He had already fallen into a deep, dreamless sleep.

Chapter Nine

The Road, June 13, 1160

The rain continued to fall into the morning, and the sun stayed hidden behind the swirling clouds. Thjostolf awoke after about four hours, and found Gabryl watching the road's northward bend with his binoculars. Edwin lay in the grass just outside the hole, watching the road with his big, brown wolf eyes. He glanced up at Thjostolf as he rolled over, rubbing his eyes wearily. Gabryl didn't seem to notice him at first, but then he said, "Sleep well, captain?"

Thjostolf grunted and opened his rucksack, grabbing some of the Elven rations and chewing hungrily at the dry crust. The rain pelted off of his hood, and the mud sucked at his boots as he shifted his weight. *Why does it always rain on us?* He liked the rain, though. It lowered visibility and made the enemy miserable, which gave the well-disciplined Jomsskari an edge. They trained for the worst possible conditions, because that was when their enemy was the least likely to notice them skulking about in the shadows. It is always easier to fight a demoralized enemy.

As he finished his breakfast, he nudged Gabryl's arm and murmured, "I got it."

Gabryl said something in response, but Thjostolf couldn't hear him over the rain. Leaning forward, he asked for the wizard to repeat himself.

Gabryl half-turned, showing his old face behind his hood. He looked annoyed. "I said, there's a convoy coming!"

Thjostolf grabbed his paper and notepad from his rucksack, shielded them from the rain, and leaned on the parapet besides Gabryl. Gabryl handed him the binoculars and he peered into them. Through the spattered lenses and the dim light, he could see a row of lamps moving through the thin fog, coming down the north highway. Gabryl said, "I counted at least twelve..."

Thjostolf nodded. "Twelve, thirteen, fourteen...This is a full convoy, all right." He handed the glasses back to Gabryl and patted his shoulder. The wizard glanced up and smiled slightly. "Another passed by here about two hours ago, with eight troop trucks and six piglets. I took notes on the piglets' appearance, and their speed, but didn't think I should wake you."

Thjostolf knew he meant well, and didn't press it. "Next time, wake me up," he said. "Does the rest of the company know?"

"Edwin told the ones that were awake," Gabryl replied.

"Edwin!"

The wolf appeared at Thjostolf's elbow. "Yes, master?"

"Go wake everybody up, be ready to break contact."

The convoy was getting closer. Thjostolf counted sixteen vehicles now, and they looked to be moving at about thirty miles an hour. That was odd. Ordinarily, a convoy would drive at around twice that speed, unless they were heavily loaded. They bobbed through the fog slowly, crawling towards the saddle. He guessed they were about two and a half miles off. Thjostolf squinted into the binoculars, readjusting his grip, and suddenly felt his mouth go dry. There was a dim outline of a large mass above the lamps. As the vehicles drew closer he saw the muzzle of a great cannon pointing towards him.

These were no trucks. These were clunkers—sixteen of them.

How did they know we were here? They had covered their holes as best they could, and had cloud cover and rain. Had they been spotted yesterday, while they were shadowing the training villages? Thjostolf couldn't believe that. The reaction was too slow and the clunkers, at least from a mile away, didn't appear to have infantry support. *Well, maybe their clunkers don't need infantrymen,* he thought, but that didn't seem plausible, either.

He looked again. They were definitely clunkers, he could see the armored turrets for sure now. But they looked bigger than any clunkers he had ever seen. He checked the range card Gabryl had made up beforehand, confirming the distance. They were less than a mile away now, and closing.

For some reason he suddenly wondered what Thorhalla was doing, and glanced at his watch. It was almost 1000, and she would be well into her morning routine. When Thjostolf had received his commission, they were able to afford a nice young thrall to help her around the house and with Aud. It was odd, as he peered through the binoculars, watching a formation of hostile clunkers bear down the highway, he didn't feel fear or even apprehension. It seemed normal to see a full-strength company of enemies headed right for him, and it seemed equally normal to wonder dejectedly about his wife. He tapped the range card, and mumbled, "One thousand two hundred yards and closing." They were almost to the bend. If they were attacking the saddle, where Thjostolf sat in his miry hole, they would slow and get into an attack formation within the next six hundred yards.

More likely, he thought, they would continue following the road and turn west, towards the training complex. But his instinct told him otherwise.

Thjostolf heard Gabryl give a low call to the other positions, telling them to prepare to break contact with clunkers. The rain pattered steadily, splashing against the mud. Thjostolf squinted into the binoculars. The whole world seemed to be moving slowly, as though the One Unsayable was holding all time still so Thjostolf could understand what was happening. The clunkers were clearly visible now, at one thousand hundred yards and closing. They were indeed larger than the Haellic versions. He estimated they were about ten yards long, four yards wide, and three yards tall.

"Nine hundred yards."

The main gun was immobile, firing forward, and looked big enough to fire a fifteen or sixteen pound shell. There was at least one machine-gun mounted on a swivel outside the main hatch on the top. But Thjostolf saw something that caught his eye, it was the face of the lead vehicle's driver.

The drivers are unprotected.

That couldn't be. It didn't make sense. Time seemed to accelerate to its normal speed, and the air went from the calm inevitability that he had felt before into an energy-charged intensity. Suddenly, the rain seemed to strike his helmet like gravel, and for the first time he was aware of the pounding of his own heart. He looked over his shoulder and called, "Snipers, forward!"

Kolskegg and Wendyll appeared through the mist, slithering along the ground. "Cap'?"

"Target drivers on number one and two vehicles—if they start fanning out for an assault, make a road block out of them and buy us time to break contact."

Wendyll flipped the covers off of his scope, leveling his rifle. "Eyes on target. Range?"

Thjostolf lowered his binoculars. "Six hundred yards and closing."

The sound of the snipers adjusting their scopes was entirely lost in the rain. The clunkers were almost at the bend. Kolskegg breathed deeply, his face relaxed impassively. "Eyes on prey. Five hundred-fifty yards, wind half value west, ten miles an hour. What do you read, Wendyll?"

"Half value west at ten, I concur."

The lead clunker slowed suddenly, and turned abruptly to the right. The second clunker swung around in a line abreast formation, and the six behind began to peel off to either side to complete the formation. Their intent was unmistakable. They were preparing to attack.

Gabryl looked over at the Thjostolf, whispering, "Should we pull back?"

Something still didn't seem right. Thjostolf didn't answer, his eyes fixed inexorably through the binoculars. The clunkers were at the bend, but they might be taking a double column formation, and if they turned with the road to head west, the Jomsskari could hold their fire and remain undetected.

The two lead clunkers hit the bend and kept coming, rolling off the road, right at the saddle. Thjostolf didn't hesitate any longer. "Snipers, fire!"

The fiery venom spat forth from the tips of their rifles at the same time, and as one, the snipers fed another round into the chamber of their weapons. "Hit," they intoned. They fired again, this time a little more staggered.

Thjostolf heard himself shouting, "Break contact! Break contact!" but it sounded to him as though someone a long way away was shouting and he was just mouthing the words. Wendyll fired a third shot without speaking, and Kolskegg paused for a second before loosing the last of his lead trio.

By now, the company had risen from their positions and were slipping quickly and quietly down the other side of the saddle, covering each other as they ran. Thjostolf took one last look through his binoculars and saw the lead clunkers slew violently, one accelerating quickly and turning to the right, the other stopping abruptly, only to be rammed in the back by those following it. The one that had accelerated turned a full ninety degrees to the right, striking the clunker beside it. Both stopped instantly from the impact. The clunkers on either side also slammed to a halt, and one began turning around in place.

The snipers had already covered their sights and were finding their way to the rear. Thjostolf followed. He was the last to leave.

The earth shifted beneath him, and rose suddenly to strike him in the face. Everything was quiet. It seemed peaceful, and he had a distantly, disconnected feeling of being excited, titillated by the sheer absence of sensation. He felt a vague touch of mud and rain falling on his back, and he felt suddenly warmer. His boots scrambled for purchase, sliding in the mud beneath the weight of his pack. Smoke filled his nostrils.

The earth shifted again, but this time he heard a deep, terrifying crash, like close thunder. He saw clearly as a patch of earth a few yards to his left sank slightly into itself, then leap straight into the air with a rush of air that pushed him down. Another shell landed far to the left, and fire leaped up from the ground as though Hell was rising.

Thjostolf jumped, and as the explosions erupted around him, he sprinted like a lunatic. In a moment, he had reached the far side of the saddle, and was on his way down. The rest of the company was grouping around Rhys, who was doing a head count.

The clunkers hadn't seen where the Jomsskari were, and their barrage was sporadic and panicked. Thjostolf knew that they had no idea how many men they were facing. Six clunkers had been taken out before they had fired a shot, and they were still blind in the rain and smoke from their battered machines. They wouldn't pursue, at least not until they got untangled. The snipers had done their job well. As he rose, Rhys grabbed him by the shoulder. "You okay?"

Thjostolf nodded shakily, glancing behind him. "Have you set up a rally point?" He was still disoriented, but he couldn't afford to wait to regain his full wits. They had to move fast.

"Yes, captain, at these coordinates," Rhys said hurriedly. He, too, struggled with his instincts, and forced himself to remain calm despite the circumstances. "We're moving in our squads, east and west, away from Feldhall, then buttonhooking back to the rally point. Correct?"

Thjostolf looked at the map and nodded. "Yes, that's good.

Company, move out! Let's get as much distance as we can between us and those feckin' clunkers! I'll see you at the rally point!"

* * *

Kolskegg, Thjostolf, Khalan, Gabryl, and Peter were together, hiking as quickly as they could in a loose formation through the tall grass. Kolskegg was aware that the captain had chosen a circumlocutious path to the rendezvous; hopefully, their pursuers would be unable to track them quickly until the rain and fog lifted. Until then, they were making clear footprints in the mud, and the enemy would follow those as long as they lasted. It was imperative that they didn't point back to Feldhall. On they went, heading east until the rain lifted, each man fingering their pace beads unconsciously, keeping track of how far they had gone. Kolskegg counted fifteen hundred yards, and the rain still came.

Kolskegg looked back and forth quickly, scanning the area to the left of the group, his bolt-action rifle slung across his back and his stubby carbine braced against the shoulder-straps of his rucksack. The rainwater ran off of his hood and down the sides of his cloak. The fog was thicker as they got away from the hills; they could only see a few dozen yards now. The mud squished beneath his feet, and the grass scratched at his exposed hands, a hundred tiny cuts stung with sweat. He wondered if they were moving with the storm. Kolskegg glanced up towards the front of the formation, and through the falling rain he saw vertical lines that looked like trees.

Peter, who had the vanguard position, suddenly turned and waved. They stopped, sinking down into the grass, and Kolskegg saw Thjostolf slip up to the halfling. They mumbled at each other for a moment, and then Thjostolf waved the rest of the group in. Kolskegg pushed himself up and sidled over, backing into the circle and keeping a watchful eye on his side. Khalan did the same, his massive back facing in at Thjostolf, and Gabryl huddled down near Thjostolf, looking forward warily. The captain had taken his map out and was consulting it. "Okay, guys, we're about one hundred yards shy of what looks like a forest. I've got 1570 yards, and Peter has 1580. What do you have?"

Kolskegg glanced at his pace beads. "Um...1570, sir."

"1560," said Khalan. "But I have been on rearguard."

Thjostolf nodded and made a note of the change in terrain on the map. "We'll see if we can turn south at the tree-line," he said. "It'll be harder to track us in there. I want to set up some booby-traps to slow down pursuers. How many explosives do we have?"

Peter whistled thoughtfully. "I reckon we've about ten pounds apiece, a few detonators, and trip-cords. That's enough to make a nice daisy-chain, inn'it?"

Thjostolf nodded. "Let's get to the forest, double back and lay a feckin' mechanical ambush."

As they reached the forest, the fog settled above the boughs, leaving the forest floor largely untouched. The raindrops spattered down on them in irregular bursts, and the thunder rolled above them. The trees were mostly some kind of maple, with a few evergreens and oaks mixed in. Everywhere they looked the ground was exploding in gnarled roots and small boulders covered in lichen and moss rising from the dark, fertile loam. There were patches of grass, and a lot of small bushes and shrubs, many of which were thorny. Thjostolf turned the group south and they began pushing through the underbrush. It was drier on the forest floor, and easier to see, but it was also harder to move quickly. Thjostolf had to take a heading every few yards and write down the terrain features on the map, and they left a painfully obvious trail. They progressed their next two hundred yards at an agonizingly slow pace. Then Thjostolf signaled for his men to stop.

They turned east and headed deeper into the forest by another twenty yards, then moved due north, parallel to their previous course. After a hundred yards, they stopped again, and Thjostolf waved them in.

With Kolskegg and Khalan watching the forest, Thjostolf and Peter took off their rucksacks and dug around in the pouches, producing several bricks of explosive wrapped in brown paper. Thjostolf counted them quickly, and, taking them in his arms, the two carefully slipped to the west, towards the path they had made earlier. They walked gingerly, leaving as little evidence of their passage as they could on the damp forest floor.

There was an old, dead oak tree, rotted and hollow on the inside, next to the path they had made. Thjostolf scraped the earth out from under it with his hands, and then took out his knife and sliced the explosives long ways, so that they were about eight inches long and an inch thick. These four he placed on the side of the trunk closest to the path, covered by a thin layer of wood fragments, pebbles, and dirt. He had a roll of black tape, which he secured the explosives to the bark with, and then sat back. To his right, Peter had done likewise, so that there was a pair of charges facing out against the trail, backed by the tree.

They primed them with a detonator to each slice, and connected the detonators to lengths of explosive cord. Then they packed the dirt behind the charges again. An explosion would follow the path of least resistance, and they had to be sure that was towards the enemy, not back under the tree.

They joined their four cords and tied them together to a single, long length, taping it to reinforce the knot. Thjostolf carefully taped this final length along the trunk moving left, with the path. Peter followed, sprinkling dirt and leaves over it to conceal them from a watchful scout. They carried on like this for about six yards before Thjostolf cut the cord and fitted it into an initiator.

The initiator was a small metal tube with a spring-loaded firing pin and a small explosive inside it. He put the detonation cord in the end with the explosives, and taped it off. Now, when the pin holding back that spring was removed, it would go off, and the smaller explosives would leap down the line until they found the main charges. The trick now was to get the enemy to pull the pin.

To that end, Thjostolf got out a spool of thin fishing line, and tied the end to the pin. Then, carefully, he crossed the path and tied the other side to a firm twig across the way, cutting it from the spool. It was practically invisible, hanging across the path at shin-level. Peter was putting the last touches on the concealment with mud and dead leaves, and when he had finished, Thjostolf deftly removed the safety on the initiator. *Armed.* They slowly made their way back, covering their tracks as best they could as they went.

Gently, they backed up to Khalan, Gabryl, and Kolskegg, and the five began moving south again, covering their trail behind them. The fog hid them from view within fifty yards, and the forest, silent save for the pitter-patter of falling droplets, stood as it always had.

Chapter Ten

The Forest, June 13, 1160

Thjostolf looked at his wrist watch, which dangled from his neck on a lanyard, and held up his hand. It was 1600, and they were almost nine hundred yards south of the trap they had placed. The rain was finally letting up. Gabryl was looking a little pale, and although he kept the pace up, he looked very tired. Thjostolf hated to stop, but he knew he had to. It was the risk he had taken when he'd agreed to take Gabryl into the field. It wasn't that the wizard was weak. On the contrary, he was immensely powerful, in his own right, and was an invaluable asset to the team. Gabryl had studied magic longer than most elves lived, and carried his three stone rucksack without complaint. But even the strongest men were hard pressed to match the pace and weight of the Jomsskari, and Gabryl wasn't a young man. An Ancient couldn't be expected to go so long without rest.

The team stopped, and Thjostolf turned to his friend. "Gabryl?"

The wizard looked up, "What's wrong?"

"You should rest a few minutes."

"We shouldn't stop..."

"We're far enough—feckin', we'll turn west-by-southwest to get to the rally point as soon as you get some color back into your face, okay?"

Gabryl knew it was useless to argue, and didn't protest as Khalan helped him get his rucksack off. The team formed a perimeter around him, and he sat down with his cloak wrapped around him. Thjostolf looked at him and nodded to himself. The wizard clearly needed a short break. Five minutes would be enough. Planting the bombs hadn't been exactly restful for anyone.

A bird chirped nearby, and although the rain still drizzled from the boughs, a spot of sunshine appeared to the west. Sunset would come in about two hours, and it looked like the storm was blowing off for the night. Thjostolf wondered if Feldhall had been hit, and though his eyes were still scanning the forest for any sign of movement, his mind slipped back home. Thorhalla would be pretty tired by now, and really appreciating their thrall's help. Aud could be a handful. For some reason, Thjostolf couldn't remember their thrall's name. She was about sixteen, he recalled, and good with kids. They had bought her for seven years when her previous master had died in a traffic accident. She had been really happy to have been reemployed to quickly, and even more so when she discovered that her new masters were undemanding. She was a good worker, but Thjostolf didn't see her much. Thorhalla let her go to bed around 2100 every night, and Thjostolf rarely got home before 2200. She served him breakfast. Gertrude, that was it. Her name was Gertrude. Thjostolf wondered why he couldn't remember that.

Suddenly, to the north, six blasts sounded in close sequence. Everybody grabbed their gear and began to get back into their formation. Khalan mumbled something crass and glanced around. "Sounds like someone found our trap."

"They're too close," said Gabryl. He was already strapped in his rucksack.

Peter looked up. "Should we set another trap?"

Thjostolf shook his head. He wished they had time to install a few spike pits, but that could take hours to do right, and an obvious trap is no trap at all. He got a heading on his compass, found his azimuth, and murmured, "Let's get the feck outta here."

There was no sign of the others when Thjostolf's team reached the rendezvous. It was a small grove of coniferous trees set awkwardly in the middle of the plains, and while it looked quiet enough, they immediately moved to secure it. Thjostolf and Gabryl hunkered down in the tall grass to provide a base of fire if the need arose, while the other three circled around and checked the rocks and foliage for enemies. Once they were satisfied, the group formed a tight perimeter among the trees and lay still waiting. The sun sank lower on the horizon, and the storm clouds to the east turned a brilliant shade of pink. Soon, the stars began to show—the tiny pricks of light starting out in the growing darkness like celestial tears.

Thjostolf was taking a bite from his rations when he heard Khalan give a low call that sounded like a distant owl. It was answered in a moment by a pair of similar calls. Rhys' team had arrived.

Rhys joined Thjostolf in a moment, and they pulled their cloaks into a tiny tent over their heads to inspect the maps under the light of a candle. "Glad you made it okay," said Thjostolf softly. "Careful!"

Rhys shielded the candle and glanced up briefly. "We almost did not, actually. We were delayed by a flight of griffins, although they didn't spot us. We spent about forty minutes hiding in a grove much like this one before Erik realized we had miscalculated our azimuth for about eight hundred yards."

Thjostolf shook his head. "That's not good."

Rhys nodded his assent. "This land all looks the same, sir. We hit a big depression that we suspect to be a collapsed mine shaft. There were stone ruins about two hundred yards off of the main formation. We investigated, and it looked a lot like an old Dionysian mining facility. At any rate, we circumvented it and in the gathering dusk we got about five degrees off."

"Did Erik catch it?"

"Yes, I believe so, although he didn't say how. I guess he suspected something was wrong but was too preoccupied to mention it until we settled in."

Thjostolf nodded. For all of his youth and his lack of formal education, Erik was astoundingly intuitive about a number of things, land navigation among them. He was surprising in more than one respect.

Thjostolf tapped the map and said, "Let's move straight back to Feldhall. Anyone who's followed us this far will have figured out the fort is in the bay, and I don't want to waste any more time. We had a close call ourselves. Someone walked into a mechanical ambush we set not five hundred yards back. That was over here, in this forested area."

"IHO, cap," said Rhys. He blew out the candle and they swept their cloaks back from their heads. Rhys gathered the men as Thjostolf folded his map and replaced it in the water-proofed leather bag. After a headcount, they set out again. Now it was familiar ground—they were less than a mile from the path they had taken coming up.

They had thirty miles between them and Feldhall, but they weren't stopping to chart the terrain anymore, and the heading wasn't hard to maintain. The stars, which were beginning to poke their heads out from behind the clouds, showed them clearly which way to go. Gabryl looked like he was doing well so far, though in the failing light even Thjostolf's half-elven eyes had a hard time telling if he was pale or not. Fear could be a powerful motivator, and even a medicine. Thjostolf had seen men walk miles on broken limbs rather than be caught by a superior force.

They pressed on a few hours until midnight, and then half of them slept while the other half stayed awake. In the morning, they started early.

*   *   *

Marching under these conditions can be introspective. Erik found his mind wandered most when he was doing nothing more than placing one foot in front of the other. While his eyes scanned his side of the formation, his thoughts strayed.

Sometimes, in the silence of the night, he would listen to his heartbeat and will it to stop. Whether waking or sleeping, he prayed, but not as one faithful. He prayed in desperation, crying out to the sky and expecting no answer. His expectations were met.

God. There was a time he would have let the idea slip, a time when he would have passed by the very mention of God, accepting it, perhaps, as a postulate, or denying it as an irrelevancy. Now he knew otherwise. There was a God, that was certain, but he knew less about this God than he had once imagined. When God was tame, he was not afraid.

The entrails around him, the distinct gurgling of blood in the lungs, screams of the wounded. He would wake in a cold sweat, afraid to sleep again. As he walked, distracted in part by his aching feet, the thought was easy enough to put aside, but he knew it would return. The moment became a fixation, a loaded gun in a trembling hand, the answer to this ultimate question lying in the twitch of a finger. In the deepening abyss he found no solace in the thought of eternity— eternity here or there, for good or ill. Only the secession of consciousness, the dreamless sleep, could have comforted him. But he knew it was not so.

The thoughts came and went. The Jomsskari did not speak on mission unless they had to, and this discipline gave him plenty of time to ruminate. But soon enough, just before dinner was to be served, they reached Feldhall.

*   *   *

That night, they found a few buckets of water and took baths, which was a welcome luxury to say the least. It helped to off-set the smell of three days in the field. Khalan had thrown on some pepperweed, the orcish deodorant. It really only served to cover the smell. It was made from mountain peppers, which grew in the rocky soil and flavored most orcish dishes. They splashed it under their armpits, and the stinging, peppery smell covered the smell of their body odor by sheer brutality. Most of the Jomsskari had learned to deal with it. It wasn't lavender, but it beat orc sweat.

Thjostolf, Rhys, and Gabryl didn't join the others for dinner. The two commanders were briefing Hoskuld Lord sen Ogmund on their findings, and receiving briefings on the other Jomsskari' discoveries. Gabryl, on the other hand, had retired a solitary place in one of the command structures, where he sat still.

Edwin came along, of course. Edwin always came with Gabryl, unless specifically told otherwise. He lay silent a few feet away, watching Gabryl and sighing occasionally in a quiet, doggish fashion. Gabryl was seated cross-legged, concentrating, his lips quivering as he murmured incantations.

Light streamed from his face, a soft glow at first, but it grew until it lighted the room. As it intensified, it enveloped his entire body, and slowly, inch by inch, he rose, as if still seated, from the ground. The air was transformed, as the pure, white light swirled around him.

He opened his eyes, they were pure azure, radiant and terrifying. Before him, as the mist collecting before him, colors assembled from all around, swirling like dust in a tornado. They formed a figure, seated like him, eyes brilliant like his, and a voice came from the air, ethereal and ancient.

"Gabryl," the voice said, "What news from El Ornahar?"

Gabryl sat, hovering, for a moment, and when he replied, his lips did not move. The words seemed to come from the same nowhere that the voice did.

"Mikhal, we have seen the Alnethar," he said, his voice gentle and rich. "We saw them ride on griffins, raid villages, and take women. It is as we feared; they are serving Irkalla, the Demon of Gob-Gerra."

At the mention of the name, the swirling white flashed green, and Edwin whimpered.

"Are you sure of it?" asked Mikhal.

"Tell me about the dragon," said Gabryl.

The image flickered, and Mikhal sighed.

"Irkalla is…powerful," he said, "Powerful, clever, vainglorious, and entirely evil. He has deceived the griffins for generations, leading them from the One Unsayable and demanding live sacrifices to curb his bloodlust. I had heard tell that his taste had turned to human flesh. Perhaps this comes from the union of griffin and Alnethar…I had hoped these rumors were false.

"His scales are thick, his eyes piercing, and his claws sharp. Fire boils within him, and when he speaks, it comes from his mouth. He has engulfed armies in flames."

"And where is his temple?"

Mikhal did not answer for several minutes. Then, slowly, as if he were telling a horrible secret, he said, "There is a mountain to the east, called the Accursed Mountain, too high for griffins to nest. It was once a volcano, pouring forth flame and ash. When it died, the dragons died, and it has left in its crater a great lake, the source of the river. On the north face of the mountain, it slopes gently for many miles, four days walk across the surface, before it plummets a thousand feet to the ground.

"This cliff, on the north side of the volcano, is called Gob-

Gerra, the Place of Fire, for into the rock he had dug out his lair. He tunneled deep into the mountain in ancient times, and has hoarded treasures for himself. All day long he admires his wealth. In his honor, the griffins and the Alnethar have built a temple to him. It stands at the very entrance of his lair so that he may feed at his leisure."

Gabryl sat for several minutes, his face tranquil, but the swirling colors betrayed his agitation. Mikhal spoke again.

"You know your mission, Gabryl. Complete it."

*   *   *

Thjostolf stepped out into the sunlight and blinked. It was about 1000, and he had been up for six hours already. The briefings had been busy. First Jomsskari had found a military installation about twenty-five miles from the training villages Thjostolf's team had found, and further west they had found a small fortified city on the coastline. After the briefings ended, he had gone to his longhouse and talked with the troops about things they could have worked on. It was the standard self-criticism drill for everybody, and Thjostolf was glad he'd made the decision to debrief the morning after. They used to do it before hitting the showers, but Brutus and Rhys thought it would be better to do it the next morning, when they were rested and could think more objectively. They had given it a try, and it had stuck.

Before briefing Lord Hoskuld, he had spoken with Gabryl about the drills they had witnessed. Gabryl had been tight-lipped, and Thjostolf didn't know why. They knew, he recalled from the voyage over, that the Alnethar and the griffins worshipped a god known as Irkalla, but there hadn't been much information provided in the dossiers. It bothered Thjostolf that they had so little information on something that was apparently important enough to the enemy to warrant specialized training.

And then the runner had come and told him to report to headquarters for his next assignment. *No rest for the best,* he reminded himself as he walked over to Lord Hoskuld's longhouse.

Gabryl was already there, and the air smelled strongly of tea and pipe tobacco. Lord Hoskuld came in from his private quarters when he heard Thjostolf greet Gabryl. "Captain," he said simply. His own sense of formality was slipping. "Gabryl has received some intelligence that we want you to verify."

Thjostolf glanced at Gabryl, then back at his commander. "I hear and obey, m'Lord," he said. "What are my orders?"

"To our east there is a large mountain, which may provide us with an observation and artillery overwatch position for the entire southern line along the river and onto Feldhall. Moreover, we believe that the river originates from the mountain, and could be diverted to starve us of fresh water. You will travel upriver to the east by boat as far as you are able," Lord Hoskuld said, "When you can no longer travel by boat, disembark and climb the mountain until you find the source of the river. We have reason to believe the griffins cannot nest so high up, but the Alnethar may have built a fortress to control the headwaters. If they have established such an outpost, you must destroy it if possible, and if they have not, you must mark a building site for our engineers."

He stood close to Thjostolf, and spoke quietly. "If the river is diverted, or enemy artillery is permitted to fire from the mountain, our expedition will be gravely endangered," he said. "You understand that mission is vital."

"I hear and obey, m'Lord."

"Good," said Hoskuld, and turned, returning to his quarters. "That is all," he called over his shoulder. "Coordinate with the Dionysians, they are surveying the area for a second fortification. They leave by first light."

When Thjostolf asked, Gabryl just shrugged. "All I told him

was where I believe the river begins," he said. "The rest was his invention."

He found Rhys in their longhouse and took him aside. "Our next mission is a long one," he said. "Go draw three pack-horses and load them up with ammunition, medical supplies, and demolitions. We're going to be a long way out, so we'll need some extra firepower, too." He stood for a moment, his hands on his hips, pondering, and then continued. "Get a two-inch mortar and one hundred rounds of high explosives, and phosphorous. You and Brutus will be my mortar team if we need an indirect fire element."

"I hear and obey, captain."

"Make sure everyone has thirty days rations on person, and add an additional thirty per man on the horses. Okay?"

Rhys just smiled and winked. "This is going to be fun, isn't it, captain?"

"Another day in feckin' paradise," said Thjostolf, and slapped his back as he left. The rest of the Jomsskari were only a few yards off, and were listening in. "Eat hearty," he told them, and grinned. "It'll be the last hot meal this month."

*   *   *

First thing the next morning, they left Feldhall. They boated upriver with a team of Dionysian surveyors and their Haellic security, a company of riflemen. It was about twenty-four miles to the site that Third Jomsskari had marked, and the trip took about six hours. When they came close, Thjostolf's team went in first, with Rhys' team following closely. The riflemen formed a perimeter and as soon as their commander gave the signal, Thjostolf waved the Jomsskari in. After a quick headcount and equipment check, they set off, moving east parallel to the river. By noon, they were in dense, deciduous woods, and about four miles from the fort site. Erik was leading the horses, Rhys was navigating, and Thjostolf had put Kolskegg on point, with Wendyll and Edwin keeping the flanks.

They covered the first fourteen miles quickly; they didn't have to map anything out, because it had already been covered. At 1845, they reached the edge of Third's maps and stopped for a meal and a look around.

Thjostolf decided to make camp. The place was defensible and there was plenty of cover, and they had a good view of the river without putting themselves at too much risk from wild animals. Predators like to hunt around water sources, when their prey bent over to drink. It was always a risk when camping near rivers. It was a clear night, and the sky brightened long before the sun rose. Before it had, the scouts were on their way again, this time moving more slowly and taking notes.

At about 0900, they spotted a mule-deer. When it saw them, it bolted. As the day wore on they saw several more, as well as some foxes and warren of rabbits. They all scared easily, so they'd been hunted by man before. They couldn't be that far from a settlement.

It was getting warm—the storm from the last few days had slacked off, but the ground was still wet under the canopy. It was a nice, clean smell. Squirrels chattered at each other, and Erik heard sparrows and jays twittering back and forth. His rucksack was heavy, but he didn't mind. There was something comfortable about these marches, despite the discomfort and danger—he always felt at home. The long months before A'kaylii had been truly transformative.

As the sun finished its climb and began to slide back down the sky, Rhys, who had taken point, held up his hand to signal *stop*. He then glanced back and waved Thjostolf forward. The forest had taken a sparser nature in the last half-mile or so, with numerous broken limbs strewn across the ground. Thjostolf scuttled forward and had a look, and Erik followed. Before he could see, he could smell, and his stomach churned.

It was a village, or had been recently. As the tree line broke, the trunks were scorched, the leaves burned from the twigs. A field stretched out before them, desolate, burned to the ground. It looked like it had been some kind of barley, and smoke still rose from the ash in some places. The charred remains stank of rot and decay, but there was a stronger scent in the air. The village was a mile or so ahead, but it was easy to see that the huts had been gutted.

The Jomsskari didn't speak to each other as they gathered at the tree-line. Hunched down, looking through their binoculars, there was a sense of expectant horror among them that Erik felt, as tangible as the smell itself. There wasn't any noise, save the wind. Even the birds were quiet.

Hesitantly, they crossed the field, spread out in a wide formation. The earth was soft and well-tended before the fires, but the ash had formed a sticky layer of carbon flakes that rose up with every step like evanescent tendrils. Stalks were piled on each other, pushed over by the growing heat wave that had destroyed them. Erik had to lift his feet high over to get over the composting heaps, and the horses whinnied in agitation as they struggled through the mess. He glanced at the sky, and prayed for rain to wash the air.

Something crunched beneath his feet, and he froze. Everything in his mind told him not to look, to move on without satiating his curious impulses, but he couldn't help himself. He regretted it immediately.

She looked about six, judging by her size. The fire had stripped the flesh from her body so that he could see the charred muscle beneath. She hadn't rotted, she had burned within the day. His boot had crushed her fingers, made brittle by the inferno, where they had reached out in her final agonized moments. She lay fallen on her side, a bit of undamaged eye still gazing in terror towards the forest. Her hair, once blonde, was now singed and sooty and her face twisted in pain. She was half buried in refuse, and over her thin frame there were pieces of red cotton that had once been a dress. One hand was outstretched towards the forest, pitiful and desperate. For a few seconds he stared, and then tore his eyes away and went on quickly. Involuntarily, his lower lip quivered, and he bit it in defiance.

As he entered the village, the smell hit him full force, as though he had walked into a putrid wall. The rotting flesh filled his nostrils, and he coughed and gagged, turning his head away and covering his nose and mouth in his sleeve. There was just no escape from it. He heard Edwin growling, and saw three skinny wolves run yipping across the field, one dragging a human leg behind. Edwin followed closely, barking and shouting, "Get away! You savage bastards, get away from them!"

Gabryl and Thjostolf had been among the first to reach the village, and they stood in the middle of it all, looking slowly back and forth. Thjostolf's shoulders were slouched, and he was running a hand through his hair over and over again in disbelief. Gabryl looked back at Erik, and Erik saw tears streaming down his face. Across the ground, corpses lay where they had fallen: shot, stabbed, burned, beaten. There was what appeared to be a woman cut into pieces, left in a pile. A man hung from a pole, impaled and suspended, a few entrails discarded on the ground beneath. Ravens and vultures hopped on the roofs, waiting for the newcomers to leave so they could return to their gorging. Empty shell casings littered the ground. There was no sound save for the breeze, the distant protests of the other wolves, and the flapping of wings. Even Khalan was speechless. He went from door to door, peering into the huts and shaking his head.

Rhys crouched on the ground, picking up shell casings and looking over them. He seemed oddly detached, and sniffed the brass. Carefully, he placed one of them in his pocket, and looked from one side of the village to the other as though tracing the order of events.

"Erik!" Brutus came hopping around a corner, his beard aquiver. "We have wounded!"

They had found a boy, no more than ten years old, coughing blood and bile. When Erik came into the hut, Wendyll was kneeling next to him, holding the child's head up. "It's a sucking chest wound," he said quietly. "He has gone into shock, I believe."

Erik had kicked into high gear. "Elevate his feet," he instructed, "and his arms."

It was a bullet wound. The exit wound was in front, and Erik realized they had shot him in the back. *Who shoots a kid in the back?*

"Pressure here," Erik instructed, and got out his kit.

The child coughed, his lips were blue and his trachea was almost to the side of his neck. He was whimpering something, and Brutus, who was holding up the boy's arms, leaned over and said, "Don't worry, my boy, don't worry; you're going to be okay."

The hut was littered with carbonated shreds and burnt embers, and the stone walls were still warm at the touch. In the corner, a man lay in a bed, shot in the head from the side. He looked strangely tranquil, relaxed, as if he had just fallen asleep and could wake up any moment. The smell of the blood was fresh, and as strong as the stench was, Erik knew they hadn't been dead for long. Like the girl in the field, his body had been rotting for less than a day. Near the entrance of the hut was a broken spear, perhaps an ill-fated counter-attack, and a few pieces of broken pottery lay to the side. From the walls, a few pinpricks of light streamed in through bullet holes, articulated by the airborne dust. Flies buzzed. In the distance, Edwin let out a long, plaintive howl.

Erik couldn't find his pulse; it was too weak. Blood was oozing gently from the wound, rather than flowing, and his skin was cold at the touch. He was sweaty and cold. If he gave him khem-khat, the drug would lower his heart rate too far, and kill him…but maybe that would be easier. Without a hospital in the next half-hour, the boy didn't stand a chance. The wound in his chest had flooded this thoracic cavity with blood, collapsing his lung. Even if he could stop the bleeding, the boy would asphyxiate. He had only moments.

"You're going to be okay, child, you'll be fine," Brutus kept saying. Nobody believed him, least of all Erik. For a few moments he debated with himself about whether or not to use precious pain killer on him. Applying bandages would be a waste, too, but Erik found the calculations difficult to bear. The boy began to cry. It sounded like a much younger child, and it was a distinctive cry reserved only for the dying—rapid little gasps, still fighting for his last few breaths. It made Erik feel horribly helpless.

It was too much. Erik muttered an oath, reached into his surgical kit and gave the child a shot of khem-khat. Then he sat down heavily, his shoulders shaking involuntarily. Wendyll and Brutus looked at him knowingly, and gently set the boy's limbs down.

Erik coddled the boy's head in his arms. Thjostolf and Gabryl were looking in through the door, and Brutus turned and walked out, his fists bunched in fury. Wendyll stood leaning against the wall, watching silently, his face blank.

They stayed with the boy for another few minutes. At first he cried, and then his hands balled up into fists, pushing feebly against Erik as if struggling one last time. Erik recognized the drugs kicking in. A moment later, the boy had gone still, breathing gently and whimpering like a newborn.

Erik held the boy and wept. There was nothing else to do. As the khem-khat circulated in his blood, he breathed more and more slowly, until finally his tear-stained face lay quiet, finally at peace.

There was no talking. Kolskegg and Khalan took the man down from the pole, and they tried to gather the bodies together as best they could. They didn't have time to bury them, but before they left they all knelt and Thjostolf prayed for the dead. As they rose, Erik spoke up.

"When we meet the enemy," he said, "remember this place."

Chapter Eleven

The Climb, June 19, 1160

They had seen the mountain the day before; indeed, it was hard to miss. It towered in the distance, to the northeast of them, but a few miles beyond the massacred village, the river turned towards the mountain. By noon the next day they had reached the foothills, and they began their ascent after a brief repast.

The river was narrower now. It wasn't deep enough to support a barge or a cargo ship. As they soon discovered, though, the depth was irrelevant. The river soon became a series of waterfalls, some five feet, some ten, and one over thirty-five. The Jomsskari circumvented them, finding paths that the horses could climb. The going was slow, but they passed the waterfalls and reached a steady slope before nightfall.

They rested and carried on the next day. The earth was rocky, and as they climbed Thjostolf estimated that they had risen some three thousand feet from the plains below. By nightfall they had risen another four thousand feet, at least. The air was thin, and they had to take their journey more slowly. It was hard to breathe; even at rest they felt as if they had just run, and they had to adjust their pace to keep from driving themselves to exhaustion. The tallest mountains in Haelhan were about seven thousand feet; this mountain could easily be twice as tall.

They had been moving steadily up the mountain all day, following the river. At about noon the slope leveled off to the east, in front of them, and as they reached this plateau Thjostolf realized they had just come up the side of a long and enormous draw. The vegetation became mostly coniferous, the ground thick with mountain ferns close to the riverbank. Every few hundred yards they had to ford another sublet running off the main river; of course, there was thick vegetation all around. Thjostolf took notes furiously. There didn't seem to be a quicker way up without backtracking several miles to find the spur, at least not that they could see, and their going was slow. It would take the engineers a long time to make effective roads. It seemed that the mountain was impassable by anything but the lightest scouts.

The river slowed as they reached the plateau. Ahead, perhaps another four or five miles, Thjostolf could see the higher peaks rising, but it seemed that the river ran between them. Perhaps there was a valley. In any event, they were getting close to the source.

Peter had point. He was a good fifteen yards ahead, and behind him, Erik and Khalan had their respective sides covered. Kolskegg followed, then Thjostolf. At 1330, Thjostolf decided to move away from the river and see if they made better time. He called everyone together, and after they had reorganized themselves they moved a few dozen yards north, walking parallel to the river, but out of the heaviest undergrowth. It was a good call. The ground cleared, and they covered more terrain in the next two hours than they had in the last five. Erik was relieved, not only because they could move more quickly and make up for their lost time, but because they left a much less obvious trail. It would be much more difficult to track them in this lighter foliage.

The earth took on an oddly rich texture as they got higher, sprinkled thick with pine needles and low-growing rhododendron trees. The ground was rocky in places, and they had to scrambled over a few patches of stone to find the same dense, dark loam waiting them on the other side.

For his part, Erik didn't mind. He had grown up in the mountains, and had spent the last few years in A'kaylii. Of course, some of the other scouts were less enthusiastic, but there was no griping, although there were sure to be muttered oaths when they bedded down for the night.

It was nearing 1500, and the slope was getting more and

more gentle. To their left and right, peaks rose high into the sky, another thousand feet of sheer cliffs. The gap between them looked about two or three miles wide, and ahead Erik could see that the cliffs formed a bowl. Maybe it was the mouth of an old volcano; at any rate, they were reaching the top.

Erik had slowed briefly to adjust the straps on his rucksack when he saw Peter freeze. The whole team stopped as one, and sank slowly down. The horses, which had been trained for scouting, settled down into the ground as well, and lay still. Erik had stopped in the middle of a patch of ferns, and he saw his Elven cloak shimmer and take on a leafy, green texture. They had done this dozens of times today, stopping for a bit of wildlife or a clearing, and Erik expected Peter to creep forward, have a look-see, and then signal the all clear.

But he didn't. Instead, the halfling remained utterly motionless, and then, slowly, he turned around and touched his eyes. *Visual contact.* The air became electric.

Almost immediately, he heard movement, and the unmistakable sound of voices. To his left, Khalan drew his cloak over his machine gun, and settled into a ditch, resting the barrel on a large tree root. Erik pulled his hood up and sank lower, crawling forward to the edge of the ferns and taking a little bit of cover behind a rotting stump. Peter vanished into the foliage, and Erik heard the light, whispering sound of the rest of the team forming a firing line and covered their flanks. Thjostolf appeared beside him, patted the air—*stay put*—then waved Kolskegg forward. The sniper slithered up, found a good spot a few yards ahead, and popped the covers off of his scope.

For several minutes, they lay. A fly landed on Erik's cheek, and he twitched. The voices chattered. They sounded loud, as though whoever was speaking wasn't trying to stay hidden. It wasn't constant, either; there were only two or three people. *Maybe a foraging party*, he thought. It couldn't be scouts, because they'd be quiet, and it couldn't be the whole unit because there would be more of them. Maybe a forward element of a larger unit? They were a little ways off, but he saw movement ahead, maybe twenty feet from Peter's position and closing. There was something else, too, some kind of animal.

Erik heard oinking and rustling. Just to the right of Peter's position, he saw the foliage part gently, and then a large black sow came into view, snuffling and swinging her head back and forth across the ground. Following the sow came two girls. They were clothed in simple peasant skirts made of a thick fabric Erik thought might be goat-wool. The younger girl's skirt was dark green, reaching halfway down the calf, with muddy stains along the hem. She was skinny, blond, no more than twelve, and had a pleasant ovular face that seemed to shine as she smiled—and smile she did, much as a twelve-year-old girl could be expected to.

The other looked about four years older. Her skirt was blue, with the same dimensions and the same stains along the hem and another across the right thigh. Her hair was a lovely shade of dark brown that could have been mistake for black if the sunlight was not poking through the trees and glowing through her tresses. It was drawn up under an embroidered scarf, and she had a shawl over her shoulders. Her eyes were a brilliant blue, and she was stocky and a little shorter than her younger sister. It was clear from the shape of their noses, Erik thought, that they were sisters. But as she drew closer, Erik found his eyes drawn towards her.

We have discovered an angel, he thought. What were they doing out here?

Suddenly, it made sense. The sow sniffing the ground, the girls following closely. At the tip of the muzzle of his carbine, he saw for the first time a cluster of ripe, full truffles barely breaking the surface of the loam. They were picking truffles, and it could only be a few seconds before he was discovered.

Eshé-ma, feck me running!

Instantly, he began trying to think of how he could stay

hidden. They were too close for him to move away. He flipped the safety back on, quietly, gently, to be sure, and glanced towards Thjostolf. The captain clearly saw what they were doing, too, and shook his head slowly. Erik suddenly realized that this wasn't so simple. They must have come from a village or outpost, but were they friend or foe? Until they could be sure, Erik knew, they couldn't risk them raising the alarm.

The sow turned towards him, snuffling furiously. She was less than three yards away, and the little bell on her collar jingled lightly as she got closer. The girls followed closely, a little distracted and chatting idly. Then, looking right at him, they gasped happily.

Eshé!

They stared at the perfect truffles in delight, and the younger girl grabbed the sow's collar and directed her away. The angel knelt before him and began picking them, stopping here and now to inspect them, all the while her excitement grew. He was struck. He thought in that moment that the greatest artists could not have captured her likeness, or her gentle features, which shone almost ethereally in the light filtering through the evergreen canopy. She was the most beautiful thing he had ever seen. More than anything, he wanted her to get up and leave, and never know he was there.

Her fingers darted towards a truffle, and brushed the barrel of his weapon lightly. Her eyebrows furrowed as her fingertips rested on the forward sight, cold metal against the warm soil. Then, tracing it back, she raised her face and looked him dead in the eye.

Erik pounced. Leaving his weapon as he jumped, he struck her shoulders with his entire weight, knocking her on her back. She screamed, of course, but his hand covered her mouth. He saw out of the corner of his eye as her sister began to turn to run, and then froze in terror as Khalan erupted from the earth itself and leveled his machine gun on her.

Tears glistened in her eyes, and she whimpered softly. The angel was trembling so much that Erik's dog-tags rattled inside his

157

tunic. The look on her face was one of such horror and fear that he couldn't help but feel like a jai-khu.

Carefully, he put his finger to his lips, and took his hand off her mouth. Then, so as not to hurt her, he got up, crouched before her, and slung his weapon. As soon as she could move, she scooted backwards frantically, looking left and right. The sight of Thjostolf covering her made her stop, and then she spotted Khalan. Erik heard her breathing quiver. She looked back and forth frantically, and her gaze stopped on Erik, as if he were the chief perpetrator. She blinked the tears out of her eyes, still trembling terribly, sizing up her situation. Erik offered her his hand, but she recoiled is if he had offered her a snake.

She had been gathering the truffles in a small leather bag, and he saw it laying a few feet away. He picked it up and offered it to her. A look of confusion crossed her face, and she looked at the bag distrustfully. Then, slowly, she reached to it, snatched it in, and clutched it close to her as if it offered her some security. She looked at him, her expression slipping further from fear and closer to bewilderment.

Erik glanced at Thjostolf, who still had his weapon pointed between her eyes. "Is that necessary?" he asked.

The half-elf glanced at him curiously, and lowered his rifle a hair. "We're not safe yet. We don't know what team they play for. Peter!"

"Clear front, cap'," came the hushed reply.

The angel looked at both of them cautiously, but she had stopped crying. Her sister still glistened with tears, staring down the wrong end of a GP-10 had rightly petrified her. Khalan had followed Thjostolf's lead and lowered his machine gun, but he still had her covered, and Brutus had appeared behind her. Neither seemed quite sure what to do. This was not a scenario they had trained for.

The angel looked to her sister, and then looked at Erik as

though pleading with him to call the orc and the dwarf off. Erik offered her his hand again, and this time, gingerly, she took it. Her hand felt in every way exactly as Erik had always expected an angel's hand to feel: soft, cool at the touch, with calluses on the palm. He pulled her to her feet and pointed her to the younger.

"Go on," he said gently, "We won't hurt you."

Seeing this, her younger sister dashed to her and buried her face in her shoulder, crying hysterically. Erik, Thjostolf, Khalan, and Brutus had formed a circle around them, and the rest fanned out into a close perimeter. Thjostolf looked around. "Okay, we need to talk to them. Where's Gabryl? Maybe he can communicate with them."

"We understand you," said the angel.

Everyone raised their eyebrows. Her Haellic was flawless, with a touch of some odd, archaic accent, but that was impossible, they were over a thousand miles from Haelhan.

Thjostolf was the first to react. "You speak Haellic?" he said, a little stupidly.

"I...what?" she stammered, as if she didn't understand the question. "Who are you? What do you want?" she asked, in the way people ask when they aren't sure they really want to know.

Erik and Thjostolf exchanged glances, and then Rhys arrived. "Captain, we don't see anyone else— "

The girls abruptly bolted for the woods. Khalan roared and raised his machine gun, and Kolskegg rose from the brush to intercept them.

Thjostolf pushed Khalan's barrel away, shouting, "Let them go!"

The girls tore through the brush and vanished into the forest. Everyone looked at Thjostolf for explanation. "We don't feckin' shoot kids," he said quietly. "And besides, they'll lead us home. They aren't Alnethar, and I want to know where they learned Haellic."

Thjostolf looked around. "Rhys, feckin', take a team and follow them. The rest of us will bring up the pack horses and sweep our flanks for enemy contact. If you get ambushed, pop flares and establish a base of fire so we can flank or break contact."

"IHO, cap." Rhys glanced around. "Kolskegg, doctor, Peter, let's go."

"Take Edwin," said Gabryl. "He can track them; you don't need to catch them."

Kolskegg, Rhys, Peter, Erik, and Edwin set out. As they left, Erik spotted the truffles again, the angel had dropped them as they went through a patch of rhododendron. He picked them up and put them in his surgical kit.

The girls had chosen a path through low-laying brush and vegetation that made it extremely easy to track them, but very difficult to overtake them. At first it was just the rhododendron, but then it turned into small sharp stones and low lying brambles. They found a scrap of green cloth, from the younger sister's skirt. Edwin ran ahead, sniffing and panting, and occasionally hopping back and whispering, "This way," or "They rested here a while." The Jomsskari's gear kept getting caught, and Erik's extra medical bag was hard to carry in a crawl. In retrospect, he thought, they really should have left their heavy loads with the packhorses.

They spent nearly half an hour crawling, and emerged on the other side bruised, torn, and grouchy, but rewarded by the sight that met their eyes.

The forest had begun to slope downwards, and a few hundred yards after the rhododendron patch, it gave way to rich, lush grassland. They stood in the entrance of a bowl-shaped valley surrounded by thousand-foot cliffs on the north, east, and south. To their south, the river cut through the trees, leading up to a large lake on the eastern side of the valley. Erik could see dozens of waterfalls coming off of the mountains and feeding the lake, but the land was higher on the edges of the cliffs, forcing the river along a path near the south. The grasslands were dotted with herds of goats and sheep, and on the southern banks of the river there were barley fields waving in the breeze. On the high ground, just west of the lake, stood a village.

"How many houses?" asked Erik.

Rhys whistled, gazing across the landscape. "Two, maybe three dozen structures—twenty families at least, and some barns and pens for the livestock." He scratched his nose and looked at Edwin. "Good job, my friend."

Edwin wagged his tail appreciatively.

Erik pulled his binoculars out of his rucksack and scanned the area. Nobody seemed alerted, as of yet, and there didn't seem to be a military presence. It looked benign, a placid little lakeside village, peaceful, quiet, and entirely secluded.

Then he spotted the girls, and distantly heard their shouts. They were nearly across the field, nearly a mile ahead of them, running as if the devil were at their heels. As he watched them run he felt like a total jackass. *It figures*, he mused, *that I meet the most gorgeous creature in the world, and scare the eshé out of her.* He lowered his binoculars and looked at Kolskegg, who was watching through his scope. Rhys began reporting what he saw as it happened.

"Girls are raising the alarm—some goatherds are taking notice, and bringing their herds in. They've reached the village...looks like several men have come to meet them...they're embracing...oh, I think it's their father. He might also be an authority figure. He's issuing instructions now. They're telling him what happened...the older girl is pointing our way...they know we followed them."

A bell began to ring in the village, and the workers in the field dropped what they were doing and ran back to the village. Erik glanced at his watch. It was 1600, sunset was in a few hours. They set up a hasty perimeter and waited for the rest of the team to arrive, each lost in thought.

"These aren't the bad guys," said Thjostolf. "I think it's pretty clear that this is one of those villages that the Alnethar have been raiding, and I'll wager they don't know the feckin' difference between Alnethar and Iaelian."

"They are all ugly bastards, I don't blame those girls a bit," quipped Brutus, and grinned. Rhys blew him a kiss.

They had gathered in the cover of the forest overlooking the valley, and were eating a little bread. For a few minutes they sat in silence, and then Gabryl spoke. "They need to know there is a difference. They are more valuable to us as friends than as neutrals."

Thjostolf nodded. "They know the land. We could use a guide or two."

Gabryl nodded. "They can guide us, yes, provide local reports and resources, yes, but more importantly, they can fight for themselves. If they believe they stand alone against an unstoppable force, they will quake in their boots and submit. But if they see that they are not alone, they will stand up to their oppressors…and they will inspire other villages to do the same."

Again, silence. Erik looked at Thjostolf. He was deep in thought. It was barely 1700, and Erik knew they would have to move within the hour or wait until morning. They wouldn't want to come in darkness or at first light, because it would look like an assault.

"Gear up," said Thjostolf abruptly. "We go in now, and try to meet with their feckin' leadership. There's the chance they'll try to attack us, so be careful. Stay in close formation, and maintain fire discipline. Don't fire unless fired on. Understood?"

Everyone nodded; this wasn't what they were used to, but

they understood the situation.

Thjostolf turned to Gabryl. "Leave your rucksack with Khalan, and stick close to me, near the front. I'll carry your rifle. You're the face of civilization out here, so they need to see you as a diplomat."

Five minutes later, they were moving. They broke the tree line as the shadows were beginning to grow long, and the field crickets began to sing their melodies. The village was silhouetted against the cliffs and lake, which shone brightly in the setting sun. The grass was knee-high in many places, and it rustled gently in the wind, waving like the sea. Erik looked back and saw Khalan, Peter, and Wendyll bringing up rear security, their cloaks shimmering with the breeze, and when they stopped, they melted into the landscape and vanished. Brutus, close to the middle of the group, lead the horses and the sow, while Erik walked behind Gabryl.

As they entered the village, Thjostolf signaled the group to stop. Nobody seemed to be around, and Erik wondered if they were walking into an ambush. It looked like everyone had gone into one of the larger buildings near the center of the village, but they may have dispersed. He knew Thjostolf was thinking the same thing, and wondered what they'd do if villagers burst from the windows, firing old rifles and heaving stones. Deadly fire was reflexive, almost instinctive for the Jomsskari. "Respond to contact" was the most frequent drill they trained on.

Thjostolf carefully walked forward, and Erik became aware of the sound of talking somewhere in the village. There were only two or three voices, but they seemed to be arguing. The village was constructed around a central square about fifty yards in diameter, with a large building made of split logs on the eastern side. There were fires burning inside, and as they drew closer it sounded like the voices were coming from within. As they entered the square, they spotted a boy standing watch outside the doorway to the building. The door was between six to eight feet wide, and was constructed of nothing but animal pelts hung above the threshold. When the boy saw them, he darted inside and shouted something. Silence fell over the building, and then, in groups and one at a time, the entire village emerged, forming a semi-circle in front of them.

There was a distinct sense of anticipation and fear that struck Erik. He had never seen so many people so silent. Four men stood forward, one of which bore a distinct, familial resemblance to the angel. He had a thick brown beard and a slightly balding head, with streaks of silver that betrayed his age. He had heavy eyebrows, large crow's feet around his eyes, and a weather-beaten face. For such a man, he spoke far more gently than Erik had anticipated. He had a very kind, almost ministerial voice, but simple words. "Welcome, strangers," he said, "to our village."

Thjostolf stepped forward, his rifle slung across his back, and opened his palms. "I am Thjostolf sen Skarp-Hedin of Haelhan, captain of the Jomsskari, in Allegiance to the Five Monarchs. We come in peace. Also," he added, gesturing behind him, "We've come to return your pig."

The villagers looked at each other wordlessly, and Erik caught sight of the angel. She was standing with her sister and an older woman who looked like their mother. The angel was looking at him, and Erik noticed a difference in how she gazed at him. There was no fear in her eyes anymore, only curiosity. It was almost as if she felt more confident on her own turf. Her sister, who had taken refuge in her arms, looked a little less confident. For whatever reason, they didn't have the same expression of horror on their faces that they had had before. Erik smiled a little sheepishly, and the angel cocked her head.

The assembly was silent again. Then the man opened his hands towards them and said, "I am called Josef. If you come in peace, then we welcome you."

There was a pause, and then, in an instant, the entire body rushed forward and each of the villagers began introducing themselves and their families. Erik found himself surrounded by men shaking his hand, women putting their hands on his chest, children jumping up and down around him, saying, "Welcome, welcome, welcome."

In the flurry of activity, Erik felt turned around and disoriented. There were so many voices, so many hands, and so many names being thrown at him that he couldn't begin to process it. "Welcome, welcome, welcome," they kept saying, and then suddenly, they were gone, disappeared into their homes around the square.

It took a moment for him to realize what had happened. They *had* to greet the newcomers, as a social obligation, but nobody wanted to stay around. That realization made him feel a little better – at least he wasn't the only one on edge.

Only Josef, the two sisters, their mother, a few older women, and three elderly men remained. Gabryl was the first to recover. "Well, I suppose the good people of this town are not convinced of our veracity."

"They are decent folk," said Josef mildly, "But there are rumors of elves and griffins destroying villages. There are some among us who have fled from the lowlands, and have seen the terrors first-hand."

Thjostolf nodded. "We understand their caution. I would ask that you forgive our conduct towards your daughters earlier this evening. We had hoped they would pass us by. I hope none of you were injured?"

Josef glanced back at them, and Erik noticed the angel suppress a half-smile. "Well," their father replied, "They are hardy. In any case, rest assured we bear you no ill will. I know you did not intend to harm them, and these are difficult times."

"If the people of the village would prefer that we not stay within your borders, we can stay in the forest," offered Gabryl, "But naturally, we are very interested to know more about this valley, and your people."

The three elders behind Josef glanced at each other, but Josef smiled. "We would be honored if you would stay the night, and join the elders for a meal. This is Sigmund," he indicated the first of the old men, "and Feodor, and an elf of our own, Abraham. And this," he turned completely, and the women stepped forward coyly, "Is my wife, Eidel, and my daughters, Shayna and Sisel."

Shayna. Erik liked the sound of it.

As Josef turned around, his eyes got big, and Erik glanced back to see Khalan approaching. The orc was back-lit from the setting sun, and his black, gnarled face was twisted into a grimace. Erik knew that grimace. Khalan felt self-conscious, and a little nervous, although he would never admit it to anyone. Next would be the gruff persona to cover for it. Really, orcs weren't so different from humans.

Khalan came to a stop, his bandoleers rattling gently. "Cap, nothing in the tree line. Peter and Wendyll are holding rear security." he growled, and cast a look at Josef, who was clearly unprepared for such a sight. His eyebrows furrowed, and his gaze leapt from Josef to the elders, then the women. "Well?" he snarled at Thjostolf, and grinned toothily. "Introduce me!"

*　　*　　*

Dinner was goat, potatoes, and a barley porridge, and some brown ale served in delicately carved steins. The Jomsskari had to be careful not to overeat their welcome. As they had gone into the meeting hall, Thjostolf had quietly passed the word down to watch their hosts' table manners and try to imitate them, but that plan broke down quickly when they were served first. Eidel and her girls bustled about serving food which, apparently, had already been cooked in a kitchen at the back of the building. When the ladies joined them, they watched everyone's reaction self-consciously, but the scouts didn't have to feign. It was simple food, but tasty, and most of it was sprinkled with some kind of peppery spice that reminded Erik of a mild pepperweed.

Erik, for his part, thought it was delicious. It called to memory the long nights of reading by candlelight in the back of the bookshop, eating reheated stew leftover from his master's evening meal. He always put pepper on it to liven the flavor; the old man Svend had a sensitive stomach, and preferred his food mild and tepid.

The hall was about seventy feet long and forty feet long, with windows every ten feet or so. The windows were nothing but holes in the wall, covered by goatskin drapes, but they seemed cozy enough. The doors, three in all, were on the north, south, and west sides of the building, facing out towards the square. There was a kind of corridor running down the center from the front door to the kitchen, and from the side doors across, and the rest of the hall was filled with long wooden tables and split-log benches that had been polished and lacquered until they were so smooth they were almost slick.

As they came in, they had removed their heavy gear, and Brutus took a seat where he could keep an eye on it. Without their packs and cloaks, they looked a lot less frightening, and Abraham dared to strike up some small talk with Khalan before the meal was served. Erik was beginning to relax. There was something pleasant about the atmosphere, and he liked it. It felt like a home...not his home, but somebody's.

As they ate, Gabryl explained the situation as far as they knew: the ancient division between the Alnethar and the Iaelians, the rise of Lord Mashatsu, the Alnethar confederation with the griffins and Irkalla, and the Alliance's expedition to prepare a first-line of defense. The villagers found it fascinating, and while they had initially seemed skeptical, they grew more and more attentive. Erik noticed that the women were paying close attention, too, although they pretended they weren't.

When the wizard had finished, the table fell silent, and the elders thought for several minutes. Eidel got up and began taking bowls away, and Erik caught himself glancing at Shayna for the hundredth time. She seemed disturbed, and yet relieved. Before, he guessed, they had no idea who or what was going on. Now, the enemy seemed less mystical. He could relate. Politics was something that he could wrap his mind around, if not probe its depths. It was finite and tangible. At least, it seemed to be.

Josef stirred abruptly, and said, "We have heard stories like this before—rumors, tales of lore, and stories for the campfire. The griffins consider this mountain sacred and cursed. It was for that reason we built our village so far up, we know that the griffins will not follow. When our families left the foothills thirty-five years ago, we didn't know we could grow the seed we brought, or feed the livestock so high in the mountains. Nobody had ever tried to climb so high. When we found this valley, we knew God Himself had led us here. It is an old volcano, long dead. The soil is good because the minerals from the mountain are washed down to us. The goats thrive, and there are few predators that come out of the mountains. This is our home, and it has been our safe haven the better part of my life."

"Does it have a name?" asked Gabryl.

Josef nodded. "We call it Stadfesta."

Gabryl nodded. "Old Haellic," he said, to the Jomsskari, "It means, 'Farmland.'"

"You mentioned predators up here?" asked Thjostolf.

"Mountain wolves," said Feodor, a little shortly.

"Oh, we've got one of those," said Gabryl. He was running his hand through Edwin's fur, and the beast looked up at him and gave a low, almost mournful *woof*. "Have you met Edwin?"

Josef smiled politely at him, and said, "How did you domesticate him?"

"Well," Edwin quipped, "It all started when I was only a pup..."

The elders gaped, and Eidel almost dropped an armload of bowls. Sisel craned her neck over the table, and Shayna, who had just emerged from the kitchen, stared in awe from across the hall. Gabryl laughed, and Edwin, sensing the sudden flux of attention, stopped talking and began wagging his tail self-consciously, which thumped loudly against the benches. "Go on," urged the wizard, "Tell them."

"That is extraordinary," murmured Abraham, and smiled. Erik noticed he didn't have front teeth.

"Well," continued Edwin, a little bashfully, "when I was just a pup I awoke to find myself being carried away from my den. I was very upset, I recall, because my mother just laid there and slept, and didn't wake up to stop him from taking me. At any rate, Gabryl, for it was he that took me, put me in a cage, and stood over me muttering and rocking back and forth. After a few hours he stopped, and left for a few moments. Now, of course I wasn't any smarter than any other wolf at that point, but I knew there was something different about this man. He returned to me and fed me a sweet potion from a vial, and sang to me all night. This pattern went on for several days, and on the fifth day, I believe, I fell into a deep sleep. When I awoke, the cage was gone, and he was sitting in a chair opposite me. I woofed at him, and then, without thinking, I said as clearly as I say now, 'May I have something to eat?'

"He offered me a leg of lamb, and we talked for some time. At length, I asked him what he had done, and he told me he had given me the wisdom of the heavenly beings and the longevity of the elves. But more than that, he had interceded on my behalf, and delivered me a soul.

"That was nine hundred years ago next week, and not a day goes by that I do not thank God for giving me such a pleasure as to serve Gabryl."

As he reached the end of his speech, the wolf's voice grew

bolder with pride, and his tail thumped enthusiastically. At the end, he looked at Gabryl, panted for a moment, and laid his chin on the wizard's leg.

There was a silence around the table, and then Brutus said, "That may be the strangest thing I have ever heard."

"You're a mage?" said Feodor quizzically.

Gabryl laughed, and shrugged. "Well, no, not as such," he said. "I'm a wizard."

"What's the difference?" Feodor asked.

Gabryl smiled cryptically, and looked away. Josef answered the question. "Mages," he said softly, "Are of this world."

*   *   *

The elders invited the Jomsskari to sleep in their homes, and they graciously accepted the invitation. As they made their way to the homes, Erik noticed prying eyes peering out from behind goatskin window covers. The doors on the houses, he noticed, were wood, and he heard latches sliding shut.

He was quartered in Josef's house. It was a one-room structure, with a loft with two rooms, one for the girls and one for the couple. In the main room, there was a fireplace and a goatskin rug, as well as a loom and spindle in the corner with a small tapestry on the wall. Khalan and Wendyll were in the house with him, and Josef offered them the only spot he could, the floor. It was a welcome change from the rocky ground, and when the candles were blown out, Khalan and Wendyll were asleep in seconds.

Erik lay awake. The home was quiet, and warm, and he had taken his armor and boots off, but he couldn't sleep. For half an hour he lay, turning over and around, unable to rest. Whenever he closed his eyes, he saw the boy's face, fresh in his mind, vivid and terrible.

He opened his eyes, and looked at the ceiling. The rafters were barely visible in the dark. He tried counting them but kept losing his place and eventually gave up. When his eyes were open, he was exhausted and ready to sleep. When he closed them, he was accosted by the image of the weeping boy and his bloody hands.

He sat up, hugging his knees and staring into the black. Khalan grunted and shifted slightly. Erik sighed deeply and, grabbing his pistol belt and cloak, got up and quietly slipped outside.

The moon was high and it was getting close to midnight. He knew that Thjostolf had left Rhys and Brutus on guard duty for a couple of hours, until they could be relieved. He trudged up the hill overlooking the lake in his bare feet, his black trousers rolled up to the knee and his revolver flapping against his thigh. He wanted to be alone, and the lookouts would be facing west; so, he went east.

The hill was grassy and cool, when he got to the top he found a rock that made a perfect stool. Sitting on it, wrapped in his cloak, Erik reached into his belt pouch and produced a small bag. Inside was a bit of tobacco and a few rolling papers. He made himself a cigarette, lit it, and took a long, indulgent draw. As he exhaled, the smoke curled from his nostrils, and he felt his body begin to relax.

He leaned back and looked at the sky. There were a few clouds, but for the most part the stars shone down unabated. Before him, the lake shimmered by their light, like dancing fireflies. Crickets chirped, and the cool breeze ran over his face and feet.

There had been a time when he could have believed that God was but a fiction, but he could not believe it anymore. He could have passed off the faith of generations for a social construct, or called it a desperate dream of a people unable to conceive of an emptier reality. At one time, before the massacre, he had wondered if it was just a way of explaining the pain in the world...pain as passing, and therefore inconsequential.

A hundred corpses on his right and left. Why had he lived? A systematic execution with but one error. It was impossible now to believe in nothing. God was – It was beyond his doubt now. But the Absurd permeated everything. To live was a greater terror than to die, and yet his life among many was spared.

He sat still, taking it in as he finished smoking. For a while he looked at the night sky, breathed the air, and let his head empty itself. It was cleansing, and felt wonderful. But as soon as he looked down and saw the peaks, his mind wandered back to the massacre, the stink of the bodies, and the decay.

He decided to keep looking at the sky.

He was so engrossed in this task that he hardly heard her come up, and startled suddenly when he heard her exclaim, "Oh!" very close to him. He looked back and saw Shayna, wrapped in a blanket, standing a few feet away.

For a second, he didn't know what to say, but she saved him the trouble. "I hope I'm not disturbing you," she said quickly, taking a small step back. "I didn't see you."

He looked at her, confused, and then realized he was wrapped in the cloak, and so was mostly camouflaged. "Oh, this, yes, it's…it's Elven magic. Makes me disappear, see?" He pulled it over his head, and then popped out again. "It's Shayna, right?"

She came a little closer, a little shy but intrigued. "Yes, sir," she said. She looked closely at the cloak, and touched it with the tip of her finger. It rippled like water when touched. A delighted smile dashed briefly across her face, and she glanced up. "That's awfully clever!"

"Yeah, we like them." Erik scooted over and patted the rock. "What are you doing out?"

She sat down as far as she could from him, leaning her back against the rock and facing the lake. "I just…I don't know, I just wanted to be alone for a few minutes. I come up here a lot during the summer." She nestled into her blanket a little deeper, and glanced sideways at him. "What about you? Are you keeping guard?"

He chuckled, and shook his head. "No, it's…basically the same reason as you."

She looked at him for a moment, and then looked back towards the lake, but she didn't say anything. He felt a little awkward, and looked away.

They sat like that for several minutes before he broke the silence. "I really am sorry we jumped you like that."

She glanced at him, and smiled a little smile on the corner of her mouth.

"We thought you'd just walk by," he went on, and plucked a piece of grass, playing with it idly. "We thought there might be an Alnethar encampment up here, and…well, we didn't know." He was quiet for a second, and looked at her again. Her eyes were enchanting, and he had to look away to recall his train of thought. "Anyway…I'm sorry I scared you, for what it's worth. I won't make a habit of it."

She was quiet and motionless, and he looked away.

There was silence. Then, soft as a whisper, she asked, "Why can't you sleep?"

He didn't want to answer. Usually when someone asked he just lied and said he had a headache. He could always make it simple by saying he was just a little restless, or it was pretty outside. Something unremarkable, something untrue, something safe. With anyone else, it would have been reflexive, but...

For whatever reason, he couldn't do it. He stared at the lake, with its shimmering wavelets and the dark cliffs and waterfalls rising beyond them. He didn't want to tell her, but the words came out regardless. "Thirty-six hours ago I held a ten-year-old boy who had been shot in the back," he murmured. "His lungs had collapsed and he suffocated to death while I watched. When it's quiet...I hear his cries."

Quiet. The wind caressed her hair, and she pushed a strand from her eyes.

"It's different," he went on suddenly, "Than seeing soldiers die. I saw my whole unit massacred once, over a hundred men killed. I dream about that, too. But when you see something like that, something so callus and senseless, it makes you think about the big questions, you know?"

He realized suddenly that he was still talking, and she was still listening. Steeling himself, he looked at her, and smiled nonchalantly. "Anyway...I just got some stuff on my mind, I suppose."

They sat quietly for a few more moments, and then she said, "I think you tell the truth."

He didn't know what to say, so he shrugged.

"I mean, about the dark elves," she continued. "Sisel, my sister, thinks you're going to take us away."

"Yeah, I can see how she'd think that."

She looked at him for a while, and he savored it. "How old are you?" he asked suddenly. There was a daisy on the ground nearby, and he pulled it out as he spoke, spinning it around between his fingers so that the pedals made a continuous white circle.

"I just turned sixteen," she said, and cocked her head slightly as she thought. "Last week, actually."

He smiled, glancing at her, and tossed her the flower. "Happy birthday, then."

It landed on her blanket and slid off onto the ground, and she reached out to pick it up. Her raven hair slipped from behind her ear as she leaned over, and she pushed it back with a graceful gesture. She smiled at him, and smelled it delicately. "Thank you."

"How do you celebrate birthdays up here?" he asked.

"Flowers," she said, and giggled. "No, we get together at dusk and our parents and siblings and the elders lay their hands on us and pray. It's all about thanking God for the past year and asking for another."

He nodded. "Wow. That's, ah...that's a pretty good way of doing it."

"Yeah, it's really nice."

"Do people give you gifts?"

"Well," she said, and laughed, "It's mostly just from within a family, but..." She held up the flower as though toasting him, "I'll accept this."

They sat still, saying nothing. She was looking idly at the lake, and he was looking at her face. Up close, she was even more beautiful than he had known—the gentle curve of her nose, and the softness of her cheek illuminated by the starlight—he lost himself in the vision of her. He'd have been content to sit there with her all night. It was more restful than sleep, more precious than anything he knew, and he'd have happily sat there until dawn if he'd had the choice.

They chatted on, about the valley and the lake and the crickets. She marveled at Edwin and he told her how none of the Jomsskari had ever heard the story of his origins. She told him how she used to pretend to be an explorer and walk all over the forest, and he told her about traveling to A'kaylii. He told her about libraries, and she told him about truffles. He told her he still had her truffles, and they bickered about what she should cook with them.

When they returned to the house, it was past midnight, and

he was sorry to see her disappear into her room. She paused on the way in to glance back, and he waved stupidly. For a few minutes he lay still, his hands behind his head, staring at the ceiling, wondering if she was thinking about him.

He decided she wasn't, and went to sleep. But he slept deeply and dreamt of her, and when he saw her the next morning, he noticed she was wearing the daisy in her hair.

Chapter Twelve

Stadfesta, June 21, 1160

The previous evening, the elders had said that they had been undisturbed in Stadfesta for more than three decades. First thing in the morning, the Jomsskari set out to find out just how likely things were to stay that way. The peaks were impassable to the north, the east, and the south; the Jomsskari had already noted how the village sat in a kind of topographical bowl. That meant that the only avenue of approach to the mountain was from the west, where the Jomsskari had first made their climb. They had found the headwaters, as ordered. Now Thjostolf's priority was to determine if the mountain had any other strategically significant features. Thjostolf estimated that they were at about twelve thousand feet of elevation, and was determined to uphold to old adage of warfare: "Hold the high ground." They needed to develop the situation before they decided where to go and what to do next.

The Jomsskari had gotten up early, and by the time the sun rose, they were already moving across the barley fields, back to the tree line. The day before, they had come in a few hundred yards north of the river, which entered the valley at the southernmost corner. Now Thjostolf wanted to investigate the northern region of the pass.

Though it was past sunrise, Stadfesta was still covered in the shadow of the eastern cliffs, and they left the village behind them in darkness. Behind them, the villagers were moving towards the meeting hall, and the smell of porridge, bread, and herbals teas rose into the air. The Jomsskari had eaten a bit of their Elven rations, and the bland taste that stuck to their tongues made the smells all the more alluring.

Erik was tired. He had seen Shayna and Josef briefly when they had first gotten up, but neither seemed talkative, and Erik had work to do. Despite his fatigue, he felt surprisingly light, and it took him a moment to realize why. For this excursion, they had left their rucksacks behind, secured in Josef's house, and Erik was shocked to remember how easy movement used to be. It felt good to get out and move, and he took the opportunity to stretch his sore limbs and breathe the brisk, thin mountain air.

They hit the tree line and dispersed into a wedge formation. Khalan had taken point; in the dim light, his orcish eyes could see clearly, and he had the most firepower at his disposal. They soon found a wide foot-path leading towards the plateau, and followed it for about half a mile before stopping to investigate the forest surrounding the trail. About five hundred yards north of the path, after a long space of thick vegetation, they found a sudden cliff face that descended vertically some two-hundred feet before tapering off to only a slightly gentler declination. Below, nearly two miles down, Erik could see the foothills, thinly shrouded in a morning mist. From the edge of the valley, the landscape formed a deep, sharp draw to the northwest. Thjostolf took notes on the area, and they decided that even a griffin would have difficulty flying so high from the lowlands. It seemed more plausible that any griffin flights would have to reach the plateau several miles west and rest before attempting to fly to the valley. That meant that the spur the Jomsskari had climbed was the only reliable way up the mountain - even for the Alnethar.

They turned south and head back to the trail. The forest was thick all around, and they couldn't see very far in any direction. In order to get a better idea of the lay of the land, they divided into teams. Erik was with Thjostolf, Gabryl, Edwin, and Wendyll, while the others went with Rhys. Staying about two hundred yards to the north and south of the trail, they followed the path for about two miles, charting clearings, elevation changes, major landmarks and smaller game trails. Then, just as the sun was rising above the mountain, they reached the plateau. Erik had been preoccupied for a moment, adjusting his medical kit as he walked. When he looked up, the sight took his breath away.

It wasn't so much that he hadn't seen it before. They had seen their position when they came up. To their left, they could see the distant river snaking in and out of the trees, with heavy brush and forest extending for over a mile around it. When they were in the trees, they couldn't see what lay to the north, where they currently stood. But now, they found themselves in a wide, open space. The land fell gently beneath their feet, the draw extending about eight or ten miles in front of them. The clear space between the forest and the northern edge of the draw, where the land turned to cliffs, looked about about two and a half miles wide. Their initial reconnaissance of the south-western approach had convinced them that only light infantry could navigate their way up the mountain. Now they knew differently. The route along the middle of the spur from the north-west could easily support vehicles, perhaps even clunkers.

But it was the view beyond the mountains that stunned him. To the north, he could barely make out the shape of a city, and the road they had seen a few days before. To the west, he could see Feldhall, just the outside shape of it, but Feldhall nonetheless. From this vantage point, with nothing more than a pair of binoculars, they could easily see any Alnethar movements towards the river and in the entire lowlands out to the coast. On a clear day, the only thing preventing them from seeing the coastline west of Feldhall was the curvature of the world itself.

Around him, the Jomsskari stared, and Edwin woofed softly in awe. Finally, Thjostolf spoke,

"Feck."

Khalan laughed raucously, and Erik shook his head in wonderment. "This is a two-edged sword, cap'," he said.

"Yes, it is." Thjostolf raised his binoculars to his eyes and scanned for a moment. "Feck. Me. Running. What a view."

Gabryl had been standing back a little ways, but now he stepped forward. "Forgive me, captain, but it seems to me that this mountain is more important than we may have anticipated."

"Oh, yes, absolutely," Thjostolf said. "Feckin', from up here we can see things three days before they reach the damn coast. The griffins may have left this mountain alone before, but that was before we built Feldhall. As soon as the Alnethar realize the importance of this position, feckin', it's only a matter of time before they send a feckin' reconnaissance team to see if anybody's up here."

Kolskegg sat down on a rock and whistled. "It's not so great a position for us," he pointed out. "Even if we can see their movements, we'd be hard-pressed to get that information to the right people, so they know what's coming their way. But with griffins, they can relay movement data within a few hours. If they control this land..."

"...They can drive us back to the sea, why not," Brutus finished.

Thjostolf nodded, lowering his binoculars as he did. "Solid gold real estate, this. We'll need to send a runner to Feldhall to get reinforcements," he said. "Feckin', we can't hold the plateau without more men. Rhys, let me see the map you've drawn up."

Gabryl interjected. "Captain, it will take some time to prepare, but I can communicate with Feldhall from here, if you like."

They all looked at him, and for a moment, the old man looked taken aback, as if their surprise surprised him. "I can conjure a portal through which we may speak to Lord Hoskuld," he explained, and then, as if he were talking to little children, "through the magical arts."

"Seriously?" said Peter. "You can do that?"

Thjostolf laughed. "You didn't think we brought him along for his looks, did you?"

"To be honest, we all kind of figured it was a public relations thing, yes?" confessed Brutus.

Thjostolf grinned. "How long will it take?" he asked Gabryl.

The wizard didn't answer for a moment. Then, his eyebrows furrowed, he replied, "I'm not sure. By the end of the day, no later. If you would, just write the message you wish me to convey."

"Yeah, sure." Thjostolf pulled out a notepad and began writing. "Well," he said as he finished, "I think we need to leave an OP in place and head back to Stadfesta. If we can't hold this plateau, then feckin', we can hold 'em off from the village. That's the best we can do with our current manpower situation, so feckin', let's head back there. Who wants to be on the OP?"

Wendyll raised his hand, and Rhys said, "I will stay as well, captain. We will report back if we see anything significant."

"Good deal," said Thjostolf. "Brutus, you'll be my second in Rhys' absence. Feckin', when we get back we can see what we can do to secure the village from assault. Once Gabryl has an update from Lord Hoskuld, feckin', we'll adjust as necessary. Questions?"

There were none.

"Okay, let's go."

It was nearly noon when they emerged from the tree line and into the barley fields. Some of the farmers looked up at them, evidently surprised to see them again. The Jomsskari waved cheerfully at them, and a few of the farmers waved back. Others, however, scowled, and several moved away distrustfully, watching the company as they made their way towards the square.

Feodor, the elder, was tearing out weeds, but when he saw them coming down the path, he set his hoe aside and came to meet them. "You've returned," he said. Though he was smiling, Erik felt that his tone of voice was taut, and he noticed that for all the polite manners, Feodor had taken the stance of someone expecting a fight. His shoulders were squared, and his feet were planted in the path between the Jomsskari and the village.

Thjostolf noticed, too, but he didn't show it. "We never left, actually," he said lightly. "Some of our gear is still in the houses. But I'm very glad to have met you. I have a matter that we must discuss with the elders. When would it be convenient for us to meet?"

Feodor glanced at Gabryl, and then back at Thjostolf. "What matter is this?" he asked cautiously.

"The matter of our continued presence," Thjostolf replied. "We do not presume to take advantage of your hospitality, but we believe that we may be required to stay a little longer then we had hoped. I will explain more fully when we are all together."

Erik glanced at Thjostolf, and then at Khalan. He knew they were both thinking, *What does it matter what they think? The mission is what it is. Like it or not, we're staying around.* But Erik knew Thjostolf wasn't this polite unless he was being shrewd. There was always a method behind the madness.

Feodor looked hard at the half-elf, and finally said, "Now is convenient. If you would join us in the meeting hall, I will call the others and we will meet you there."

"Good. Thank you." Thjostolf nodded graciously, and turned to the Jomsskari. "Okay, guys, feckin', disperse and get a feel for the land. Try to figure out how they'll hit this place, and get your fields of fire down. Oh, and Brutus −" he pointed at the dwarf and nodded. "Set up the feckin' mortar tube and pre-sight their main avenues of approach, landing sites...you know how to do your job. Gabryl, go ahead and send that message. I'll be in the meeting hall."

As Thjostolf followed Feodor back to the village square, Erik slapped Khalan on the back. "Come on," he said, "Oi, Brutus, Khalan and I are checking out the goat fields across the river."

"Excellent, excellent," Brutus said. "Only don't be too long, yes? Everybody meet me in the square in forty-five minutes."

They all intoned the obligatory "IHO," and set off. The village was essentially split into three sections. To the north and the west, there were plowed fields bearing barley. The farmers had built their houses in this area, and there were three large barns built just north of the square, by about five hundred yards. Near the center of the village, around the square, woodworkers and smiths had built their homes. On the southwest corner, a blacksmithy stood, an anvil out front. There was a tannery to the western edge of the village, and the central hall on the eastern corner. Beyond that, the river left the lake and flowed southwest for a few hundred yards before turning west and cutting a path through the mountain pass. South of the river were goat pens and grazing fields, with the homes of the goatherds built near the pens. A wooden bridge spanned the river just south of the meeting hall, a few dozen yards from the lake.

Erik and Khalan set off towards the river. Coming to the edge of the field, they moved between the village and the riverbank, passing the tannery and chatting idly in orcish as they went. Across the river, the goatherds kept their vigil as their flocks grazed.

"How fast do you think that river is flowing?" Khalan asked suddenly.

Erik glanced at it. "Let's go see."

On closer examination, they could see eddies near the center of the river. The whole thing spanned nearly a hundred yards, and looked about eight or ten feet deep at the most.

Erik pointed at the eddies. "There's a strong undercurrent," he said. "You'd want to be a strong swimmer to negotiate that."

Khalan nodded. "So," he said slowly, "They have to take the far side of the river, yes? They must control the goatherd's homes, so they must land in the goat fields, and push east and then north, across the bridge."

Erik nodded. "The other team will land near the barley fields, then."

"How do you come to that?" asked Khalan.

Erik glanced at him, and held up his hands in an "L" shape. "They won't attack from the north and the south at the same time. That'd put their own teams in crossfire. Unless they're just stupid, they'll land to the west and push east. That way, they hit the main body of the village from two sides, without getting in each other's fields of fire."

Khalan nodded. "Yes, I see what you mean."

Erik picked up a stone from the bank and began to toss it up and down in his hand. They resumed walking towards the bridge. Ahead of them, over a rise, they could hear the sound of women singing. Erik listened as the melody floated over the water. It was strangely beautiful, if a little melancholy. He couldn't tell what they were saying, but the sound, next to the rush of the river, was refreshing.

They came over the rise. Twenty or so women were washing clothes in the river, wicker baskets on the banks and washboards in hand. Erik spotted Shayna in a cluster of girls her age, talking together. She was speaking to a red-haired girl, and as he watched, Shayna reached up and touched the daisy in her hair ever so lightly. The other girl smiled knowingly at her and then caught sight of them walking up. She said something quickly, and Shayna glanced over, blushed, and began to scrub vigorously.

One of the older women spotted them, too, a very pregnant brunette, with curly hair and bare feet. She rose, a little unsteadily, and came towards them. Erik saw her eyes dart to his carbine, and then to Khalan's GP-10.

"How are you this fine morning?" Erik asked in greeting, "I don't believe we've met. I'm Erik, and this is my brother, Khalan."

The pregnant woman cocked her head slightly and smiled warily. "Good morning, Erik," she said. "Your brother? I wouldn't have guessed."

Erik grinned and looked at Khalan. "Well, brothers of

different blood, I suppose."

She nodded, and after a brief hesitation said, "We didn't know you'd be returning. Will you be staying long?"

"Yeah, we're staying in the area a little while longer, I think. We don't mean to outstay our welcome, but we've still got some work to do." Erik skipped the stone into the water and dusted his hands. "You've all been very hospitable. We thank you for that." He glanced at the river, and noticed Shayna sneaking a look at him. All of the others were watching cautiously, and he noticed that the singing had stopped. They were listening, too.

"And your name is...?" he went on.

"Anya." She followed his gaze. "Are you looking for something?" There was a deliberate pause in her intonation.

"Just looking around," Erik replied glibly. "Actually, we were wondering if anyone swims in the river. It looks like it's got a little bit of a current to it."

"I think it would be a bad idea," Anya said.

Khalan raised an eyebrow. "A bad idea?" he asked. "As in, it is uncomfortable to swim in? Or as in, they find your body washed up a few miles downriver?" Erik knew the orc didn't mean to, but he sounded harsh in comparison to Anya's feminine voice.

"I don't swim much," said Anya coolly. "But the boys swim in the lake."

"Fair enough," said Erik. "I might catch a swim later on, if we get some time." He pointed to her belly, and said, "Looks like you got a little one coming. How soon?"

Anya laughed, and rested a hand on her stomach. "Yes, I do. A few weeks at most. Any day now, really."

"Well, congratulations. Is it your first?"

"Yes, it is."

"One of our guys, Kolskegg, has his first coming soon too," Erik said. "And Thjostolf, our captain, he's got a little girl at home."

Anya nodded, and glanced over towards the others briefly before asking, "Are either of you family men?"

Erik shook his head, and Khalan laughed. "Erik here has asked me to be his bride, but I am waiting for a rich man with a nice shiny ring."

"Well, you're a damn flirt," Erik returned accusingly. "Always flaunting your stuff."

Khalan grinned toothily. "I am beautiful, aren't I."

Anya glanced back and forth between them as if trying to discern if they were serious. Erik grinned. "Anyway, moving on. Thank you for your help. We're going to get back to work now."

He looked over at Shayna and caught her eye. Indicating the daisy, he said, "I like it!" before turning to go. Behind him, he heard the girls giggling amongst themselves.

When they were out of earshot, Khalan leaned over and said in a low voice, "The girl, the daughter of Josef. You see how she looks at you?"

Erik smiled. "Yeah, I noticed."

"You should purchase her," Khalan said, as if he were giving financial advice. "She is probably fertile."

Erik stopped walking and looked at him with evident surprise. "Wait, *what*?" he said incredulously.

"You know, with the birthing hips. She can bear you many children, many sons. Her father would probably take thirty goats for her, I think?"

Erik blinked. This was one part of orcish culture he was aware of, but had never come in direct contact with. "Um...well, Khalan, that's...I'm not doing that."

He looked over at Shayna, who was trying not to look at him. Khalan seemed confused. "Does she not please you?"

Erik laughed. "Don't get me wrong, she's quite a lady. It's just not, you know, a *barter* thing so much."

"Haellics do not purchase their wives?" This was clearly a revolutionary concept to Khalan. "Then how do you marry?"

Erik laughed again and shook his head. "I don't...It doesn't matter anyway, I haven't got thirty goats."

Khalan cocked an eyebrow. "I could lend you some goats."

"Just leave it, man."

Khalan looked back at them, and shrugged. "Very well." After a moment of walking, he added, "I just thought you'd be interested."

Erik smiled, but didn't reply at first. As he thought about it, though, it occurred to him that such an arrangement would be a rather good deal. Beyond her obvious beauty, she struck him as very intelligent, and their conversation the night before had been more than mere pleasantries. There weren't a lot of people outside the Jomsskari whose presence Erik truly enjoyed. "Maybe later," he said after a moment. "There's a war on now. This isn't the time to consider building a family."

They reached the bridge. While Khalan began to walk across, stomping every so often to hear the quality of the wood, Erik examined the beams and pondered.

Khalan leaned over the railing and looked down at him as he walked down the bank. "What is it?"

"They've got an awful lot of metal around here," Erik said.

"I assume this has significance to you." Erik grinned to himself. Khalan was too polite sometimes. It didn't match the rest of his persona.

"It means they've got an economy outside this village," he explained. "Look, there's no mine shafts here, but they have a blacksmith's shop with an anvil. An *anvil*, Khalan, that's a lot of metal. Besides which, they use a bell to signal. That's some sophisticated metallurgy that goes into that."

Khalan nodded. "This is true."

"And look at these planks," Erik went on. "They were cut cleanly, not split by an axe. They looked like they've been sawed in half. These nails are big and thick, not the little ones."

"So, there are other villages nearby?"

"Yeah, maybe further up those cliffs," mused Erik. "Or else they had trade with the people in the lowlands. They talk like they're entirely self-sufficient up here, but they may depend on resources down the mountain. The Alnethar may be choking them even now."

They had reached the other side now, and Khalan looked out over the goat fields. "There isn't a lot of cover out there," he said, "Besides the houses. I think that if the enemy lands in the fields, we ought to wait until they have reached the bridge before engaging them. They will be bottlenecked on the bridge."

Erik walked down to the river bank and looked up underneath the bridge. "We could blow the bridge, if we had to. What do you think? Twenty, thirty pounds of explosives?"

Khalan nodded. "Yes, that would suffice."

"I'd hate to do that," Erik went on, as they climbed the bank and headed towards the goat pens. "Who knows how long it'd take them to rebuild it."

"Yes, of course. As a last resort." Khalan waved to a goatherd, who nodded in greeting. For a few minutes, they walked across the fields, and finally Khalan said, "They will not land any further away than this."

They were about five hundred yards from the nearest goatherd's house, and all the ground between was open grass. Erik looked around a nodded, "Yeah, I think you're right. They'll want to land close enough that they can hit their objectives quickly."

The soldiers stood for a few moments, looking across the fields. "They will have no cover for a few hundred yards at least," Khalan said, more to himself then to Erik. "And when they move to the bridge they will be exposed..." He considered it for a moment longer, and then looked at his watch. "We should head back, brother."

"Right."

When they reached the bridge, Erik saw that the women had finished their washing and were moving back up towards the square. They had resumed their singing. He couldn't see Shayna.

"Do you have a firing position for your '10?" asked Erik as they crossed back over.

Khalan pointed to a large structure a few buildings down. "That one there would give me cover of the entire southern bank," he said. "These buildings directly ahead of us are too small to provide good cover," he went on, indicating the buildings closest to the bridge. "And I assume you wish the use the meeting hall as a field hospital?"

Erik nodded. "It's the only one big enough to hold multiple casualties, and it's got facilities to boil water and bandages. It's probably best if we draw fire away from the center of the village anyway."

Khalan nodded. "That is what I thought."

They found Brutus, Kolskegg, and Peter gathering in the square, and went up to join them. For a few minutes, they conferred. All things considered, there were three places the Alnethar were likely to land. They could land on the bare ground around the barns and attack from north to south, which would drive the villagers into the river. They could land near the goat pens to contain them: they decided that this landing site would be mandatory, to keep their quarry from escaping across the water.

"They'll take the bridge," said Khalan confidently.

The last spot they could land was the northwest corner of the village; this would give them high ground over the lake, and enable them to force the villagers into a corner between the lake and the bridge.

"What about the bombers?" asked Peter. "They'll be dropping their bombs right in the middle of us."

"Snipers can deal with griffins," said Kolskegg. "I was watching them when they trained. They hover a little as they turn, and they aren't very fast unless they're diving. I think we can take them out before they let their bombs go, and we can certainly deal with any of them on the ground. I mean, if we hit a wing, they're down, so..."

Brutus nodded. "Excellent, excellent. I shall tell Thjostolf what we have found, why not. The rest of you, stay close, yes? And we will call you when we need you."

Brutus headed for the meeting hall, and Erik followed. "I want to get a better look at these facilities," he explained when Brutus asked. "If I'm turning it into a field hospital, I want to have some kind of plan."

*   *   *

It was dark inside the meeting hall, at least compared to the midday light outside. As Erik's eyes adjusted, he saw Thjostolf sitting at a table to the far left. The elders were with him. One of them, Sigmund, was talking quietly. As Erik and Brutus drew near, Sigmund finished. Then Abraham, the elf, began to speak.

"I must disagree with you, Sigmund. I do not mean for us to put our trust in our own strength, but we must prepare for our future. Now all of us agree that we must choose what is best for our children, and our children's children, and most of all for..." He stopped when he saw Brutus and Erik. "Ah, welcome. Brutus, is it?" He looked at Sigmund and smiled. "A Dionysian, if I am not mistaken."

"Race and faith are separate, Abraham," said Feodor. "You of all people know this best."

"What's up, guys?" asked Thjostolf.

Erik could see that Thjostolf was being put through the wringer. Brutus did, too, because he replied, "We are ready to brief you, captain, whenever you are ready. But, if now is not good..."

Erik glanced at the elders, and noticed Josef looking at him rather oddly. Their gazes met, and for a brief instant Erik felt as if the man's eyes were going to bore through his skull and into his mind. He wasn't sure what to make of it, until Josef spoke.

"I trust you slept well, doctor?"

He knows. Suddenly, Erik recognized the look, it was the look of a loving father with a lovely daughter. It struck him rather sharply that this was not Havenstead. Idle flirtation might fly twelve hundred miles south, but here in El Ornahar, it could be a grave breach of honor.

But, it had been a long time since Erik had been apologetic. Kowtowing of any sort just wasn't orcish, and it didn't have a place in the Jomsskari, either. Erik met him head-on. "I did, sir," he said pointedly. "Thank you."

There was the slightest pause as they regarded each other, as if each of them were waiting for the other to make a move. Then a broad, genial smile spread across Josef's face, and Erik caught a glint in his eye. "I am glad to hear it," he said, his voice betraying just a hint of amusement. "I heard you had some trouble sleeping."

"It comes and goes," Erik said simply. "But we don't mean to interrupt."

Feodor held up his hand, "I would like to hear what your men have come to tell you."

Thjostolf glanced at him, and then to Brutus. "Go ahead," he said. "What's your analysis?"

Brutus briefly explained the Jomsskari' findings, and as he did so, Erik noted that each of the elders reacted differently. Feodor and Sigmund seemed almost exasperated – Abraham, resigned. Josef's face fell, as if remembering a great sorrow from his youth. When Brutus had finished, they all sat in silence for a moment.

Thjostolf looked up at Erik. "And where do you want to put casualties?"

"Right here," said Erik. "Lots of space, hot water to sanitize things..."

Feodor put his face in the palms of his hands and sighed deeply. "Remind me again," he said wearily, "Why you believe that, after more than thirty years of solitude, we will suddenly be subject to attack by the Alnethar."

Thjostolf weighed his words patiently. "The Alnethar are building an army to move south and attack Iaelian, Haelhan, and Humbridge. We have come to investigate their capabilities and provide a first line of defense. Now that we are here, the Alnethar will attempt to either rout us, capture us, or kill us. This mountain gives them a clear view of all of our positions along the river and in the lowlands. It is strategically significant. They want it, and we can't let them have it."

"To be clear," Feodor said sharply, "you have brought this evil to us. If you had never come –"

"What's done is done," Abraham interrupted. "And it is not the fault of these men either way. The Alnethar have been building their war machine for a hundred of years, and the nations of the Alliance are responding. It is the way of the world."

"I do not require a lecture, Abraham," Feodor said, forcing his voice into a calm. "The truth is, we have no idea who these men actually are. They come here with elves, and dwarves, halflings and orcs. Has anyone seen such a company before? Who then can know their purpose? We have their story and nothing else. If the Alnethar and the griffins intended to occupy the Accursed Mountain, they would have done so much earlier in our lifetimes."

Josef held up his hand. "Brothers," he said. "We have all spoken our piece. I believe we all have good reasons to offer our recommendations. But we are still divided. So, then, let us go and pray, and come together in a few hours. Then we will cast our votes, and if we are still unable to come to a decision, we will gather the congregation tonight and we will all of us decide."

Abraham nodded. "I agree with Josef."

Feodor took a deep, cleansing breath, and stood. Sigmund looked at Thjostolf and said, "Captain, we will inform you of our decision this afternoon. Until then I hope you and your men are comfortable, and that you will all join us for lunch."

"Absolutely," Thjostolf said, standing and extending his hand to each of them. "Two of my men are keeping watch, but the rest of us would be honored to share a meal with the people of Stadfesta."

He's never polite unless he's being shrewd. So, what's he up to?

Erik soon found out. As they stepped out into the sun, Thjostolf blew his whistle, the signal for the Jomsskari to gather. In a few moments, they had all arrived from different corners of the village and formed a half-circle around him. Only Edwin and Gabryl didn't show. They were probably still working on that whole "magic" deal. Erik had no idea what to make of that…first a talking wolf, then this? Gabryl was a strange old man.

"Take a knee, guys," Thjostolf said heavily. "Here's the situation."

He squatted, pulling out his pipe and stuffing the bowl with tobacco. "The elders are undecided as to whether or not we can stay in their village. And feckin', as much as I'd like to just point out that we have really big guns and they don't, we're not acting as an feckin' occupying force. Lord Hoskuld gave orders that, should we contact local, non-hostile governments, we're to respect their feckin' sovereignty and attempt to ally ourselves with them."

He struck a match, and took several long draws, until he had a good burn. Then, flicking the match aside, he continued, "You all remember the briefing on the ships. Now, Stadfesta may not be much, but it qualifies. Besides, I don't want to have to deal with a riot. Even if that was the best course of action, feckin', we don't have the manpower. And sleeping in the woods for a little while may be worth it, if it proves to them that we're not hostile."

He sniffed, rubbing his nose. "I think I'm allergic to something up here," he muttered, half to himself. "Anyway," he went on, "Where we stand now is, they'll have an answer for us sometime in the next few hours. Now, I heard your plan to defend the village. Feckin' solid work. It turns out, we're probably going to need that plan."

He held up a piece of paper from one of the Jomsskari' notepads. "Rhys came running in about twenty minutes after we got back," he said darkly. "They've spotted activity in the lowlands north of Feldhall. We don't have any kind of details at this time, but it may be a troop build-up. Feckin', if that's the case, we may have to hold this feckin' mountain until reinforcements can break out from whatever's going on down there. There's no telling how long that could be."

Nobody spoke.

"Now, as of yet, there's no indication that the Alnethar will send a raiding party up here. So, time is both our friend, and our enemy." Thjostolf looked around to make sure nobody was listening, and then said quietly, "No matter what these morons decide, we've got to feckin' hold this village. It's the only defensible position. The alternative is to feckin' mount a guerrilla war from the brush, and that would leave Stadfesta open to occupation, or worse. They may suffer the same fate as that fecked up village we saw coming up here."

Kolskegg shook his head. "That's not happening here."

"Damn right it's not. I'm not leaving these people to their deaths. That's just not decent."

Kolskegg raised his hand. "Cap, what about Gabryl? Has he been able to contact Feldhall?"

"I haven't heard from him." Thjostolf checked over his shoulders again. "And fecking, we need to be realistic here. I know he has powers, and he's been alive for-feckin'-ever, but everything I've seen so far is pretty much feckin' pretty lights and talking dogs. No offense to Edwin, I think he's great and everything. But if this magic trick doesn't work, we'll need an old-fashioned runner to get down the Feldhall. It's about a seventy-mile hump. Who wants it? Erik, not you, I need you here."

Kolskegg said, "I'll do it."

Peter raised his hand. "I'll go with him. If we book it, we can reach Feldhall in less than forty-eight hours."

"Can I get a look at the maps?" asked Kolskegg. "I'll get a

route selected, and we can strip down our kits to the bare essentials."

Thjostolf pulled a folded-up map from his breast pocket and passed it to the sniper. "Okay, feckin', Khalan, Erik, Brutus, and I will stand by. And you two, once you've got your route selected and your kits stripped down, feckin', go somewhere quiet and try to sleep."

"IHO, cap."

Thjostolf gestured to the remainder. "Come on, I'm going to go sit by the lake for a minute. Chill out or something."

They walked to the other side of the meeting hall and walked down the bank to the water's edge. Thjostolf relit his pipe and offered the others some of his tobacco and rolling papers. As they rolled their cigarettes, Thjostolf sat back against the bank, laying his rifle across his knees. "These are some odd folks, I tell you."

"How so, cap'?" asked Khalan.

"Well, none of their arguments were practical," said Thjostolf. "I mean, they're talking about feckin' faith and doctrine and crap. I tried to point out that having us around has – I don't know – some tangible utility, but feckin', they always went back to whether or not their God wanted them to do this or that."

"What do they worship? The dragons perhaps, like the Alnethar?" asked Brutus.

"No, I don't think so. For a second there I thought they might worship the One Unsayable, but they talk about 'Father' and 'God' like he's their buddy or something. I don't know."

Erik lit his cigarette and passed the book of matches to Khalan. "You know what these guys look like?" he said. "They're like West Haellics. You know, the coastal fishermen, like those just south of Fjordstead."

Thjostolf nodded. "Yeah, they do, kind of."

"Maybe they are the descendants of fishermen that got lost or something," said Khalan.

They sat in silence for a few minutes. Brutus began tossing stones into the lake. The smell of the midday meal began creeping out of the kitchen at the rear of the meeting hall behind them.

Thjostolf pulled out his binoculars suddenly and began gazing across the lake. For a few moments, he scanned wordlessly. Then he said, "Isn't it beautiful," as more a statement than a question.

The clouds were beginning to thin as the sun burned through them, and for the first time, Erik got a good look at the rock face. The lake was bigger than it looked, nearly a mile square.

"Yes, it is," he replied.

"There's a cave over there," said Thjostolf. "It's hard to spot; just looks like a shadow."

"Where?"

"Um...okay, do you see that feckin' light spot that looks like an old man?"

Erik laughed. "Yeah?"

"It's right under his ear."

"Oh, okay, yeah." He squinted. "That's a cave?"

"Yeah. Here, look." Thjostolf passed his binoculars.

Through the binoculars, Erik could see the cave clearly. It was about fifteen feet above the water, on the north-east corner of the valley.

"Notice anything odd?" asked Thjostolf.

"No..."

"Look at the waterline," the half-elf prompted.

He looked. At first, he didn't see it. There were a few horizontal shadows, and a stalagmite, and what looked like a...

"Whoa."

"Yeah, that's what I thought."

"That's a dock," Erik said, "carved right into the rock, leading into the cave."

Khalan took the binoculars, and after a moment of peering gave a low grunt of assent. "Well, that is interesting."

"Is that a back-door to the mountain?" asked Erik.

"I have no idea," Thjostolf replied. "Could just be a storehouse, or it could be something a little more interesting. If we stay here, I want to check it out."

"Might be a mine shaft," said Erik. He told Thjostolf about the odd presence of forged metals in the village.

The captain nodded. "Perhaps," he said. "Or maybe there's another village through there. But you know, these guys have been really feckin' elusive about what all's up here. Feckin', I can't help but wonder if these guys are trying to keep us out of something or other."

They heard footsteps coming up from behind, and saw Peter coming up behind them. He was rolling a cigar as he walked. "Hey, guys."

"You got a route?" asked Thjostolf.

Peter nodded, flopping down next to Brutus and taking the matches. "We'll hug the tree line down the spur, then cut south through the forest to the river and follow it back. It's not a straight line, but it's close enough and we can make better time if we don't have to constantly recheck our azimuth."

Thjostolf nodded. "Good." He seemed to be thinking deeply.

Suddenly he turned to Erik. "Hey, what was that with Josef?"

Erik glanced at him. "What now?"

"Josef, you and he had a little exchange there."

"Oh, that," Erik took a drag and shrugged. "I couldn't sleep last night, so I took a walk and ran into Shayna, you know, his daughter, the older one?"

"Yeah. What happened?"

"We chatted. Nothing deep." Erik laughed suddenly. "I didn't even think about whether or not it'd be okay to talk to her."

Thjostolf looked at him quizzically. "What do you mean?"

"I mean, we don't know anything about these people and their culture. I wasn't trying to be forward or anything, but I suppose I should have...I don't know." He shrugged again. "It's really amazing to me how little we know about where we are. You know?"

Thjostolf nodded. "Yeah," he said softly. "I know."

Khalan spoke up suddenly. "Thirty goats. I tell you, brother, it is a good offer."

Brutus laughed, and Thjostolf looked at them as if they had lost their minds. "What the hell are you talking about, Khalan?" he asked.

Erik grinned. "He thinks I should buy Shayna. You know, how orcs give a bride-price?"

"Ah. Thirty goats? Really?" Thjostolf considered it. "That seems kind of cheap."

Peter threw a stone into the water. "Hell, I've a hundred goats at home. At that price, I could get three wives, and one for the weekends." He paused, considering it, and then grinned widely. "Not such a bad idea, really."

"I pray for your soul, Peter," said Thjostolf. "I really do."

"What? Okay, so I like women. Is it such a crime?"

Erik pointed at Thjostolf emphatically. "Chastity, that's the warrior virtue you forgot. Forgot all that brutality and courage and eshé, we gotta work on our chastity."

"You know what this village needs?" said Peter, ignoring Erik. "A midget! All these girls are too tall. They need a damn midget."

Brutus slapped the halfling on the back. "My friend, you do not like tall women? But think of it! You could make nice medium-sized babies, with hairy feet, no less!"

"You're right!" Peter said, taking a heroic stance. "I could create the new master-race! Half man, half halfling!"

"What, three-quarterlings?" asked Erik.

"Yes!" Peter laughed. "We'll need a better name, though. Three-quarterlings is bollocks."

Thjostolf shook his head. "Feck, you guys, you're embarrassing me." He looked behind them and got to his feet. "Come on, then," he said. "They're serving lunch – let's be good guests."

*   *   *

Gabryl found them as they left the meeting hall, their stomachs full of barley stew and bread. He looked exhausted, and Erik noticed that his robes, usually dull and rough, seemed slightly radiant as if they were freshly cleaned, although they clearly were not.

"Thjostolf Captain," Gabryl said as he drew close, "I've had contact with Feldhall and delivered your message."

"What orders from Lord Hoskuld?" asked Thjostolf.

Gabryl beckoned them in, and he spoke to them in a low voice. "He agrees with your assessment, captain. We must hold this mountain until reinforcements arrive. However, First Jomsskari observed at least three companies of clunkers assembling north of Feldhall. They may shortly be under attack. Lord Hoskuld warns that he cannot say how soon help will arrive, but promises to dispatch a sufficient contingent as soon as possible. They will establish fortifications on the plateau."

Thjostolf nodded, "So, now we know what we already knew." He glanced at Kolskegg and Peter, and smiled. "At least you guys don't have to run all feckin' night, right?"

They spent the next few hours training. First by drawing lines in the sand, and then by actually running around the village, they rehearsed their defensive plan. Then they cleaned their weapons and did physical exercises. The villagers watched from a distance as they lifted logs over their heads and ran the mile from the village to the wood line and back. It was the first time these quiet, mountain folk had seen soldiers train, and they seemed a little taken aback. Erik spotted Shayna and a young farmer watching from the edge of the barley fields as the Jomsskari did wind sprints down by the river.

But Erik knew what the training was really all about. They were all frustrated. There were conflicting orders – to respect the local governments and to hold the territory – and the simple matter of staying in a village where their presence had apparently become an issue of deep theological import. And when the Alnethar did come, and the Jomsskari knew they would, the Jomsskari would be outnumbered and understrength against a disciplined and well trained enemy. To fight them off for a time was one thing. To completely eliminate the enemy was something else entirely. In the absence of orders, professional soldiers defaulted to training.

It was late afternoon when Wendyll arrived. When they saw

him, they gathered quickly.

"What news?" asked Thjostolf.

"About an hour ago," Wendyll said, "I observed Feldhall in the distance through my rifle scope. Because of the clearness of the day I could also observe the roadway we examined on our last mission, as well as a distant city to the north."

Wendyll's voice was soft and lilting, it sounded as though he was reciting poetry. He had a cadence to his voice and a gentle timbre that gave his words a lovely air. Erik could almost imagine a wildflower speaking in such a voice. His words, however, were somewhat more ominous.

"The Alnethar are assembling," he went on. "They have gathered at least four companies of clunkers and an additional six of infantry near the main road. It is my belief that they intend to attack Feldhall."

"Feck," Thjostolf spat on the ground.

"That's not enough men," Kolskegg interjected. "They can't take Feldhall with so few."

"That's something we know that they may not," said Thjostolf, referring to Kolskegg's comment. "But they have to know they have us isolated up here until the assault's over."

He ran a hand through his hand, and looked at Wendyll for a moment. "Thank you," he said. "Do you or Rhys need relief?"

Wendyll shook his head and smiled. "No, captain."

"Okay. I'll be up there in the morning. I'll bring you some hot chow if I can, alright?"

Wendyll nodded in reply, and without another word he turned and disappeared into the barley.

They were talking quietly amongst themselves when the

elders emerged from the meeting hall at last and approached Thjostolf. The half-elf was drenched in sweat, and at the high altitude, they were all far more beat then they would have been at Feldhall. Erik was checking everyone to make sure they had taken their salt tablets and were drinking water, but when the elders stopped in front of their captain, they all listened in.

"Good captain," said Josef, and bowed slightly. "We have reached a decision."

Erik raised his eyebrows, and glanced at Khalan. Khalan was paying close attention, and had locked Josef with his stare. It wasn't meant to be intimidating, but Erik always found it a little unnerving.

"We are split evenly over the matter," Josef went on. At this, Erik shifted petulantly, glancing at Khalan and grinning. Thjostolf inhaled deeply, and let it out very slowly and very quietly.

"We are split," Josef said again, this time more forcefully, "and so we will bring the matter before the households tonight. If the elders cannot reach a consensus, then the congregation will. We will vote after dinner. Again, we would be honored if you would join us for our meal."

Thjostolf nodded, and bowed in return. "We thank you for this," he said. Erik could tell he was frustrated, but he did a good job of sounding gracious. "I hope the people of this village are convinced of our good intentions."

The elders turned and left. Around the square, the villagers looked on silently. Thjostolf looked at him men and shrugged.

"Let's get washed up," he said. "No sense smelling like arse for dinner."

Chapter Thirteen

The Meeting, June 21, 1160

When the villagers came together for their evening meal, the Jomsskari slipped in with them and took seats near the rear of the hall. Dinner was barley bread and a thin soup of vegetables and goat…most of the food seemed to be made of these two ingredients. Erik spotted Shayna with her family, and admired her for a moment before digging in. For his part, he didn't have a problem with staying until relieved. It was more time with Shayna, if all went well tonight.

As the meal ended, Feodor stood up and announced that the vote was to be taken. The villagers became quiet, and Shayna glanced back at Erik. He caught her eye, and, somewhat impulsively, winked. She blushed and looked away.

Abraham stood. He was the only elf in the village, but had a different look than Rhys or Wendyll. His cheekbones were higher, and he had a shorter build. His wispy white hair was braided in much the same fashion as Erik had seen in Iaelia, but it was his eyes that were most noticeably different – almond shaped, grey, and always slightly squinted. He leaned on a cane, and spoke in a rich baritone. "We all know the issue to be considered tonight," he began, "And I feel it is my duty as your elder, and an Alnethar by blood, to assure you of the dangers we would face should we be discovered here."

The Jomsskari glanced at each other. Brutus smirked a little, and Thjostolf glanced at Kolskegg. "I *told* you," he murmured. It hadn't occurred to Erik that Abraham was Alnethar, he didn't seem to fit the physical profile they had seen.

"I do not know how true it is that the Dark Elves have made war on our visitors," he continued. "And I do not know if they will venture so high on the mountain. We established this settlement to isolate ourselves from the constant feuding of the river-peoples, and to live peacefully without fear of raiders from the wilderness. We came here to preserve the gift that has been entrusted to us. For forty years, we have done so.

"The Alnethar are worshipers of the Great Demon, and if they make war on us, we will likely be annihilated. Our weapons are primitive, and we are unversed in the art of war. I ask that you consider the danger we face, should we be discovered."

He sat down, and the room buzzed softly for a moment as families talked. Sigmund stood up and, spreading his arms wide, called for attention. "There is no reason to fear the Alnethar! Our strength is of no consequence," he declared. "Have we forgotten to whom we belong? Have we lost our faith? We are a small settlement, established for a single purpose. Was that purpose to merely live? Or are we called to live faithfully, peacefully, and in keeping with the doctrines we have worked so hard to preserve and propagate? I say, let the newcomers take their war elsewhere; I will have no part of it!"

This elicited cheers from some and groans from others. A man called out, "Sigmund is right! Are we not the children of God, and have we not established our homes here for peace? The newcomers will bring war to our village!"

"Do you hear yourself?" retorted another, "as if they profit from this!"

"Here we go," muttered Kolskegg, and took a long swig of ale. The room erupted in shouting and for a few minutes Erik watched, bemused, as half the room swore the Jomsskari had come to destroy them and the other half proclaimed their good intentions.

In the midst of it all, he saw Shayna watching him. For a moment, amid the shouting turmoil around them, they just looked at each other. There was a pleading hint in her gaze that he didn't quite understand. The shouting seemed to grieve her, and she seemed to be begging him to put a stop to it. Then Eidel leaned over to her and said something, and she turned, pretending she hadn't been looking. Eidel hadn't noticed, but Sisel did. She narrowed her eyes suspiciously, and stuck her tongue out at him before laying her head on the table as if exhausted.

The debate continued for nearly three hours. Someone would stand up and give an argument, and everybody would argue amongst themselves. It was still light outside when they had first sat down to eat. Now the sun set, the moon had risen, and the smell of night invaded the room. Finally, Feodor stood up and everybody simmered down for a moment.

"Friends," he began, "I want you to remember our situation and remember the reason we came here. We came to leave the warring of the tribes behind us, to retain the pure doctrines of our faith and keep it unspoiled by violence. We built a new village in the heights of this mountain to protect our children from the warring ways of the lowlanders. We have set ourselves apart so that we may raise a generation in peace. How do we benefit, then, by bringing warriors into our midst? How do we intend to remain faithful to our purpose if we contradict ourselves? And how do we hope to give a good example to our children if we are inconsistent?

"Friends, I have nothing against the newcomers. I do not wish them ill. But I ask that you join with me and respectfully request their timely departure."

The vote was taken, and it was decided, twelve households to seven. The Jomsskari would leave in the morning.

* * *

Erik had first watch. He sat at the edge of the barley fields, fifty yards from the outskirts of Stadfesta, his back against an old tree stump. For a summer night, it seemed strangely cold. All the nights on the mountain seemed cold. He wrapped himself in his cloak, his carbine hugged close to his body and his feet tucked in. Khalan was a few yards south, his hood drawn over his head. Erik could see his stubby nose and underbitten jaw protruding from the shrouds.

The sky was clear, at least, and the starscape was beautiful. The rough peaks to his left and right didn't inhibit the view at all, since he was looking towards the lowlands. He hadn't noticed just how frightening the tree line looked from here. Maybe the villagers were superstitious about it. That would explain a lot.

He tried to stay focused on the task at hand, and watched for movement. He always felt edgy on watch. His eyes traced the outlines of the forest, but of course, he didn't see anything. His eyes weren't orcish or Elven, and didn't adjust to the dark as well. Even the dwarves had better night vision than him. Khalan was the real lookout. Erik was just company.

He smelled something out of place, and heard light footsteps behind him. He looked back. Shayna was coming, two cups of steaming tea in her hands. Erik glanced at Khalan, who was looking back as well. The orc glanced at him, and winked. In the dark, Erik could barely make out his lips, but he was sure that Khalan mouthed, *Thirty goats.*

"Cheeky bastard," he muttered to himself, but couldn't help but smile a little.

Shayna found Khalan first, and offered him a cup, which he accepted graciously. For a moment they spoke together in low voices, and then Khalan pointed towards Erik. Erik stared straight ahead. Although he couldn't explain why, he tried to look as if he didn't notice her, all the way up to when she crouched beside him and said, "Sir?"

He looked up, spotted the cup, and took it. "Thank you," he said, and, blowing on the liquid inside gently, took a sip. It scalded him a little, but it was welcome.

She hesitated, and he scooted over. "Can you stay a while?"

he asked. There was no sense being shy, he'd be gone in the morning anyway.

She glanced back towards the village, and sat down, resting her back on the stump, her shoulder pressed against his. Her face was more than a little troubled, and she didn't look at him directly.

They sat in silence for a few minutes. Erik's original boldness had fled as soon as she had taken her seat. He found himself suddenly tongue-tied. For a while he just watched her out of the corner of his eye, and caught her doing the same. After a while he decided it was time to talk.

"So, your father's a cobbler?" he asked. It was a stupid thing to say, but it was something.

She glanced at him, and nodded, "Yes, sir."

"My name's not 'sir'," Erik said gently.

She didn't reply.

There were crickets in the field. They seemed happy enough. Erik didn't know quite what to feel. He tried not to feel anything, but that didn't work.

She spoke up. "Where will you be going?" she asked.

He sighed, and took another sip before answering. He didn't want to tell her too much, but it seemed wrong to mislead her. "Back to the forest, I suppose," he said finally. "Cap's got a better idea than I do."

She looked out on the barley fields, and he couldn't help but watch her. She looked like she wanted to say something terribly, but couldn't find the words.

"I wish…" she began, and then looked down as though ashamed.

"What?"

She looked up again, and, taking in a long breath, turned to face him. "Where did you say you were from?"

"Haelhan," replied Erik. He found himself staring into her eyes, and melted.

"Haelhan," she repeated, and then again, more softly, "Haelhan." She dropped her eyes for a second, and then looked up. "Tell me about it."

"Oh, I…"

"Please?"

How could he refuse? Erik laughed nervously, and tried to gather his thoughts. "It has mountains, like this one. Not so big, though. It's really not so different from here. The weather's a bit warmer, I think." He sat still for a moment, collecting his thoughts. Then he laughed again. "I wasn't ever at home there. It's in my blood, I guess, but Haelhan isn't…you know, home."

She dropped her eyes, and then, as if trying to change the subject, poked his arm with her forefinger. "What do these mean?"

She was pointing to the tattoos. He pulled his sleeve up to his shoulder so she could see them all. "They're old orcish runes," he said.

"What do they say?"

"Well, my left arm reads, 'He that lives with honor is honored in eternity,' and the right arm reads, 'May the blessing of our ancestors follow you in war and peace.' And here—" he pulled out his revolver, "—It reads, 'May the Spirit of the Weapon guide you.'"

"Oh."

She looked confused, so he explained. "Whenever a young orc passes his trials, he's given these tattoos and a weapon engraved with these words. They've been doing it for hundreds of years. When

I passed the tests, I got them, too."

"What are the spirits?'"

He smiled. "Well..."

She waited expectantly.

"Orcs," he said slowly, "believe that everything has a spirit. This blade of grass has a spirit, the moon has a spirit, and so does this handgun. So, the blessing engraved on it is to...you know, give me the upper hand in combat."

"Do you believe in the spirits?"

Erik laughed. "Oh, I don't know...It's a little hard to say."

She cocked an eyebrow. "Well, either you do or you don't, right? How can it be hard to say?"

Erik took a moment to formulate his thoughts. "In Haelhan," he started slowly, "There's this idea that all reality is split into two kingdoms, the material kingdom and the spiritual kingdom."

She smiled, confused. "What are you talking about?"

"Well, like this world—what we experience by smell, by sight, or by touch—is material. And the idea is that it's not affected by the spirits at all, and it doesn't affect the spirits at all. The two are mutually exclusive." He took a sip of tea. "Mm. This is really good."

"Thank you." She looked genuinely pleased.

"Anyway, the orcs see the world differently. They see the two kingdoms joined. And there are times when I think it must be that way. It just doesn't make sense that our senses could possibly tell us everything there is to know about the universe; that just seems so arrogant."

"And this is what you think about when you're on watch?" she asked. She sounded amused.

He smiled distantly. "Gotta think about something," he murmured.

She sat silently. "Do you think the Alnethar will come?" she whispered.

Erik looked at her. She didn't look afraid...there was something else in her eyes, something that he couldn't quite see.

"They may come, or they may not," he said. "I know they won't come tonight."

She waited for him to go on. He cleared his throat, and tried again. "No matter when or if they come, we'll be nearby."

She looked at him for a while. A gentle breeze brushed a strand of hair from her head, and she rolled her head a little to get it out of her eyes. "You look so tired," she said.

Erik smiled.

"Is it because you can't sleep?"

Erik nodded. "Well..."

"Because you dream?"

He sighed. "I'm tired...not just from being awake. I'm tired from carrying memories." For a moment he considered it, and then added, "It's not the kind of tired that make you sleepy. It's the kind of tired that makes a man old."

She looked up at him, and Erik looked back. For a while she looked back and forth between his eyes, as though trying to discern something hidden.

Softly, she whispered, "Will you ever come back?"

"Back here? To see you?"

All was silent. She dropped her eyes, furtively looked up

again, and nodded.

Erik took a breath, and, gently, reached out his hand. A strand of hair had blown into her face, and he pushed it behind her ear. As his fingertips touched her forehead, she held his gaze, and he drew them lightly down her cheek before withdrawing his hand to his cloak once more.

"Yes," he said confidently, "I'll come back."

"When?"

He thought about it. "I don't know," he admitted. Her face fell, so he hurriedly added, "As soon as I can, for sure."

She managed a half-smile, but it wasn't committed. He tried again. "We'll be around," he said, "And I promise, we'll watch over you as long as we can. If anything happens, we'll be nearby."

They sat for a few more minutes, and she took his cup, lingering a moment at his hand before removing it from his grasp. "Erik of A'kaylii," she said, and rose.

"Shayna," Erik responded.

"Please be careful." There was shine in her eyes, not from joy or excitement.

He nodded, "I will."

Without another word, she turned and walked quickly back into the village.

The breeze picked up, and he watched her go. As she reached her house, she turned and looked back before disappearing in the door.

Khalan came over, and crouched beside him. His machine gun's bandoleers jangled musically as he situated himself, and he wrapped the ammunition belt like a brass snake around his arm. Erik glanced at him, and said something softly in orcish. Khalan laughed, and replied in kind.

For a moment, they looked out across the field, and then Khalan said, "Are you going to be okay, brother?"

Erik didn't reply for a few seconds. Khalan repeated his question, and Erik looked up as though he'd just heard it. "Oh, yeah, I'll be fine," he said.

"She forgot to get my cup," observed Khalan, and drained it. "I do not think she was thinking of me when she made this."

Erik smiled.

"Her father is amiable, and a friend of ours in this village," continued Khalan. "Sigmund and Feodor wanted us to leave. That means that Abraham and Josef would have had us stay. Perhaps we can visit here again, when fortifications are established on the ridge."

"That'd be nice."

"Many Jomsskari are building homes in El Ornahar," Khalan said. "Perhaps the One Unsayable has guided you here for this purpose."

Erik grunted and glanced at his watch. It was hard to make out in the dark. "What time do you have?" he asked.

"Almost midnight."

Crickets chirped. There was a gust of wind, and the barley rippled like ocean waves.

"She told me to be careful," Erik said suddenly.

"Hm." Khalan nodded. "It is nice to have someone care, is it not?"

"You wanker, you know you love me."

"Eshé. I would not buy you for one goat."

*   *   *

They were up before sunrise. They assembled in front of Josef's house, and Brutus got a headcount. As he was strapping on his gear, Erik noticed a few people emerging from their houses. Most stayed some ways back, and a few waved. One woman came over and gave Thjostolf a skin of ale, wishing them well on their journey.

Josef came out, his family behind. Erik was helping Peter get his heavy rucksack on his back, and when he turned around he found Shayna standing close by. She had taken a small scarf in her hand, the same she had worn over her hair the last few days. Before he could say a word, she stepped forward, and taking his hand she pressed it in his grip. Behind her, Josef and Eidel watched, while Sisel stood with her arms folded.

He gazed at her for a second, and smiled a little. Slinging his carbine, he tied the scarf to an ammunition pouch over his left rib. She bowed her head slightly and stepped back before turning and scurrying back to her father.

Erik glanced at Josef, a little unsure. Then, a little abruptly, Brutus slapped his shoulder. "Here you are," he said, "Careful now."

Four stone of gear crushed him, and he grunted loudly as it settled on his back. He pulled the straps tight, and looked around. The last of the Jomsskari were ready to go. Thjostolf waved his hand forward without a word. *Move out.* He signaled a "Y" shape with his thumb and little finger—*wedge formation.*

Erik glanced back, caught her eye one last time, and waved. The whole family waved back, except for Sisel, who stuck her tongue out again. Erik stuck his out in return, winked at Shayna, turned and walked away.

They were in the trees before the sunrise cast an amber glow in the boughs, and the village, now two miles behind, seemed as distant as Feldhall. Erik noticed some of the other Jomsskari glancing at the scarf, and Kolskegg grinned at him and cocked an eyebrow. He decided to ignore them. The scarf was white, with blue embroideries on the hem, and it smelled of her.

They pressed on until they were about a mile from the edge of the plateau, where they had left Rhys and Wendyll in the OP. There was a heavy mist from the clouds that veiled the scene. Erik wondered if Feldhall was under attack even now.

They were just gathering up to push through the last of the forest when Edwin's ears pricked up. "Masters," he whined, "Listen."

Erik listened. The wind blew gently, and the treetops rustled. Everybody had frozen—Peter, kneeling in a patch of ferns, turned his head slowly back and forth. It took him a moment to realize what Edwin had heard. It wasn't a sound, it was that all the sound stopped. The birds stopped chirping, and as he turned his head slowly, he heard a deathly silence fall over the forest.

Then, clearly, soaring over the air, they heard the cry of a griffin.

They sank into the foliage, looking around. The cry was distant, but not distant enough. The echoes bounced the sound around, clear as day. Erik mouthed an expletive, but made no sound.

There was flapping of great wings. *Whoosh, whoosh, whoosh.* Over the trees ahead, they spotted three griffins with figures on their backs.

They were in good cover, and Erik couldn't see any of his compatriots, but he heard the gentle, metallic *clicks* of safeties coming off. His fingers performed the same motion, and he carefully wrapped his fingers around the grip of his carbine. They were two hundred yards away, and closing fast.

Stay low.

The griffins pumped their wings, pushing their lion's bodies into the air. On their backs, Erik could see the Alnethar quite well. They had long, black hair and tan uniforms, with long rifles strapped to their backs. Their black, knee-high boots were in stirrups, and they leaned back on stuffed saddlebags.

In a few seconds, they passed overhead, and Erik felt the wind of their wings as they flapped by. As they went, one of the griffins called out to another in a high-pitched shriek, and Erik gritted his teeth to keep from moving. It was so loud and shrill that it was painful.

Then, in a few powerful flaps, they were gone.

For a second, nobody moved. Deafened by the calling, they hesitated, trying to hear if there were more. Then slowly, the birds in the forest began to call to each other, and Thjostolf whistled softly. They gathered up, and Erik, rubbing his ears and glancing warily upwards, slipped over to join them.

"Scouts," hissed Thjostolf, once everybody was close enough that he could whisper. "As soon as they spot that village they're going to send out a raiding party."

"*Psst!*" Out of the brush to the west, two figures emerged. It was Rhys and Wendyll.

"Where have you been?" asked Thjostolf. "We should have known about them by now!"

"They roosted for the night on the plateau, as you anticipated," Rhys said. "But they arrived well after dark, and under cloud cover. I misjudged their distance, and believed them to be owls. I will make no such mistake again."

Thjostolf opened his mouth to rebuke him, but caught himself. "It's not your fault," he said. "It's done. Feckin', we move on."

"So, what are your orders, captain?" asked Peter.

"Well, I had planned on holing up at the OP until we spotted trouble or relief," he said, "But that part of the plan just got expedited. Let's get back to Stadfesta."

"We just left four hours ago," said Brutus. "I do not think they will be happy to see us again."

"I really don't feckin' care if they're happy to see us or not. Let's go." Thjostolf started to get up. "Let's get to the tree line, outside the valley," he said, "And get a hold of the situation. Rhys, take point. Brutus, rear guard. Move out!"

They headed back again, through the forest, sticking to the game trails to avoid leaving telltale signs of their presence. As they drew to the edge of the valley, they saw the griffins circling and heard the bells ringing in Stadfesta.

They watched, incredulously, as the townspeople stood in the square, shaking their muskets and shouting. None of them even fired; they just yelled and shook them above their heads. The griffins called to each other as they swooped lazily through the air. They seemed to be getting a good idea of the layout of the land, and were completely unperturbed by the display below them.

Finally, after an agonizing few minutes, the griffins turned and flapped back over the Jomsskaris' position. Erik watched them go, and looked back towards the village. The people were celebrating, whooping and hollering like they had just vanquished their enemies in the open field.

Rhys shook his head. "They think they won."

"Can you read their lips?" asked Brutus.

"Some of them are saying it is our fault," Rhys said. He sounded a little hurt. "And others are saying they have defeated the enemy. They believe that they scared the Alnethar away."

Wendyll turned to Thjostolf. "Orders, captain?"

Thjostolf shook his head. "Let's dig in," he said, "Camouflage your positions and watch for scavenging villagers. I need two lookouts watching the town and two watching the forest. Khalan, make your position towards the forest." He ran his hand over his beard and shook his head.

"Our orders are to hold this mountain," he said. "We have a good plan to defend the village, so, we feckin' use the plan. Whether they like it or not, those morons have our protection."

Chapter Fourteen

The Trees, June 27, 1160

God had become something other than savior. God forced him to choose between eternal judgment and temporal misery. God was, as far he could see, the Great Trickster; a malicious clown. The thought in itself was terrifying. Unable to deny God, but unable to trust Him, he felt himself learning to resent. Submission to God was only accomplished to save face—the act of submission was done in defiance. A bitter slave.

And yet, he was dishonest. He did not tell himself the truth, and he knew it. He defied God, but he longed to love Him. He held a pistol to his head, and yet he broke his body to survive the harshest conditions.

He hated the falling, but he hated the thought of stability.

Little by little, he had come to realize that the fall into the depths was more efficient to his sanity than the stability offered by ignorance. Although he could not place it, there was something in the terror, something in the shadow, that kept him breathing. Were it not for the darkness, he would have shot himself long ago. Were it not for the tumbling, twisting, tumultuous descend into the black, he would have given up.

It was nothing—but not merely nothing.

It was morbid curiosity perhaps, or perhaps it was part and parcel with his defiance. He reasoned that to die would be to give in to God, but that didn't make sense. God had spared him among hundreds. Then he reasoned that to live would be to give in to God, but that didn't make sense either, as every day he struggled for life.

And in this land, so far from whatever home he could

imagine, that struggle became harder with each passing day. Either way, it was either to give in or to defy God. Whether he would serve or exasperate the Almighty by living or dying, he could not guess. In his spinning descent, he could change nothing.

That was the Absurd: the failure of his will, the inability to alter his course, the uncertainty of whether or not his actions were to defy or give in. It was his purest anger confused with his deepest ambivalence. It was complete uncertainty, not only was he unsure of his origin, but unsure of his destination, and entirely unaware of what he accomplished by his action. In the face of God, he was sure he had a "who," but he did not know his own "who." He was sure he had a "how," a "when," and a "why," but these things eluded him. Even if he was to learn the ultimate answer, he could not recognize the ultimate question.

So, he stopped asking what the ultimate anything was. He returned to the problem of the "now." "Now," should he live or die? There was nothing more to do than to live. To die would propel him into the ultimate, to live would let him linger in the "now." There was nothing more that he could do.

*   *   *

They laid low for the next six days. They dug foxholes and covered them with their cloaks, and took turns watching. For the most part, they only talked at night, and then in short, hushed exchanges. Peter and Khalan had the same position, and Peter had brought some cards, so they started a game. By and large, they were bored more than anything else. The sun rose, and they watched the villagers go about their daily work, oblivious to the danger they were in, oblivious to their protectors on the tree line. The sun set on another uneventful day; crickets sang, owls hooted, the Jomsskari tried to catch a wink, and then do it all over again.

They had chosen a spot of ground that was completely inhospitable: the tangled mess of rocks and rhododendrons that the girls had fled through on that first day. In the thicket, they were concealed, and those on the interior of the perimeter could rest without being seen.

None of them minded it, though. For patrols like this one, they carried eighty pounds of equipment, and it was no joy to struggle across rough terrain with all of that. The horses seemed especially relieved, although they did get antsy in the daytime. They had to feed at night, which spooked them, and it was always frustrating to be in charge of their care.

One day a couple of girls and a sow came looking for more truffles, and this time an older man accompanied them. They walked right past the Jomsskari position without noticing. They returned a few hours later, and the man tripped over Khalan's machine gun, but thought it was just a root and didn't even look back. When they had gone, Khalan muttered a curse and began stripping the weapon to clean it. The muddy shoe had jammed the muzzle into the dirt.

Thjostolf had decided to stick to the trees. He disliked the idea of trying to locate an Alnethar assault team in the dark and they would only have a few hours to prepare an attack. However, he liked even less the prospect of crossing open fields with griffins circling overhead. So if they could, they would try to attack the enemy as they bedded down for the night. Otherwise, they would have to return to the village in force.

He was a little concerned about his unit. The Iaelians were a stoic civilization, but the stress of this particular mission was even beginning to show in their faces. Thjostolf knew why, too. In training, it was still theoretical, to some degree. They were practicing fighting a long way from home and a long way from help. Making the transition to real conditions was rough on all of them.

Nobody relished the idea of being cut off and forgotten. Feldhall was seventy miles away, and had its own problems. They had all been prepared for this sort of situation – it was their entire purpose, in fact. But seventy miles never seemed so far, and the overwhelming sense of isolation was beginning to erode the team's confidence.

To that end, he decided to risk the quiet. Erik was alone in his foxhole. Edwin was supposed to be with him, but had decided to stay with Gabryl. Thjostolf slipped over and slid down. "Erik," he said.

Erik looked a little surprised, and nodded in greeting.

"So?" Thjostolf said, tapping the scarf with his forefinger, "You seem to have made a friend."

Erik smiled a little and shrugged. "I guess so."

The talking had attracted attention, and the other Jomsskari were glancing around. Thjostolf pressed on. "She's Josef's daughter, right? The older one?"

"That's right, cap."

"That's really great." He noticed Khalan craning his neck, and ignored it. "You never know when you're going to meet someone like that."

Erik cocked his head quizzically. "How do you mean, cap?"

Thjostolf settled in. "I met my wife at the feckin' worst possible moment," he said, and chuckled as he recalled. "You see, it was just after the Belvade campaign, but before I assumed command of Second Jomsskari. Feckin', I had gone to visit my parents, who run a farm on the banks of the Ahaern River, north of Havenstead. There were about a dozen goats that needed to be slaughtered, so I offered to do it. My father has a lot of feckin' arthritis and it's hard for him to do that kind of manual labor. He was in the process of hiring some hands, but at that time, feckin', I was it.

"So anyway, I slaughtered and hung about a dozen of these

goats, and I was completely soaked. I'd gotten blood and feckin' guts and stuff all over myself."

By now a few of the Jomsskari had gathered, and Kolskegg, who had apparently heard the story, laughed to himself.

Thjostolf pointed at him. "Yeah, Kolskegg was there, too. He was being feckin' lazy—hanging out indoors."

"It turns out his dad had a friend coming into town," Kolskegg chimed in, "An elf named Beli ap Caradoc, from across the river. For this particular visit Beli brought over his family as well."

"So, I went back into the house, all soaked, and I was cracking some lousy joke about feckin' killing babies or something, in really bad taste," Thjostolf acknowledged, "And the first person I saw was this feckin' vision of feminine beauty, Beli's daughter, Thorhalla, now my wife. I think I made her cry. But…" Thjostolf nodded pensively, "It worked out in the end. Three weeks later our families made the arrangements."

"I'm afraid Erik still has you beat, captain," commented Brutus, punching Erik in the arm. "When I look for a wife I will take my lessons from the doctor. I will attack her straightaway, why not?"

By now most of the Jomsskari had gathered, and Kolskegg looked around. "Well, you remember when I met my wife, don't you?"

Thjostolf laughed, and nodded. "Hey, now I told you, I know I was wrong. Don't dwell on it."

"We had just come back from the Belvade," Kolskegg explained, "And had arrived at Brandstead to get orders about starting the Jomsskari. We got out of the truck and I spotted this gorgeous brunette checking me out, so Thjostolf here, in all his captainly wisdom— "

"Oh, feck you."

"—He told me, 'Oh, no, Kolskegg, that's Sir Harold's niece, she's out of your league.' So after we received our orders from Njal General, he told us to clean up and we ended up at this fancy officer's ball. I was the only sergeant in the room, and I pretty much just tried not to get in anyone's way. And guess who walked up and introduced herself, eh?" He jerked his thumbs back at himself, and nodded coolly. "Helene döttir Kai, the very same."

"Well, well," Rhys said, grinning. "Thjostolf, you never told me you'd made a mistake."

Thjostolf grinned, and shrugged. "I can't be perfect all the time, now."

"It was a long courtship, though," Kolskegg went on. "I must say, her parents had some questions. It must've been four months before they were compelled."

Rhys shook his head. "You Haellics," he muttered, "You marry so quickly. An elf wouldn't dare be so bold. My father courted my mother for seventeen years before asking for her hand."

"Life is short," Erik replied. "And doesn't the Philosopher say, 'Do not waste your years; seek a wife in your youth, and you shall age joyfully with children'?"

"What a pretentious arse," Peter said, "That's just an educated way of saying, 'Get a bit of skirt before your wanker stops working.'"

They discussed the merits of the philosopher's advice at length.

As the banter died down, Kolskegg sighed pensively. "She's pregnant, now, with our firstborn. Due in three weeks."

They fell silent, and after a few moments Khalan punched his arm gently in commiseration.

Kolskegg shrugged. "What can you do?" he asked, and laughed the laugh of a man who doesn't find anything funny. "Orders are orders."

He paused for a second, and then, "I just really hate El Ornahar."

They sat quietly for a few seconds, each man lost in his own thoughts. Thjostolf watched them. He had learned, from a lifetime of military service, that even the most mature, competent, and skilled soldiers had a singular need— to voice their frustrations. After weeks of silence, broken only by the occasional whisper or murmur, he could feel their tension. A few moments of decompression were all they needed to find their hearts again.

His own thoughts strayed to Thorhalla, and little Aud. He missed them intensely, and wondered if his own daughter would know him when he returned. Thorhalla had been worried that Aud would be afraid of him, but Thjostolf was sure she would have some memory, even if not at first. Either way, he looked forward to doting on her. He'd win the heart of his daughter, one way or another.

Erik ran his fingers over the scarf, and Brutus was chewing on a stick. He spat out a small piece of wood, and cleared his throat. Everybody looked up.

"You know," he said, "I do believe we are all homesick, we are. But we are here, and there's no sense in complaining."

There was another moment of silence, and then Wendyll stood up. "Let's stay focused," he said. "And earn the right to go home."

* * *

Thjostolf had sent pairs of scouts out to try to locate a raiding party all week, but there was no sign of the Alnethar. They talked in low voices back and forth when they could, and Peter kept beating

Khalan at cards. Besides the occasional animal that supplemented their diets, there was nothing to report.

On the afternoon of the tenth day, Erik was cleaning his M27 when he heard Edwin and Wendyll slip back into the perimeter. They had been out all day on patrol, and weren't due back until nightfall. He watched as they found Thjostolf, and whispered something to him.

Erik knew something was up. Thjostolf started tapping his forefinger quickly, a personal twitch that only manifested when the captain was under a lot of stress. Dropping the bolt carrier back into his carbine and locking it shut, Erik began to do a functions check, just to make sure he had assembled it properly. It was habitual, and he didn't even watch his fingers as they flipped the safety off, cocked the weapon, squeezed the trigger, and listened for the *click*. His eyes were on Thjostolf, and when he whistled softly for the Jomsskari to gather in, Erik was already on his feet.

Thjostolf waited until they were all together, and looked at them intensely. "They're here," he said, "Two miles west-northwest, on the other side of an extended clearing about a half mile off the edge of the spur. Wendyll doesn't think we'll be able to eliminate them; they've set up a perimeter and are able to defend their position. If we attack, some will escape. And, of course, we're at greater risk of taking casualties. I don't want to assault an entrenched position unless we outnumber them at least two to one."

Khalan spat derisively. Brutus said, "So we stick to our original plan, then?"

"Yes, we do. We'll move in and secure the village at first light. Feckin', they always gather for breakfast. It'll be a helluva lot easier to contain them if they've already contained their own selves." Thjostolf wiped his nose as he spoke. His eyes were a little puffy, too. Erik wished he had something to give him. Those allergies were no joke.

Kolskegg thought for a second. "Let's go over it again. Erik, you still have that map?"

"Yeah, here you go."

Kolskegg unfolded it on the ground, orienting it. "Okay, the barley fields end about a hundred yards from the west end of the village, right?"

Everybody nodded.

"So we know they'll take the bridge, on the southeast side," he continued. "We'll be in position to cut them off in order to secure the south side. Now, their second team will land on the high ground, either on the northwest corner or by the barns. Either way, they'll have to sweep the village from the northwest to the southeast, assuming that the first team will have secured the south. If they don't, they'll have villagers escaping into the barley fields.

"So Khalan's GP-10 will engage the first team as they try to cross the bridge. We can bog the second team down here, at the outskirts of the village, and try to inflict catastrophic casualties as they're making their landing. The village itself will keep the enemy from seeing what happened to their buddies; all the buildings will block their line of sight. We can use that lack of communication to our advantage."

Thjostolf pointed to the map. "The village is basically just two parts," he said. "Feckin', there's a distinct north half and south half, cut down the middle by the square. Looks like a damn walnut from the top. Now, the griffins will be dropping their bombs in the center of the village, or near the meeting hall. With a little luck, they'll be making their feckin' approach before we open up on their guys on the ground. Feckin', we hit all of their elements at once, and communications breakdown, panic, and the good old feckin' fog of war will take care of the rest. From there, we adjust and maneuver, make short work of 'em."

Everybody nodded. Kolskegg let out a long breath and said, "So we've got our two firing lines in the hard structures, and Brutus and Rhys by the lake with the mortar. They've already pre-sighted their avenues of approach. Once the griffins start to land, sniper and mortar fire will converge on them. It's a classic combined arms ambush. If we kill the griffins, we can isolate the elves and adapt our plan as necessary."

Thjostolf gave the thumbs up. "Sounds good. Brutus, can you put mortar rounds on the northwest landing site on your first try?"

"There should be no difficulty. As Kolskegg has said, we have already pre-sighted those positions."

"What's the best rate of fire you can do without cooking off a round?"

Brutus waffled. "I can push it to twelve rounds a minute, perhaps, but only for a short time. And should we require sustained fire, I will need to allow the tube to cool..."

Thjostolf shook his head. "No, let's not be foolish. Feckin', just run her as fast as you can safely."

"We're going to get civilians in the mix," Erik said. "These two house have young children, and this—" He touched Josef's house, directly across the western edge of the square from the tannery, "—I sure would appreciate if we don't put rounds through this structure."

"Well, we might have to," said Thjostolf. "It's the best firing point on the northwest corner."

"They'll ring the bells, am I right?" offered Brutus. "They will lock themselves in their homes. Will that not get most of the civilians out of the streets?"

Thjostolf nodded, thinking. "Feckin', if we come in the morning, then they'll all be at breakfast. If we keep them in the meeting hall, then we'll be drawing fire away from them. Now we can't feckin' make them stay anywhere, but feckin', that's the best we can do to keep them out of the crossfire."

"So where does the machine gun go? South side?" asked Peter.

Thjostolf nodded. "What's this building, here?"

"That's the smithy," said Khalan. "It's a good building, quite strong, about three hundred yards from the bridge. That is the building I selected for our firing position."

"Okay, Khalan, you and Peter occupy the smithy. Wendyll, you take the tannery. Gabryl, you and Edwin stay with Khalan and Peter."

"Yes, master Thjostolf," Edwin said, smiling.

"Rhys, you and Brutus take up your position by the feckin' lake and be ready to put some indirect fire on the northwest landing zone. Feckin', we've only got one crew-served weapon and it's pointing towards the bridge, so feckin', I want overwhelming mortar fire by the barns first. Erik and Kolskegg, stick with me. Myself and the doctor'll occupy this structure." he pointed to Josef's house. "Kolskegg, you take a spot in this building behind. That'll give us feckin' interlocking fields and fire superiority on those landing sites."

"What about the bombers?" asked Erik. "How do we take them down?"

"We got it," said Kolskegg. "Wendyll and I can bring them down, one way or another."

For a few seconds, they didn't say anything, and then Rhys spoke up. His voice was quiet, and unnervingly calm.

"Target the officers first," he said, "Deprive them of their leadership. We must ensure that not one of them escapes."

Kolskegg and Wendyll nodded.

"We move out at 0230, then," said Thjostolf. "Be in position at the edge of the field before daybreak, and move up to secure the area when the villagers go to breakfast. Wendyll will be able to see both landing sites, so he initiates the ambush. When he takes the first shot, we feckin' drop hellfire and brimstone on these bastards, understood? Rhys, that means you feckin' make it rain on the northwest landing site."

"IHO, cap."

"Wendyll, did you get an idea of how many we're up against?"

"There were six griffins," Wendyll reported, "And twelve elves. They looked like they have three on each griffin, with the two bomber griffins reserved to take prisoners."

"That sounds right," muttered Thjostolf. "Feckin', leave your heavy gear with the pack horses. We'll settle them down in one of the hard structures." He examined his watch, "It is now 1550; try to get a little sleep."

Chapter Fifteen

The Village, 2 July 1160

He dreamed about Shayna. They were together in Havenstead, standing outside the castle walls. Everything was deserted, and the wind was blowing gently through the stones. It sounded like ghosts whispering.

She looked at him, and laid a hand on his cheek. She had a smile across her face, and he smiled back.

"What are you thinking?" he asked.

She gazed at him for a moment, and laughed lightly.

Erik?

"I know you'll take care of me," she said softly.

Erik, we're moving.

He opened his eyes. Brutus hunched over him, his carbine braced against his leg. "Come on, Erik," he said, shaking him gently by the vest, "Rise and shine."

Erik rubbed his eyes groggily and looked at his watch. It was too dark to see clearly, but Brutus filled him in. "It's almost two," he said. "Come on, get a bite to eat."

They prepared themselves in silence, each one checking his comrade's equipment. Once he had shaken the sleep from his eyes, Erik felt electrically awake. He ate some of his rations and took a long drink, splashing a little on his face.

They gathered up and Thjostolf offered a short prayer before

231

they moved out. The tree line broke at the very edge of the barley fields, and they slipped out onto the narrow paths that led to the village, walking furtively in single file. Everything was quiet; even the crickets had taken their leave. It was that special time of night when all the nocturnal animals had gone to bed, but the birds hadn't woken up yet. There was a distinct silence and tranquility that was almost haunting. Overhead, the stars peeked through the clouds, as if curious.

Thjostolf, Erik, and Kolskegg slipped north, while Khalan, Peter, Wendyll, Gabryl, and Edwin turned towards the smithy. Rhys and Brutus, the pack-horses behind them, settled in a few yards behind Thjostolf's team. They paused at the edge of the barley fields, looking out at the buildings. They were about one-hundred-fifty yards from the houses, and a hundred yards from each other.

Thjostolf signaled for them to get down, and they sank into the grass, their cloaks shimmering and vanishing into the foliage. Erik watched the houses closely.

It was serene. The silence was as beautiful as any aria, and the wind gently caressed them. The earth was cold and moist from the forming dew, and Erik smelled the fresh aroma and smiled. The stars shone brightly enough, though not enough to illuminate the darkness. He could barely see the hands of his watch, even with his eyes adjusted to the dark.

A thought occurred to him—*why don't the Alnethar attack at night?* They could see in the dark, couldn't they? Perhaps the griffins couldn't, or perhaps the term "dark elf" was a misnomer. He stowed the thought in the back of his mind, and lay still.

There is an art to stillness. It must be practiced. The ability to lay quietly, unmoving, for hours, and then act quickly and aggressively, was one of the hardest things Erik had learned with the Jomsskari. He had learned to stalk as he had journeyed from Brandstead to A'kaylii, and there was an element of stillness to that, but Erik had never stalked for more than a few hours. The snipers could do it for days. For now, though, he concentrated on being a stone. He imagined himself sinking slowly into the earth. In his mind's eye, he saw the plants covering him, and the ground itself forgetting he was there. The mental image helped, Kolskegg had taught him how to do it.

Time passed slowly. One by one, the stars began to fade, ever so slightly, until they vanished into the cloudscape. The sky in the distant east seemed a lighter shade of black, and then grey. In the distant forest, a bird twittered, and then another. The morning had arrived.

Erik saw movement in the middle of the square. A villager emerged, an older woman, stepping off of her porch as the sound of her closing door reached Erik's ears. She rubbed her eyes and walked towards the meeting hall. Soon she was joined by another, and then another. They disappeared into the hall, and there was no more motion.

He then watched the sky turn slightly pink on the horizon, and bit his lip, glancing at Thjostolf. Thjostolf was thinking, too. In the light, Erik could see it was now nearly 0500. The griffins would be coming soon; they had to get into position.

The smell of porridge and tea wafted through the air, and the villagers began to emerge, one by one, then by families. Erik saw the blacksmith emerge, with three children and a wife close behind. They shuffled off towards the food, and Erik drummed his hands gently against the grip of his M27.

Josef came out, glancing right at Erik without seeing him, and turned to take Eidel's hand. Shayna came out next, clothed in a light blue dress, her hair drawn up in a bun. Sisel was next to her, and skipped ahead energetically. They disappeared into the meeting hall, and Thjostolf raised himself up slightly.

Erik kept watching the village. There was no movement now, nobody was in the square or the grassy space between the buildings.

Thjostolf raised his hand. To the south, Khalan gave thumbs up. *All clear.*

Erik coiled himself up, ready.

There was a slight pause, as Thjostolf's hand lingered—then, he waved it forward, gently. They rose, silent as the night they had left behind, and in the shadow of the mountain, they loped towards the houses. Erik heard his footfalls coming loudly, too loudly, and his heart pounded in his ears. His index finger pressed tightly against the trigger guard, ready to descend at a moment's notice, and his surgical kit bounced off of his left thigh while his revolver bounced off his right.

They reached the house, and Erik turned to look west, towards the forest. Kolskegg slipped off to the east, passing Josef's house and entering the adjacent structure. Erik heard the door lock behind him, and then Thjostolf patted his shoulder, the signal to follow.

Rhys and Brutus led the horses towards the meeting hall, and Thjostolf and Erik followed. As they drew near, the mortar team broke left, heading for the defilade behind the hill. Thjostolf didn't hesitate. He strode into the meeting hall and shouted, "May I have your attention, please!"

All talk stopped. Erik saw faces all around, wide-eyed, confused, looking at them with perturbation. He couldn't see Shayna, but he spotted Josef, a hunk of bread held up to his mouth, his jaw gaping in surprise.

Thjostolf didn't wait for anyone to react. "The Alnethar are coming," he said, "They will be here any minute. My men are securing Stadfesta from attack. All of you, stay low to the ground and stay in the meeting hall. We'll come and get you when it's safe."

"Clear off these tables," Erik added. "We'll need them for the wounded."

They spun on their heels and walked out. Behind them, the stunned silence lingered.

They entered Josef's house and bolted the door behind them. Across the square, Wendyll had disappeared into the tannery, and the other four had moved to the smithy. Erik hurriedly turned his attention to creating a fighting position. He overturned the family's table, pushing it up to the wall beside the window. Opening the shutters, he pulled out a canteen and poured a little water over the window sill, so that the muzzle-flash from his rifle wouldn't kick up dust and give away his position. Thjostolf had headed upstairs and disappeared into Josef and Eidel's room.

Erik took off his cloak and hung it across the top half of the window, letting it drape down. It shimmered, taking on the look of a darkened house. Kneeling, he peeked out. He could see the barns clearly, a hundred yards away, and the northwest landing site on the hilltop a hundred-fifty yards out. He could hit both positions accurately from this distance, without sticking his muzzle out. For the first few, panicked moments of the battle, the enemy would have no idea where the fire was coming from. That would give them the edge they needed; there were six Alnethar, and only three Jomsskari on this flank.

He settled back, and breathed deeply before flipping his safety off. Thjostolf poked his head out and gave the thumbs up. "The other team's in position," he said. "Let's feckin' do this."

*   *   *

Rhys was checking a range card they'd worked up before. Gazing over the top of the hill, he estimated they were five-hundred-fifty yards from the northwest landing site and four hundred-eighty yards from the southern landing site. He did his calculations, and had Brutus double-checked them. "That should do it," Brutus agreed.

The use of the mortar bothered Rhys. He would be dropping explosives within a hundred yards of friendly positions, and while the shells only had a kill radius of thirty-five yards, the shrapnel could reach out to a hundred easily. That was far too close for comfort, but they didn't have any other options for achieving fire superiority over a larger element.

The stubby dwarf had laid out six mortar rounds, and had another six several yards away. They had settled the horses down a little ways off. Their elven cloaks covered the mortar and ammunition by the lake's shore. They knelt, silent, unmoving, and listening. The sky was distinctively pink now, and the bird calls were more plentiful. Rhys glanced at his watch. It was 0515. Any minute now.

A small lizard scurried through the brush. Rhys spotted a tick on Brutus' sleeve and brushed it off. They'd have to check themselves again; they'd been checking themselves constantly all week. No sense getting dog-sick up here.

Brutus turned his head slightly. "Here we go," he murmured.

Rhys listened. At first it was indistinct, but then he heard it clearly. Wings beating, powerful rushes of air. Over the tree line, six specks rose up, close to each other.

They were here.

*   *   *

Thjostolf saw them, too, and looked across the square. The people were peeking out of the windows, looking skyward and talking together in low voices. But they stayed inside. That was perfect; they'd be out of harm's way in there. He looked towards the smithy and caught Wendyll's eye. Wendyll nodded at him, and popped the covers of his sights. He was ready.

One of the flights turned south, across the river, and then another turned north towards the barns. The third flight climbed high in the air, and let out of a blood-curdling screech.

Thjostolf heard the talk in the meeting hall slack off. The griffins were already halfway across the field, flying low, their shadows streaking across the swaying sheaves. The other two flights were hugging the earth, gliding low. Thjostolf could see the Alnethar on their backs, three per griffin, ready to dismount.

He couldn't see the southern landing site, but he'd told Wendyll not to let them get off the ground. He trusted Wendyll to do that.

*   *   *

From his position, Wendyll could see the griffins sail over the goat pens and begin to touch down. Quickly, with the smoothness of endless drills, the Alnethar leapt from their backs, fanned out, and headed toward the bridge to their northeast.

He chose the griffin on the right. The griffin on the left was slightly forward and looking the other way, and wouldn't react as quickly to the sound. His cross-hairs hovered over the griffin's eye. It was a beautiful eye, brilliant blue, almost human—and yet it had an avian quality, a soulless vacancy, that seemed alien and strange to Wendyll. It was almost as if he was looking into an eye that was already dead.

He breathed out—*squeeze*.

As he fed another round into the chamber, the empty brass spun lazily across the room, and he saw the griffin vanish, as if the earth had swallowed it up. The second griffin was coiling to take off, and glanced back in surprise. It let out a terrified shriek, and then—*squeeze*.

Another piece of brass flew, ringing merrily on the floor, and he saw the Alnethar running forward, oblivious. They hadn't noticed, probably mistaking the two shots for their team to the north. Wendyll watched them, and noticed that one of them had an ornate symbol on his shoulder, and carried a pistol instead of a rifle. That had to be their officer.

He aimed, breathed out, and—*squeeze*.

*   *   *

Rhys heard the shots, but he couldn't see if the northeast team had landed. They were flying too close to the earth to tell. High above, the bombers hung in the air for a second, and then began to dive, tucking their wings behind them. They were headed for the square, where, Rhys saw, some of the villagers were beginning to emerge, debating with each other whether to make a break for their homes.

"Ready! Hang!" he ordered. Brutus snatched up a shell and held it up.

"Fire!"

THUNK.

"Hang! Fire!"

THUNK.

*   *   *

Erik could see the griffins to the north preparing to land,

when a patch of earth a few yards from the griffins erupted in flame. The first mortar round had struck home. Rhys had started firing.

The griffins screamed – there was no other word that could describe that sound – and then toppled over. Erik saw Alnethar falling off their mounts, and then one of the griffins shot skyward. A single shot sounded from the east, and the griffin spun out of control, slamming headlong into the barns nearly seventy yards to the right.

To the south, Khalan's machine-gun began chattering, and Erik spotted a group of three Alnethar gathering near one of the fallen griffins. They were disoriented and struggling with their weapons; one of them was already limping, another was missing his helmet. Erik lined up, and squeezed off his shots—*bang, bang, bang.* One of them fell, and the others grabbed him and headed for the barley.

As they were running, Erik heard a brief whistle, and then they were engulfed in a tower of fiery dust. When the dust cleared, they were gone. Whether they had escaped or not, he couldn't tell, but he kept firing nonetheless. Another mortar round landed a few yards ahead, and he saw a body with no legs sail several feet. It fell slowly, almost as if it was being set down gently by an invisible hand. It was surreal.

The first griffin lay still, but the second, the one who had hit the barn, stirred, scratching the ground, trying to limp for cover inside the building it had struck. Erik saw two figures rush to help it move, and then he heard a hiss as a bullet passed by his head. There was a muzzle-flash from the door of the barn, and he fired a burst in response.

"Erik, two in the barn, one by the griffin!" Thjostolf's yells came above the din of gunfire, his voice strangely calm.

Erik kept firing, focusing on keeping his fire accurate and precise. The griffin flopped heavily on its side, its belly exposed, its feet clawing the air, and Erik shot it four times. The dirt beneath it grew red, and it lay still. At a hundred yards, it was hard to see much detail, but Erik was sure it was out for good.

He turned his attention to the barn again, squeezing the trigger—*click*—nothing happened, the bolt was locked to the rear, out of ammunition. He dropped his magazine.

"Loading!" he called, while fishing another out of his vest. His fingers brushed against Shayna's scarf. *Focus*. Then the magazine was in the well and he pulled the charging handle. "I'm up!" he yelled and resumed firing.

He'd worry about her later.

*   *   *

After the griffins had gone down, Kolskegg stopping paying attention to the northwest landing site. From his position in the second story of the house, he was gazing skyward, watching the two bombers as they swooped down. It was a majestic sight. The griffin's wings stretched nearly thirty feet when they were gliding, but in a dive, they compacted to their sides. He could see the bombs clutched in their talons, and their shrieks pierced the air. They were moving too fast to see or hear the mayhem beneath them. If they caught on, they might use the bombs more tactically, dropping them on the Jomsskari instead of using them to intimidate the villagers.

He couldn't hit them with a single bullet, they were moving too fast. Wendyll might be able to, but not him. He had set his sniper rifle to the side and drawn his carbine, and had the selector switch flipped to full auto. The griffins were only a hundred feet over the ground when he fired three, short bursts, raking the air with lead. Feathers sprayed, and the war-shriek transformed suddenly to a shriek of horror. One of the griffins spun out, flipping over backwards and upside-down, while the other wheeled hard left, still gripping its bomb tightly. He fired another burst, catching the outstretched wings as they began to pump, and then there was a frightful explosion as the first griffin struck the earth.

The world rocked, and filled with acrid dust. Kolskegg felt as if a great storm had cropped up and vanished in a second, pushing him back into the room. Bits of blood and feather began to float through the air.

That was no flash bomb.

The blast was so powerful it rattled the window frame, and Kolskegg felt the heat and pressure of it on his face as if he'd been punched by a boxer. The second griffin, its wing wounded, somehow managed to flop to the ground in the middle of the square, and as dust and feathers fell from the explosion, Kolskegg saw it tuck its wings back and begin to run. It ran like a lion, with long powerful strides. It was headed straight for the meeting hall.

That was no flash bomb! They weren't taking prisoners on this raid; this was an extermination. They were out to kill.

He couldn't shoot it; he'd be putting rounds into Khalan and Peter's backs. But Kolskegg could see the villagers to the east, shouting to each other and running for their houses. In the heat of the moment, he suddenly remembered that the griffin still had a bomb, and realized that it intended to detonate it among the villagers. The griffin was trying to accomplish its mission.

There was nothing else to do. He lined up, and fired.

*   *   *

Khalan was set up a few feet back from the window. The elves had been crossing the bridge when their officer had gone down. As they began to panic, he had lit them up, killing two outright and wounding a third. Gabryl was hand-signaling with Thjostolf, while

241

Edwin lay calmly by his side, his eyes were alert and his ears laid back against his head. On Khalan's left side, Peter was feeding the brass snake into the machine-gun.

There was a lull in the shooting. Several elves had grabbed their wounded comrades and taken cover by the bridge. They had nowhere else to go. Wendyll hadn't fired at them yet, so they must have found cover.

The barrel on his machine-gun was smoking slightly, he had fired a few long bursts. "Peter, barrel change," he snarled.

As Peter grabbed the spare barrel from the table beside him, Khalan twisted off the hot barrel, and laid it aside. Peter had just finished screwing the fresh barrel in when a bullet struck him in the shoulder, knocking him down. Gabryl began to fire, one eye squeezed shut, his lips pursed in concentration. Khalan saw the muzzle-flash, it came from underneath the bridge, in the cattails. Roaring, he squeezed the trigger, but nothing happened. He'd forgotten to charge it. He pulled the charging handle, and began to fire. The tracers arced over the water, and the cattails shook and snapped as the bullets found their mark.

He saw one of them emerge from above the bridge, and heard Wendyll fire. The elf spun as if punched, and vanished down again. One down, maybe three left total.

"We need indirect fire!" he shouted. "Edwin, run to Rhys and get some mortar fire on that bridge!"

Gabryl shouted, "Get down!" and then there was a massive explosion.

Black, swirling, silent. Khalan found himself on the ground, his helmet gone. Dust was everywhere, and he couldn't hear anything. There was a distant hum, as if his ears were ringing, but it was strangely quiet. The world spun slowly in circles, and he saw spots.

Peter was nowhere to be found. The table he had set his machine-gun up on was overturned, and he tasted blood in his mouth.

He struggled to his feet, looking around. The blast had come from behind, perhaps a hand grenade. Then he saw Gabryl, crouched low by the window, his rifle on the ground, trembling and sputtering, feeling through the dust. Khalan heard Edwin's muffled barking, but he couldn't see where he was.

The spots began to fade, and he began to hear again, slowly. As he snatched up his machine-gun, he heard the cracks of gunfire coming back. As the dust settled, he spotted Peter's feet sticking out from under the table. He fired a burst towards the bridge, just to keep their heads down, and then pushed the table off of the halfling.

Peter had blood running down his face, and he was dazed, his eyes squeezed shut. His helmet had a dent in it. Edwin appeared suddenly, and shouted, "It was a griffin! A griffin hit the ground and exploded!" Then, "You keep shooting, master, I'll take Peter to safety!" He clamped his jaws on the halfling's collar, and started pulling him to the door.

Gabryl crawled over, his old face ashen, slinging his rifle. "I'll assist for you!" he shouted.

"Get the spare ammo from the ruck," Khalan ordered. "Be ready to reload!" He began firing.

*   *   *

The explosion had knocked Erik off his feet, and when he got up again he saw that the front door had been thrown open by the blast, landing several feet inside the room. Above him, Thjostolf shouted, "What the hell was that?" Erik didn't know what to tell him. It was too big to be a mortar shell or a grenade.

Things had quieted down on the north flank. The elves had taken up defensive positions in the barn, and their two griffins lay dead. From all that Erik could figure, there were three elves alive in the barn, one of which was probably wounded. Thjostolf claimed he could see three bodies when the mortars had landed, two of which were in multiple pieces; that meant they didn't have to worry about elves in the barley. Rhys' mortar barrage had slacked off, too, and now it was quiet except for the occasional burst across the river from Khalan's position, and the isolated snap of the sniper rifles.

Thjostolf appeared on the loft. "I think one of the feckin' griffins blew up!" he called down. "Feckin', Kolskegg says the other is wounded, but it still has a bomb. He doesn't have a shot, and neither does Wendyll. It crawled into a ditch on the south edge of the square, between two buildings." He glanced out the window again, and then said, "Go across the square and feckin' check on the other team. I can't see Gabryl anymore. Kolskegg and I have this corner locked down."

"IHO, cap!" Erik hopped up and ran to the door. The sight that greeted him was shocking.

Bits and pieces of the griffin lay strewn about, some of them smoldering. It had landed near the middle of the square, which kept the blast from destroying any of the houses, but the damage to the lawn was extensive. Erik could see the villagers. Most of them were still in the meeting hall, while some had escaped to the cover of their houses in the northeast. He couldn't see Shayna, or the rest of her family.

He saw Wendyll, and got his attention. He indicated himself, then made a thrusting motion towards the smithy. *I'm coming over.* Patted his helmet. *Cover me.* Wendyll gave thumbs up.

He braced himself, took a deep breath, and bolted across the square. It was less than a hundred yards, but it seemed like miles. Once on the other side, he hit the wall and stopped to catch his breath. Then, switching his carbine to his left hand, he began advancing slowly down the sides of the house. As he reached the edge of the house, he checked around the corner, ducked back, and then, gingerly, checked again. Then he ran across. He was at Khalan's building now, and he saw that the explosion had broken several of the planks that formed the siding. It looked like the whole wall had caved in slightly from the concussion.

"Friendlies coming in!" He pounded on the door and burst inside.

It was a mess. Khalan and Gabryl were manning the machine-gun, set up back from the window. Gabryl looked back at him, and then returned his attention to the firing line. Edwin and Peter were on the ground at Erik's feet. It looked as if Peter had been dragged to the door. The halfling was sputtering angrily and bloody.

Erik got to work. It looked superficial. Peter had been struck in the shoulder, but the bullet hadn't penetrated his armor, leaving only a huge purple bruise across his chest. A chunk of something had struck his helmet, leaving a dent the size of a fist, and he had broken a lip and lost a couple of teeth. Erik splashed some water on him, and Peter opened his eyes and struggled to get up as if waking from a deep sleep. "Son of a – what the feck!" he cried, and coughed violently.

Erik laughed, slapped him on the shoulder, and handed him his helmet. "You're a lucky little man," he said. "Listen, there's a live griffin around the corner. Let's go get him."

Peter blinked a few times, staring at the helmet, and then put a hand to his mouth, and spat a tooth. "Damn," he muttered, and put his helmet on. Edwin wagged his tail and licked his face.

"Okay, okay, I'm up!" Peter stood, a little unsteadily, and Erik handed him his carbine. "We're moving out," he called. "Where are the bad guys?"

"I have several beneath the bridge," reported Khalan. "Be careful crossing open space. Are all the griffins down?"

"Yeah, they're down, but one's still alive. Kolskegg wounded it, so we have to finish it off."

"Kill the jai-khu twice for me," Khalan said, and fired a burst. Erik pushed the door open, and they stepped out into the square.

They moved quietly. Peter was still dazed, and occasionally put his hand against the wall to steady himself. They reached the edge of the house, and while Peter covered, Erik ran across. Then they reversed it, with Erik covering while Peter ran.

They were half-way down the square, only a hundred yards to the meeting hall, and Erik spotted Shayna. She was crouched down, peering out one of the windows of the meeting hall; she looked terrified. He motioned for her to get down, and she ducked out of sight.

He spotted Kolskegg, and saw him waving. Kolskegg indicated his eyes, then pointed around the corner, and held up a finger. *One around the corner.*

Erik crept closer, and looked back at Kolskegg. The sniper was looking through his scope, and Erik mouthed, *Griffin?*

Kolskegg nodded vigorously. Then he held up both fists, one behind the other, and opened and closed the one in the back several times. Erik didn't understand at first. Then he realized—*he's got a bomb.*

Peter had pulled out a hand grenade, but Erik waved him off and mouthed, *Bomb.* Peter rolled his eyes, and put the grenade away. Then he sidled around Erik, taking point, and knelt. He hand-signaled: *You go high, I go low.*

They got close up to the corner, and Erik was practically straddling him. For a few seconds they paused, listening. Erik could hear the griffin breathing in ragged gasps, and heard scratching. Maybe it was trying to dig itself in.

Peter patted Erik's boot, the signal that he was ready. Erik took a breath, and gently tapped his foot. *One...two...three...*

They swung the muzzles of their weapons around the corner, lining up, the griffin turned – *It was right there* – They fired and it shrieked so loud that Erik could hardly hear the pounding of his weapon, the griffin shook and fell over and Erik's carbine clicked, a malfunction, and he swept around the bend, drawing his revolver – *Bang! Bang*—two shots in the griffin's head, it fell back heavily, twitching. And suddenly the air was full of bullets, hissing and snapping all around him, and he dropped to the ground, scrambling back as the elves under the bridge opened fire. Peter grabbed his hand and jerked him to cover, and then he was laughing and he didn't know why.

"Hot damn!" Peter yelled. He was laughing, too. "That was fun, wasn't it?"

Erik hurriedly cleared the jam and put in a fresh magazine. The bullets kept hissing and snapping past, and suddenly they stopped.

"Guess they're low on ammo," said Peter. "Or else they're regrouping for a counter-attack. Khalan's right, we gotta get mortar fire on that bridge."

"We don't want to lose the bridge," Erik said. He noticed Peter blinking rapidly, and remembered his head injury. "Are you okay?"

"Yeah, all I needed was a little thrill." Peter spat some more blood, and added, "Wouldn't mind some whiskey, either. Hot damn!"

*   *   *

Thjostolf scanned the barn and thought. He was sure there

were at least two of them still alive, but he wasn't sure if they were wounded or not. Clearing out the barn without destroying it would be difficult at best. Across the river, Kolskegg said that the last griffin had been taken out, and now there were several Alnethar trapped in a hole on the other side of the bridge.

He decided to put a mortar round in the cattails by the bridge. He could see Edwin in the building with Khalan, and called for him. Edwin's ears pricked up, and he looked around. Then, lightly, he jumped through the window and raced across the square. In a few moments, he came trotting up the stairs. "Master Thjostolf?" he asked. He sounded calm, as if he was performing some routine errand.

"Hey, Edwin. Listen, I need you to tell Rhys that I need a mortar round on the south-east bank of the river, just behind the bridge, to flush those guys out. Tell Khalan that as soon as he hears the blast, he needs to put a burst on them, and Wendyll needs to look out for guys making a run for the goat pens, okay?"

"Yes, master." Edwin turned and trotted off. As he ran across the open space between the field and the village, Thjostolf fired a burst into the barn, just in case anyone wanted to take a pot-shot at the wolf. He saw the wood doors splinter, but there was no return fire. Thjostolf watched him run to the tannery, then to Khalan's position in the smithy, and finally lope off towards the lake. "Okay," he said to himself, "Let's get this done."

*   *   *

Erik was in cover near Josef's cobbler shop. He could see the meeting hall directly, and tried to ignore the eyes that watched him from the windows.

Blast after blast sounded from the banks of the river. Rhys

and Brutus were lighting the Alnethar up, but Erik wasn't sure if it was doing any good. They could easily have defilade from the shrapnel, and even if they were wounded, it didn't mean they wouldn't fight to the death.

The *thunks* of the mortar stopped, and a few moments later the explosions stopped. Erik peeked around the corner, his carbine trained on the bridge, and watched. There was no movement, but he wasn't convinced. He'd have to see bodies before he'd believe the Alnethar had been eliminated.

He heard footfalls behind him, and Wendyll and Gabryl appeared behind him. They circled up, Erik keeping his cover on the bridge, and Wendyll took a drink from his canteen. "We need to clear the far bank," he said. "Gabryl and I will establish a base of fire by the meeting hall. Erik and Peter, you maneuver."

Erik turned. "Get the villagers away from the walls," he said. "Get them low. They're going to want to see what's going on and get themselves shot."

Gabryl nodded. "I'll be sure of it, doctor."

Peter checked his ammunition and nodded. "Let's go."

Erik covered Wendyll and Gabryl as they rushed across the open space between the cobbler's shop and the meeting hall. There was a depression between the hall and the river, and Wendyll disappeared inside. Gabryl ran to the windows and called inside for the villagers to get down. Erik saw the heads disappear, but as soon as Gabryl had joined Wendyll, a few of the younger men and boys poked their heads out again.

Erik shook his head. As long as Shayna got down and stayed down, he didn't have time to care about the others. Peter patted his shoulder and they moved out.

It was a long walk in the open. Erik kept his weapon up, Peter a few feet off to his side, and they reached the bridge without incident. Erik could feel his heart pounding in his chest, but the bank below was silent.

Carefully, they began to cross. Erik was watching the left side, and Peter was covering forward and right. The sound of his boots against the wood was so loud, he tried to walk more quietly but —*holy feck!* The floor erupted, splinters, bullets snapping by, and Erik didn't know what he was doing but he rushed forward. Over his left side, he saw an Alnethar, his rifle raised, and heard Gabryl and Wendyll shooting. Erik shot him, and his feet were pounding, Peter was shouting, "Come on!" and Erik found himself on the opposite side, sliding down the right bank. There was no conscious thought now. Every action was instinctual.

"Shift fire left!" Erik bellowed, as Peter threw a grenade under the bridge. There was a blast, and Erik threw another, followed by another blast, the shrapnel hissed and rattled through the cattails at his feet. Then they were pushing forward, sweeping under the bridge. Erik saw a bleeding body – whether it was alive or not he didn't care, he shot it and kept moving. Peter was shouting, "Lift fire!" and Erik kept shooting them and suddenly they were through.

Erik couldn't catch him breath. His whole body felt as if every muscle had seized. Peter smacked his helmet, and Erik spun around. "Clear the bodies," Peter said. "Make sure we got them all."

Erik was beginning to see things clearly, and he saw the enemy dead. Each of the bodies had sustained dozens of shrapnel wounds and all of them had suffered several bullet wounds to their legs and torsos, some hurriedly bandaged. These elves had fought to the end.

He counted bodies, and came up with two on the field, two in the cattails, and one more across the bridge. That left one unaccounted for. Peter called over that there was another body face-down and in the river, and Erik quickly confirmed. Their team had been eliminated.

The Jomsskari crossed back, and as they passed the meeting

hall, Erik heard someone ask what was going on. Erik jogged over and leaned in the window. "Everybody stay where you are," he called out. He was dimly aware of how strained and unnatural his voice sounded, as if he were choking. "We'll let you know when it's safe."

"What's happening?" asked one of the men in the back.

He glanced back at the devastation in the courtyard. "They came to kill you," Erik said simply. "So, we killed them first." And he turned and ran back towards the rest of the team.

*   *   *

They gathered inside Josef's house. Kolskegg kept his position, but Rhys and Brutus packed up their mortar. Under a burst of covering fire, they reached the rest of the Jomsskari. Thjostolf briefed them. "We've got possibly three bad guys in the barn," he said. "I need a security element, a breaching element, and my two snipers."

Erik, Khalan, Thjostolf, and Brutus volunteered to go in as the breaching element. Edwin asked to go, too, and Thjostolf let him. Gabryl and Peter manned the machine-gun from Erik's firing position, and Rhys took Thjostolf's position in the loft. Wendyll went with the breaching team to support their entrance.

They planned to flank right, using the village to cover their approach, and then hit the barn from the east side. The base of fire element stayed in and around Josef's house, to prevent the elves from escaping out back, while the snipers watched over everything from the south and the east. If any of them made a break for the barley, they would be cut down by machine-gun and sniper fire. If they broke north, they were in Wendyll's territory, and there was no escape from him.

They set out. Khalan had taken Peter's carbine, which looked ridiculously small on him. Thjostolf had taken Gabryl's carbine as well, so that they all had maneuverable weapons in the close quarters of the barn. So far, there had been no movement in the barn since Erik had left, and Thjostolf suspected they were laying low to conserve ammunition and wait for the Jomsskari to get out in the open.

They headed towards the meeting hall, and then turned north, moving between the houses cautiously. A few of the villagers had taken refuge in the houses, and they told them to either stay hidden or go back to the meeting hall. Most chose to stay in their homes, casting suspicious glances at them as they swept past.

Wendyll entered an unoccupied house and took up a position on the second floor. Once he was ready, the rest of them slipped forward to the last house before the barns. There was seventy yards at least between them and the enemy—a long way to be caught in the open.

They double-checked their ammunition, and gave each other the signal that they were ready. Erik was still tense from his experience on the bridge, and shook his head vigorously, trying to clear it. Then, taking a deep breath, he steadied himself.

They turned the corner, and walked cautiously up to the barn. Erik kept his weapon up, watching his side. Behind them, Wendyll scanned the cracks, looking for movement. They paused by the side door, and Thjostolf, who was in front, glanced back. Edwin followed, sniffing the air.

They paused for another instant as Thjostolf tried the door, and then they burst inside, dodging to the sides of the threshold. Erik flung himself through the door right behind Peter, and Khalan, practically on top of them, followed.

There was no gunfire, no sound at all, except for the pounding of his heart.

It was dark in the barn. Streams of dusty light filtered in from the walls, and the loft above was just beginning to be illuminated by the sun. It was quiet in the barn—baskets of barley were stacked to their left and right.

Peter whispered, "Corpse by the door."

Erik glanced back. An elf was laying still, his rifle stuck uncomfortably in his face, the earth beneath him bloody and wet. Erik focused on his side of the loft.

Nothing.

"He's been dead for a few minutes," Edwin murmured. "But…" He sniffed again, and fell silent.

They inched down the corridor. Their footfalls, gentle as they were, came loudly, as their boots crushed tidbits of hay and dried barley stalks. It looked like they were on a threshing floor, and Erik spotted a large rake in the corner of his eye.

Then he saw something. It wasn't much, but it looked like a hand. He lined up on it, and saw thick, globular blood running slowly down the supporting beams underneath it. Looked like another corpse.

Khalan growled softly. Erik couldn't see, but he heard a scuffle. Suddenly Khalan's gun barked, and Erik glanced back to see a body pitch headlong over the side— "*Contact left*!"— landing a few feet in front of them. It was an elf, and he was still alive, struggling to his feet, raising a pistol up. Then Edwin hit him, growling, and the pistol slid across the floor and the elf screamed. Erik couldn't help but stare as Edwin tore his throat open and the scream came to a sudden end.

When the big grey wolf turned around, he didn't say a word. He just dropped his eyes and trotted lightly past them, and disappeared outside.

They searched the rest of the barn. All of the Alnethar had been killed or had succumbed to their wounds from the crash. As they emerged from the barn and gave the thumbs up to the rest of the Jomsskari, Erik glanced at his watch. It was 0608, just over a half an hour.

Chapter Sixteen

The Bomb, 2 July 1160

She came out, and saw the devastation on the riverbank. There was a body lying in the cattails, most of its head and arms gone, and she covered her mouth in horror. Her ears were still ringing. She had never heard a sound so loud, even in the worst thunderstorms. She heard flies buzzing, attracted to the decay. There was a stench in the air, as if the slaughterhouse had caught fire.

The foreigners were coming out of her house, and her papa laid his hand on her shoulder. "Stay back, Shayna," he told her.

Sisel was crying softly, holding her arms tightly, and around her she could hear her friends and family murmuring together in shock. Her cousin Anya was breathing oddly. She had been terrified that her baby would be harmed, and had covered her belly with her arms during the fight.

She didn't understand. She couldn't tell what had happened. They had looked away for a moment, and when they looked back, hell itself had erupted in their village. It was all so sudden, and so furious, and the eerie silence that followed scared her almost as much as the battle had.

She put her hand on the threshold, looking out. There he was, coming from the houses to the north, with the giant one, Khalan and the captain, and the little one that looked like a strangely aged child. Despite everything else, she felt her spirits rise to see him unharmed. Erik held his weapon close, like he wasn't sure if it was safe. When he saw her, he smiled and came towards her.

"Are you okay?" he said, when he was close enough. Then, looking at her papa, he asked, "Is everybody okay? Was anybody injured?"

"I'm okay," she whispered back. Sisel squeezed her arm. The orc was coming.

Her papa looked back into the meeting hall, and said, "Hindelle was struck; we haven't the medicine to mend her wounds."

It surprised her. She didn't know Hindelle had been hurt. Hindelle was an older widow, and she had played with Shayna as a girl, taking care of her when her parents needed to be alone. She suddenly felt ashamed of herself, for being so preoccupied with him that she hadn't noticed before.

Erik took off his helmet, running a hand through his messy hair. "Take me to her," he said.

He looked so tired, as if he hadn't slept a wink the night before. His arms were dirty and greasy, and his face was dusty, with rivulets of sweat making streaks of mud on his cheeks and neck. And yet he looked exhilarated, almost giddy, as if he had just received some excellent bit of news. He let his rifle dangle at his side, but as he passed Shayna, his hand brushed hers, and she thought she felt him squeeze it for the slightest instant.

The captain was in front on her, and she started when she noticed him. "Josef," he said, "There's still a live bomb out here. Please get your people up to the lake; stay out of the village for now, okay?"

"What do you mean?" her papa asked. "A live bomb?"

The orc answered. "The griffins had bombs. They meant to drop them on the meeting hall. That was the big explosion you heard, the one that was so much louder than the others. It was meant to land among you."

"One of them is still waiting to explode," said the captain, "And we have to move it somewhere safe, so that it doesn't destroy those two houses over there." He pointed to Grigori the carpenter's house, and the home of Abraham.

The memory of the explosion was strangely fragmented. She could only remember the sensation of heat and sound, but she couldn't think of what it had actually looked like. The thought of two of the bombs sounding among them gave her chills. She could see the crater in the earth where the first had gone off, and she saw how the door of her own home had been blown off, even though it was more than twenty paces away from the crater. She decided to stay in the meeting hall for now.

She looked around for Erik. He was near one of the windows on the south wall, and she could see he was with Hindelle. He had lifted her onto a table, and was pulling things out of the satchel he was always carrying. Shayna left her papa to talk to the captain, and pushed through the crowd to get a closer look. Her friend Rachel took her hand and said, "Shayna! Shayna, I'm so scared."

Shayna embraced her. Hindelle was Rachel's aunt by marriage. Rachel was fifteen, a year younger than her, and she loved Hindelle very much. As they came closer, Shayna held her hand tightly. "He's a good doctor," she said softly. "I'm sure she will be okay."

Erik called out, "Brother! I need an IV!" She didn't understand what he meant, but she could hear Hindelle coughing as if she had a bad cold. Rachel's father, Andrei, was standing close by, and Erik grabbed his hand, pressing it to Hindelle's breast. "You need to keep pressure here," he said. "No, both hands. Everybody, we need some room. Can we get some room?"

On the other side of the hall, her papa and Sigmund had started urging people to go to the hilltop overlooking the lake. As the hall emptied, Rachel and Shayna moved closer and sat down to watch. Now the scene didn't look so good. Hindelle had a lot of blood on her blouse, and her breathing sounded funny, even when she wasn't coughing. Andrei's eyes were tearing up. She felt Rachel's grip tighten sharply, and she heard herself praying out loud, "Lord, Lord, please don't take her from us."

Erik took a big needle from his satchel and stabbed her hard in the chest. Andrei stared at him in shock, but as he pulled the needle out she saw that he had left a small tube, like a cut reed, sticking out of her flesh several inches above the wound. As Hindelle breathed, blood spurted out of the tube, quite a lot at first, and then less and less, until it was just a gentle trickle. Her breathing started to sound different, too. It sounded less raspy, and more regular. She was gasping less.

The first spurt had landed on Erik's cheek, and he wiped it off on his wrist as if it were nothing more than a bead of sweat. Andrei looked away, gagging, and Erik pressed a bandage against her chest. Then he said something quietly to Andrei, who nodded. The captain appeared beside her, watching with concern, and Erik came over. Rachel and Shayna listened carefully as they talked.

"What is it?"

"Bullet went right through her chest, cap. Collapsed her lungs. I sealed off the wounds and decompressed her chest cavity, but I don't know what kind of damage is on the inside."

"What's your best guess?"

"Man, cap... it's too far right to be her heart or any major arteries, so I don't think she'll bleed out. And that side of her chest sounds like it's inflating, so...I don't think she lost a lung. Anyway, I need to insert a flutter valve and get to stitching these holes up."

"What's the worst-case scenario, doctor?"

He sighed. "I'll see how much fluid she sucks up. I'm going to get a test strip to see what type she needs. We have to do a field transfusion. Worst case...I guess I might have to put her to sleep, crack her sternum, and sew her up from the inside out."

"Are you up to that?"

"Yeah, I mean...I'm not the liability here, cap. The risk of infection is crazy, who knows what's on my hands that these people have never been exposed to. And the same goes for us, if we get injured. I can only do so much to sterilize this environment."

The captain sighed. "That's the last thing we need."

Erik nodded. "Any casualties for us?"

"Peter got hit, but his armor stopped it. Most everybody got a little cooked, but nothing too bad. Mostly small cuts and abrasions, and maybe a few concussions. Hey, Khalan, over here." The orc had arrived, with a strange, clear bottle filled with water in his hand. Erik took the bottle and said, "I need to hook this up and get that valve in."

"Is there anything you need?" asked the captain.

Erik hesitated, and grinned. "Wouldn't say no to a bite to eat," he said. "And tea, if there's any available. Oh, and see if you can get some liquor or pure-grain alcohol."

"You want to start drinking?" the orc asked, a little suspiciously.

"Yeah, could do," Erik grinned again. "No, if it's strong enough I can use it to sterilize some stuff, and wash my hands. Soap will do, but I'd rather have alcohol." He glanced at her, and when he saw Rachel, his expression changed to concern. "Are you all right?"

Rachel's shoulders were trembling. "Is Aunt Hindelle going to be okay?"

Erik blinked. "She's your aunt?" Then he smiled reassuringly and put a hand on her shoulder. "She'll be fine, I promise," he said. "I won't leave her until she's recovered, okay?"

Rachel nodded dumbly. He nodded in response, gave her shoulder a squeeze, and looked at Shayna. "I have to work," he said. For a moment, his eyes searched her face, and then he said, "I'm glad you're okay."

*   *   *

Brutus looked over the situation and ran his fingers through his beard. From the opposite edge of the square, he could see the dead griffin, and the bomb was clutched tightly in the talons. Although he was only a hundred yards away, he was using his binoculars to get a closer look. He didn't want to get too close before he knew what he was dealing with.

If he wasn't mistaken, the bomb was nothing more than a very large grenade. The pin was attached to a lanyard, which was looped around the griffin's foot. Brutus guessed that when the griffin let go, gravity would pull the pin and arm the bomb. He couldn't tell if it was a time fuse or a contact fuse, but he guessed it was a time fuse. With the flash bombs, he remembered, they had gone off before they hit the ground. It was reasonable to think that these were set to air-burst, too. They were bound to be more effective that way—less energy upwards, more energy sideways, so a larger blast radius.

Brutus had an idea for how to deal with it. He wasn't just an expert at placing demolitions, he had also spent five years with an explosives device removal company in White Mountain, defusing dud shells and clearing old minefields. This was completely doable, but he wasn't looking forward to it. "Rhys?" he said.

Rhys, who was standing beside him, looked over expectantly.

"I believe I will require a small cart," Brutus said. "If possible, I do not wish to detonate it here, so maybe we could bring it to the northern fields, and destroy it there. This will contain the damage, yes? Of course, yes." He lowered his binoculars and said, "Unfortunately, I will be required to put it on the cart personally. I certainly hope it is not destabilized."

"Would you like our armor?" Rhys offered.

"There is no such need, my friend." Brutus looked up and smiled serenely. "As close as I will be, the concussion alone will shatter every bone in my body and jelly my brain. Armor will not save me, I think." He took off his carbine and vest, and set his helmet down. "I need also two hundred feet of strong rope," he added.

"Rope we have," said Rhys. "I'll see if one of the children has a wagon. Would that do?"

"Quite well, of course." Brutus began to take off his gear, laying it to the side. He patted his pockets, and pulled an envelope from his tunic. "As usual, you'll take this for me?"

"As usual." Rhys took the envelope and set off. It didn't take him long before he was back, with a wagon in tow. "I found this under a porch," he said. "Here, I got some rope from the pack-horses, too."

Brutus tied the rope securely to the wagon, and then, wagon in hand, walked toward the griffin.

Fifty yards out, he saw the amount of blood on the ground, and as he drew closer he noted that it was thick and congealed, like a runny pudding. That was good; the griffin was dead, not faking. About ten yards out, he could see the lanyard clearly.

He slowed, taking each step carefully, pulling the wagon gently behind. When he was within arm's reach of the bomb, he lowered himself carefully to his knees, and thought the situation was over. The griffin was gripping the bomb tightly in its talons, with the lanyard looped around its slender ankle.

He decided to cut the lanyard first, to prevent the bomb from arming itself. Drawing his knife, he leaned forwards and, ever so lightly, put the blade next to the griffin's—

It twitched. Brutus froze and glanced up sharply. The griffin lay still, but at the touch of his knife-edge, the foot had tightened its grip.

Gently, and much more carefully, he cut the lanyard, and it fell away. Now he wasn't so sure how to loosen the grip on the bomb itself. He had hoped the grip had loosened after the griffin had died. If he didn't do something soon, the rigor mortis would lock the bomb tightly.

Maybe not such a bad idea. He could cut the whole foot off. Brutus examined it, and nodded to himself. They would just have to cut the whole foot off. That would prevent the griffin from snagging the dangling lanyard and pulling the pin, and it would keep the bomb from rolling around in the wagon.

He got up, and walked back. Rhys watched his approach, and raised his eyebrows. "Forget something?"

"I know this may not be comforting," said Brutus, grinning. "But I now need a hack saw, or a hatchet."

Rhys laughed nervously. "Would an orcish kukri do?"

Brutus thought about it. "I think, yes," he said. "Why not? Yes, a kukri will do fine."

*   *   *

In the meeting hall, Erik pondered.

Hindelle had been hit during the firefight. That meant she had been bleeding for between fifteen and thirty minutes before Erik had arrived to care for her. She had already sucked a quart of IV fluid into her system, and it didn't look like she was done yet. Erik estimated that she had lost at least three quarts of blood. To the villager's credit, they had put pressure on the wound, and tried to stem the bleeding with bandages. They had even tried to seal off the wounds, but didn't have anything sufficiently airtight to keep the lung from collapsing. Still, such rudimentary measures may have been just enough to give her a fighting chance.

Most of the villagers had gone out to the lake to get accountability of their families, but there were several of the villagers still lingering in the meeting hall, wringing their hands and praying. Andrei was struggling to keep himself together, and was talking to Hindelle, telling her to stay awake. Erik wasn't sure if she was in any real danger; it was hard to tell how severe the trauma was to her body. At the very least, he reasoned, it was a good sign that she had made it this far.

He had already punctured the intercostal tissue between her ribs, and inserted a flutter valve. The valve opened and drew air out of the chest cavity as she breathed in, and closed when she exhaled, keeping her lungs from re-collapsing.

He was sure it was a simple lung injury—apparently, the lung hadn't been punctured, because she wasn't coughing blood. That was a good sign. He was worried, though, that the bullet had hit a vein or artery. But if that had been the case, he was sure she wouldn't be alive right now, at least not conscious and mumbling.

He was waiting for the blood type test to respond. It was a little chemical strip, and while he waited for it to change colors, he washed his hands thoroughly, first with soap and water, and then in a strong liquor that smelled vaguely of juniper berries that Khalan had found. He put his scalpel and several sets of forceps and hemostats in the alcohol, too.

The test was done; her blood was O-positive. That was lucky, Erik thought. He was O-positive, too.

"Cap, who on the team is O-positive?" he asked.

Thjostolf, who was sitting nearby, pursed his lips. "I think Kolskegg is," he said. "And maybe Peter, and Rhys. One of us has O-negative, too."

"That's Brutus," Erik said. "I remember because he's my pin-cushion if we take a lot of wounded." He began to get out the field transfusion kit and rolled up his sleeve. "She needs a unit now, though. Help me out, please?"

The villagers craned their necks as Thjostolf tied Erik's left arm off and held the vacuum bottle over his head. "I've never been good at sticking people," the captain confessed.

"I can do it." Erik attached the needle to the bag, stripped off the seal, and balled his fist. He was glad he had big veins, it made this whole process easier.

Shayna was watching intently, and winced as he jabbed the needle into his arm. Thjostolf knelt, holding the bottle low and rocking it gently. Deep red fluid rushed into the bottle, and he heard a quiet murmur move about the hall. Andrei watched in fascination. "What are you...?"

Erik glanced up. "She needs some blood, and... Well, I've got plenty." He grinned, and looked at Hindelle. She was watching, a little detached. "How you doing?"

She didn't answer for a moment, but smiled weakly. Then she whispered something. Erik leaned forward, and heard her say again, "I am precious in His sight."

"Yeah, that's right, you are." Erik patted her shoulder reassuringly.

Andrei glanced at the others, and then at Erik. Thjostolf asked, "Now, if she does need surgery, you can still do it, right?"

Erik laughed. "Yeah, I'll be good. I may need a sugar fix, but otherwise I'll be fine."

"We have honey," offered Andrei quickly, "We could add it to your tea."

"Honey. Sounds good. How are we doing, cap?"

"Almost full."

"Can you hand me a cotton ball? In the side pocket."

Thjostolf set the bottle down and they removed the needle. As Erik switched the needle for a fresh one, Thjostolf took some iodine and began cleaning her arm. "Doctor, this vein is pretty flaccid," he said. He sounded worried.

"There are other ways." Erik stripped the seal off of the new needle. "Hindelle? Hold still."

Deftly, he inserted the needling into the top of her hand, and taped it down. Then he straightened, and said, "Okay, hang it up. Can you get someone try to find Kolskegg? She's going to need another quart or two before this is all over."

Then, from the river, there came an explosion.

Thjostolf dashed to the window and looked out, his rifle ready. Erik was securing the bottle to a stand when Thjostolf shouted, "Are you okay?"

He heard someone shout in response, and Thjostolf shouted back, "Give us a heads up next time, you feck-head!"

"What was that?" asked Andrei.

"One of the bodies by the river was booby-trapped," Thjostolf said. "They put a grenade under him."

"Nobody hurt?" asked Erik.

"No, Peter's tying a rope to their feet and dragging them off. He says he's got another body to check, and I don't think that includes the bodies in the barn. Khalan's out there with him, now." Thjostolf picked up his helmet and started towards the door leading to the square. "I hope we can get some good intel off these corpses," he said, "Maps or documents, something that will tell us about their capabilities and locations. Kolskegg!"

He had stopped by the threshold, and shouted again. "Rhys, where's Kolskegg?"

Erik heard Rhys yell back, "I have him and Wendyll watching for a reaction force. Do you need him?"

"We need a blood transfusion! Are you O-positive?"

There was a pause, and then Rhys came inside. "Yes, captain, my blood is O-positive." He was rolling up his sleeve, until he saw that Hindelle was already hooked up. "Not now, I take it? In the meantime, Erik, may I borrow your kukri?"

Erik fished it out. "What for?" he asked.

"You don't want to know," Rhys replied. He came over, taking the kurki in hand, and looked down at Hindelle. "How is she?"

"She'll be fine. I just need to keep an eye on her. Who's the kukri for?"

Rhys hefted it, and grinned. "Brutus wanted it. He asked for an ax, but this should do."

"I thought he was taking care of a bomb!" exclaimed Thjostolf.

"I don't know, captain, ask the dwarf. Doctor, I'll be back in a few minutes to get you that blood you need. Or do you need it now?"

Erik shook his head. He was watching the bottle closely. "No, you're fine. I want to make sure she's getting a good amount of liquids with her blood. I don't want the blood she has left to coagulate. Anyway, it looks like this'll take a couple hours."

"Well, let me know." Rhys turned and walked off. Erik yelled over his shoulder, "Hey, you blow up my kukri, I'll spank you, you hear?"

"You can't threaten me with a good time!" Rhys replied, and

vanished into the square.

*　　*　　*

Brutus arrived back at the griffin with the kukri in hand and knelt. For a few seconds, he pondered his course. He knew that if the bomb had destabilized – the striker pin loosened, or the detonator pinched – then his next few actions could be his last. Finally, steeling himself, he took hold the foot at the ankle and raised the kukri above his head. He paused only a second longer, and then, decisively, he struck downwards.

The bone splintered, but didn't break. More importantly, and to his delight, the bomb didn't go off. Brutus tried again, careful to strike the same place. The second stroke cut deep, and the third severed the last few strands of flesh. As gently as he could, he set the ankle, talons still clutching the bomb, on the ground, and breathed again. Now that it was detached, he could move it.

He wiped off the blade before sheathing it, and then, ever so gingerly, he lifted the grotesque unit, setting it down on a pillow in the bed of the wagon. He had found it while Rhys had fetched the kukri, and he hoped that it would cushion the bumps. The villagers would have to forgive him for stealing a pillow and wagon. The ground was far from level, and he would have to drag it over three hundred yards to an outcrop of fallow land. Only there would it be safe to detonate.

He took out a spool of cord, and wrapped it under the wagon and over the bomb, until it was securely fastened to the wagon. Then, taking the rope, he walked back to the opposite edge of the square, and began to pull it towards the center. Rhys picked up his discarded gear and started to leave. "I'll tell the villagers to get by the lake."

"Excellent, excellent." Brutus wasn't really listening, though.

The sun began to rise over the peaks, casting the first direct sunlight of the day onto the valley. It was almost 0900, and Brutus could hear the smooth wooden axle of the wagon creaking under the weight of the bomb. It was at least forty pounds, perhaps more. The wagon was not large, but it was strongly built. He thought it unfortunate that so strong a wagon should meet such an untimely end.

He pulled the bomb past Josef's house, keeping it as far from the houses as possible. When it was between the village and the barley, he walked around in a wide circle, carrying the rope with him, until he was north of the bomb and just west of the barns. He began pulling it again, now away from the village and into the fallow fields to the north.

He found a ditch in the middle of the fields, and maneuvered the wagon into it. The walls of the ditch would deflect most of the blast upwards, and would keep the bomb from sending chunks of earth flying through the air. He was three hundred yards from the northern edge of the village now, and a hundred yards from the cliff face. It occurred to him that an explosion so close to the cliffs might cause a rockslide. He decided to take the risk. After all, the morning's action hadn't brought down the mountain.

Cautiously, he approached the bomb, and knelt carefully by the wagon, cutting off the rope and then coiling it over his shoulder as he walked back to the village. Gabryl and Edwin were near the barns, and Brutus told them to keep the area cordoned off. "In a few minutes, I'm going to make a real big mess," he said, with a twinkle in his eye.

*　　*　　*

Peter had finished searching the bodies. It was grisly work, and many of the documents he found were spattered with blood. They were all in a strange Elven script, as well; Peter couldn't make out any of the words.

He and Khalan had been dragging the bodies out of their positions to search them, and had them in two piles—one across the river, the other outside the barn. He wasn't sure where they should bury them. All of their weapons and equipment were piled in the square, near the packhorses. In all, there were seven rifles, two machine-guns, and a pair of pistols still working, with about fifteen-hundred rounds of ammunition between them. The other small-arms had been destroyed by the fighting. The Alnethar who had been trapped under the bridge lost a rifle to mortar fire, and apparently made their last stand with only a single rifle, twenty odd rounds, and a few hand grenades. Peter had yet to search the saddlebags of the fallen griffins, but he hoped for more ammunition.

Thjostolf was in the meeting hall, and Peter walked up to him with an armload of documents. "I got you a little something, cap," he said, "Just 'cause I love you so much." Dropping the armload on a table, he flopped down on a bench and began going through them. "These look like operational orders. Here's a map of the entire lowlands, and a map of this area. You can see their campsite from last night, marked here." He held up another paper, while Thjostolf took the maps and looked over them. "I think what we have here is a cargo manifest for the griffins. If I'm correct, here's where they drew their gear, and here's where they signed for it." He set the papers down and broke out in a satisfied grin. "This should give us a pretty good idea of what they carry, and what they're for, if we can translate any of it."

Thjostolf nodded. He pointed to the map and said, "This icon here—that's the built-up area we spotted on our first patrol. The clunkers came from there." The image looked like a castle with a letter superimposed over it. Underneath the castle was an image composed of a rectangle and a smaller square set on top, like a step pyramid. Out of the square there was a thin line. "Looks like a clunker base," Thjostolf concluded. "They were probably headed somewhere for a training exercise. That must be why they didn't have any infantry support."

Peter nodded. Erik, who had been caring for a woman in the corner, came over and looked over their shoulders. "Hey, good find," he said. "Do you think we could get Abraham to translate this?"

"Worth a shot." Thjostolf spread the map of their immediate area out and looked closely. "This is very rough," he said. "That first flight of griffins could have been a surveying team. Look, the contour lines are approximate, and there are a lot of major terrain features they just simply missed." He traced the river with his finger, and laughed. "They know less about this area than we do."

Erik grunted. "Then they might think the raiding party went down in bad weather, or just got lost. They won't send a reactionary force They'll send a search party."

"We can always hope." Thjostolf thought for a few moments, and then gathered up the papers and headed towards the door. "Good work, Peter," he said as he went. "Have you checked the griffins yet?"

"Not yet, cap."

"Okay, get to that. I've got to talk to Gabryl about this." He vanished outside, brushing past Khalan, who had just arrived in the threshold.

The orc came in, and saw Hindelle lying on the table. "How is she?" he inquired.

"She's fine," said Erik, "Or at least she will be. Just give her a little space, this is hardly a sterile environment to begin with." At her side, a young girl was sitting, talking softly to her. Peter got up, and came a little closer, just to get a look. When the girl saw him, she gave him a funny look, as if she was repulsed by him. It took minute for Peter to realize how much he smelled like the corpses he had been handling. He kept his distance.

The elder's daughter, Shayna, was sitting nearby, and smiled at him in greeting. He nodded in reply, and looked back at Erik.

"Whose blood is that?" he asked.

"Mine. Are you O-positive?"

"No, I'm AB-negative." He looked back at her and asked, "How long to recovery?"

"A week at least." Erik sat down. He had a mug of tea in his hand, and took a long drink before continuing. "She should be able to feed herself and sit up by tomorrow evening, but for now she needs to just rest and get plenty of fluids. I can't imagine she'll be able to swallow much at a time." He grinned, and cocked his eyebrow. "You let me know directly if any of those griffins have IV's on them. We're going to need them."

"Bandages, tourniquets?"

Erik nodded. "Any drugs, too."

Peter grinned. "Oh, no, if I find drugs, they're mine. Have you ever seen a halfling tweaking?"

Erik lolled his head around to gaze at him sardonically. "You start tripping, you'd better share. Don't you hold out on us."

Peter shrugged. "Maybe I will, maybe I won't." Then, with a quick glance at Shayna, he said, "And who knows? Since we haven't got thirty goats, maybe you could just trade recreational narcotics. Out here, you could sell a hit for a goat, you think?"

Erik laughed. "Why do you have to be like that? What did I ever do to you?"

"Hey, I'm just saying..."

Erik shook his head and took another drink of tea. "Feck off, *jai-khu*. Go build your master race of three-quarterlings."

Peter jumped up and gestured bombastically. "You know what? You know what?"

"What?" Erik challenged.

"I will! I'm going right now! I'll get right on it!"

Erik laughed. "But seriously, medical equipment, please."

Peter waved him off. "Yeah, you got it, doc."

*   *   *

Thjostolf went north, towards the lake shore. He knew that Gabryl and Edwin had moved the villagers up to the lake, to keep them far from the blast radius. Brutus was making his way up to the fallow fields with a roll of det cord and a few bricks of explosives, and in the middle of the field, Thjostolf could see a small rectangular object.

Gabryl was talking to Abraham. They stood on the top of the hill, chatting quietly. Edwin was talking to a group of villagers a few yards off, while the rest sat on the hillside, looking out at the lake. A few of the boys had ventured up to look out at the village, ignoring their mothers calls to come back. Gabryl looked up as Thjostolf approached, and smiled warmly. "Captain," he said. "The families have accounted for their children, and there are no further injuries. How long until it is safe for them to return to their homes?"

A few of the other villagers looked up expectantly, and Thjostolf realized that they had been huddled on the shoreline for almost an hour and a half. He glanced over at Brutus. At about four hundred yards, it was hard to tell, but it looked like he was setting up the charge. "Brutus is preparing to blow it now, out in the fields," he said. "I need somebody to keep guard over the salvaged armaments, but I think we should start moving back into the cover of the buildings now." He turned to Abraham and held up a handful of the captured documents. "Abraham, can you translate these?"

The elf looked at the stack and nodded. "Yes, I think so. It has been years since I read this pagan script, but I think I can make sense of them."

Thjostolf turned to Gabryl. "Once we have hard intelligence, can you relay it to Feldhall?" he asked.

Gabryl frowned. "I cannot send them physically," he said slowly, "I can convey a few words, but we must condense the message. I cannot communicate the whole, I'm afraid."

The Jomsskari began moving the villagers back to their homes. As they did so, Thjostolf questioned Gabryl more. "Are you sure?" he insisted. "How long can you talk to them?"

Gabryl looked at him as if he were asking a ridiculous question. "A minute or two, captain Thjostolf, at the longest. There is something different about this mountain. My powers are limited here. There are forces at work here beyond what we see. You must understand," he added, a bit more gently, "These things are not simple."

*   *   *

Shayna had stepped into the square. The decapitated body was gone and a blood trail lead across the bridge. She spotted a pile of corpses across the river. The others were coming back, and the foreigners were moving from family to family, instructing them quietly. She couldn't hear what they were saying.

She saw the talking dog, Edwin, and the old man and the captain coming down from the hillside, and her papa and mama lingering nearby. When her mama saw her, she extended her arms, and Shayna crossed the square to embrace her. Sisel was close by, looking back and forth cautiously. Her eyes were still red from crying, but she looked okay. Shayna gave her a hug, too.

The silent elf approached them. He frightened Shayna; his face was as blank as a stone, and his eyes were cold, as though he had no soul. When he came close, he said in a quiet voice, "We are preparing to destroy the bomb. Please get inside a building and cover your ears."

The captain came close, and said to the silent elf, "Wendyll, spread the word. After the blast, Kolskegg and Peter are to stand by the ammunition salvage and keep an eye on the forest. Everybody else gather at the meeting hall."

"IHO, cap." The silent elf turned and walked away.

Shayna didn't know what he had said, and she asked, "What's that mean?"

The captain glanced at her. "What, IHO? 'I hear and obey.'" He looked towards the fallow fields to the north, and said, "Josef, we need to talk sometime about where we can bury the dead."

"Of course," her papa said.

"Come on, get to your house. It's not long now. Be sure to cover your ears." He walked towards the meeting hall.

They went into their home, and Shayna bit her lip. The table had been upturned, and there was a cloak hanging above the window. Pieces of wood were torn from the walls, and the door lay on the ground, the hinges shattered. It was dusty and smelled vaguely like something had been burning.

They could see the fallow fields. Shayna looked out at them, and saw the dwarf walking behind the barn. He waved at her, and she waved back. Then he shouted, "Fire in the hole!"

The other foreigners echoed him, shouting back and forth several times. She looked towards the fallow fields, and spotted a wagon. That was odd, she thought. *What on earth was a child's wagon doing out in the—*

The earth seemed to sink, and for a moment it looked like the air had turned to water. A line of dust leapt up, and a pillar of smoke erupted from the ground. The air around her shivered, as if a gale had swept in and dissipated in an instant, and she saw the dust around her leap into the air several inches—and then she felt the shock wave hit her, and for a single instant she thought she was flying. A flash of fiery light belched upwards and vanished into the cloud, and the crash of a hundred thunderstorms sounded in her ears.

Then it began to rain—or, at least, it sounded like rain. Then she saw the pebbles falling, and the dust drifting across the wind. She stood in awe. It was the most terrifying, powerful thing she had ever seen.

By the barn, the dwarf stood calmly, and looked towards the field with his binoculars. Then he turned and shouted, "All clear!" several times before walking back towards the meeting hall, lighting a cigarette as he went. He looked as if he had just taken the tea off: entirely unconcerned, entirely relaxed, and almost unaware of the immense cloud that had only now begun to settle.

She realized her family was standing by her, gazing out the window. Her mama placed a hand on her shoulder, and Sisel stood speechless. Her papa spoke.

"There is no going back now," he said gravely. "The world has found us again."

Chapter Seventeen

The Tunnel, 2 July 1160

By noon, the bodies were buried and the stench of death was beginning to lift. Erik and Andrei had carried Hindelle on a stretcher to her own bed, where she now lay sleeping. She was stable, and Erik was sure she would be fine, barring infection. In the event that her condition worsened, Erik had given Andrei a whistle. He could hear it anywhere in the village.

He was exhausted. As he stepped out of Hindelle's home and into the square, the sun directly overhead, he felt a distinct sense of fatigue that started in his bones and worked its way outward. He shook his head vigorously, and turned his tea-cup upside down. It was depressingly empty. *Time for a refill.*

The few of the Jomsskari had assembled in the meeting hall, off in one corner, while a few of the younger men and women in the village had clustered on the other side of the hall, talking together in low voices. When Erik came in, he spotted Shayna, Anya, and Rachel among them. They looked up at him, and all smiled as if they were genuinely happy to see him. Some of the young men seemed less thrilled. One of them scowled darkly, and Erik noticed him shift slightly towards Shayna. It reminded him of a wild dog he had met while he was traveling to A'kaylii, who stood defiantly between Erik and a fresh deer carcass. Erik tucked the impression away in his mind, waved cordially, and turned to the Jomsskari.

Brutus, Wendyll, and Peter were sitting, chatting with Khalan. They were cleaning their weapons, and the smell of lubricant, pungent in the enclosed space, was strangely familiar to Erik. It smelled like the barracks, which had been a comfort and a home for the last five years. The realization startled him.

He flopped down next to Peter and began disassembling his carbine. They were talking about cheese, something Erik didn't spend much time thinking about, although Peter and Wendyll apparently did. They bickered for a few minutes about something or other, and Erik phased out. His weapon was dirty, and he began twisting together the thin steel rods in his cleaning kit to swab the barrel. He had a tune in his head, and couldn't remember where it came from.

They fell silent for a few minutes. "I have this stupid song stuck in my head," Erik said presently. "Did any of you see that opera where the two couples tried to elope, and they got switched somehow and ended up with the wrong one?"

"Yeah, they were sisters. I saw that." Peter laughed and held up his bolt carrier to the light. "Yeah, and then the parents come chasing after 'em. That was a pretty funny opera."

"It wasn't supposed to be funny," Brutus pointed out.

"Yeah, well, I have the song about how they're going to elope stuck in my head, and I can't get it out. It's driving me crazy."

"Well, it's a catchy tune." Peter said.

"I did not see it," said Khalan. "I cannot understand opera."

They cleaned for a while. "It's just...you know, they're just singing instead of talking," said Peter. "You don't like opera?"

"No, I mean I cannot understand them," explained Khalan. "Haellic is not my first language. When they sing, it all sounds like babble to me."

"Oh," Peter set the bolt down and frowned. "This pollen is a pain in the arse. No wonder cap's got allergies."

Erik inspected his own weapon. There was oil everywhere, and a thin film of greenish-gold pollen stuck fast. When he tried to wipe it off, it just smeared. Khalan was having a particularly hard time. His machine-gun fired from an open bolt, and that meant that the pollen had direct access to the chamber. He was scrubbing vigorously.

Peter looked up mischievously and began to sing again. "So can you understand me now?" he warbled. Khalan glanced up at him and shook his head, "You little *jai-khu*."

"Hey, be nice."

"Do you have more patches?" asked Brutus. A pile of filthy rag fragments had accumulated in the middle of the table, and he poked through them in search of a clean corner.

They patted their pockets and found that they didn't. Across the hall, the cluster of villagers sat, murmured among themselves. Khalan muttered, "Well, maybe they have a few," and he got up and started towards them, his machinegun tucked underneath his arm. Erik hopped up and followed, holding his carbine up to the light as he walked.

The villagers looked up as Khalan drew near, and fell silent. The orc, apparently not noticing, asked, "Do you know where we can find some scrap cloth?"

"What for?" demanded one of the young men.

Erik handed the man the bolt carrier assembly. "Cleaning time," he said simply.

Anya, her hands rested on her belly, wrinkled her nose at the smell of cordite and oil. The young man held the piece of steel as if it were a surprising piece of garbage, and when Erik took it back, the man stared unhappily at the residue on his hand.

Shayna said there were some dishrags in the kitchen, and got up to fetch them. Rachel went with her. As they disappeared behind the curtain that separated the kitchen from the rest of the hall, the young man spoke suddenly. "So, you have a thing for our Shayna, do you?"

Erik raised his eyebrows. The table fell silent, and Anya shifted uncomfortably. "Asvald, you needn't—"

"Oh, but I must. You see, he wears her favor." Asvald smiled the stiff smile of a man who doesn't find anything amusing, and pointed accusingly at the scarf tied to his vest.

Khalan glanced at Erik and muttered something in orcish. Erik laughed before responding in kind. "Why do you ask?" he asked, "Does that offend you?"

The outburst had piqued the interest of the other Jomsskari, who crossed the hall curiously. Asvald saw them coming, and sneered.

Anya laid her hand Asvald's shoulder, speaking softly. "Asvald, speak to the elders. There's no sense in this."

Asvald glared at Erik, and then looked out the window.

"Hey, what's happening?" asked Peter, who had just arrived. "Anything a friendly drink would fix?"

Khalan started to say something rude, but the curtain to the kitchen opencd again and Shayna emerged. "I'll tell you about it later," said Erik.

They fell into an awkward silencc as the two girls drew close. Shayna gave a stack of rags to Erik, and as she pressed them into his hand, he noticed her smile a little. Everybody else noticed, too.

Rachel had noticed the tension in the air immediately, but didn't seem to realize where it had come from. "How is my aunt?" she asked Erik.

Erik wasn't paying attention to her, and it took him a moment to react. "Oh, yeah," he said, "She'll be fine. She's just resting now."

"Are you sure she won't die?" she pressed, "How can you be sure?"

Erik leaned against the edge of the table, wiping off his bolt carrier as he spoke. "Well, I've got her on a couple antibiotics, but her fluids look okay and I don't see any signs of major trauma or infection," he said. "To be honest, I've seen much worse." He recalled an orc in A'kaylii who snapped his legs in a bad fall. Both legs had went gangrenous and required amputation. He decided not to share that story.

"Will you give her more of your blood?"

Erik shrugged. "If she needs it, sure. But not mine. I'll take somebody else's." He tapped his arm and added with a grin, "I need blood, too, you know."

Rachel raised her eyesbrows but did not reply.

They offered their thanks for the rags, returned to their table, and resumed cleaning. After a few minutes, the villagers rose and left, leaving the Jomsskari alone in the hall.

There is a point in time after the battle, when the adrenalin begins to wear off and the nervous jitters stop, when soldiers become calm and even morose. For a while the Jomsskari joked among themselves, targeting Erik especially for the strange confrontation, but gradually the talk grew less and less. Soon each of them scrubbed, lost in their thoughts, and Erik felt the weight of fatigue on his body. Peter began to sing something softly, an odd halfling folk song, and Khalan hummed along. Wendyll moved his fingers fluidly and precisely, finished cleaning his rifle and stood to leave.

Rhys and Thjostolf came in, talking quietly together. Edwin followed behind, and Erik noticed that they were carrying satchels of ammunition and hand grenades. Kolskegg and Gabryl were still on watch, he reminded himself. The whole team was here.

"Refit and rearm," said Thjostolf as he drew near. "Rhys,

Khalan, Brutus, Erik, and Edwin—get ready to move out."

"Where to?" asked Peter.

"We have a mission for you," Thjostolf said simply. "We need to scout out the cave and see if there's feckin' anything significant back there."

"What, the cave on the lake?" asked Erik.

"That's the one."

"Have you asked any of the locals?"

"Yeah," Thjostolf said. "They say they don't mess with it. Who knows if that's true, though."

Khalan began reassembling his machine-gun. "Is this just a curiosity, or did you see something?"

Thjostolf winked at him, but didn't answer. "Wendyll, I need you on overwatch. Feckin', Peter, you and I will secure the village." Thjostolf began to reload his magazines, snapping the cartridges down rhythmically. "Let's do this quickly," he went on. "When you're ready, assemble by the docks and get it done. Rhys, you've got lead on this one. Unless you'd rather deal with the public relations nightmare…"

"My present assignment will suffice, cap'," Rhys said with a smile. He turned to Wendyll and said, "When you are ready, let me know. We won't move until you're in position."

Wendyll picked up his rifle, bowed slightly, and said softly, "Ready." Then he turned and walked silently from the hall.

"Let's go to it," said Khalan, as Wendyll disappeared through the threshold. "And be back for lunch."

They gathered their gear and headed out. Erik and the rest of the scouting detachment made their way down to the lake, and after a quick look around, located a simple dock with a pair of rowboats tied up to them. Neither of them were large enough to hold all of them, so Rhys and Khalan got into one while Erik, Edwin, and Brutus took the other. Wendyll was out of sight, on the hilltop overlooking the village, and Rhys waited for Thjostolf to give them the signal to move.

The activity was strangely reassuring to Erik. He found that staying busy kept him from the weariness he had felt before, and while he was sure he would feel twice as tired later, he was happy to have his energy back. He and Brutus did a quick equipment check on each other, made sure their weapons were locked and loaded, and waited.

For a few minutes, they sat in the boats. Edwin lay down carefully, unsteady on his feet, and whimpered slightly. Erik looked him over. "Are you okay?" he asked quietly.

"Sir?"

"Are you okay? You look pretty down."

Edwin laid his ears back and rested his head on his paws. For a moment he sat still, and then, a little reservedly, he said, "Sir, I wish I had fingers, so I could shoot a gun like you. I do not enjoy tasting blood."

Erik glanced at Brutus. The dwarf glanced at him, and looked away.

Edwin fell silent for a moment, and then said, "I have killed three hundred and seventy-four souls since I came into Gabryl's service, and I remember each of their tastes. They were all different, you know. These elves are…metallic, almost, and a little sweet. I do not fear to serve, but I wish I could be free of my memory of it."

"Let's go," called Rhys. Thjostolf had come into view, and flashed a thumbs up.

For his part, Erik was glad they were underway. He really didn't know what to say to Edwin, so he just ran his hands through the wolf's thick neck fur. Edwin didn't seem to expect an answer, and sat quietly as Brutus and Erik dipped their oars into the water and pushed off.

The lake was bigger than it looked. They rowed for a half hour, and when Erik looked back the village seemed as far away as the rock face. In another half-hour, they had drawn close to the cave. Erik saw that it, too, was larger than it appeared from the shore. In fact, the stairway leading up was at least thirty feet. There was a slab of stone that projected from the edge of the rock face, with a tall natural knob on the top of it. Rhys tied his boat off on the knob, and Erik tied his off to Rhys'. After an unsteady disembarkation, they were all ashore.

The landing was only about four feet wide and six feet long, and Rhys had to start the climb to make room for the rest. Khalan followed, then Erik, Edwin, and Brutus. When they reached the top of the landing, they spread out, with Rhys and Khalan on one side of the cave and the dwarf, the doctor and the wolf on the other.

Erik crouched in the shadow of the cave's mouth and peered inside, his carbine raised cautiously. All was darkness in its gaping maw. It reminded him of the mountains of A'kaylii, and the thought of encountering a spider again made him shiver, even though he was confident they could easily take it down. No matter how many times he faced a cave spider, he could never get used to it. The prospect of being devoured alive had a way of holding one's attention.

Rhys glanced over at them. "Edwin, what do you smell?"

The wolf sniffed the air, and a look of concern crossed his face. "Master Rhys," he said slowly, "I do not recognize this smell."

Rhys pursed his lips and turned at Brutus. "You have point. Khalan, you're next, then me, then Erik. Edwin, keep sniffing. Let us know directly if you think something's up."

Erik had an oil lamp in his gear, and they lit it up. Rhys did a final glance around, and gave Brutus the go-ahead.

The dwarf huffed a little, and then moved into the darkness. As they slipped forward, Erik heard Edwin growl, ever so softly, and he wondered what it was that the wolf smelled. He checked his safety; it was on. He decided not to flip it off. In the darkness he could easily stumble, and an accidental trigger pull could cost one of the other Jomsskari their life. Still, he rested his thumb over it, ready to switch it to "fire" in an instant.

He wasn't the only one on edge. Maybe it was the recent action, or maybe something else, but everybody seemed ready to snap. Khalan was walking softly, as though stalking a deer, and Rhys crouched slightly as though he expected to be shot at any moment. Brutus was moving so cautiously and carefully that he appeared to glide along the surface of the stone beneath.

The oil lamp flickered, and Erik held it carefully, peering into the shadows. Brutus and Khalan disappeared forward, out of the feeble light, and Rhys lingered at its edge. Only Erik and Edwin remained in the illuminated circle, and it made Erik feel surprisingly vulnerable. He rested the front of his carbine on his forearm, so that he could hold his weapon and the light at the same time.

The cave turned uphill, and the ambient light dropped off quickly to murky shadow. Erik could hardly see a thing except for Rhys' back, and he stayed close. The others could see in the dark, but he couldn't. He didn't want to get left behind, or fall into a chasm.

The walls of the cave were strangely smooth, and he noticed some runes scratched into the rock as they passed by. He could smell the faint scent of the lake behind, and the cold breeze blowing up the tunnel gave him chills. Ahead, the sound of Khalan's footsteps were barely audible, and he heard Edwin's paws padding softly at his side. The ground was damp, and mostly stone, with a few patches of sandy earth here and there.

They stopped for a moment. Erik couldn't see what was happening, so he sat tight and tried to see the path behind them. After a few minutes, he heard Rhys whisper, "Moving," and they resumed their climb. As he passed the spot that Brutus had stopped, he saw another set of runes, and paused briefly. It looked like some kind of picture with a caption: a mountain summit and some kind of eye. He didn't know what to make of it.

The path took a sudden downward turn, and began to turn hard to the right. After a few yards it turned hard left, and continued this pattern several times. Rhys told Erik that the cave ceiling was dropping, and soon they had to get on their hands and knees to continue negotiating the path. It was difficult to keep a hold of his gear in the space, and he almost spilled the lamp oil on several occasions.

And then the cave opened up again. Erik stood, quietly muttering oaths, and saw Khalan and Brutus standing a few yards ahead. They were looking around as though they were looking for something. Rhys went up to join them, and Erik followed. As he drew closer, he saw amazement on their faces.

"What is it?" he asked.

Rhys just shook his head in wonderment. Khalan finally answered him: "Brother, we are standing in a city."

*   *   *

Thjostolf consulted his map and scowled.

The mountaintop had only one entrance—the spur the Jomsskari had climbed, starting in the foothills to the west and ending at the mouth of the bowl of the mountaintop. While the mouth of the bowl was only about three quarters of a mile wide, much of the spur itself was five miles across, of which only two or three miles were negotiable by vehicles. Thjostolf had hoped to push the first line of defense down a few miles, but it was simply impossible. He'd need a battalion-sized force to defend the mountain that way. The terrain put him in a difficult position, more so than he'd believed.

He knew what the Alnethar would do. Once they realized an Alliance unit had taken the valley on the mountain, they'd try to get within howitzer range and shell the village defenses relentlessly. It wouldn't be difficult, either. They only need to get a few cannons to the plateau, and they would be able to both assault the village and defend themselves from a counterattack from Feldhall. What was more, the ability to ferry troops and supplies up and down the mountain by griffin gave the Alnethar a serious advantage in deploying reinforcements. It would be two weeks at best before an Alliance unit could move to reinforce, and if they had to break through the lines to do it, it could take much longer.

He was looking for choke points, places where the Alnethar would be unable to flank the Jomsskari, places that were narrow enough that the Jomsskari could defend without overextending and isolating themselves. It was the only chance they had to hold the mountain.

Only there were no such places. A few miles down the mountain, there was a waterfall, and the only passage through there was only about two hundred yards wide. It would be perfect to defend from there, except that it was only a few thousand feet above sea level. Thjostolf was sure the griffins could deploy flanking elements to the rear of his positions, and then they'd be trapped. He needed a way to prevent the griffins from being able to effectively move behind them. He was drawing a blank. There didn't seem to be an effective way to hold the mountain without more men.

He set the map down and ran a hand throughout his hair. The final count on the weapons was seven bolt-action rifles, two crew-served machineguns, two pistols, and fifty odd grenades. They had about eight-hundred-sixty rounds for the rifles, just over fifteen-hundred for the machineguns, and about thirty rounds for the pistols.

He reasoned he could outfit two fire-teams from the villagers, each one with a machinegun and an assistant with a rifle.

The rest of the five rifles would be divided up and put into the fire-teams, one with three riflemen and the other two. At the very least, the villagers could bolster the ranks of the Jomsskari and provide some additional firepower. He made a mental note to ask for volunteers later, or perhaps conscript a few young men, if they proved too timid to step out on their own.

He was sitting in the shade of Josef's house, his back rested against the outer walls. Gabryl and Kolskegg were a few yards off, watching the tree line and the sky. On the other side of the house, Peter was looking out at the village. Nobody seemed to have noticed the departure of Rhys' detachment as they went about gathering wood to patch the bullet holes in their walls. Even now, Josef was inside his house, and Thjostolf could hear him shuffling about and moving furniture. He heard Eidel as well, talking softly, apparently to herself, because Josef never responded. By the river, the young women in the village had gathered and were singing hymns.

They had to evacuate, he decided. There was just no way the Jomsskari could defend the village and protect its inhabitants without more men. He just didn't know where to send them. The lowlands weren't secure, and the road to the bottom of the mountain was open and vulnerable to attack. The lower they got, the higher the risk of being assaulted from the air.

It used to be that combat was two-dimensional. It hadn't fully registered to Thjostolf how valuable a third dimension would be. It completely changed the dynamics of warfare, and it left him befuddled.

So, he had to move the villagers. He had to convince them that it was necessary, and figure out how to get them security as they passed down the spur. He ran a hand through his hair again, and shook his head. If they couldn't get the villagers out before the Alnethar laid siege to the mountain, then there was no question what the end would be: every last one of them would be killed. He tried not to think about the fact that he was in no different a position.

He rose, and went to speak to Gabryl.

Gabryl was smoking his pipe. Even from a distance, Thjostolf saw him breath smoke from his nostrils and sigh. He paused a moment, and watched. Gabryl seemed entirely relaxed.

The air was warm, it was nearly 1400, and the village was bathed in sunlight. The laborers in the field moved about, pulling weeds and tending to the goats. He heard birds calling to each other, and felt the cool breeze run over his head. The wind drew the wisps of Gabryl's hair up, and for a moment it like he was becoming a vapor. Then the wind died down, and the impression faded.

It was an idyllic sight, tainted only by the distant stench of the morning's violence. The sun passed behind a cloud and reemerged a second later. Flies buzzed about, confused by the disappearance of the corpses they had smelled earlier. But while Thjostolf was still several paces away, the wizard said plainly, "You are planning to evacuate the village."

The interjection broke Thjostolf's stride, but only for a second. "Yes," he said. "Yes, I am. Only I do not know how."

He came forward, squatted next to the wizard, and showed him the map, explaining the situation. Gabryl listened quietly, letting the smoke escape his nostrils in wisps as he breathed. "It seems we've inadvertently trapped ourselves," Thjostolf finished, "And I don't see a way to move them out."

Gabryl looked at him. Thjostolf would never speak so frankly in front of the others, but when it was just the two of them, the young captain could express his doubts. Gabryl had seen a side of Thjostolf that none of the others could—a vulnerable side, the side that was fearful and wanted more than anything to go home. But Gabryl didn't offer any advice. He simply told Thjostolf that they'd think of something, and told him to get some rest.

It was abnormally unhelpful. Thjostolf left their meeting more disquieted than before, and he glanced back at the wizard as he went. There was something else on the wizard's mind, he could tell. But this raised a more troubling question – what could so preoccupy Gabryl that this problem, so immediate and concerning the very lives of a hundred or more people, was nothing to him?

*   *   *

Erik peered into the darkness. While the others stood, transfixed, he could see nothing. Presently, however, he began to notice a strange smell that hung in the air, accompanied by a faint hissing. "What do you see?" he asked.

Khalan only laughed in awe, and the sound echoed in the depths.

The hissing continued, so quietly Erik thought he was just imagining it. He swung his lamp around to see. It seemed to be coming from his right. Carefully, he stepped towards the sound, holding his breath so that he could hear it. Along the smooth stone, he saw the circle of light casting dark shapes. An ornate pipe emerged from the murky black, projecting straight out of the stone. It stood about five feet high, and appeared to be made of copper or gold. Erik stared at it, and ran his hand lightly over its surface. The hissing, ever so faint as it was, seemed to be coming from inside it.

Edwin stood beside him, and panted lightly. "Open your lamp, master," he said.

Erik glanced at him, a little surprised, and opened the glass face of the lamp.

"Bring the flame close to the top of the pole," Edwin said, "And shield your face."

Erik did so, and immediately understood the wolf's instructions. A tongue of flame leapt from the lamp to the top of the pole, and the hissing abruptly changed to the deep roar of fire. The pole-torch shone brightly, as if the flame was traveling through it— and then a flame erupted a few yards ahead on a second pole he had not seen, and then another and another. All around the cavern, pole-torches awoke, and the darkness was illuminated like a starry night.

And he saw that they were indeed in a city. Towering above them and descending into a sheer chasm, the rock had been hewn and carved into pillars and landings, balconies and causeways. The thousands of tongues of flame bathed the city in golden-red light, and Erik could do nothing but stare as the others had. It was intensely beautiful, immensely large, and it took his breath away.

They were on one side of the city. Before them lay a great chasm, about one hundred feet in width and so deep that Erik couldn't see the bottom, separated them from the other side. There didn't seem to be a way across to either side – no sign of a bridge or a crossing. There were no guardrails on the landings or at the side of the chasm, either. As he took it in, he saw that although the city towered upwards for hundreds of yards, there were no stairscases.

But the city was, above all else, empty and silent. For several minutes the Jomsskari stood at the edge of the precipice and looked out over the city, and heard nothing. As he stood, Erik thought that the whole place seemed ancient; even the air tasted unused and old. It was dry, too – dry as a bone.

Edwin whimpered softly.

They gathered together, and since there wasn't a bridge, Rhys decided to try to cross the chasm where they were. They made a lasso from one of their lengths of rope and spent a few minutes throwing it at a sturdy stalagmite on the other side. Once it was hooked, they fastened it to another stalagmite on their end.

Brutus went first. They tied a harness to him and he dragged a second rope across, crawling upside down across the empty black. Once across, the dwarf secured the second rope above the first. Rhys went next, standing on one rope and holding onto the second, shuffling across. When he had brought across a third rope, Erik carried much of the gear they had left across to them, with his feet on one rope and his hands on two others. Finally, Khalan carried Edwin across, and they took a breather on the other side.

They left the ropes where they were, and moved into the city. Now that the lights were burning, Erik could find his way quite easily, and the team adopted a looser formation. Erik began to wonder. The city was much larger than any city he had seen before— not only in size, but in scale. The streets were tall and open, and the lowest ceiling looked to be thirty feet. The doors to the buildings were at least ten feet wide, and when they entered one of the buildings, they found stone formations that looked like large chairs. Each of these was at least fifteen feet long and six feet wide. And, as Erik had noticed before, there were no stairs, and no apparent way to reach the upper levels.

They moved through the city, passing several rows of buildings. The buildings were nothing more than enormous pillars rising to the cave roof, hollowed out and given doors, windows, and balconies. Each of them was marked with strange runes that Erik couldn't read.

They came to what looked like a city square, a vast open space. The columns around them formed a circle about eight hundred yards in diameter, and the stone floor seemed to swirl in etchings leading to the center. There was a large object in the middle of the floor, and they moved towards it.

It was a giant stone slab, covered in runes. Edwin hopped up onto it, and began sniffing.

Rhys looked around, and sat down. "So," he said gently, "What is this place?"

"A griffin city, perhaps?" asked Brutus. They had circled up, forming a perimeter. Edwin continued to sniff.

Rhys shook his head. "Griffins are nowhere near this size,"

he said slowly. "And they nest in the trees. These runes...I cannot read them." He ran his hand over them and shook his head. "How long has this been here?" he wondered aloud.

Erik was looking up at the columns when suddenly, Edwin began to speak. They all turned to looked at him, and saw him lying quite peacefully in the center of the stone slab, tracing the runes with his paw as he read.

" 'I am King of Sky and Rock,

Lord of Stone,

Master of the Clouds themselves.

There is none like me.

I am the Leviathan,

And all that see me tremble.

I am the Warrior, King, Lord, Master.

Yet I die,

I perish, I burn, and I am forgotten.' "

They glanced at each other. "You can read these?" asked Khalan.

Edwin sat still for a moment, and stood up, moving to another part of the slab. "Yes," he said simply.

"What tongue is it?" asked Rhys. "I have never heard it."

Edwin looked at him, and smiled. "This is a great city," he said softly. "It is called Gob-Heshem, the Place of Nesting. This is the last resting place of their greatest king."

"Nesting?" asked Erik. "So, it is a griffin city after all?"

"Oh, no, master," said Edwin. "This is the City of Dragons."

Chapter Eighteen

The Egg, 2 July 1160

"This entire realm was once ruled by dragons," Edwin explained. "Thousands of years ago, before the griffins were made, the dragons ruled this entire continent by fire and claw, from El Ornahar to the southern coast of Haelhan. They built this city at the peak of their empire: Gob-Heshem, their fortress in the boiling remains of a dying volcano. There were thousands of them. Oh, that you could see them in their glory! They soared through the air, enormous, majestic, fire and lightning pouring from their nostrils! They were the greatest of all creatures, blessed by the One Unsayable with wisdom, power, and knowledge. They built other cities, too. The castle Havenstead was built on the ruins of Gob-Kuresh, and other broods were built also.

"But the dragons were arrogant, and made a pact with the Great Demon. They set up pillars and altars to their kings. They even dared to claim power over heaven and earth, and they did not fear the One Unsayable. They mutilated lions and goats and eagles, and made griffins to serve them—twisted, miserable abominations. But the One Unsayable cursed the dragons for their pride, and delivered them over to disease and famine. The One Unsayable parched the ground between Gob-Heshem and Gob-Kuresh and split their empire. I speak of the land you now call the Wilderness. It is a vast desolation, reeking of death and decay.

"The dragons were devastated. A few returned to the One Unsayable, and were forgiven. The One Unsayable appointed them as the servants of his warriors, of whom I will speak of later. But the vast majority of the dragons refused reconciliation, and stood firmly in their haughty ways. They raised sacrifices to the demons and made vows to them. And their hatred for the One Unsayable was unquenchable. They sought out and enslaved and killed all they found that worshiped the One Unsayable.

"The dragons were destroyed for their evil. One by one, the mighty beasts fell to their disease, cursing the One Unsayable with their last breaths, until only three remained. Isikar-Benham and Urryah-Hezek were the last sons of the great king entombed here beneath us, and Rah-Tamar was the daughter of his most trusted warrior. Both of the princes sought to woo the she-dragon, but she feared them both, for they were violent and deceitful.

"So Isikar-Benham made a pact with the Great Demon himself. In exchange for the strength to kill his brother, Urryah-Hezek, and win the last she-dragon as his mate, Isikar-Benham promised to give his body to the demons. The Great Demon took his offer, and Isikar-Benham murdered Urryah-Hezek. But Rah-Tamar feared him all the more, and fled from his presence. Isikar-Benham was so enraged by her insolence that he raped her viciously and left her to die.

"After he had raped her, the demons came and entered his body, and he was filled by them. He took the name Irkalla, retreated to the caves beneath the Mountain, and was tormented by them. But unbeknownst to the Demon-Dragon, Rah-Tamar lived. She hid in Gob-Hemesh, and made vows to the One Unsayable. She was a lonely soul, broken and wounded, until she breathed her last. But it is said that she bore her egg, and left it in these ruins—the bastard heir to the throne of Irkalla, and the dishonorable birthright of the dragons."

The city was silent. The only sound was the gentle breath of the lamps, and the heavy thumping of his heart beating in his ears. Erik listened to the wolf, captivated. As his story ended, Edwin laid his head back down on the runes and sighed a heavy, doggish sigh.

"So..." Brutus began, a little hesitantly. "To be clear: we are in a cave-city...with a dragon's egg?"

"If I am correct, master Brutus," replied Edwin, "It is not more than two hundred yards to our northeast. And, if my nose is not lying, it is not alone."

*   *   *

It was nestled in the back of the room, behind a stone structure that looked like a dragon's chair. It was in a nest made of torn cloth, bones, mud daub, and what looked like snake's scales, nearly ten feet across. A strange odor filled the room, a predator's odor, the taste of rotting flesh. On the ground around the room, dried plants were scattered about like spilled potpourri. The room had a faint orange glow near the windows, from the torches outside, but around the nest there was a blue haze. It was almost violet and cast dark, still shadows across the floor, until it all faded to black on the ceiling.

They stacked on the doorway, and rushed inside, each of them training their weapons on the four corners of the room. When they were satisfied that there was no immediate threat, they left Khalan to guard the door while they cleared around the furniture. Finally, they crept up to the nest itself. The air was noticeably warmer as they drew close, and Erik noticed steam rising from the sides of the mound. It stood seven or eight feet high, and when they began to climb it, Erik was struck by how hard the nest was. It felt like petrified wood, solid as stone, but with a different quality. As they rose over the lip and looked down into the nest, they all stood silently.

It was the most beautiful thing Erik had ever seen. The egg was a perfect sphere, deep blue in color, mottled in red and purple. The surface was smooth, and looked as if it had been polished painstakingly. It was almost as big as a man, and through the shell Erik almost thought he could see something flicker, like a distant tongue of flame. For a few moments, they could do nothing but stare at it.

"We should go, masters," said Edwin. He sounded worried.

"Just a moment," pressed Rhys, and knelt, his eyes fixated.

Edwin sighed, and sniffed the air. "Masters..."

Erik suddenly thought of Khalan – they couldn't leave without him seeing it. For a few seconds longer, he took in the sight of the egg, and then, a little painfully, tore his gaze off and headed back to the door. He found Khalan crouched by the threshold, his machinegun braced and ready. "Go on," Erik said, "You have to see it."

Khalan seemed eager enough to comply, and trotted off.

It was several minutes before they regrouped. Rhys and Brutus couldn't stop smiling, and even Khalan seemed to be in an unusually good mood. Only Edwin seemed unnerved. While the wolf had been calm before, he now glanced about quickly, his eyes darting from shadow to shadow, and said with a low snarl, "Masters, we really must go!"

They formed up, and returned the way they had come. As they passed through the square, Brutus held up his fist, and they all dropped down. Erik looked up ahead to see what Brutus had seen, and he suddenly understood the wolf's consternation. There was something, some kind of creature, walking slowly at the far north edge of the square.

The creature looked to be seven or eight feet tall. It had long, grisly arms, a lumbering gait, and short, stubby legs like hewn-off tree trunks. It was dressed in nothing but a black garment wrapped around its waist. It was dragging something behind it on a kind of sled, and had a long object in its hand—either a spear, or perhaps an antique rifle. Even from across the square, Erik could hear the creature's huffing and puffing, and it vanished into the shadows to the north a few seconds later.

They had only seen a glimpse of the beast, but the sight burned in Erik's mind. There was a new stillness to the air that he had not known before. He had never seen anything like it. Just as he had been drawn to the egg, Erik caught himself longing for a second look at it, but it was not beauty or wonder that enticed him. He felt a stifling horror in not seeing it, the same kind of horror he felt in stalking the cave-spider in the dark. He felt hunted, and he wanted to look the beast in the eye. Although it had been over a hundred yards off, he suddenly felt as if it were watching him, close enough to reach out and touch him. He shuddered involuntarily and glanced back into the gloom, but saw nothing.

They paused, concealed behind a pillar, unmoving. Finally, Rhys patted Brutus' shoulder and they rose, circling around the south edge of the square until they had reached the other side. Now they could see the rope bridge they had erected, and they ran to it and crossed quickly. Rhys laid his hands on the rope and spoke a few words in Elvish, and it loosed itself so that they could pull it in.

Then, across the still air, they heard the huffing and puffing again.

"Movement left!" hissed Khalan, "It's on this side of the chasm!"

Erik looked. He couldn't see anything, but the sounds seemed to be coming closer. They spread out, and made a firing line.

It stopped. All at once, there was silence, and Erik held his breath, listening.

Something scratched the rock, a quiet, slow squeak of stone and steel.

A tiny, grey field mouse scampered across the floor, emerging from the shadows ahead. It ran about, sniffing left and right, and stopped in front of them. Then it sat upright, looked directly at Erik, and cocked its head. Its gaze jumped to Rhys, then Brutus and Khalan, and finally rested on Edwin.

Its tail curled impishly around its feet.

And then it seemed to scowl, and creep a bit closer. Erik

looked at the wolf, who seemed to draw back in fear, and then back at the mouse, who held his gaze steadily.

And then the mouse drew back, shook its head, and said in a deep, rich voice, "I might have known." And then it turned, scurried away into the shadows, and the silence returned once more.

They all looked at Edwin. The wolf was quivering as if a bullet had just missed his head. Without looking at them, he said softly but emphatically, "Masters, we *really must go.*"

They emerged from the cave and paddled across the lake in silence. Erik felt the tension; he knew the others were as eager as he was to ask Edwin a thousand questions. For some reason he couldn't explain, nobody did. In fact, they all seemed lost in thought. Edwin lay on the floor of the boat, motionless, his eyes unfocused and his tail limp.

They tied their boats up on the dock and moved up the shore, back into the village. Erik looked at his watch, and shook his head. It was nearly 1530, so much for getting back by lunch. His stomach had started to growl, although he hadn't realized it before. Edwin loped off, presumably in search of Gabryl, and Rhys wanted to brief Thjostolf immediately.

They found Thjostolf poring over his maps in the shade of Josef's house, and told him everything they'd seen. At first, he was almost disinterested, but when Rhys got to Edwin reading the inscriptions at God-Heshem, his half-elf ears pricked up and he began tapping his finger. When he heard of the egg, he pursed his lips, ran a hand through his hair, and asked in a quiet, tense voice, "And Edwin knew all of this?"

"That is correct, captain."

"So Gabryl knows all of this, as well," Thjostolf shook his head and spat. "Feckin' hell."

"That's not all, sir," added Khalan. They told him of the creature, and the mouse, and Thjostolf shook his head in wonderment. "Now that can't be good," he said musingly. "I don't like being around unnatural things. Come on. We'll form up on the perimeter and figure this crap out. Gabryl should be on guard just by the fields."

They gathered Peter and Kolskegg, who were on watch by the barns, and the entire team gathered by Gabryl. He was sitting on a rock, Edwin at his side, talking softly. As they drew close, Thjostolf held up his hand; he wanted to listen.

"And you are sure of it?" Gabryl was saying.

Edwin replied, "I am sure, master. The nest was steaming, and the egg had traces of fire inside it."

Gabryl mused for a moment. "So. The flame has lit. This changes things, I'm afraid." Then, without turning around, "Captain, no doubt you seek some sort of explanation for all this."

"We should have had an explanation before we left Feldhall." Thjostolf's face was calm, but there was a touch of anger in his voice.

Gabryl turned around, and waved them over. "Come on, come on," he said. "I cannot explain everything, but I can bring a little more to light."

They gathered up, and Gabryl looked at each of them. "I am not a soldier of Haelhan," he started. "I bear no allegiance to White Mountain or Iaelia, and the banners of A'kaylii and Humbridge do not command me. I am with you to affect a mission of my own, beyond that which you have been tasked with. You were to conduct reconnaissance of El Ornahar. I have been tasked to locate Gob-Heshem and see if the rumors were true. And—" he smiled wryly, "—I have found them to be true."

"What rumors?" asked Brutus, but Thjostolf interrupted.

"Tell us of the rumors later. First, tell us where your allegiance lies."

Erik noticed that Thjostolf had switched the safety off on his carbine. His voice was low and strained, and he was watching Gabryl closely.

Gabryl smiled at him. He had noticed the safety, too, but he didn't look frightened. "I am a servant of the Master, Thjostolf Captain. Do you not know? The wizards were sent down from the One Unsayable when the first of you denied Him. When the parents of elf, dwarf, man, and halfling left His presence, He sent His warriors to wage war on the demons of this world. That is why I am here. I remain in this land to destroy the demons wherever they are found."

"And we are just a means to that end?" Thjostolf asked hotly. "What the feck is that supposed to mean?"

"Everything is a means to some end," said Gabryl gently. "I serve a purpose for you, and you serve a purpose to me. Do not reduce our camaraderie to mere use and disuse. Such is the nature of every partnership."

"A partnership entails trust," Thjostolf shot back. He started to say something else, but checked himself. "And what are your objectives now?" he asked, a little more levelly. "Why were you sent so far to find Gob-Heshem?"

"And the rumors?" pressed Brutus.

Gabryl shifted uncomfortably, and measured his words carefully. "A troll in the Far North told a barkeep that his cousin had discovered a dragon's egg. This was perhaps thirty years ago. Since I heard this tale, I have spent twelve years tracking that troll down, and finally made contact with him in the Wilderness. He is an old acquaintance of mine by the name of Ulmudh the Sly, and I have had many a run-in with his cousin, who they call Ulrich Bearslayer.

"Ulrich and I have dealt together on several occasions. He

has turned up in Haelhan, Iaelia, White Mountain, the Wilderness, El Ornahar, and even on a galleon in the North Seas—this was before steam boats, you see. His cousin, Ulmudh, sells information, but Ulrich has always been wary of us. Unlike other trolls, he has never been interested in money. Whenever I see him, there is something afoot; he is never idle. I do not understand why he has laid claim to the egg."

"The beast in the city," said Erik, "The seven-foot-tall monkey thing? That was a troll?"

"Not just any troll," said Gabryl, still musing. "Ulrich has magical powers almost equal to mine, and his wits are sharp. It is clear that he recognized Edwin, and knows I am nearby. He will speak to us tonight, I suspect, or earlier."

There was a brief silence. Then, Khalan said slowly, "You mean to say the talking mouse was a troll?"

"Trolls can shape-shift," said Gabryl. "That is why they are so difficult to find. Indeed, witnessing Ulrich in his natural form was a rare treat, if you see it that way."

Erik looked at Edwin. The wolf was hanging his head slightly, and had a strange look on his face.

"So, the rumor is that a troll has a dragon's egg?" Thjostolf said, a little suspiciously. "I don't see the significance."

Gabryl took a deep breath. He explained, "The rumor was that the heir to the Dragons had been found. If it is so, we would have to either destroy the egg or raise the dragon-prince ourselves. Ulrich may not understand the power he is dealing with, or worse, perhaps he knows all too well.

"If we preserve the life of the dragon-prince, he could take his place as the Lord of the Griffins and King of El Ornahar. He could destroy the Alnethar and the evil that is Irkalla. But he could also continue in his father's steps." He sighed, and added, "I must seek council with the other wizards and I suppose I must meet with Ulrich, as well. You may recall that I have had trouble casting my spells on this mountain. There is no doubt in my mind that Ulrich is to blame for this."

Peter spoke. "Begging pardon and all that, but how about feck the troll, feck the egg, let's back into the fecking cave, yeah? At least get the villagers back there. Am I crazy for thinking that?"

Erik shook his head. "I think we should consider that, too. The griffins can't hit them in there, and seriously, what's one troll going to do to stop us?"

Edwin whined, thumped his tail once, and said pleadingly, "Master Erik...no offense to you, sir, but have you ever encountered a troll?"

There was a long silence.

Gabryl spoke, his voice low and extremely serious. "I would not pick a fight with Ulrich," he said, "Unless we had no other options available to us."

Thjostolf let out a long, strained breath. "I will take your word on that," he said tersely, "But am I to understand we must now guard two fronts?"

"Not as of yet," Gabryl replied. "Ulrich and I are old friends, of a sort. He will not attack us, though he may visit. When he does, I must be sure to meet him."

Edwin sniffed the air. "The troll has a distinctive smell, master," he said. "I will alert you if he leaves the cave, whatever form he takes."

"Thank you." Gabryl ran a hand through Edwin's fur, and smiled at him. He looked up at the Jomsskari and gazed back and forth, regarding them each in turn. His eyes rested on Erik, and for the briefest moment he saw the wizard's eyes quiver, as though he wanted to say something but couldn't. Then he looked at Thjostolf.

"The villagers are holding a feast tonight," he said. "You were worried about gathering enough men to defend the valley. I will be gone for a couple of hours, but do not fret, there are other forces we can gather."

The sun began to set. Erik had taken watch, gazing towards the distant forest, sitting on his rucksack with his cloak draped loosely across his shoulders. He had felt fear before, and learned to deal with it. The khem-khat in his bag was proof enough. But this was something different. It wasn't fear that ate at his mind now, it was dread, a deep dread. It wasn't the Alnethar, either. It was the feeling of thinking you were in a bath, and suddenly realizing you were in the middle of the ocean while sea monsters circled about.

He heard voices approaching, and looked back to see Josef and his family approaching. Shayna was half hidden behind her mother, but Erik caught a nervous, little smile on her face. He turned to look at them, and waved as they drew close.

"Where have you been?" asked Josef. "You did not join us for lunch."

Erik didn't think it wise to disclose too much. "We had a look around," he said simply.

Josef looked at him curiously, but didn't inquire further. "The village has called for a feast in celebration of our deliverance," he said. "Of course, your company is to be honored. It is the desire of this household that you, Erik, would join us for dinner."

Erik didn't know what to say. He glanced back and forth at them, and mumbled, "Well, if you want me to…"

"They are calling you 'Erik Blood-giver,'" Eidel added. There was a shine in her eyes that Erik couldn't quite identify. "We would be honored by your presence."

It took Erik a moment to realize what she was talking about, then he remembered Hindelle. He hadn't thought of her since they'd gone into the cave. "Oh, no," he said hurriedly, "That's nothing special; it's just a field transfusion. We do it all the time."

Josef smiled and shook his head. "We know what it was, Erik," he said softly. "It has not been so long since we left your world, you know. But it is your heart that you have shown us. It is clear to us now that you would give up your life-blood for someone you do not know. That is why we honor you, not because we have failed to understand the technicalities of your work."

Erik didn't know what he was talking about, and he said so.

"Did you not wonder how it was that we speak Haellic?" asked Josef, "Or the similarities in our faiths?"

Erik cocked an eyebrow. "To be honest, I haven't taken the time to consider," he replied, a little defensively. "I've plenty enough to worry about without all that."

In fact, he realized, they had all noticed it immediately, from the moment Shayna first spoke to them in the forest. But since then, the issue hadn't arisen, and with the attacks and the wounded and everything else, nobody had thought to revisit it. In a place where dragons and trolls and griffins were roaming around every corner, a colony of Haellics in the middle of El Ornahar was by far the least of their concerns.

Eidel whispered something under her breath, and Josef nodded. "We will tell you of our history later," he said. "We must prepare ourselves for tonight. But you will join us?"

Erik glanced at Shayna, and saw her blush. "Yeah," he said, shifting his gaze back to Josef. "Yeah, I'd be happy to."

An hour or so later, Wendyll came to relieve him. Erik knew better than to draw Wendyll into conversation – it was a futile endeavor. Instead, he sought out and found Thjostolf, talking quietly with Brutus and Khalan. They glanced up as he drew close, and

Thjostolf waved him over. "Gabryl's up in the forest," he said, a little darkly, "Talking to trees or something. I think he may have lost his mind."

"It is possible," admitted Brutus, "However, maybe we shouldn't assume, no? I've always had an eye for dishonest people, and I do not think Gabryl is one. We give him some time, why not, and see what the trees have told him."

Khalan snorted. "I would have liked to know we were going to meet a troll," he said irritably. "It could have been quite a fight, if he had been less friendly. This Ulrich—"

"Ulrich is not our concern right now," said Thjostolf stoutly. "He's just another variable, but our mission is the same as it ever was. I'll address the whole company presently, but don't get it in your minds that our job is different. We hold this mountaintop, not for some feckin' troll and his pet dragon, but for the Alliance."

That seemed to put an end to it. Brutus and Khalan glanced away but didn't respond, and Erik felt obligated to move on. "Josef said something weird," he broke in. He told them about Josef's comment, and Thjostolf shook his head. "'Left your world,' huh? Well, that's interesting. Let me know what he tells you. And all of you, keep your ears open about the egg. I'm curious to know how much the villagers know."

"IHO, cap," said Erik.

They dispersed, Thjostolf and Brutus heading off to gather the rest of the Jomsskari. Erik spotted Rachel, Hindelle's niece, moving through the square, and went to meet her. Khalan followed.

"Rachel! It's Rachel, right?" he asked.

She nodded, a little wary but much less so than before. "Yes, doctor."

"How's your aunt doing?"

"She's sleeping," she replied. "I left about half an hour ago, and was just returning to sit with her."

Erik glanced at Khalan and said, "I want to go check on her. You coming?"

Khalan grunted affirmatively, and the three of them went into the house she was resting in. It was basically the same structure as Josef's house, but a little larger, with simple tapestries decorating the walls. A spinning wheel sat in the corner, similar to the one in Josef's home. Erik followed Rachel up the stairs and into the second bedroom, where Hindelle was laying still. Andrei sat by her side, twiddling his thumbs. He didn't say anything as they came in, but he smiled in recognition.

Erik took her pulse, listened to her breathing, and checked the IV in her arm. It was close to empty, but her veins looked normal. Her pulse was stronger than it had been that morning. Carefully, he checked all the bandages and sutures for any sign of infection, and was surprised to see how clean the injuries looked. After checking the antibiotic levels on the IV drip, he told Andrei to give her water if she asked for it. "She looks like she's doing well," he said, "Better than I expected."

As they left, Erik caught a whiff of the upcoming meal, and his stomach growled aggressively. Khalan grinned at him. They'd both missed lunch. They opened the door and stepped out, Erik standing aside to let Rachel pass by. When he turned around, he found himself face to face with Asvald.

It startled him, and he felt his body tense reflexively. Asvald was scowling again, a few feet off the porch, holding a shovel in one hand. It looked like he had been working in the fields for most of the day, and he eyed Erik and Khalan suspiciously. "What are you doing?" he demanded.

Erik was hungry, tired, and footsore, and his temper flared in indignation. But before he could open his mouth to tell Asvald to go feck himself, Khalan stepped in, and, to Erik's surprise, answered coolly. "We were checking on the welfare of Hindelle," he said. "You'll be delighted to know she is well."

Rachel glanced back and forth between them and murmured, "Excuse me, sirs." Then, she backed away.

Asvald squared up as if he was going to attack, shifted the shovel to his other hand, and started forward. Erik didn't wait. He drew his revolver and pointed it between Asvald's eyes. Khalan snarled, drawing his pistol, too. Asvald stopped, stunned.

For a few seconds they glared at each other, and then Erik said softly, "I don't know what your feckin problem is, but I didn't come this far to have you take me out with a shovel. So how about you walk away, and I don't waste a bullet on you?"

Asvald sneered and leaned forward, pointing accusingly at him. "You can't fool me, Erik," he snarled. "I know you and your Jomsskari are in league with the Alnethar, that you staged the attacks this morning. Now you're the big heroes, and you can turn us over to our enemies whenever you wish!"

"Walk away," growled Khalan, but Erik laughed. The accusation seemed so ridiculous that he really wasn't offended.

Asvald's knuckles were white with anger. "I have no illusions, and neither do the elders," he snapped. "You'll see soon enough!" And he spun on his heel and stalked off.

They watched him go, and only when he had vanished around a corner did Erik return his pistol to its holster. "That guy is starting to tick me off," he said heatedly. "'In league with the Alnethar?' Really? That's so stupid I don't even know how to respond to it!"

"He is only a fool," said Khalan quietly, "He is not worth your anger."

Erik shook his head. "Well, if he comes at me again, I'm handling my business."

He glanced back and saw Rachel a few yards off, watching them nervously. "What's his problem?" asked Erik. "Seriously, do you know?"

Rachel seemed reluctant to answer at first. She came forward slowly, and said something in a low voice.

"I'm sorry, I couldn't hear you," said Erik. He tried not to sound as angry as he was.

"Sir, it's just…well, this is no city, sir, and it's such a little village…" she stammered, "I-I only mean to say, there are certain expectations from certain families…"

"Come on, now, don't be afraid," said Khalan, doing his best to sound fatherly.

He only succeeded in sounding vaguely drunk, but Rachel didn't seem to notice, and plunged onward. "You see, sirs, Asvald is the first son of Feodor, and it has always been presumed, and I don't mean to say promised, that he and Shayna would be betrothed, once he goes to the Wilderness to study and…well, sirs, she's taken such a favor to the doctor, and some of the villagers, those who were presuming, you see…well, some of them think you'll serve no better than to upset everybody's plans, sirs…that's all."

She fell silent and stared at the ground. After a moment of silence, Erik laughed, and she glanced up quizzically.

"Well, that's a bit of an understatement, isn't it? I mean, we're on the brink of a massive war. I think everybody's plans are a bit upset."

"I think the Alnethar will be far more instrumental in 'changing plans' than we will be," replied Khalan. "Anyway, we'd best keep an eye on young Asvald. I do not wish to harm him over something so petty."

Thjostolf's whistle sounded, and they met between the village and the fields. Thjostolf gave them a brief pep talk, and they reviewed their actions that morning: criticizing their mistakes, planning to correct them, and imagining how much worse it could have been. Thjostolf asserted again the mission at hand, "We are here to protect this mountaintop, not some feckin' egg a troll found!"

Erik and Khalan briefed the rest of them on Asvald's outburst and Rachel's explanation. Thjostolf looked irritated. "I had hoped to dodge clear of local politics," he said. "I don't understand exactly how this little society works, but it sounds like Feodor is trying to join two of the elder's families together, and that means some kind of power-struggle. We've got to be careful, now more than ever. We'll hold out a lot longer against an outside attacker than we will from internal dissent."

There was a murmur of agreement, and Erik, struggling a little, spoke up. "Josef has asked me to eat with his family tonight," he said. "I can go back to him and tell him I'm on guard or something."

"What for? To defuse the situation?" asked Rhys. "We've no idea how offensive it may be to reject such an offer, and we can't risk alienating our supporters in the village."

Thjostolf nodded. "That won't be necessary. Just don't propose or anything, all right?"

Erik gave a thumbs up. "I don't have enough goats anyway."

"I'm telling you," Peter interjected, "Trade drugs. A dram of recreational khem-khat goes for about the price of a goat on the street. Once you get the elders hooked on that junk, they won't give a damn what you do with the girl."

They all began to laugh. "You need help, Peter," Rhys said.

"Your mother needs help! And I'll be the one to give it her," Peter returned impudently, and held out his hand. "Ten goats for your mother! Full disclosure, the goats are addicts."

"Deal!" Rhys slapped the halfling's palm enthusiastically. "It is a pleasure doing business with you, my petite friend."

They gathered themselves, and Thjostolf shaking his head, continued. "Anyway...Just keep your ears open and your wits about you." The captain glanced around, and added seriously, "And keep an eye out for Gabryl. I want to see him the minute he gets back."

*   *   *

The sun had begun to set, and the villagers were gathered near the central hall. They had donned bright, colorful garments. The men wore embroidered cloaks and clean, polished boots. The women wrapped themselves in long, radiant shawls, and had taken off their aprons. As they gathered, groups here and there burst into song periodically.

Erik and Khalan were together, and they moved gingerly across the square towards the cluster. They had dropped their vests and their armor, and left their rifles behind, but the two had chosen to wear their gun belts and kukris. Erik hadn't been able to properly wash his uniform, and while he had taken a moment that afternoon to bathe, he was acutely aware that he, as well as all the Jomsskari, smelled like two weeks in the field. He had put on some of Khalan's pepperweed; it helped hold down the smell of filthy body, but he knew it could make the eyes water. He hoped he had been circumspect in its application.

They stepped through the threshold and paused to take in the sight. The tables had been adorned with candles and bowls of potpourri floating on water. Simple tapestries hung from the rafters, wafting gently in the evening air, and the smell of roast goat, fresh bread, and fruits filled Erik's nostrils. Platters and bowls lay across the tables, bearing their provisions handsomely. Some of the villagers were playing fiddles and pipes in the corner, and all around the hall, the crowd mingled and chattered. Erik immediately felt uncomfortable. He had never liked crowds, and he was acutely aware that Shayna was looking for him, and that her family would scrutinize him. He felt inexplicably sure that they would disapprove of their findings. Khalan, hanging back slightly, growled softly, and Erik knew he felt the same way.

They moved through the crowd. Every so often a villager or two would slap them on the back or grab their hand and shake, and say something like, "Erik Blood-giver, so good of you to come," or "Erik and Khalan, you must meet my family!" Erik had no idea who he was talking to most of the time, but he smiled as convincingly as he could and hoped the pepperweed wasn't too overwhelming. He caught a glimpse of Peter, chatting animatedly with a group of goatherds, and saw Thjostolf speaking quietly with Abraham and his wife.

"Erik!"

She was coming through the crowd to his right, and for a moment the rest of the room seemed to disappear. She had tied her hair back with a blue ribbon, and wore a white dress with floral embroidery along the hem. A blue and gold shawl was tied about her waist, and her bare feet were peeking out from beneath her garments as she walked. Erik couldn't help himself. He grinned like an idiot.

She grabbed his hand and led him back to her table. Erik saw Josef and Eidel sitting close together, and Sisel sat across from them. There was a vacant spot by Josef, and Erik guessed he was supposed to take it. Sure enough, as they drew close, Shayna indicated the place and, with an excited little smile, hurried around the edge of the table and took her seat next to Sisel.

Feodor rose at the far end of the hall. There were a few shouts from some of the men to quiet everybody down. Feodor prayed over the food and they started in. Khalan had taken a seat a few away from Shayna. As Erik conversed with the family, the orc-brothers caught each other's eyes every so often, and Khalan would grin knowingly. Erik didn't remember most of the conversation, it was pleasant small talk, jovial and easy. Even Sisel piped up a few times, although she spent most of the meal eying Erik distrustfully.

As for Shayna, she was quiet throughout, saying almost nothing. She watched Erik and her parents talk but didn't join in. But whenever Erik would look at her, and this was quite often, she would blush ever so slightly and nod encouragingly. As their appetites waned, the sounds of eating grew less while the chatter of talking grew more, and Shayna rested her chin on her hands and sat listening. Erik tried not to look at her too often, because it became harder to look away every time.

Finally, Josef sat back and sighed contentedly. For a few seconds he looked at Erik benignly and, Erik thought, rather detachedly. But then his expression changed. He looked at Erik very hard, as if trying to piece something together. Erik returned the gaze, a little put off but not wanting to appear disrespectful.

"What do you think about God?" Josef asked.

The question caught Erik completely off guard, and he realized with a vague shock that it had wiped the smile right off his face. "What do...I'm sorry, about God?"

"Yes." Josef looked placid, but something told Erik that everything depended on his answer.

What did he think about God? *Nothing. Nothing. Nothing, nothing, no thing, no one, nowhere, no why. What was there to think?* The question of God was clear to him: *yes, God was.* The question was not *God,* but *why God;* or perhaps, *who God,* or *what the hell, God.* A thousand years is too short a time to work it all out.

And now, in an instant, the answer must be perfect.

Yet he was aware, though perhaps only in the deepest crevice of his mind, that the question itself was wrong. It didn't matter what he thought about God—what mattered was what he did with the reality of God. And that same deepest crevice bore another thought, a thought so full of shame that it stung him: to think that he would dare pursue the perfect answer about the Creator to win the approval of a creature, a Divine means to a mortal end. As if the answer itself was not worth the study and toil of a hundred lifetimes.

The Holy Book was empty. Knowledge of God was impossible, the Words nothing but babble, if the simplicity of this was not embraced. The One Unsayable—Unsayable, Unspeakable, Unknowable—could only be pursued for His own sake. And therein once more lay the Absurdity: the only thing that he knew for sure could give him a "who," required only that the "who" be given up.

What did he think of God?

He answered honestly. "I don't really know," he said. "I mean…some days I think the One Unsayable is just how we handle our inability to deal with how badly life sucks." He hesitated, and drove on. "I do believe. But I know that I neither love nor know the One Unsayable half as I well as I should."

He had expected Josef to be disappointed, but Josef actually smiled. "I've been there, too." He folded his hands on his belly, and nodded to himself as though appraising something. "I've seen you pray, you and your company. It is good for warriors to pray together."

Erik didn't know how to respond, so he kept his mouth shut.

"I ask," Josef said abruptly, "Because you are undoubtedly wondering who we are and where we came from. We spoke earlier on the topic. Would you like to know?"

Erik nodded. "Yes, of course."

"You know of the Dragons, do you not?" asked Josef.

Khalan shifted closer. Suddenly alert, Erik tried not to show his surprise. "Yes," he said, "A little, at least."

"When the dragons reigned," said Josef, apparently unaware

of the piqued interest he had caused, "They created the griffins by black magic and made them their servants. The griffins were the perfect servant to the dragons. They had ferocity and wings, yet were unable to withstand fire. They were useful, but inferior. Gradually, the griffins began to worship the dragons as gods, and the dragons, in their pride, rewarded them for it. They gave them permission to enslave whatever other creatures suited them.

"The griffins chose the nomads. In the Wilderness, tribes and villages, not so different from this one, lined the waterways and formed a loose trading network up and down the river. With the backing of the dragons, the griffins gathered the nomads and put them to work, building great nests and breeding livestock. And of course, the nomads were made to worship the dragons as well.

"By the time the Alnethar fled from Iaelia, this government of dragons and griffins was beginning to collapse. The dragons were weakening, though the enslaved humans were not aware of it, and the griffins were becoming a coherent society without them. When the Alnethar arrived in El Ornahar, they saw the weaknesses of griffin politics. Because of their longevity, the elves could afford to wait for the perfect moment. When the time was ripe, they staged a coup. The griffins found themselves divided, between those who allied themselves with the Alnethar and those that wished to become a power unto themselves.

"The Alnethar succeeded in establishing themselves as overlords by claiming faith in the Dragons, for although the dragons were no longer lords of the world, they were still the lords of the griffins. The Alnethar then bought the approval of the dragons through honeyed words, gold, and abominable sacrifices. When the dragons finally died out, it was the Alnethar that stood as kings.

"The Alnethar are shrewd, you see. They had not totally subjugated the griffins, as the dragons had done, but set them up as near-equals instead. By maintaining a delicate equilibrium between the two races, they quickly unified the entire land of El Ornahar under a single banner. Rather than rule with an iron fist, they made their races symbiotic. They depend on each other."

Josef paused, and Erik glanced at Shayna. None of this seemed to alarm her; in fact, she looked as if she could have picked up the story where he left off. Erik looked back at Josef and said, "I'm not sure if I understand...I mean, all this is fascinating," he added, "But it doesn't sound like *your* story."

"It is because of the plight of the nomads that we came here from Haelhan," Josef explained. "The nomads had been living in paganism for generations. They needed the Word."

"The Word," Erik repeated. "You mean the scriptures?"

Josef nodded. "In a sense, yes. Let me explain. Three hundred years ago, there was a rift in the Haellic churches, between two schools of theology. No doubt you're familiar with the rift?"

"You mean the Appollonians and the Dionysians? Of course," said Erik. It was basic church history.

"Yes. Father Apollonius saw God as primarily...distant. The Apollonians focused on the qualities of God that are apart from human experience: eternality, for instance, and omniscience. It was the Apollonians that used the phrase, 'The One Unsayable' because they were so committed to the other-ness of God. The Apollonian theology became dominant in Haelhan. You yourself call God by the name they used.

"Now, Father Apollonius had a student named Brother Markko, who studied the ancient Dionysian writings. Because it was the dwarves that first had knowledge of God, Markko felt that they had special insight into His nature. He and his followers called themselves the Dionysian Church, and centered their theology on the personal, relatable qualities of God. They wrote on God's love and nurture, and put proselytizing at the forefront of the faith. They rejected the Apollonian reverence for high theology, and sought to establish a faith based on action.

"Many of these early Dionysian missionaries only traveled as far as Iaelia and Humbridge. But Markko had heard of the slaves in El Ornahar, and decided to live the word he had preached. He and a dozen or so families left Haelhan and sailed north."

Erik looked at him. "You're the descendants of the Dionysian missionaries?" He had read about them. They were often portrayed as religious fanatics and were ridiculed in the contemporary editorials. They were one of the pieces of Haellic history that everybody knew, but nobody cared much about. After all, when they left, they took their doctrines with them, and only the Apollonian schools remained.

Josef smiled. "My grandfather, Brother Markko."

"And the other elders? Are they descendants as well?"

Josef shook his head. "When the missionaries made landfall, they burned their ships so that they could not return, and began living with the locals. As they converted villages, they would intermarry, raising a generation of believers at every turn. Whenever there were too many of them in one place, they would send out preachers to the next villagers. My father, Markko's third son, converted three villages on the south edge of the river before marrying my mother, a local from the river-village at the foot of the mountain."

Erik thought of the desolated settlement, the whimpering boy. He winced imperceptibly and glanced at Shayna. It was hard to tell, but Erik didn't think she knew. *Her grandmother was in that village.*

"When I was of age, my father left me with a task," Josef went on. "He was getting along in years, and was worried that the faith was losing some of its grounding. Grandfather Markko had built a seminary in the Wilderness, but my father was worried that the Alnethar would destroy it. He was adamant that we needed a second seminary. He wanted me to build it. There was petty warring between the settlements of the Dionysian church and the locals, and I wanted to be apart from it, in a place where we could study the doctrines of the faith in peace, a bulwark of learning. So, me and three others, two local preachers, Feodor and Sigmund, and an Alnethar convert, Abraham, took our families and a few others and climbed the mountain."

"This is a seminary?" Erik asked, a little incredulously. It didn't look like one.

Josef looked weary and discouraged. There was a sorrow behind his eyes that seemed to have dried up all the tears in his body, as if his soul was many decades older than his body. "It used to be," he said softly. "The Alnethar began raiding the villages, just as father predicted, and many of our books were burned. We have copies of the Holy Books, and we have fostered the faith in our community, but in El Ornahar and the lowlands our numbers grow fewer and fewer. We knew it was only a matter of time before Haelhan arrived," he added. "The war of empires has brewed for hundreds of years."

Erik nodded. "That's what they told us," he said.

"We have had limited contact with the lowlands," Josef said, almost to himself, "It has been too dangerous to venture past the plateau. We've no word from the seminary in the Wilderness, and even the villages close to the foothills have not sent word in months. I feel our missionary zeal is waning in the face of war. If we go out as boldly as we once did, the Alnethar will stamp us out. And I fear the faith would die with us."

"You've become preoccupied with maintaining the doctrines," Erik said, and grinned. "A very Apollonian concern, isn't it?"

Josef glanced up at him, and smiled a little wryly in return. "It is," he confessed. "Every evening we gather, men, women, and children, to read the Holy Books, sing and pray…"

He trailed off, and Erik thought he looked desperate for an encouraging word. Erik obliged. "You've protected a treasure," he said gently. "An entire generation of believers with solid faith and sound theology. You've raised a generation that can carry that Word forward, as your ancestors did. That's nothing to be ashamed of."

Josef smiled a humorless, uncommitted smile. "You are too kind," he said. "The elders have discussed this at length, and we all agree that we have failed to follow the teachings that we ourselves have espoused." He looked at Erik for several seconds, and smiled. "We only disagree on what we should do about it."

A bonfire was lit in the square, and they gathered around it and sat, squatting or sitting on the ground, as some of the older men told fables and tales. Erik hardly listened to them.

The music picked up, and the missionaries began to dance. Erik was sitting on a porch out of the way, his hands folded pensively, going over everything Josef had told him. The warmth of the fire and the coolness of the night were beginning to blend, and he watched, detached, as the villagers formed lines and skipped about clapping. He spotted Shayna among them, dancing with Peter, and he smiled a little to himself. Erik had never been much of a dancer, but Peter would never pass up an opportunity for amusement.

Thjostolf came and sat down next to him, saying nothing. They sat in silence for a few minutes.

"They're missionaries," said Erik.

"Yes, Khalan told me." Thjostolf had a cup of ale in his hand, and took a slow sip. "It makes sense."

"Mm."

"They didn't mention the egg, though?"

Erik shook his head. "No, but they must know about it. They've intermarried with the locals, they must know about Gob-Heshem."

"You'd think," Thjostolf said and looked around. "But if

they did, why would they build a seminary right next door?"

Erik shrugged. "Maybe they thought it would symbolic."

Thjostolf didn't say anything for a moment. "No sign of Gabryl," he said abruptly. "I wonder if he's ducked out on us."

"It's possible." Erik didn't want to think about it. "You don't trust him anymore?"

"I shouldn't have to question the motives of any of my men," Thjostolf said sharply. "That's the whole feckin' point of Selection. That's why we weed out the bad apples. Out here, all we've feckin' got is each other, and now Gabryl and Edwin want to go and do their own thing." He sat quietly for a second, and added, "I do trust him, I suppose. It's just a bit of a shock. I never got a good answer from anyone as to why they were with us. I doubt even Lord Hoskuld knows. Feckin' hell…It's no use dwelling on it. We just need to keep an eye on them."

Erik nodded. "IHO, cap."

"What are you so pensive about?" asked Thjostolf. He was looking at Erik closely.

Erik weighed his words carefully. "The village at the foot of the mountain," he said slowly, "Was the home of most of these people's extended families. They don't know it was hit. Josef spoke of the place without any kind of sorrow in his voice."

Thjostolf didn't say anything.

"We're going to have to tell them, aren't we?" asked Erik.

Thjostolf tapped his fingers petulantly. "The Alnethar raiding party will be due back soon," he said. "They'll send out a search party in the next couple of days. So, I suppose we'd better tell them tonight, so they can mourn before the next assault." He laughed bitterly and shook his head. "What a buzz killer."

"I could tell Josef," Erik said. He hated himself for volunteering but he felt like it was right thing to do. "I'll take him aside and he can tell the other elders. There's no need to broadcast it."

Thjostolf glanced at him. "What, now?"

Erik nodded.

Thjostolf thought about, and then, standing, said, "Do it."

Erik did. He found Josef conversing with a few of the older men, and asked if they could talk. The other men looked at him curiously, and Erik supposed they thought it had something to do with Shayna. He didn't care.

He led Josef to the outskirts of the feast and sat him down before breaking the news. He told him how they had been tasked with climbing the mountain, and how they had discovered the village. He told him about the training villages they'd seen on their first mission in the lowlands, and he told him how the village had been burned. He didn't go into detail about the little girl in the fields, or the brutal execution of the villagers, but he did mention that they had gathered the bodies and tried to lay them to rest in peace.

As he spoke, Josef's face transformed to the deepest sorrow, and before Erik had finished, he began to weep openly. For a long while after Erik had stopped speaking, Josef just sat there with his head in his hands. Erik could only imagine what he must be thinking. He didn't say anything further. He was afraid, suddenly, of cheapening their deaths by offering any consolation.

Finally, almost not knowing what he was doing, he said, "I wanted to be the one to tell you, sir. I think you know by now that I want to be a part of your family, and...I guess I just wanted you to hear it from me."

Josef didn't look at him. He fell strangely silent and, although his tears still rolled down his cheeks, he no longer trembled.

He just stared ahead, blankly, into the fire.

"And," Josef said abruptly, "What are you willing to give for my Shayna?"

Erik didn't know what to say. "Khalan thought you might take thirty goats for her. Quite the orcish solution, isn't it?"

Josef glanced at him, a strange smile on his face. "Thirty goats." He looked away, and laughed, wiping the last of the tears from his eyes. "That's a lot of goats."

"Well, no such luck, sir, I haven't got any goats."

Josef smiled. "I wasn't talking about dowry."

Erik cocked his head. "Then, I don't take your meaning, sir."

Josef took a breath. "I could easily give you my blessing," he said, softly now. "You seem a fine young man, and though your faith is - " Erik cringed a bit " - undeveloped, I believe you are genuine. And I feel sure she would find the arrangement...amicable.

"Erik, today has changed everything for us. I know now that we cannot hide, and I feel so *faithless* to think...to think that to hide is what God would have us do." He sat in silence a moment before continuing. "I am not ignorant enough to think that so few of you can hold off the enemy forever. But we are a community of faith. Our purpose is not merely to continue surviving, but to send out missionaries to the lowlands, and resume preaching the Word. Our dedication to that has always been, and continues to be, our devoted act of faith.

"For now, I must be single-minded. We must contact the seminary in the Wilderness, if it still exists. Until we have returned to our original purpose, I cannot promise anything else to you. After all," he added, "In the grand scheme of our lives, nothing else but faith really matters."

Erik thought for a moment, and nodded. "That's fair," he

said. *That's a hard line to take.*

Josef looked at him. "Thank you," he said suddenly, "For telling me."

"You'll be okay?"

Josef smiled, only a little this time.

"Erik," he said, "I may weep for a while for my friends and my family who have died, but I do not mourn as one who has no hope. I am assured that each and every one of them has gone to His rest."

*   *   *

Erik found Khalan at the edge of the village, watching the festivities. He took his seat by the orc, and sat in silence for a few moments. Khalan said something in orcish, and Erik smiled but didn't respond.

Shayna found Erik and sat down with them. She had never really conversed with Khalan before, but after the first few minutes, they found they got along quite well. Khalan told her about how Erik had fought the cave spider, and Erik explained how to make khem-khat. She reproached him for not telling her about the trials earlier, and demanded he disclose all the details.

The villagers danced and sang long into the night, until the bonfire had died down to the embers. The moon had begun to set before the last of the villagers finally went to bed, and Shayna fell asleep on the porch where they sat. Erik covered her in his cloak, and he sat with Khalan in silence once more. They didn't speak, but Erik knew they were both thinking the same thing.

Before the week was out, they would be attacked again, and

this time, the Alnethar would be ready.

Chapter Nineteen

The Greenhorns, 3 July 1160

Shayna awoke with a start. Erik and Khalan had been talking in soft voices, and he saw her jerk upright and look around, disoriented. It wasn't quite light yet, but the moon had set, and the stars had begun to fade.

She looked around and Erik smiled at her. "Morning," he said briefly. "Sleep well?"

She stared at him, bewildered at first, then smiled sleepily, and flopped back down, rubbing her eyes. "Oh, my back is stiff."

Khalan laughed a raucous, orcish laugh, but in good humor. "It takes a few nights to grow accustomed to sleeping on the ground," he said, getting up. "Here." He offered his enormous hand.

She took it and Khalan pulled her to her feet. Erik admired her from the other end of the porch. She ran a hand through her disheveled hair, blushed a little, and said something about cleaning up. A moment later she was across the square and in her house.

Erik picked up his cloak where she had left it and sat back down on the stoop. The two brothers had stayed up all night, talking about nothing in particular. Now they were silent, and watched the sky change from dark blue to reddish grey. The village began to stir, as it had the morning before, before the assault. The missionaries rose and went to breakfast, and presently the Jomsskari emerged as well. Thjostolf assigned Peter and Kolskegg to keep watch, and the rest followed the missionaries into the central hall for breakfast.

Josef broke the news of the massacred village over breakfast. Erik and the rest of the Jomsskari stood in the rear of the hall, silently watching the proceedings. Most of the missionaries reacted the same way as Josef had, and wept openly. Others just stared blankly at him as if he was speaking nonsense. Josef chose his words carefully, and Erik noticed that none of the other elders appeared surprised. They must have learned the night before, and decided together when to tell the rest. As Josef finished, Erik saw Shayna burying her face into her mother's shoulder, and Sisel had laid her head on the table. Eidel put her arms around both of them and whispered something to them.

Josef led them in a long, fervent prayer, and they sat in tearful silence for several minutes afterwards. Finally, Abraham stood to speak. "Brothers," he said, "I do not doubt that the Alnethar intend the same fate for us. Surely, these strangers were sent to us in good time. But we are now faced with a struggle of the heart. We will be tempted to hate the Alnethar. We will be tempted to take pleasure when they die. We will be tempted to fear them when we ought to fear only God. I implore you all, hold fast to the faith."

He paused to clear his throat, and continued, "Captain Thjostolf?"

Thjostolf was leaning against the wall, his arms folded. "Yes?"

"How long do we have?" asked Abraham levelly, "Before they return?"

The entire hall turned to look at the Jomsskari. Thjostolf didn't hesitate. "We can expect a scout party to arrive within the next forty-eight hours," he said, "And a second assault by the end of the week, unless they are delayed."

A murmur ran through the hall, and Thjostolf walked up towards the front, speaking as he went. "My men, the Jomsskari, are excellent warriors. We have dedicated ourselves to the art of war, and each of us has proven our mettle again and again. We are trained and accustomed to fighting an enemy far superior in numbers, and have the will to survive against all odds. But I fear even we are too few. The Alnethar will return, and when they do, they will make sure they have enough men to overwhelm us."

He stood in front of them all, next to the elders. "Abraham is right, we must not act from hatred, anger, or vengeance. We must hold true to the faith that we share. But war is upon you. This is no longer my war, or Haelhan's war. It is your war now. You must stand in your own defense, or everything you have sought to build, including the doctrines and mission of the Word, will perish." He looked around, and Erik was impressed by the air of authority he conveyed. Erik had always known him as their commander, but today, Thjostolf's presence seemed more resolute, more stout, then it had ever before.

"I need eleven young men," he said, "who can shoot a rifle and are willing to stand with us."

For a second, nobody moved. Then a young man stood in the far corner, and another stood up a few seats down. Erik saw Asvald stand next, his face ashen but his jaw set, and then, almost as one, another two or three dozen rose. Thjostolf looked over them, and then walked around the hall, choosing out eleven. As he chose them, they went to the back of the hall and stood, a little awkwardly, a few yards from the Jomsskari.

Erik immediately saw the pattern. Thjostolf did not choose any husbands or fathers, and he took only one from each family. No one family would sacrifice more than the others.

Those who were left behind showed mixed expressions: some relief, others resignation, and a few, disappointment. Those who had been selected all had the same expression: nervous, biting their lips, looking back at their families. Asvald stood among them. Their gaze met. Asvald was scared, his eyes wide and his face taut. For a moment, Erik felt a burst of disdain and superiority welling up from his chest, and he started to smirk. And then, much to his surprise, he was ashamed. This boy was as young as he was when he joined the Haellic Fusilliers, and he knew he had been afraid when they told him Haelhan was at war. Asvald had stepped forward despite his fear. He deserved respect for that, even if he was a little *jai-khu*.

They issued them the Alnethar weapons. For the rest of the morning, the Jomsskari familiarized the greenhorns with the tools of their new trade. Khalan taught them all how to run the machine-guns and then Wendyll gave a class on rifle fundamentals. It was difficult, because they didn't have enough ammunition to actually fire the weapons. Wendyll balanced a small pebble on the tip of the barrels, and had the greenhorns practice holding the weapon stable and squeezing the trigger correctly, so that the pebble didn't fall. Then they'd work the action, reset the pebble, and try again. After that, they worked on battle drills, and everywhere they went they ran.

At the end of the day, Erik was almost as tired as the greenhorns were. The Jomsskari sent them to the meeting hall, where the rest of the villagers were almost finished with dinner, and they heard cheers erupt from the families as the recruits stumbled in, muddy, exhausted, carrying their weapons slung to their backs. The Jomsskari gathered in a small cluster in the square and began to discuss the next day's training.

For all the day's activity, none of them were encouraged. For several minutes, they reviewed what the greenhorns knew and what they had to work on. Then they sat silently.

Kolskegg broke the silence. "They're decent at tracking, they have acceptable marksmanship skills, and they know the land. That's all they have going for them. Basic battle drills? Nothing. And none of them have been shot at before."

"I could say, they are not prepared for the stress of combat," Brutus offered. "But there is little we can do about that."

Thjostolf had joined them, but he hadn't said anything. He was puffing away on his pipe, grim and preoccupied. Erik watched him expectantly. He felt sure that Thjostolf would say something soon.

He was right. "They're no good at fighting," the half-elf said coolly. "That's not a feckin' surprise, we knew that already. But they won't last a minute in open combat with the Alnethar, you can be sure of that. Feckin', we need to use them to their full potential. They're good at tracking? They know the land? So let's get them to show us where the griffins can land in the forest and plant obstacles: sharp spikes so they can't land, pitfalls, snares, the works. Let's get them to feckin' set up observation positions to give us early warning and help us figure out how to evacuate this village. Let's get them to help us set up feckin' phase lines with command detonated mines. How much explosives do we have?"

Brutus said, "Sixty pounds."

"Can we make some more?"

Brutus thought about it. "Not without nitric acid, I think," he said slowly, "Although, if the goatherds make fertilizer from the goat droppings, it may be suitable for ammonia nitrate, why not?"

Rhys cocked an eyebrow. "You think so?"

"Why not? Yes, if their fertilizer is suitable I could make many anti-personnel bombs. And I'm sure they have reserves of sawdust. I will have to inventory our initiators and det cord," he added. "I will have an answer for you by nightfall."

Thjostolf nodded. "We're going to have to rely on confusion and feckin' harassment," he said. "We need to convince the enemy that they are up against a much larger force, and throw them off balance. That means we need to force them to land much further down the mountain than they did last time, and feckin' engage them sporadically. Sniper fire, mechanical ambushes, feckin' mortars, targeting officers, you know the drill." He took a long drag from his pipe, and blew smoke from his nostrils. "Gentlemen," he said roughly, "We need to kill them with a thousand tiny cuts."

The Jomsskari nodded. Thjostolf looked around at them and said, "I guess we'll just teach the feckin' new guys how to break contact, and keep that simple. And Rhys, I'll get a volunteer to learn to assist you on that mortar so we can put Brutus up on the line. Sound good?"

"Sounds smart," said Peter, "And I hope you recognize the damn difference."

Thjostolf laughed. "Yeah," he said, "We're probably all going to die, but damn it if we don't make 'em remember us for generations to come."

Though they all laughed, Erik was vaguely aware that referencing their imminent demise wouldn't seem amusing to anyone else in their position. Perhaps, he thought, they had all been doing this far too long to worry about it anymore. Or perhaps laughing at death was the only way they could face it.

They walked into the central hall, and as they crossed the threshold all the talk died down. The villagers were watching them expectantly. Erik guessed that they were anticipating some terrible news. So far, the Jomsskari hadn't been the harbingers of glad tidings. Thjostolf didn't say anything to the assembly, but he walked right up to the elders and began talking to them in a low voice. The rest of them sat down and wordlessly helped themselves to the food. Slowly, the babble resumed. The Jomsskari ate in silence, hunched over their plates. They knew they would be up most of the night. They had very little time to booby-trap all the clearings on the plateau, and although none of the them said a word, Erik knew that they were all thinking the same thing: with limited ammunition and only a few dozen hours to prepare, they would be working around the clock. This would be the decisive moment for the Jomsskari. Selection had proven that each and every one of them would not give in to fatigue, and now they would be depending on each other to function in combat after days of grueling labor.

They were so preoccupied they didn't notice Gabryl until he had sat down with them. The wizard looked pale and tired. His face was dirty, and the years showed themselves in the wrinkles on his face. He didn't say anything either. The others looked at him for a few moments, and resumed eating.

Presently, Thjostolf spotted him and came over. Leaning

down close to him, the captain said, "Where have you been?"

Gabryl smiled wanly. "I have spoken to the trees," he said.

Thjostolf waited for further explanation, and when none came, he asked sardonically, "What did they tell you?"

Gabryl looked up at him, and Erik noticed the familiar twinkle in his eyes had returned. "Captain," he said, "If I have anticipated your intent, you mean to prevent the Alnethar from landing close to the village. Your intent is to create space between them and this valley. Am I right?"

Thjostolf nodded. "Yes, that's correct."

"The trees have agreed," said Gabryl, "To grow out over the clearings. It will take time, but the smallest clearings may be filled in as early as by tomorrow morning. By the end of the week, the forest should extend, unbroken, to the western edge of the plateau."

The Jomsskari stared at him, and Thjostolf broke into a broad grin. "You're not feckin' with me?"

Gabryl shook his head, smiling. "Captain, I assure you, the trees were quite adamant. They have heard whispers from their brethren in the lowlands, how the Alnethar have burned forest and field to root out their enemies, and they know that the Dark Elves are no friends. They have already begun to seed, and the incantations I have cast in the forest will cause them to grow most rapidly."

"You were talking to trees?" said Rhys. His expression was blank, but Erik thought he caught a ring of skepticism in it. The magic of the Iaelians did not deal with such things. If Erik understood correctly, the Iaelians used magic as an element. Gabryl spoke of it as if it were an organism.

"Well, in a sense," Gabryl said with a light laugh. "Driads – tree spirits, you know – are not prone to hear simple words, although they do enjoy good music." He picked up a cup and took a long drink. "But there are ways, when one has studied them as I have, to make them hear you, and to hear what they say in return."

"Will they fight for us?" asked Thjostolf.

"They are not animals, captain," said Gabryl, a little reproachfully. "But they will do what they can."

Erik couldn't process what he was hearing. They had never known what Gabryl was capable of. Now, his dread of the coming days eased, if only for a moment, and he looked out into the assembly and saw that they were eating, unaware of the wizard's work, unaware of what it meant, unaware that now they had fighting chance...

Thjostolf was still grinning. "That's...that's good. Good work." He looked at the Jomsskari. "We still need to put out traps in the larger clearings, but...well, feck, I knew we brought you along for a reason." He thumped the table with his fist, and turned, walking back up to the elders looking much more cheerful than he had in days.

Rhys began to talk with Gabryl, asking him about tree-talking, and Erik saw Shayna for the first time that night. She was at the far end of the hall, barely visible through the crowd, talking to...he blinked. She was talking to Asvald, and Erik wondered what he was telling her. He hated, suddenly, the knowledge that he cared so much, and he hated how much he wanted to leap up and interrupt them, and how he just *knew* that Asvald was much safer for her anyway, how much more likely he was to survive long enough to see the next year...

She saw him looking, and smiled briefly before returning her attention to Asvald. Erik tried to resume eating, but found he wasn't hungry. The news of the trees had uplifted him for a moment, but now he felt heavy, as if his kit had gained a two stone. For a few minutes he nursed his ale, and then decided he wanted to get some air. "You need me for anything, Rhys?" he asked.

Rhys looked up. "No, not presently," he said.

"I'm going to take a walk," said Erik, and taking up his weapon he headed for the door.

He was experiencing something he hadn't felt in a long time, a kind of panic, a lost memory clawing its way to the surface. He had fled from it all his life, but it always caught him. It had cost him his pride, it had cost him his life as a bookkeeper's assistant, it had stolen his dreams of academia and had even cost him his career in the Haellic army. The truth was, he was a bastard, and nothing he did could ever change that. Not even his service in the Jomsskari could save him from the fact of his lineage. His mother...he tried not to think of her. He had resolutely put her out of his mind for years, and he wasn't going to let his thoughts stray to her know.

Feck it all.

He told himself he had no right to infect Shayna with such a disease. Asvald was a much safer choice, for every reason. Asvald knew her better, Asvald was so much less likely to be killed in some muddy hole in the middle of nowhere, and the families would be so much more content with such an expected union. And whatever Asvald was, he wasn't a bastard. Rachel had spoken truthfully. If he were to persist, then he stood to do nothing more than upset an otherwise stable order. If that wasn't bad enough, his involvement with Shayna could do nothing but lock her in the same isolation he had been locking in his whole life. It would be better, he felt sure of it, if he stayed with the Jomsskari and just let her live her life peaceably.

He was almost halfway across the square when he heard her call out to him. "Erik!"

He turned. She was coming across the square, a curious smile on her face, barefooted again. His chest felt like it was filled with lead. It must have showed, for as she drew close she reached out and touched his shoulder gently. "You look distressed."

Erik smiled noncommittally, "It's been a long day."

Her hand was still on his shoulder.

"Asvald and you are good friends, I suppose," he said. He realized as he said it how hostile it sounded, and hoped she didn't notice.

She cocked her head. "We're all old friends here," she said. Then, "He told me you tried to shoot him."

"He's being dramatic. After all, he's still alive, isn't he?" *Why am I so proud of being dangerous?*

She shook her head, and a look of reproach crossed her face. "There's no need to be rude."

Erik caught himself, and measured his words carefully. "It's nothing personal," That was a bald-faced lie. "He came at me with a shovel. That's a direct threat and I'm going to handle it."

She didn't say anything.

He tried again. "We don't always have the luxury of time," he said. "We react to threats, engage the enemy...and if we hesitate, we die. Asvald was acting like an enemy, like he wanted to attack me, so I reacted. I'm not saying it was the most appropriate way of handling it," he added, "But I don't know him. I don't know what he will or will not do. And I'm not going to wait to find out. I'm going to live."

They stood in silence for a moment, her eyes searching his face. Then, still touching his arm, she began to walk slowly. He went with her.

"He wouldn't attack you. He's not a killer. He's just...zealous, for the sake of the village. He's the son of an elder, after all."

Erik pursed his lips, exasperated, but held his tongue.

She was watching his face closely, and noticed. "I guess you know how he feels about me," she said.

"Rachel mentioned something about it."

"He *is* my friend, you know."

Erik didn't say anything.

"You're jealous, aren't you?" she asked. She had slipped her arm into his.

"Of course, I am," said Erik. "I could search the whole damn world and never find another girl like you."

She laughed, a little girlishly, and didn't say anything for a moment. Then, "That's very sweet."

"What? I'm serious." He stopped and they looked at each other. Suddenly he grinned. "I mean, I've been to A'kaylii and you're far prettier than an orc."

"Oh, okay, that's not very nice." She tried to scowl at him but her smile kept breaking in.

Erik looked at her for several moments, and brushed her cheek with his hand. "I am jealous," he said softly, "That he's known you all his life, that he could see you every day...I'm jealous that you can know for sure that he would be there for the rest of your life, that you won't have to deal with...Well, if I'm not batshit crazy now I will be soon. You don't deserve that." His fingertips rested in her hair. "In short, I'm jealous of him because, if I were your father, I'd rather you be with him then with me."

She looked at him quizzically, "Why would you say that?"

"Because I'm a bastard," he said bitterly.

"I don't care."

"You should."

"I don't," she said firmly. "And neither does my father. Everyone here is the descendent of pagans and pariahs, Erik. Where you come from means nothing to us. You can't dwell on that. No matter where you came from, you were made in the image of God, and nobody can take that dignity away from you."

"You'd be surprised."

Her eyes searched his. "This is a deep scar, isn't it?"

Erik didn't say anything.

"Come on," she said, and taking his hand she led him through the village, past the barn, and into the fallow fields beneath the cliff face. They walked for some time, not speaking. Erik watched her. She didn't seem agitated, and being in her presence, feeling her cool, soft hand in his, he felt his own disquiet recede. The sun had already set, but the horizon was still a brilliant gold, and there was a slight breeze from the west that played in her hair as it did in the grass at their feet.

She led him right up to the cliff wall, and they both gazed up. Then, slowly, she reached out and touched it, resting her palm against the stone. He watched her.

"Do you know how this mountain valley came to be?" she asked. Her voice was so soft it was as if she were asking herself.

"Someone said it was a volcano."

"Yes," she murmured, with a strange, almost melancholy smile on her face. "Yes, it was a volcano. Fire boiled in its belly for eons. It died a long time ago, when the Dragons ruled. The stone's cold now, but it used to flow like water. Sometimes, when you look closely, you can see the droplets"

She squeezed his hand, and looked at him. "This was an extremely violent place once. When it erupted, it killed everything within a hundred miles. Every living thing between here and the coast was burned alive or buried in the singeing ash. The stories say that Hell itself vomited from the peaks."

Erik listened, transfixed by her voice.

"For decades, it was nothing but bare rock, ash, and petrified wood. There's quite a lot of it, still, if you know where to look. It was desolate. Accursed, the natives in the lowlands called it, even after the forest grew up again. They've told stories about the Accursed Mountain for generations. Nobody dared even to approach the foothills, and the pagans would perform rites to banish the evil spirits they believe live up here. Nowhere in all of El Ornahar is there a place so reviled.

"But God made it my home. I love this place. I don't care where it came from or what it did before it was formed into what it is now. God does that, you know." Her eyes shone so brilliantly in the failing light. "He pours Himself out in mercy and love where we least expect it. He heals the broken and makes saints out of miscreants."

Erik didn't reply.

She watched him for a few moments, and then, coyly asked, "Would you like to know something?"

"Yes?"

"When you first jumped up and... introduced yourself," Erik laughed, and she did too, "I was only afraid of you for a second. When I looked into your eyes I just couldn't believe you wanted to harm me." Her eyes twinkled. "I couldn't believe you were a bad person. From the moment I looked up and saw you, I wanted to know you. I wanted to hear your story. And the more I know of you..." She bit her lip just a little, "...the more I want to be a part of that story."

Erik wasn't sure what to say.

"There's a lot we haven't spoken of," she said softly. "Isn't there?"

"Like what?"

Now it was her turn to be silent.

"I've spoken to your father about you," he said.

Her eyes widened, and a surprised smile spread across her face.

"It's not the right time. He wants the seminary to return to its original purpose. He wants to resume preaching in the lowlands. And there's this whole war thing going on."

Her smile didn't falter. "You spoke to him." It was a statement, not a question.

Erik nodded. She was just looking at him, so happy he didn't know what to do.

"I'm just not sure if..." he started, but he felt he had opened up a conversation he didn't want to have.

"Not sure if what?"

He didn't know how to start. "I want...I want the best for you, Shayna. I really do. I'm just not convinced I'm...you know, the best one for you."

She cocked an eyebrow. "What?"

"You don't think there are others, you know, here? That would be a better choice for you?"

"Like who, Asvald?" She laughed, and he found himself strangely comforted by the kind of laugh it was. She wasn't derisive, or surprised. She actually thought it was funny. "Erik, no. No, I don't think that. And I think I'll be the judge of what is best for me."

Erik felt her hand trembling inside of his.

"He said he would give his blessing," Erik said.

Shayna uttered a happy little squeak and bit her lip again. For a moment, she didn't say anything. "Then," she said suddenly, "I suppose there's only one other person you need to ask."

Erik laughed, and pulled her close. He felt entirely out of control. Every movement, every breath, was purely instinct. Despite the battle of the morning, despite the A'kayliian trials and the Belvade campaign, despite everything he had been though, now, for the first time, he felt truly afraid, afraid that this moment would be snatched away, or she would think better of it and leave.

But she stayed. For a few minutes they stood, her head resting on his collar, their arms around each other. He could feel her heart beating, hear her breathing in his ear, he could smell her hair, and he took in every sensation, cherishing the milliseconds. He was dimly aware of the pounding of his own heart, and felt a thrill in his spine as her lips brushed his temple.

"Will you?" he asked.

"Yes," she whispered, close in his ear.

"I don't know when."

"I'll wait."

He kissed her.

*   *   *

When they returned, they found the square a beehive of activity.

The Jomsskari had gathered, with the greenhorns assembled a few yards off. It was full dark, but the work day had only just begun. The missionaries were bringing armloads of scrap wood from all corners of the village and had begun to cut and split it into stakes. The plan was to set up three to four foot spikes in the large clearings and camouflage them. It would be effective against the griffins, and prevent them from staging for the attack. The enemies fatigue would be a valuable asset.

Shayna broke off as they entered the square, lingering only a moment to give Erik one last kiss. Then she ran off and disappeared into the crowd. Erik turned to the Jomsskari. Thjostolf was getting a headcount, and waved him over impatiently. "Come on, we've been looking for you," he said testily.

Josef was with the captain, as was Feodor. They were discussing the rest plan for the village; about half of them, Erik understood, would work until about 0100, and then they would be relieved by the others. It was already nearly 2200; Erik hadn't realized how much time he had spent away with Shayna.

Thjostolf clearly had. He pulled Erik aside and demanded to know where he had been. Erik wasn't even sorry. He told Thjostolf what had transpired and, to his pleasant surprise, the half-elf laughed. "Well, I guess congratulations are in order."

"Thank you, cap."

"Of course, you realize that feckin', I just told you to not do that exact thing, just last feckin' night." He didn't look angry, though.

"What could I to do?" asked Erik with a shrug. "It came up in conversation."

"You mention anything to Josef?"

"Probably should," Erik realized he couldn't stop smiling.

"Well, it'll have to wait because we've got an arse-ton of work ahead. The villagers might get half a night's rest but feckin', I think you know better than to hope for that."

They spent the night working. Half of them pulled security while the other half assisted and supervised the men of the village in placing the obstacles. The goatherd's supplied fresh dung from the livestock and they smeared the stakes with it to ensure infection. "If we kill one, the others will drive on," said Thjostolf, "But if we maim one, it'll take two to evacuate the casualty. That takes three out of the fight. Simple math."

The work was backbreaking, and even in the cool of the night, they were pouring sweat. Gradually they began to fill the clearing, and when the second shift arrived, the razor-sharp forest in miniature, concealed by discarded leaves and mud, covered the better part of the area.

As they worked, they heard strange sounds issuing from the earth and the trees, and when it came to Erik's turn to watch the perimeter, he could just barely see the branches and undergrowth pushing up and into the clearings. Gabryl had been on the level, there was no doubt. Erik had never heard such groaning from plants. It sounded as if a strong wind was buffeting the boughs, but there was no wind. The first clearing they addressed was by no means small. It was the same clearing the griffins had landed in to stage for their first assault, almost five miles from the village, near the edge of the plateau. It was several hundred yards square, but as the minutes ticked away, the forest closed in. They called it "North Pitch," and the second clearing, further south and only large enough to land three griffins at a time, they called "South Pitch." As the sun rose, Erik saw that the clearing had already shrank. The first rows of stakes were now ten feet inside the wood line. At least now, at first light, the job here was done. The clearings were completely booby-trapped now, a deadly forest of hidden barbs. The first griffin to land would serve as warning to the rest.

At dawn, the villagers retired back to their homes, but the greenhorns and the Jomsskari remained. Thjostolf assigned Wendyll and one of the greenhorn gun crews to keep watch over North Pitch, which afforded a view of the sky west of the spur. The rest of them fell back into the wood line a hundred yards or so and took a breather.

Erik could see the greenhorns were hurting. They stared vapidly at their food, their eyes puffy, struggling to stay awake. Erik, for his part, was far too happy to care about his fatigue. Her scent was still on his collar.

The rest of the Jomsskari had apparently learned of Erik and Shayna's engagement, because as he was sitting and musing to himself they all rushed up and jumped on him. For several minutes they crushed him, whooping and hollering like playful wolves. Khalan spanked him for a while and then they made the mistake of letting him up. As soon as he was upright, Erik tackled Kolskegg and was winning until Brutus jumped in. Then they hog-tied him and told him that they were preparing him for a life of monogamous bliss. Peter and Khalan argued about which of them would be his "maid of honor". Wendyll, who had come up from the clearing only a few minutes into the affair, chose this moment to kneel down next to him and say, with his characteristically blank expression and in his perfectly level voice, "I wish you every joy, young doctor." Eventually, Thjostolf made them untie him, but not before he emptied his canteen into Erik's trousers.

After they had had their fun, they gathered their composure and returned to business. The experience hadn't dampened Erik's spirits at all, although he distinctly looked as if he had urinated on himself. The greenhorns, who had been almost as alarmed as Erik was, had moved some distance away, watching the Jomsskari with wary disapproval. Erik noticed Gabryl smoking his pipe beneath a tree a few yards off, a bemused smile on his face, and Edwin, sitting at his feet, was wagging his tail uncontrollably.

Thjostolf had just begun to brief them on their next project when the sound in the forest ceased.

They all froze.

A breeze blew gently. Only, it was not a breeze, though Erik could not explain why he knew it. Then Gabryl stood. His eyes were focused towards the clearing, and when he opened his mouth Erik heard not words, but the same breeze blowing, gentle but intense. For several minutes, the trees and Gabryl murmured to each other.

"The driads have seen the enemy," he said. "There is a flight of griffins reaching the foot of the mountain…Three strong, bearing six riders. They are coming."

"Rhys, take Khalan, Peter, and Wendyll and reinforce the gun crew at North Pitch," Thjostolf ordered. "Everybody else, we gotta feckin' beat feet back the village. You guys," he called to the greenhorns nearby, "You'd better keep up!"

They ran. Single file, rushing through the brush, sticking to the game trails the greenhorns had shown them. Erik could feel his lungs burning, tight against the altitude, but this was no time to give anything less than everything. The greenhorns were right behind them and they seemed to understand the urgency of the situation.

They covered the five miles to the village in just over a half hour, and tore across the fields in a full sprint. Erik saw Josef and Eidel emerging from their house ahead. As they broke out of the barley and into the square, he saw several others standing on their porches, their expressions taut, waiting for word.

Thjostolf was gasping, but he still managed to shout, "Raise the alarm! Griffins on approach!"

Erik retched, and when he looked up, he saw Shayna rushing to him.

"Are you okay?" she cried.

Erik waved her off, still bent double. "I'm good, I'm good! They're coming, you need to get to cover!"

He was only dimly aware of the chaos in the square, but he could see every detail on her face. Her eyes were wide with fear, and she turned and grabbed Sisel and they ran back into the house. Josef ran up to Thjostolf and they began talking intensely in low voices. He heard Kolskegg yelling to the greenhorns. "Get that machine gun here! Set it up – no, *inside!* Erik!"

"Yeah!"

"Pick up the south side, and get your dispersal!" Kolskegg shouted.

Erik waved to the first two greenhorns he saw and yelled, "Come on!" They ran south, to the blacksmith's shop. As they ran inside he turned to them and began to issue instructions. They began to set up their firing positions, and Erik saw that one of them was Asvald. The farmer was soaked in sweat and fumbling from the exertion.

He grabbed him by the shoulder. "Your sector of fire is from that fence to the edge of the barn. Do you see?"

"Yes, I see," Asvald spat angrily.

Erik didn't have time to be bothered by his attitude. He gave instructions to the other greenhorn, a farmer's boy named Yolf, the son of Oleg, and took a quick azimuth on the sectors of fire. Edwin bounded in a moment later and Erik told him to relay to Thjostolf that they had the bridge covered. Then he set up his own position facing the southern fields.

And then it was quiet. Erik checked the square and saw that it was empty. The missionaries were gathering in the central hall, while the Jomsskari had established a perimeter around the edge of the village. Thjostolf appeared from the north of the village and walked up to him.

"We've got our perimeter up," he said, still panting. "So now we just wait."

"Where are our guys?"

"Kolskegg's facing the wood line, and we've got a feckin' machine gun crew facing the landing zone where they touched down last time. The rest of us are placed around in feckin' interlocking fields of fire, so we've got the best possible chance of repelling."

He took a long drink from his canteen and went on. "I've already briefed the other guys, but feckin', we're not going to engage unless I sound the whistle. Make sure your guys are clear on that, okay? We want them to think the last team got lost. The longer they're in the feckin' dark about an Alliance unit on this mountaintop, the more time we have for reinforcements to feckin' get up here."

Erik nodded. "I'll tell them."

Thjostolf looked at him. "Where's Shayna?"

.

"Central hall, I think."

"Did you get to see her?"

He looked towards the hall, across the square, and felt an unfamiliar knot in his stomach. "Not really. But they'll be here any minute," he said ruefully.

Thjostolf looked at him for a moment, and nodded. "We'll be all right. There's only six of the feckers."

Chapter Twenty

The Probe, 4 July 1160

The sound of beating wings reached their ears only minutes later.

Erik couldn't see them. From his position in the blacksmith's shop, he could only see the southern shore of the river, and the goat pens beyond, but he heard them. The shriek of the griffins sounded to the west, close, no more than five hundred yards away. Moments later he heard a rush of wind, saw a shadow streak across the water, and then, only briefly, he caught the shape of three griffins wheeling over the southeast landing site. Then they turned again, climbing out of sight, and he heard them calling to each other above the central hall.

He glanced at Yolf and Asvald. Asvald had his finger inside the trigger guard, poor weapon discipline, a negligent discharge waiting to happen. Yolf, was wide-eyed, and his lips began to turn blue...

"Yolf!" Erik hissed.

Yolf startled, and looked at him as if struck.

"Breathe, man!"

It took a moment for Erik's words to register to him, then the farmer took a gasping breath, and returned his attention to his sector.

"Asvald, finger outside the trigger well."

Asvald shot him a hateful look, but did as he was told. Erik heard a shriek from the north, and then another from the east. They were circling.

The griffins continued to circle for several minutes, calling out to each other and making low passes through the village. Then, abruptly, all the sound stopped.

He held his breath, listening.

A cry came out from the northwest. They must have landing on the hilltop, where the assault team had landed for the assault.

He heard distant voices but he couldn't understand them. Then, after a few minutes, there was a flurry of beating wings that faded to the west, slowly, until there was nothing but silence.

They waited.

For several minutes, Erik remained in position, listening for any indication of the griffin's continued presence. Then he heard a snuffling, and a moment later Edwin slipped over the threshold and next to him.

"Master, they have gone. Thjostolf Captain is collapsing the perimeter. He's at the west edge of the square now."

Erik thanked him and, beckoning for the greenhorns to follow, he loped from the shop and over to where Thjostolf was standing.

Thjostolf had his rifle slung, and was talking in a low voice to Feodor. Erik overheard them talking about the next clearings, and prioritizing them. As he drew near, however, the half-elf captain turned and said, "Erik, how much time do you need to convert the central hall into a field hospital?"

Erik thought it over. "It won't take long to make it functional," he said after a moment's pause, "But we need it hardened. Sandbags, if we have them. The real issue is that I haven't got enough antibiotics and sanitizers to sustain more than a few casualties."

Thjostolf frowned. "How many?"

"I carry enough gear to sustain routine and priority injuries within the company," Erik responded. "Eight or nine casualties at a maximum. Now, we've recovered a few additional supplies from the raiding party the other day, but it's little more than a couple of IV's and a few bandages. It didn't appear as if they had brought a medic with them."

"Probably because they can evacuate their wounded so quickly," Thjostolf said, more to himself then to anyone else. "What can you do for urgent casualties?"

"I might be able to keep them stable for a few days, but we'd have to evacuate them as soon as possible. I'd say two or three days at a maximum, if I can stay on top of fluids and blood loss."

The rest of the Jomsskari had gathered, and the greenhorns were pressing in around them. Josef and Abraham emerged from the central hall and began to cross the square towards them.

"Okay," Thjostolf said, "Feckin', here's the situation. We gambled against engaging to try to conserve ammunition and keep them in the dark about the Alliance being up here. Well, I don't think the Alnethar bought it. They landed near the impact craters and if they know anything, then they know there was mortar fire here. Maybe we still get lucky and they think it's their own bombs but I'm not counting on luck.

"Looking forward, then, I want a feckin' choke point we can hold with the manpower we have, but there simply isn't one. Any position we can hold, closer to the top of the mountain, puts the village within mortar and howitzer range of an attacking force, so if we're going to feckin' hold this mountaintop without getting everybody on it killed, we need to evacuate the civilians."

"Leave our homes?" asked Feodor incredulously. "We have no desire to do so! And even if we were to comply, where would we go? To the lowlands? The Alnethar control that land!"

"You can do what you want, but I think every household is

going to have to decide for themselves on this," said Thjostolf flatly. "I'll make it simple for you: you stay, you die. If they haul big guns up here, I can feckin' guarantee that."

He turned to Gabryl. "I've got a question," he said, "And you're not going to like it."

Gabryl smiled. "I think I know what you ask."

"What's on the other side of Gob-Heshem?"

Erik glanced at Feodor, and noticed that the elder looked bewildered, as if Thjostolf had suddenly changed the subject.

Gabryl shook his head. "I do not know, captain. But I do know that the main gates of the city open to the southeast, looking down over the Wilderness. The entrance through the cave was neither original, nor designed for the griffins."

"What are you talking about?" demanded Feodor. Abraham and Josef had arrived by this time, and a look of concern had crossed all of their faces.

"How unfriendly is that troll?" asked Thjostolf, to Gabryl.

"Ulrich is not...prone to consider the needs of others, captain," the old wizard said tactfully. "Not unless there was something we had that he might want."

"Such as?"

Gabryl shook his head. "As I have said, Ulrich is not like any troll I have met. He is not enticed by money or gifts. His agenda has been a mystery to me for centuries. Indeed, I neither know where he came from, or what he did before I met him. It has been nearly three hundred-eighty years since we were first introduced, and his purpose still eludes me. But to save Stadfesta, I may have an offer he could take."

"Then do it. I want to evacuate the villagers through the

cave, through Gob-Heshem," said Thjostolf, "And out to the Wilderness. I don't give a damn about whatever else might be in that cave. Is that doable?"

Now Gabryl smiled in a humorless way. "I cannot say, captain. Until Ulrich has given his permission, even I would be most wary of crossing into his territory. I would not risk women and children in such a place. Ulrich would not hesitate to destroy them, for no reason but their intrusion."

Thjostolf shook his head and looked away. "You said you knew him?"

"Yes," Gabryl replied.

"Then contact him. Ask. Offer what you need to, just get us a route to the other side."

Gabryl nodded and, murmuring something to Edwin, walked away.

Thjostolf turned to the elders. "Where's Sigmund?"

"I am here," The fourth elder had come up undetected, and stood a few feet from the gathering, frowning.

"Okay, elders," Thjostolf said, "I want to make this clear to you. If those clearings are not booby-trapped within the next forty-eight hours, the Alnethar will move masses of soldiers and heavy weapons onto the plateau, where they will begin to shell the village. So, we need to accomplish two things really feckin' soon. The booby-traps need to be set, and you all need to start packing. I'll get with you all and discuss anything else you need from us, but for now I'm going to have my men begin building defenses. Are we all tracking?"

Everyone nodded.

"Okay, then," said Thjostolf, "Let's get to it."

*   *   *

A runner arrived from Rhys' position a half hour later. Gasping for breath, he passed a small piece of paper to Thjostolf, who read it over. Erik was helping Brutus gather fertilizer and carry it to the barn to the north, where the villagers had grindstones for the barley. As he looked on, he saw Thjostolf standing outside the central hall.

Brutus dropped two sacks from his shoulders and, seeing Erik's preoccupation, followed his gaze. "They have sent their report," he said factually. "Perhaps it will be good news, for once."

Erik nodded. "How long does it take to make this stuff into serviceable explosives?" he asked.

Brutus sighed. "It is not a difficult process, you know, though it takes time. I think, before the day after tomorrow, I shall have a few dozen pounds, why not."

"How low-grade are we talking about?"

"Quite." Brutus tore open a bag and ran his hand through the tiny pebbles inside. "Even with fertilizer produced in factories, ammonia nitrate is a low explosive, already. We can augment it with sawdust. It will increase the power and sensitivity of the material, why not, but at best it is still a pushing charge, not a cutting charge."

"So...what? Anti-personnel mines?"

"Perhaps. Though I have had another thought. Look," Brutus said, taking out his map. "Here are the game-trails along the plateau, the ones the greenhorns have shown us. You see?" He pointed to a prominent path leading across the northern edge of the plateau. "This pathway here, this is the only one that could support a clunker. Thjostolf has been looking for a bottleneck, yes? And here it is: one trail, and only one. Yes, I see, it will not prevent foot-soldiers from maneuvering, but it directs their vehicles, yes? And their heavy-weapons. We must plant a sizable charge in such a place, to destroy their armored vehicles, should they bring them up."

Erik didn't like the thought of it, "Clunkers."

"If they can find a path to bring them up the plateau, yes. I say, if I were to assault a position such as ours, I would greatly desire to bring clunkers, why not."

"Why not?" Erik nodded. "How much of this would you need to kill a clunker?"

"One hundred and fifty pounds, no less." Brutus was looking at the fertilizer grimly. "I will be fortunate to gather so much fertilizer as to make that much. But to disable one will require much less. It may be enough. We need only crack open the treads."

Erik looked back at Thjostolf. Gabryl and Edwin had come over to him, and they were talking together. Then Brutus piped up, "On an unrelated note, I was wondering. Of course, you and the young lady are betrothed now. But have you spoken to her father?"

Erik laughed, "Yeah, we talked about it a couple of days ago."

"So he gave his blessing? Most fortunate, most fortunate."

Erik raised his eyebrows. "Well, actually..." He hadn't thought of it; he was very tired, he wasn't thinking clearly. "I suppose he hasn't yet. He said he would give his blessing, but..."

Now Brutus laughed. "You ask her, without the blessing! My friend, you should speak to him, he should at least know of it. Go on, there are greenhorns to help me, and we must begin grinding."

Erik picked up his helmet and, setting it loosely on his head, he set off towards the cobbler's shop.

He found Josef staring dejectedly at a single pair of shoes. At Erik's arrival, he looked up and smiled broadly. "Erik Blood-giver," he said, "I wondered when you were going to come see me."

Erik set his helmet and carbine down. "Only one pair today?" he asked.

"There are more pressing matters at hand, I'm afraid," Josef said with a sigh. "But I find refuge in this. You know, I enjoy cobbling. I love to see my work on the feet of my friends."

He fixed Erik with a piercing look. "Shayna has been quite happy all day," he said, with an amused ring in his voice. "But she will not tell me why. Perhaps you can enlighten me?"

Erik was too exhausted for subtlety, "Well, sir, we got to talking and I, uh...I told her what you said, about how the time wasn't right. What with, you know, what you said about the seminary returning to its original purpose, and the war, and everything."

Josef nodded. "And what did my Shayna say to that?"

"She said she'd wait." Erik didn't quite know what to do with his hands.

Josef smiled, "She'll wait." He looked back at the shoes, and nodded to himself. "She'll wait." Then, with a chuckle, he murmured, "Oh, she has her mother's audacity."

"So, I suppose," Erik continued, when Josef had been silent for a moment, "That I'm here to ask you for permission to marry your daughter."

Josef didn't look at him for a moment. Then, lifting his gaze, he said, "She could do worse. I have two daughters. I suppose it's about time I had a son as well." He smiled, a little resignedly.

Erik nodded. "Thank you, sir."

They spoke for a few minutes more, chatting almost idly. Then, suddenly serious, Josef said, "I don't think Feodor will be pleased. You're no doubt aware."

"Asvald? Yeah."

"You should understand," Josef went on, "That Feodor and his household do not support your continued presence here. But I do not think it is because of Shayna. Feodor's concerns are higher than mere human relationships. He is far more distrustful of the Haellics than any of us. He has intimated to the rest of us that he does not consider your faith to be pure. He is afraid that the return of Haellics to our community will threaten our doctrines."

"Well..." Erik said, considering it. "He's not wrong. But I tend to think we were made to struggle. And if I recall, Brother Markko's chief complaint against the Appollonians was the stagnation of doctrine."

"Yes...We are aware. It has been a point of discussion these past years." Josef paused for a moment, and then said, "He's a good man, you know. Asvald. Competitive, and hot-tempered, perhaps, and set in his ways. But he is brave, a good worker, and he means well."

"Would you have given your blessing to him? If he had asked?"

Josef thought about it. "No," he said. "But not due to any fault in him. Shayna has never wanted him. I could not give my blessing to any union that would disagree with her."

Erik smiled. "Fair enough."

"Erik!"

It was Kolskegg. He peered in through the threshold. "You're needed," he said. "And you, Josef."

Thjostolf had gathered the soldiers and the elders in the center of the square. He still had the paper in his hand, and the runner, still sweating profusely, stood a few feet off. Their expressions were grim, and Erik braced himself.

When they had accounted for themselves, Thjostolf held up the paper and read. "This is a report from Rhys. 'Feldhall visible in binoculars. Currently engaged in battle with two battalion-sized elements. Enemy artillery largely ineffective, friendly artillery bracketing. Sighted three barges traveling east on the river towards our position. Unknown if friendly. Griffin scout flight returned north. Holding until further instructions.'" He folded the paper and, taking his pipe from his pocket, he said, "We don't know if our reinforcements are coming or not. But we do know one thing."

He lit his pipe and took a long draw. Then, the smoke billowed from his nostrils as he spoke, "If the Alnethar didn't know we're here before, they're going to find out. They will have to hold this feckin' mountain to shell the valley below. It's their best chance at directing accurate fire on our outposts along the river, which they have to do in order to encircle Feldhall and push us back into the damn ocean. The way I figure it, they've no time to lose. They'll be here in the next forty-eight hours."

"Any idea what sized element they'll send?" asked Kolskegg.

"No idea," said Thjostolf, "But we'll assume they'll send at least a company or more. They know we have mortars; they saw the feckin' impact craters. So, they'll bring artillery if they can – clunkers, if they find a way to roll up the mountain – and I'd guess no less than eighty infantry."

"Eshé-ma." Erik spat.

"The evacuation must happen within the next twenty-four hours," said Thjostolf. "We can only hold a force that size back for a few days. So, everyone not actively engaged in the defense, pack your bags. Jomsskari and militia, get all the ammo from the pack horses, and five days worth of rations. We're headed back to the forest, and we're not coming back until this is over."

* * *

Erik was able to see Shayna for only a moment before they left, as he was stuffing his pack with all the spare ammunition could. She ran up to him and threw her arms around his neck, and whispered, "Be careful," in his ear.

"You know I will," he said, and kissed her forehead.

He shouldered his gear, and they set off. The greenhorns all saw it, but Erik was far too preoccupied to care. In a few hours' time, none of that eshé would matter anyway.

They marched in silence, and returned to the clearing before noon. Brutus had stayed back to make the bombs, with the help of a few of the villagers, and Erik had left instructions with Oleg, Yolf's father, on how to fortify the central hall with sandbags and rearrange the kitchen and dining areas to form a make-shift hospital. The dwarf would rejoin them with the horses carrying the explosives, and send the horses back to help carry gear across Gob-Heshem.

Gabryl had stayed behind, too. Erik didn't know why, but he was sure it had to do with meeting the troll. Until that time, he knew they would have to rely on observation posts in the forest to detect the enemy. The language of the trees would not be an asset until the wizard returned.

They set up a patrol base in the dense canopy, placing their machine guns to the north, west, and south. To their northwest, about a mile, was North Pitch. South Pitch lay three-quarters of a mile to the southwest. It was just large enough to land a few griffins at a time and both had been booby-trapped heavily. These were the only two clearings that remained on the plateau. All of the smaller clearings had either been filled in by the magic of the driads or were too small to land in. From their base, they could maneuver to either or both of the clearings in a matter of minutes, and ambush the enemy as they landed.

They settled in and began their rest plan. Erik caught a few merciful hours of sleep before being awoken by Peter. Then he and half of the greenhorns kept watch until nightfall.

Under the cover of darkness, Thjostolf and Wendyll took several greenhorns to the southern clearing and continued to improve the booby-traps and their camouflage. They were gone for the better part of the night. The Jomsskari took turns walking the perimeter and ensuring that the greenhorns were not asleep. When it was Erik's turn, he was pleased to find that most of them were alert and vigilant. Asvald and Yolf, who were on the south side of the base, were talking quietly between themselves as he walked the line. When they saw him coming they fell silent.

Erik knelt in the darkness next to their position. "Everything good?" he asked in a whisper.

Asvald didn't look at him or say anything, but Yolf nodded. "All good, doctor."

Erik looked out over the dark forest and grunted. "That's what I like to hear. You holler if you need me."

Around 0330, Thjostolf's party returned to the base. Erik heard them reach the entry point at the apex of their perimeter, at the west corner, and whisper the password to the guards. A moment later they had joined him in the center. Thjostolf made sure all of his greenhorns had got a spot to sleep, and then turned to Wendyll. "You going to sleep?" he asked.

"I slept earlier, captain. I'll keep watch until the sun rises."

Thjostolf didn't seem to mind, and was snoring softly in a matter of seconds. Erik realized the half-elf hadn't slept since before the previous night. Kneeling in the darkness, Erik felt his own fatigue gnawing at him, but he forced himself to stay awake. He looked skyward.

He remembered the whimpering boy in the desolate village. He had found solace in the stars their first night on the mountain. He thought of the stars, and her company. For a moment, he stared up at them, fading as they were against the coming of morning, and pondered them. Eternal pricks of light...

It seemed that the long wait for eternity was coming to a close. Every moment he felt it draw nearer, felt the weight of death crushing down on him. And what better time to face death, than when he had at long last found something, someone. that he was willing to live for?

It was the Absurd. It was the futility, the descent into the deep. But her words echoed to him from the black. He reached for them, and found the smallest bit of consolation.

"I'll wait."

He found himself repeating the words, not to her, not to himself, but to God.

I'll wait.

The Absurd was less daunting now. He could never have found the "who" he had searched for in the dark. But the more he found himself loving her and forgetting himself, the clearer the shadow of "who" became. She could not provide the "who" any more than he could. But, the decision to love her, the conscious dedication to give himself to another, brought to light a fact that surprised him.

The "who" had be given up. Only then could it be seen, if only in shadow.

Perhaps there was something to it.

Nothing.

Nothing.

Nothing. Nothing, nothing, no thing, no one, no where, no why.

It was curiously like despair. Despairing of finding the who, the where, despairing of finding the God that could make sense of the who, the where, and even the why.

I'll wait.

Despair and faith. The lines between them were blurring, the nothingness blending seamlessly into somethingness – something intangible, but present nonetheless.

Despair and faith. Despair as faith.

Faith is despair.

Eternity may come. It may draw near, it may destroy all, death may devour him, but God, the trickster, the One Unsayable, did not ask that he understand.

Will you?

Yes.

I cannot say how long.

I'll wait.

Faith is despair.

*　　*　　*

They stayed in position all day, and the following night. It wasn't until daybreak on the next day, the sixth of July, that Wendyll called out from his roost in the treetops.

"I see a flight of griffins approaching," he said.

Thjostolf leapt to his feet, and all eyes turned to them. "How many?"

Wendyll didn't answer for a moment, peering through his binoculars with a look of intense concentration on his face. Then, as calmly as before, "Sixteen."

"Sixteen griffins," Thjostolf repeated to himself. "How far out?" he called.

"I cannot tell," said Wendyll, lowering the binoculars for a moment. "Maybe fifteen or twenty miles. It is hard to judge."

"Everybody check your ammo!" called Kolskegg, "Be ready to redeploy! Come on, people, this is the real deal!"

Erik strapped on his vest, checking his magazines and his gear. Then he and Khalan began checking the greenhorns, ensuring their weapons were loaded, inspecting their camouflage and their spare clips. As soon as they were all ready, they gave Thjostolf a thumbs up.

"Everybody, collapse in on me," Thjostolf ordered. "Get where you can see."

He drew a simple map in the dirt. "Let's go over this one more time, okay? Here's the clearing. Feckin', either one, we'll handle it the same. We set up with our three machine-guns providing a feckin' base of fire. Each gunner will have an assistant. Kolskegg, I'm putting you in charge of the base of fire element."

"IHO, cap."

"Maintain your feckin' dispersion and stay low because they are sure to bring bombs with them. Now, by my count, that puts four militia and three Jomsskari on the base of fire, correct?"

The machine-gun crews nodded. Erik noticed they all looked terrified, their faces ashen but set. He tried to remember their names. There was Georgi, a short blonde-headed kid, one of the gunners. Then there was Lenka, a broad-shouldered man of about twenty-three

360

years; he was Georgi's assistant. He couldn't remember the other gunner's name, but he was sure that the other assistant was named Pavel.

"I'll take Asvald, Ansel, Sacha, and Vladamir with me," Thjostolf continued, speaking to the militia's riflemen. "Yolf, Sergei, and Yuri, you stay with the base of fire. Understood?"

The greenhorns nodded dumbly.

"Erik, you'll be with me. Wendyll, I need you to provide precision targeting of their griffins in flight. Rhys, you and Hirsch will run your mortar from this clearing we discussed earlier. You've got both landing sites pre-sighted?"

"Correct, cap."

"My team, we'll be maneuvering. We'll set up on the feckin' south edge of the clearing. If they land, we feckin' flank. Stay with me, stay on line, and for feck sake, nobody – I'll say that again, nobody – engage until I do! We want as many of them stuck in the spikes as we can before we show ourselves."

He looked around. "Now, if they split their forces and try to land at both clearings, then we'll split our forces, too. Khalan, you and Peter will handle the northern clearing with Wendyll, Yolf, Sergei, and Yuri. Myself, Kolskegg, Erik and the remaining militiamen will break off to the southern clearing. This is our rally point, right where we're standing, in this patrol base. If any of us fires a red flare, that means we're being overrun. Break contact and meet us at the rally point here, at the patrol base. Rhys, if we do end up having to split up, wait to drop the feckin' mortars until you see the flare and target the position that's being overrun. Are there any questions?"

Erik raised his hand. "Just a point, captain. If they do split up, make sure you guys at the north clearing flank left, and we'll flank right. That'll keep us out of each other's sectors of fire."

Thjostolf nodded. "Anything else?"

Nobody said anything.

"Wendyll, you hear all that?" asked Thjostolf.

Wendyll didn't say anything, only gave a thumbs up. Then, "They've reached the base of the mountain. They're coming in from the northwest. It looks like they've got three to a griffin, with four griffins carrying bombs."

Thjostolf did some quick math. "That's thirty-six personnel," he said. "Where are they headed?"

"It is too early to say, captain."

"Keep me posted."

They sat in agonizing silence for a few minutes. Finally, Wendyll spoke again. "They are headed for North Pitch," he said. "I do not think they know about South Pitch."

"Keep eyes on 'em and let me know if they split," Thjostolf ordered. "Everybody else, move out!"

They formed up in the cover of trees, hidden in the thick brush at the edge of North Pitch. Even as they were pulling brush over themselves and settling in, they heard the griffin's calls, less than a mile away, echoing across the landscape. The clearing was almost two hundred yards long, and one hundred yards wide. It was easily large enough to six or eight griffins to land simultaneously.

Wendyll arrived as Kolskegg ran down the line, checking the headspace and timing on the greenhorns' machine-guns, and the two snipers bumped fists as they passed. The elf-sniper scurried up a tree, looking back towards Rhys' position, and then flashed Thjostolf a thumbs up.

The Jomsskari waited, but not for long.

They flew in high, two flights of six and a flight of four,

bursting up over the tree line. They were less than a thousand yards away when Erik first saw them, and they wasted no time. The first flight formed in a line, their riders visible on their backs, and dove down towards the clearing.

They are beautiful creatures, he thought. They were so majestic, and sailed so smoothly through the air, that even now, after having met them battle, it seemed surreal to think about killing them.

They wheeled around in a tight circle, descending rapidly, flared their wings, preparing to land.

Then an unearthly scream pierced the air. Two of the griffins near the center of the formation crashed cumbersomely to the ground. They had been stabbed by the spikes, meticulously concealed in the tall grass, and as they beat their wings in a frantic attempt to lift off again, they impaled themselves further. The riders were tossed, and Erik saw one of the Alnethar land on a stake, the sharp wood jabbing up. They were eighty yards away, but he could see the blood running down the wood, the tip raising up above the elf's shoulders, and the body quiver for a moment before it fell limp.

The other four griffins heard the screams and broke off, but not in time. One of them was already too low; his wing caught the tip of a stake on the down thrust and he shrieked in pain. Erik watched as the beast faltered, the weight of his riders and his own momentum dragging him down. He, too, collapsed onto the stakes and lay screaming.

The Jomsskari, ever patient, held their fire.

There was pandemonium in the sky. The three downed griffins were crying for help, and those still in flight circled helplessly, calling to each other in hoots, trying to decide what to do. The bombers, who had been near the back of the formation, began to climb, wheeling around and around, searching for a target to unleash their hatred upon.

Erik saw the greenhorns to his left and right, sweat dripping from their faces, unmoving and tense, watching Thjostolf for the order to fire. Thjostolf was still. "Let them try to recover their wounded," he said softly. "Then we hit 'em."

Two of the Alnethar had dismounted between the stakes, and began to disperse, pulling security towards the forest. Another dark-elf, his leg bleeding, began to shout to the sky.

Finally, as the elf issued commands, the griffins began to organize. Two of them began to fly low, slowly circling their stranded comrades. Then one of the riders dropped two ropes, and the griffins began to hover, beating their wings frantically.

The wounded Alnethar began to secure the ropes to the saddle of one of the wounded griffins.

"See," Thjostolf said softly, "They'll teach us their tactics, if we let them."

Another griffin began hovering, just behind the first two, and its riders threw down ropes as well. Erik watched in awe as the Alnethar on the ground began to slowly, painfully push the wounded beast up and off the stakes. After a few moments of struggling, one of them fetched an ax from the saddlebags and began to chop the griffin free, while the other two struggled to hold it steady.

The griffins above, with great effort, began to pull the injured one upwards.

It rose, a few feet at first, and then ten, fifteen feet into the air. Big droplets of blood dripped onto the elves below. The wounded griffin's wings were shattered, its body pierced a dozen times.

The other griffins were flying low, screeching encouragement and direction. Only the bombers maintained a safe distance, circling overhead, watching.

Thjostolf turned back to Wendyll and nodded. *Do it.*

A single shot rang out from the brush. One of the hovering

griffins simply went limp, falling like a rock, and with a terrified scream the others were dragged down by the weight of two, crashing into the stakes below. There was a sickening *splat* of wood against flesh and the scream was cut short.

At once, the entire line opened fire. Bullets raked the air, striking another griffin, and Erik squeezed off a shot at one of the stranded Alnethar and saw him fall heavily to the ground.

Shrieks of anger filled the sky. Six of the sixteen griffins were now dying on the spikes, and with them, nearly half of the enemy element, but the rest were now transformed. The griffins began to wheel about sharply, beating their wings like a swarm of wasps. The Alnethar immediately began to shoot, and Erik heard the *snap, snap, snap* of bullets passing close to his head. They were accurate, and well-disciplined, and they immediately tried to rally themselves for an attack.

At his side, Asvald worked the action on his captured rifle, lined up and fired. Erik saw that the shot was good. Another Alnethar fell, struck squarely in the heart.

There was no cover in the clearing. One after another, the Alnethar and griffins trapped on the ground were shot. Erik looked up towards the sky, looking for a target, looking for –

"Bombers!" he shouted, "Take cover!"

The bombers were in a dive already, straight towards the machine-guns, their wings tucked back, hawk-like. One after another, they dropped their ordinance.

There was a massive concussion, the shock of an explosion. Then there was another, too far into the clearing to be effective, but Erik still heard the rattle of shrapnel cutting into the leaves above his head. The third detonation was deep in the forest, but the fourth landed directly in the middle of the machine-guns.

Two of the guns stopped. Only one continued to fire. Erik

prayed it was Khalan who was shooting, prayed that his brother was safe. He didn't even realize that he was reloading, didn't notice himself put his front sight on the chest of an Alnethar that staggered forward bravely, his mouth open in a shout. He only became aware of it when his own gun sounded. The Alnethar stumbled but did not fall, and their eyes met. Erik saw a look of fury on the elf's face, his lips contorted in pain, his tan uniform torn and bloody. The Alnethar was not young; he had the look of an old salt, with a thin moustache and old scars. Despite the chaos, the stinging smoke of the bomb blasts and the gunfire, Erik noticed every detail about the elf: his watch chain in his jacket, his freshly shined boots, and a wedding band on his finger...

Erik fired again, and again, but the Alnethar kept struggling forward. his eyes were wild and his mouth uttered his final battle-cry, until one of Erik's bullets struck him in the belly and he collapsed, shuddered, and lay still.

The machine-guns sounded again, all three of them. Their chatter erupted in defiance of the bombs. Over the din, Erik heard the shrieks of the creatures, and saw the remaining griffins bank to the west and vanish over the treetops. Those that could were fleeing the field.

"Shift fire right! Shift fire right!" The order came from Thjostolf, and it echoed down the line. The machine-gun tracers shifted, and Thjostolf shouted, "Forward!"

Erik leapt to his feet, and the greenhorns jumped up with him. "Stay on line!" Erik shouted. They pushed forward, into the clearing. "Watch your lane," Erik called out, "Don't collapse! Stay on line, damn it!"

The greenhorns were displaying their inexperience. They tried to follow Erik and Thjostolf instead of covering their sectors, clustering into a tighter and tighter group, and only by such repetitious reminders did they keep their dispersion and cover the whole clearing. Erik slipped in and out of the stakes, and when he came up on a dead enemy, he shot them where they lay. As they went, they called, "Lift fire!" to the machine-guns, and the chattering stopped.

One of the Alnethar was propped up on a stake, next to a griffin. His eyes were glassy, but he was breathing, and raised his trembling hands up, his weapon at his knees. Erik shot him twice and passed him by. He caught the sight of Asvald staring at him in horror, but there was no time to talk about it. The griffins, for their part, were certainly dead. Their mangled, bullet-ridden bodies dripped blood across the ground.

They passed the last corpse and kept moving, clearing to the edge of the kill zone. Erik could hardly believe how fast it had been. They had only been in contact for a few minutes. It was a good ambush, decisive, violent, and aggressive.

They reached the far edge of the clearing and called out, "Limit! Limit!" Then the base of fire pushed through the clearing as well, and when they had reached the far side, Kolskegg came running back to Thjostolf. Erik was close enough to hear him say, "We've got two wounded, but it's all routine, just minor shrapnel injuries. Between eight-hundred and a thousand rounds left for the machine-guns, all equipment accounted for."

"We'll get more ammo from the corpses," said Thjostolf. "Wendyll! What do you see?"

Wendyll's voice came from the tree line. "They're regrouping! Two thousand yards to the west!" A few moments later, he came running up. "Captain, with your permission, I will advance to within eight hundred yards and engage from them a distance."

"Kolskegg, go with him. Feckin, everybody else, salvage weapons, ammo, and any feckin' medical equipment from the dead! Machine-gunners, redeploy and pull security. Get to it!"

*　　*　　*

Kolskegg and Wendyll ran through the forest.

"They are landing in the clear ground, on the draw before the plateau," said Wendyll. "They are no doubt attempting to account for their lost personnel and equipment."

"We've got high ground and cover," returned Kolskegg, between gasps for breath. "You target officers, I'll target machine-gunners. Two volley's, then we displace and reevaluate. Sound good?"

"Certainly," Wendyll replied, ducked under a fallen tree, and fell silent.

They ran for another few minutes, until the ground began to slope downwards. Then, slowing to a cautious creep, they spread out to ten yards apart and pushed forward.

The vegetation broke, and Kolskegg saw the draw below. The river path they had negotiated coming up the mountain was to their left, and Kolskegg saw that the north side of the draw was decently clear. *They might be able to drive a clunker or two up that hill.* After this engagement, that would no doubt be their next move.

There they were, a small perimeter, in a rocky outcrop by the edge of a waterfall. The elves had dismounted and the griffins were catching their breaths. The two Jomsskari dropped to their bellies and slithered forward, their cloaks fading into the shrubs around them.

Kolskegg looked through his scope. There were nineteen elves that he counted, with two machine-gun crews and three officers. The griffins were foaming, like race horses at the end of their track, and the elven officers were gathered together, yelling angrily at each other and waving their arms in frustration. They were debating what to do next.

Wendyll called softly, "I've got the officer with the braids."

Kolskegg found him. Yes, he looked like he was in charge. He was consulting a map, and gesturing emphatically with his free hand. When he spoke, the others quieted down. That was the one they needed to kill.

Kolskegg scanned the perimeter. Both machine-gunners were facing the mountain, in good cover. But the sniper's superior elevation made their enemy's cover useless. He could clearly see his target, the heavy-set one, with the touches of grey in his hair.

"Range?" he called.

"I estimate 1100 yards." Wendyll was calm.

Kolskegg scanned the ground. "I read 1200 even," he said, still catching his breath. "Let's call it 1150...I've got the heavy-set gunner, the one on the left. I'll try to get the other gunner with my next shot."

"Very well. I have some mirage in my scope. Wind at target, seven miles per hour, three-quarters value. Wind at shooter, five miles per hour, half value. We have an updraft from the terrain."

"I read the same." Kolskegg began to adjust his scope. "Gyroscopic spin will move the impact about one minute of an angle to the right, facing due west. So, remember the Coriolis effect..." At this range, they had to adjust the scopes to compensate for the spin of their bullets and the rotation of the earth itself – long range precision shooting was as much science as art.

He consulted the bubble level on the side of his scope. Wendyll had a pad of paper out, ready to calculate.

"Downward angle is 36 degrees, range 1150."

Wendyll did the geometry. "Corrected bullet flight path will be 930 yards."

"Is your bore cold?" Kolskegg asked as he dialed in the last adjustments and settled in behind his weapon.

"No, it should be fine." Wendyll sounded bored. "Fire in three."

Kolskegg started counting. *Breath in...one...breath out...two...hold breath...three.*

His finger pressed the trigger, the recoil pushed against him, and the report of the weapon sounded in his ears. As his scope settled back on target, he saw the maelstrom of air, swirling for a second behind the speeding bullet. And then, it swallowed the gunner, striking him in the throat.

"Hit," he reported, as he worked the action.

"Hit," replied Wendyll. Then, "Hold fire, hold fire. Something's not right."

Kolskegg saw that his target, still struggling weakly as he bled out, was being attended by his assistant, who was trying to pull him to cover and render first aid. It would be useless. Even from this distance, Kolskegg could see the characteristic spurting from his target's carotid artery. He continued to scan the perimeter for the threat that Wendyll had found. It took a moment, but then, the glint of sunlight on optics. He saw an Alnethar sniper, laying low in the brush, trying to find the source of the shots. "Sniper, far right," he called. "In concealment, by the holly bushes."

"I'll take the shot." Wendyll let out a breath, and fired. Kolskegg watched the bullet sail, and strike the enemy sniper in the top of the shoulder. He vanished an instant later, slumped behind his cover. A perfect kill.

"Displace," Kolskegg ordered. As they slipped back, the Alnethar scrambled back to the griffins. As the two snipers faded back into the forest, they saw the whole flight take off and streak towards the north as if the devil were at their heels.

And then, something caught his eye. He raised his weapon to his shoulder and looked down to the valley to the north, looking to see what it might be.

"Oh, feck me," he said.

*   *   *

Erik was supervising the greenhorns as they stripped the ammunition and weapons from the enemy. There were easily another two thousand rounds for the machine-guns, and hundreds of rounds for the rifles. Hand grenades were in plenty, too; these elves had come far more heavily armed than their predecessors. They found a medical bag, packed with bandages and IV's, and some bottles containing some kind of drug that Erik suspected was a pain killer. He didn't have time to revel in their finds. They had to get away from North Pitch, before the enemy called in an artillery strike on their position. They had already lingered too long.

They fell back to the rally point, linked up with Rhys and Hirsch, and began to redistribute their ammunition. The greenhorns were chatting animatedly to each other, and Erik noticed that Asvald was grinning almost stupidly and trembling. It was the post-battle euphoria.

"Asvald!" he called.

He looked up and, seeing Erik, his joyous expression changed to a sneer.

Erik ignored the attitude. "I saw you drop that fecker - nice shot!"

Asvald couldn't help himself. He grinned again and said, "Thank you."

"You all did well," said Khalan. "Damn proud of each of you!"

They established a perimeter and waited for the snipers to return, but there was a new flavor to the air, the taste of victory. The greenhorns were loving it. Keeping their voices low at the urging of the Jomsskari, they traded adulation and all of them, without exception, had the look of one who has been thrilled beyond their imagination.

In the distance, they heard three distinct shots, and then, silence. That was a good sign. That meant the snipers had engaged and slipped away.

Half of them pulled security, while the other half cleaned their weapons. Erik was checking the wounded. Kolskegg had been right; the worst injury was a piece of shrapnel in Georgi's thigh, but the wound was superficial. As he was bandaging the hole, he saw Asvald come up from his post and kneel a few feet off.

"What's up, Asvald?" he asked, without looking up.

There was a moment's pause. Then, "Georgi, how are you?"

Georgi shrugged. "It's not so bad. It feels like a bee sting."

"Yeah, you'll be fine," Erik said. He finished the bandage and rose. "Clean up that weapon real good, and make sure you have the headspace and timing right, okay?"

He turned to go, but Asvald cleared his throat. "Doctor?" he asked.

"Yeah, what's up?" Erik didn't really want to talk to him.

Asvald was looking at him as if he didn't know how to start. Then he said, "Why did you shoot that man?"

Erik tried to think of which one Asvald was referring to.

"The wounded one, the one that surrendered." Asvald was

trembling still from the excitement, but his face was taut and bothered. "Why didn't you take him prisoner? Why didn't you help him?"

Erik blinked. For a moment, he thought about why he had done it. It was obvious to him, but he had never tried to explain that mindset to anyone before.

"Well, think about what we'd have to do if we were to take him prisoner," he said. "We haven't got enough guys to keep guard over him, and any soldier worth his salt will try to escape. That's what I'd do, if I was captured. I'd use every last breath I had to try to escape. That means somebody would have to babysit him, instead of fighting the fight. And besides, I haven't got the means to keep him alive. I'm sure not using what little medical resources I have to keep an enemy alive. Feck that. You'll see what I mean once we start taking real casualties. And that's all assuming he didn't have a grenade in his hand; he might have tried to take us with him. Goblins did that all the time in the Belvade. Hell, I'd probably do it myself rather than risk capture. Beats getting tortured, and it's an honorable death."

Asvald looked at him blankly, and Erik felt a pang of humanity.

"Don't dwell on it now," he said, softening. "We'll have plenty of time to think about that later. Believe me, you'll have the rest of your life to figure out if *how* you survived was the right way. For now, just do what you have to do so you can have that time."

"It isn't right. We should be merciful."

Erik shrugged. "Yeah, well, mercy's a tricky concept. You spare the enemy's life and he takes your compassion and kills you with it. Then they break our lines and kill your whole village. That's not merciful to the guys to your left and right and it's not merciful to the folks back at Stadfesta counting on you." He glanced towards the perimeter. there was movement coming from the west. It was Wendyll and Kolskegg. "You gotta remember," he went on, "War isn't anything like how we were created to be. Right and wrong get so blurred out here that most times you can't tell them apart. It's either do the bad thing or do the worse thing. So just trust me, don't dwell on it. Now go on, get back on the line," he said. "We can finish this talk later, if we live long enough."

Wendyll and Kolskegg had just passed by the line, and they beckoned for the Jomsskari to gather. Erik went to join them. Asvald stood silent for a moment, watching him go, before slowly heading back to his position.

"Captain," said Kolskegg, as they all drew in, "I've got good news and I've got bad news."

"What is it?" asked Thjostolf, tapping his fingertips against his knee.

"The good news is, we engaged the enemy on the draw and killed their commanding officer, a machine-gunner, and a sniper. The bad news is, as they withdrew, we saw a column approaching from the north. From what we can see, there's a clear and level enough approach on the northern half of the spur. They have access to the mountain, and at the rate they're going, they'll reach the plateau by sunrise."

Thjostolf pursed his lips. "How many?"

"Four clunkers and seventy infantry, give or take a few."

"Feck!" Thjostolf wasn't smiling any more. For a few minutes he sat still, thinking. Then he spoke, "Okay, we need those explosives Brutus was cooking up."

Erik noticed the greenhorns on the perimeter craning their necks to eavesdrop. They couldn't hear what was being said, but they could tell from the look on Thjostolf's face that something had gone wrong.

"We'll engage them as they try to get up the draw, where the forest really starts to close in and they can't disperse their damn firepower," Thjostolf said after a moment. "There's only one feckin' trail they can take, right? So, we get the explosives, bury them with a fast fuse, and then meet them ahead of the bomb. Once they engage us, we break contact and fall back. They roll over the bomb, we set it off, then they can't use their clunkers because the road is blocked. They'll have to tow the clunker out of the way, and that'll take time and manpower away from the fight. Meanwhile, we engage them at their flanks and isolate their feckin' infantry, cut 'em up bit by bit and hide back in the forest."

"Cap', Brutus didn't think he could make enough to kill a clunker," Erik pointed out.

"We don't have to kill it," said Thjostolf, "We just have to disable it. A kill is better, but we can work on that as we go."

The Jomsskari all nodded.

"We'll win this fight if we can split them up and feckin' cut off their communications," Thjostolf went on. "Inflict such catastrophic casualties on them that they have to withdraw. Feckin', we killed eighteen Alnethar and six griffins in the clearing today, and three more Alnethar in the draw. That's almost two-thirds of their force. We keep pressing 'em like that, we'll win this fight. We'll have 'em so scared on this mountain they can't get their foot soldiers to march forward. Mark my words."

They organized themselves into teams. Thjostolf and Erik led a group with a machine-gun crew and one rifleman. Khalan and Peter took charge of four more riflemen. Kolskegg and Wendyll were to alternately snipe the enemy and direct Rhys' mortar fire, while Thjostolf dedicated the remaining two riflemen and the last machine-gun crew to go with Brutus when he returned. Gabryl and Edwin would accompany Thjostolf. This gave them three teams, each with a machine-gun, and a mortar crew. They planned to establish a supply cache at the patrol base, and alternate engaging from all sides. While one team engaged, one of the others would refit and regroup, while the third team moved into position.

They would be able to rest, while the enemy would not. They would be able to replenish their ammunition, while the enemy would be at a loss. *A thousand tiny cuts.*

It was nearly nightfall when Brutus and Gabryl arrived. Edwin came trotting ahead, panting doggishly and his eyes fixed rigidly ahead. Behind him, the dwarf came, leading the two horses laden with four large bags each. Gabryl was behind, and the four elders were with them. There was a fifth man that Erik did not recognize at first. Then, as they drew closer, Erik saw the look on Edwin's face. His lip was raised and a low growl sounded from his throat. Gabryl walked serenely, but Erik felt the tension palpably.

The man was dark-skinned, over six feet tall, and strongly built. He wore a simple great-kilt, and was barefooted. His bald head gleamed in the failing light. Erik saw his expression; he was bored, almost, as if he did not care at all about what he saw. But it was his eyes that betrayed him. They were black as night, beady, just as they had been when he had shown himself as a field mouse. It was Ulrich.

Chapter Twenty-One

The Letter, 6 July 1160

Thjostolf had never seen the troll, but Erik knew he would not miss anything. Sure enough, Thjostolf only looked at him for a moment before he said, "You must be Ulrich."

The troll smiled, a charming and strangely disconcerting smile. When he spoke, his voice was deep, rich, and articulate, as if he already commanded total authority over everything he laid eyes on.

"I have been called by that name, yes," he said. "And you are Thjostolf, son of Skarp-Hedin, the half-breed who has made...quite a commotion on my doorstep."

Thjostolf extended his hand in greeting. "We asked the enemy to die quietly, but they were uncooperative. I am so sorry for the commotion."

Ulrich laughed – a dark, cruel laugh, one that lingered in the dusky air – and did not take the captain's outstretched hand. "I have spoken to my old friend, Gabryl, but these were mere pleasantries. We have yet to discuss business. The time has come for war, I see. Rest assured your struggle is of no concern to me; yet, it is true that we have some common interests. The Alnethar are quite a nuisance, and I would prefer if they were...kept from occupying this mountain."

Thjostolf smiled and replied, "Then we are in agreement. But before we proceed, I have a request that only you can fulfill."

Ulrich raised an eyebrow.

"I know you have something of value in the caverns of Gob-Heshem, and I assure you that I could not care less. Your business is yours and yours alone. Gabryl might care," Thjostolf added, "But the Alliance of the Five has no such interest. This mountain is populated by an innocent group of unarmed civilians. In the upcoming battle, many of them will be killed unless they may escape. All I ask of you is safe passage for the people of Stadfesta through Gob-Heshem and to the Wilderness beyond."

Ulrich was silent for a moment. Then, cocking his head in an animal kind of way, he said softly, "I'm afraid that I will not suffer anyone to pass through the caverns. For Edwin's sake, I spared your men when they trespassed, but I will not be so merciful in the future."

There was a tense silence. Josef and Sigmund, standing a bit aside, murmured to each other, while Feodor and Abraham stood silently with their arms folded. Then, Thjostolf sighed and looked at his fingernails. "I have no interest in dying to protect Gob-Heshem from the prying eyes of the Dark Elves. If I cannot evacuate the village through the caverns, I suppose I must withdraw from the mountain altogether, and bring the civilians down the river."

"You cannot," Ulrich spoke flatly, but his black eyes gleamed.

"You leave me no choice," replied Thjostolf. "My priority is to protect these descendants of Haellic citizenry."

"That is not your purpose," said Ulrich disdainfully. "Do not dare lie to me. I know of your mission. There is strategic value to this mountain, in many ways. You have been ordered to hold it against attack. Otherwise you would have withdrawn two weeks ago."

Gabryl stepped forward. "Ulrich, we are responsible for both objectives. We only ask that you guide the people through Gob-Heshem, thereby ensuring with your own eyes that the treasure you protect –"

"I have given my answer!" Ulrich snarled. "We may have a common enemy but that is the limit of our comradery! I am not running a charity for pathetic beings facing their overdue extinction, and you will not convince me by appealing to your infantile concepts of morality!"

"And what of the dragon's egg?" asked Gabryl, his voice unshaken. "The heir of Irkalla? You have laid claim to him, have you not?"

"That bears no relevance," said Ulrich, and turned to leave.

"If you cannot help us, then you will either face the armies of the Alnethar or the armies of the Alliance," said Gabryl matter-of-factly. "If, as you say, our comradery is so shallow, then I suppose I must inform the Haellic commanders of what you guard. I'm sure they would have as deep an interest in the dragon-prince as the Alnethar. Clearly you have seen the opportunity to control his fate. Do you believe the Alnethar, or the Five, will not?"

Ulrich spun around and glared at him.

"You speak of Irkalla as if you read about him in a book," he spat. "And you presume too much of my motives."

Gabryl smiled calmly. "You do not know what I presume."

"You are in danger of my displeasure." Ulrich pointed at Gabryl and let out a long, low growl. "I will not succumb to blackmail."

"Then enlighten us," said Gabryl. "What do you need?"

"I need nothing from you."

"Yes, you do," Gabryl said. "Your anger betrays you. You hate Irkalla – curious, as I have never known you to feel strongly about anyone, not even the Master. So perhaps it would interest you to know that it is my mission to destroy the dragon."

Every eye swung to Gabryl. Erik felt his mouth grow dry. *Another secret?* And this was no small matter.

"It is commanded of me," continued Gabryl, his voice now soft, "By the Alliance of the Five, and by the Master Himself."

Thjostolf took a step back, looking back and forth between them as if they had both lost their minds. "What the feck are you on about?" he hissed.

"You would kill Irkalla?" asked Ulrich. There was a look on his face, a look of surprise, even consternation.

"Yes," Gabryl replied.

"He is not easily killed."

Gabryl nodded. "It is your desire as well, is it not? But you have not done it yet. I suspect it is because you are not able to do it alone."

Ulrich looked at him for several minutes. Then, almost imperceptibly, he nodded.

"The Demon-Dragon is strong," said Gabryl. "But the enemy of my enemy is my friend, is he not? You see, we have more in common than you wish to admit."

Ulrich looked around, his eyes settling on the Jomsskari. "You have already brought a company of warriors."

"It is not their mission."

"Yes, it is." Ulrich smiled, the same cruel smile, almost triumphant. "Yes, you brought them at the authority of the Five Monarchs. They wear no unit patch. They wear no banner, no names, as is the custom. These are not ordinary soldiers, and they have no ordinary purpose. You brought them to die in Gob-Gerra, to give their lives to this endeavor."

Gabryl looked at him for a moment, then at the Jomsskari. They all stared at him expectantly, their faces taut with anticipation.

And then, taking a deep breath as he did, the wizard reached into his pocket and produced a small, worn envelope. It was sealed in wax five times, with the royal seals of the Five Monarchs: the Haellic seal in brilliant red, the Iaelian seal in deep blue, the seal of Humbridge in purple, the seal of the Dionysians in white, and the seal of A'kaylii in black. Almost reluctantly, he extended it to the captain.

Thjostolf snatched it from his hand and tore it open. Then, with a suspicious glance at both the wizard and the troll, he began to read:

To Gabryl, Slave of the One Unsayable, Bond Servant to the Master,

From the Five Monarchs, convened in secret this 3rd Day of December, in the Year 1159.

Greetings to you from A'kaylii, Iaelia, Haelhan, Humbridge, and White Mountain. We have prepared a unit of men, elves, dwarves, halflings and orcs, the greatest warriors within our realms. We have equipped them as best we could in accordance to your humble request. Of these warriors, we have selected the best company to perform their duties as you require them. This company is under the capable command of Thjostolf Captain sen Skarp-Hedin, and all within the unit have displayed the virtues of courage, brutality, wisdom, and honor. We have deemed them worthy of the glorious task you must accomplish.

With this letter bearing our seals and signatures, we entrust to you all governing authority and all command over the Second Company of the Jomsskari until such a time as you see fit to release them from service. Henceforth, Second Company of the Jomsskari shall be dedicated to you and you alone. All previous orders and commands shall be rescinded at your discretion. Moreover, Lord Hoskuld has been informed of this directive, and will defer command of Second Jomsskari as you require them.

May you ride on the wings of the wind, and may the One Unsayable remember your prayers in life and death.

Thjostolf stood, the letter held in front of him, staring at it blankly as if he could not comprehend what he was seeing. Then, his jaw tight, he said, "It bears the signatures of our kings."

Erik was reeling. He saw Brutus sit down on a log, his lips pursed. They were all looking at Gabryl.

Ulrich stood, smiling as he had before, his teeth gleaming and his empty eyes surveying the scene with satisfaction. "Not the friend you took him for, is he?" he hissed, his voice almost serpentine.

At long last, Gabryl spoke, not to the troll, but to the Jomsskari. "You have all been the best of companions for these long months that we have spent together," he said quietly. "You are all good men. It is true that I have been granted the authority to command you. But the task to kill the demon-dragon was given to me, and me alone. I will not order anyone to accompany me. I will only ask. If any of you would refuse to go, I will neither judge you nor will I allow your overseers to judge you. I will personally release you from my service, this very moment, and give you a letter in my own hand to carry back to your king, detailing each exceptional act of valor and courage you have displayed."

"What are we volunteering for?" asked Peter.

"To come with me to Gob-Gerra and kill the dragon," said Gabryl simply. "The task is immensely difficult, and dangerous, but it must be done, and I do not believe that I can do it alone. But you are my friends, and I cannot command you to take such a risk. I will leave it to each of you to decide."

He turned to Ulrich, and his tone hardened. "I must warn you, Ulrich, that my mission does not include you or your priorities. If you wish to join me in killing the dragon, then you must help us. You must allow these people to pass unharmed through your realm."

Ulrich shook his head mockingly, and sneered. "My old friend," he whispered, "You are as foolish as ever. You risk all for the weak, when you ought to cherish the strong. When you command the strong, you permit them to be weak at their leisure." He paused, considering, and then, a wry smile crossed his face. He said, "Very well. They may pass through Gob-Heshem. But I will accompany you on this mission. We will kill the dragon together. And the egg shall be untouched by the Alnethar and Alliance alike. You are bound by your word, Gabryl. Swear to me that the foolish kings who have trusted you with their minions will not learn of the child, and I will allow the village safe passage."

Gabryl extended his hand, and Ulrich took it. "I swear that much and no more."

"We have an accord, then," said the troll. Then, abruptly, he turned to the elders. "I will open the mountain tomorrow," he said tersely. "Have your people ready by then, for I will not keep it open for long. There is a steppe at the opening of Gob-Heshem, a wide plateau with fields and rivers for your flocks, forests for building, and safety from the Alnethar. You will find what you need to live there." He looked back at the Jomsskari, and, with a sly smile on his face, said, "And to you, good hunting."

Before their eyes, he began to change: melting like a candle, his colors changing, he was shrinking down. Almost before Erik could understand what he was seeing, the man had transformed into a hawk, which, sounding the same cruel laugh, shot upward into the sky and vanished over the trees towards the village.

The Jomsskari sat in silence. After a few moments of awkward silence, the elders excused themselves and, taking the pack-horses, they turned back and began to return to their homes. Gabryl called to Edwin and they moved some ways off, talking together in low voices. Thjostolf waited for them to get out of earshot, and beckoned everyone in. They formed a close huddle and Thjostolf passed the letter to Rhys, who read it and reread it several times before passing it down the line.

Nobody spoke for several minutes. They were all trying to process what had happened. Erik, for his part, almost felt like laughing.

They had been abandoned.

Their kings had turned them over to another, gifted them without so much as mentioning it. It was strangely like being defiled. Erik felt that a part of him had been taken away, that whatever trust he had started to regain in the Alliance had shriveled up in that instant. He shook his head.

"It bears the signatures of our kings," murmured Thjostolf.

"We swore an oath to our kings," said Peter. "We are bound to obey."

"I don't believe they'd sign this," said Kolskegg. "I can't believe they'd –" He silenced himself, and shook his head. "I'm sorry," he said presently. "Peter is right. We were always expendable. We just never knew how much."

"We can back out," said Thjostolf.

They all looked at him, waiting for him to speak, waiting for a word from their captain.

"We have that option," Thjostolf went on. "We can back out. We don't have to do it."

"What, let Gabryl go alone?" asked Rhys.

"I'm just saying it's an option," their captain replied.

"Perhaps…However, we have been tasked with such a mission for a reason, yes?" said Brutus. "We have unique training. We were specially selected; we know this better than anyone, yes? Gabryl has been with us this long. If he goes alone, who is to say he would return?"

"He's not one of us, Brutus," said Rhys gently. "We don't

have to give our lives for him."

Wendyll smiled, and began to hum a tune.

Erik didn't know what to think. "It's clearly important," he said.

Everyone looked at him.

"I mean, the letter bears the signatures and seals of each of our kings," he continued. "Think about that. Everything the Jomsskari stand for, everything we are, was made for this mission. And we were selected above all the others."

"It is a high honor," said Khalan. "I would be grateful for such an opportunity."

"I am not honored by a suicidal death," murmured Kolskegg.

They sat in silence for a few minutes. Then, Peter cleared his throat.

"I'll go," he said, "but only if the rest of you do. I say it's all of us, or none of us. We're the Jomsskari, and we need to stay together."

Thjostolf nodded. "I agree."

They all murmured their assent.

"Here's my thinking on the matter," continued the captain, "Feckin', we don't have to decide now. Probably best if we don't, seeing the magnitude of it and given we've got a feckin' full strength cohort of clunkers and infantry knocking at the door. I mean for feck sake, until we get relieved up here, it's feckin' irrelevant anyway."

They all nodded, and Thjostolf stood. "So, let's get this trap set, shall we?"

Putting the distant future out of their minds, they agreed and began to prepare their ambush. Brutus had managed to manufacture some eighty-five pounds of ammonia nitrate, and they decided to place the charges on the backside of a small rise in the clunker's path. The plan was for the driver to be unable to see where the charge was buried until the clunker had already rolled on top of it.

Brutus began to prepare the charges. He took three of the fertilizer bags, just over sixty pounds, and tied them together so that they formed a bundle. In the center of the bundle, he placed a block of the Jomsskari's high explosives and primed it with a detonator connected to a rope of det cord.

"Det cord," he explained to the watching greenhorns, "is filled with a powdered explosive, so that it is flexible, why not. You see," he went on, wrapping the entire bundle a few times in det cord and leaving a fifteen-foot length laying out, "The bombs I have made are not sensitive enough to explode from a mere blasting cap, so I must add a booster charge. That is detonated by the detonator, yes, which is detonated by the det cord, to which I will attach a blasting cap. I will set off the blasting cap with a fast fuse."

He added another booster charge and more det cord, and then they buried the charge in the spot they had selected, leaving the two lengths of det cord leading off to the brush on the left side of the trail. "Always prime twice," he said with a wink.

Erik and Edwin camouflaged the charge, covering it was about two inches of dirt, and then covered that with leaves and twigs. Then they sprinkled loose dirt and leaves over the det cord, until it disappeared into the brush.

Brutus found a firing point, about two hundred-fifty yards from the charge, where he had a clear line of sight to where the blast would occur. Then he walked about in the forest, cutting the bark from trees, so that he could judge the speed of the approaching vehicle, and aim his detonation.

"I've tested my fuse," he explained. "So, I know that this length of fuse will take five to seven seconds to burn that distance. In case the first fuse fails, it is coiled around a second fuse. I will light both at the same time, you see? So I will lead my target, wait until they are six seconds away from the charge, and light. It burns, the det cord blows up, and in turn, the main charge will destroy the target."

The rest of them established a firing line a few yards forward of Brutus' firing point, on either side of the trail. They had divided into their three teams. Thjostolf, Gabryl, and Erik took their team on the right flank, while Kolskegg, Wendyll, and Brutus' team occupied the left flank. Khalan, Peter, and their team were to lead the enemy into the trap. They were to set up a small position on the slopes, fire a few shots at the lead element, and then break contact and fall back by running down the trail. Once out of sight of the enemy, they would break off and circle south and west, and take up a position in the forest near Brutus' element. Once there, Khalan's team would provide rear security for the ambush.

Some of the greenhorns were skeptical. "How can you be sure they'll take the bait?" asked Pavel. "What if they smell the trap, and find another route?"

Peter answered him. "You would be surprised how unclearly people think then they've been shot at. It's a simple ruse, to be sure, but there are no other paths."

"But why not just let them come? Why shoot at them?"

"As soon as they are nearing the top of the plateau I want them feckin' stressed," said Thjostolf. "They need to be looking over their shoulder every second they're up here, and I want them burning their ammo reserves from the get go. But Peter is right, we scouted this land coming up, and there are no other trails that could support a feckin' clunker. Gabryl has assured me that the driads have blocked any other inlets, as well. Feckin', if they want a different path, they'll have to carve one themselves, and that could take weeks – weeks they don't have."

They were gathered in a circle, and sat in silence for a moment. Then, gingerly, Yolf raised his hand and spoke, "Captain?"

"What is it, Yolf?"

"What's a clunker?"

It took several minutes to explain to the greenhorns what they were up against, and when they were done, the greenhorns lapsed into a shocked silence and traded wide-eyed looks. It was nearly midnight, but Thjostolf ordered the teams into position. With a terrified look at their friends, Yolf, Ansel, Sergei, and Sacha followed Khalan and Peter down the trail, and the rest of the teams fanned out of the flanks and began to camouflage their positions. By 0100 that morning, they had settled in, and lay waiting. Kolskegg and Wendyll had advanced to the edge of the plateau, where they lay, watching over Khalan's bait team. Wendyll sent back word that the clunkers had stopped at the base of the mountain, and so they lay in place throughout the night.

Gabryl and Edwin had joined Thjostolf and Erik, as well as Asvald, Dimitri, and Pavel. Erik took over the machine-gun so that Dimitri and Pavel could sleep the first shift, and Edwin came and joined him. For an hour or so they lay in silence, staring into the black. Even if they weren't maintaining noise discipline, Erik wouldn't have known what to say to the wolf. There were too many things in his mind to organize them, too many things unknown, too many questions that vied for answers.

The trees groaned. Gabryl had begun to cast more spells over the forest; he said they would make the trees stronger, and bring briars and vines up from the ground to channel the enemy towards the ambush's kill zone. Erik could hear the whispering breeze of the driads speaking to each other, and felt an occasional warmth, as if an invisible body had passed close by him. He supposed it was the tree-spirits, and tried not to dwell on it.

Edwin broke the silence as the moon began to set. "You must be very angry with Gabryl."

Erik, surprised by the voice at his side, took a moment to answer. "I don't know what I think, Edwin."

"You know he is a good person," said Edwin, almost pleadingly. "Whatever else you may think of him, I ask that you remember that."

"I know," Erik replied and reached over to scratch the wolf's ears. Edwin's tail began to wag gently.

"I just don't understand why he didn't tell us earlier," Erik went on. "Did he not trust us?"

Edwin woofed doggishly. "He trusts you all implicitly," he said. "And I cannot hope to speak for him. But I have thought that he wanted to be absolutely sure that he needed you before he brought you along."

"What do you mean?"

"I only mean to say, master, that this mission is exceedingly dangerous. Ulrich speaks of Gabryl as if he is weak for choosing to love his friends, but there is far more strength in what Gabryl does than the troll could ever know. Greater love has no man than he who lays down his life for his friends."

"You quote the scriptures," Erik said with a smile.

"Yes, sir."

Erik was quiet for a few moments. Then a thought occurred to him. "So, you're saying that he needs us?"

"I am sure he would not trouble you if he did not, master Erik."

"But he still expects to give his life on this mission?" asked Erik.

"The dragon has many demons, master Erik. That is trouble you've not known."

Erik looked at him. "Have you fought a demon before?"

Edwin nodded. "It is our only purpose here, sir."

"Huh," Erik wasn't sure what to say to that. "What...what is a wizard, Edwin?"

Edwin looked up at him and replied, "He is an angelic being, sir."

"Angelic?"

"Yes, sir," Edwin replied

"Like, he's an angel?"

"There are many kinds of angels, sir. Some are given to serve at the Master's table, others are given to guard his people, and a very few are given to take physical form and live on this world."

"And Gabryl is one of those few?" asked Erik.

"One of seven, sir."

Erik nodded slowly. "Seven wizards?"

"Yes, sir."

"Can he die?" Erik asked.

"Only the Master cannot die, sir," Edwin replied.

Erik was silent.

"Do not trouble yourself with these things, master Erik," Edwin said kindly. "I have served Gabryl for centuries, and I cannot tell you more than I have. It is all mystery, you see. It is above our ability to know."

Erik chuckled. "Spoken like a faithful servant, Edwin."

"Thank you, sir." The canine's tail thumped enthusiastically, and Erik decided not to tell him that his comment had been sarcastic.

*   *   *

Shayna had spent the last few hours packing bundles of barley and wool. Around her, friends and family worked feverishly. The children watched the proceedings with wide-eyed enchantment. Never before had the village been so busy. In clusters of ten or fifteen, small working parties tackled different tasks. She didn't know how they would get the flocks across the lake, but her father said the magician – this Ulrich – was making arrangements. She put it out of her mind and focused on her work. Others took stock of the tools, the saws and hammers, axes and adzes, and the drills they would need to rebuild their lives. They had no idea where they were going, but it seemed that they must flee or die.

She tried to keep her mind off of Erik, but she couldn't. Her heart felt like a stone in her chest, heavy and pounding. She was determined, though, to be strong. Even now, she felt eyes watching her; eyes like her mother, and dear Rachel, and Anya, her cousin.

As night fell, her father came to her and laid his hand on her shoulder. "Take Sisel," he said. "Go across. I'll see you tomorrow."

He was exhausted, but his face was as kind as ever. She embraced him and, taking a bundle of her belongings and her sister's hand, she went to the lake and climbed aboard the last raft.

Grigori the blacksmith, and Andrei and Hindelle were aboard, with Rachel and several of the young men. Hindelle looked weak, but far improved. She leaned on her cane and smiled warmly to all around her. If not for the bandages, Shayna would never have guessed that she had recently been shot.

The voyage across the lake was quiet. Hardly anyone spoke. By the time they reached the cave, it was dark. As they disembarked, Shayna looked up and saw a crow sitting on the stone. It looked at her appraisingly, and then flew into the cave.

Each of them carried a torch in hand as they entered the cavern. Rachel walked beside her. As the sky above disappeared, replaced by the stone ceiling, she said, "Shayna?"

"Yes?"

"Do you know where we are going?"

Shayna shook her head. "I'm afraid not."

Rachel was silent for a moment. "I'm scared."

Shayna reached out and took her hand. "Me, too," she said.

Eventually the path grew narrow and low, and they had to stoop to walk. As they went, they chatted quietly, about nothing in particular.

Then Rachel said, "Shayna? Is it true, about you and the doctor?"

Shayna blushed in the darkness, and felt herself smiling uncontrollably. "Is what true?" she asked.

"Come on, now, don't pretend you don't know."

Shayna looked back at her, and laughed. "It is true."

Rachel squeezed her hand. "Do you love him?"

Shayna considered. "I think I do," she said presently. "I mean…all that I know of him, I love."

Rachel was quiet for a moment. Then she said, "You've always been bold, you know."

"What? How so?"

"When you decided to study midwifery you never gave it a second thought," said Rachel. "You never considered any other specialty. Nor have I ever seen you think about what to eat, or what to drink. You just do things. Whatever you like, you like, and that's that."

"Are you reproaching me?"

"Of course not," said Rachel. "I just...I don't understand."

The path opened up, and the ceiling suddenly soared above. For a moment they stood, dazzled by the lights of Gob-Heshem. Shayna had never seen buildings larger than the meeting hall before. The dragon's pillars captivated her. Beside her, Rachel gasped, and they all stood, transfixed at the edge of the darkened chasm between them and the city.

She had been staring for quite some time before she realized that the crow was with them. She was certain at once that it was the same crow, for it was regarding her with the same clinical detachment. All at once, it flew into the air and across the chasm. Beneath it, a brilliant structure appeared, straddling the space between the two cliffs. It had an ethereal quality to it, like light passing through pure ice, and before her eyes it became quite solid; a bridge, materializing from thin air.

They crossed, a little carefully at first, and then with delight. As soon as they were over, the crow returned, circling in tight wheels overhead. It then landed in front of them, and spoke in a deep, rich and cruel voice: "Follow me."

They did as they were told. The crow led them through buildings and squares, and they strained their necks looking up and down, gazing at the structures and murals in fascination. Soon, though, the novelty began to wane, and the fatigue began to set in. They rested for a time, and then pressed on.

Finally, they reached a long, dark corridor that seemed to extend into an empty sky beneath the mountain. At the end of this corridor they smelled the fresh air of the outside world, and moments later, felt the wind on their faces.

Ahead, across a darkened plateau, they saw campfires

burning. As they went on, she heard a voice at her ear, and felt the crow alight on her shoulder.

"You – what do they call you?"

She felt her blood chill at his voice. "Shayna," she replied. She hoped her voice didn't tremble.

There was no reply. Ulrich took off again, wheeled around, and disappeared back into the mountain, leaving her standing in the cool air. Beside her, Rachel grasped her hand. "What was that about?" she asked.

Shayna shook her head. "I don't know."

*   *   *

By sunrise, the clunkers had resumed moving. Gabryl spoke continuously to the trees, and reported their movements throughout the day. About midmorning, the Alnethar unit halted for half an hour, and then backtracked almost a mile and circumvented a pathway that was apparently too steep for their tracks. At noon, Wendyll reported that there were five clunkers, not four, and no fewer than a hundred infantry divided into two companies. Two of the clunkers lead the way, with a thirty-man element sweeping ahead and twenty men on the flanks. The other three clunkers lingered some two hundred yards behind with another fifty men forming a berth on the flanks and rear. Thjostolf moved up to Wendyll's position and watched them for about an hour. When he returned, he went to Brutus' position first, and then returned to his place.

"They're taking their time," he told Erik. "But I sent coordinates to Rhys. If they don't take the bait and start cutting south, we'll drop some feckin' mortars on them and see if we can't get them to make some quick, foolish decisions."

"I'm okay with that," Erik replied. "Do they have mortars?"

"We think we see a three to five tube battery moving with them, but feck, they could be grenade launchers or spare ammo for the clunkers. Anyway, if there are mortars, they still can't target us without a spotter, and we'll make short work of anyone trying to run corrections up and down the line. It'd be different, perhaps, if they had any feckin' griffins, but we haven't seen any so far."

"Maybe they can't convince the griffins to return," Erik offered. "They're superstitious about this mountain, and they've taken heavy casualties every time they've come up here."

"Well, we can always hope," Thjostolf said, and slipped back down the line to his hole.

Erik could hear the clunkers now, their churning engines echoed in the distance. Every passing minute they grew louder. Then, just before 1500, he heard machine-gun fire. It was Khalan.

"Get ready," he hissed to the greenhorns.

Dimitri charged his machine-gun.

The Alnethar returned fire. Erik could hear the high-pitched cracks of their rifles sounding over the edge of the plateau. Khalan's machine-gun fired another burst, and then he heard shouts, indistinct and distant.

He took a drink from his canteen, and noticed the greenhorns imitate him. Then he settled in, chewing absently on a stalk of grass. He wanted a cigarette, but he only had enough tobacco left for one more; besides, he didn't want to give them away with the smell.

Wendyll's rifle sounded once. The seconds passed, agonizingly slow. There was another volley of fire from Khalan's team, much closer this time. They were breaking contact.

There was an explosion, just on the other side of the hill, then another, and another. A tower of dust and smoke rose into the air.

Erik glanced at Gabryl. The wizard was still, his eyes darting back and forth over the ridge ahead.

Two silhouettes emerged, running full tilt, and then another. They dropped down and began to shoot back towards the advancing clunkers, and then another three appeared off to the right, and the six of them came sprinting down the trail, hidden from the enemy by the landscape.

Khalan was limping slightly, and Erik saw that as they passed by their position, Yolf was bleeding from the head. He made a mental note of it; they were all running, so they didn't require immediate attention. *Fight the fight, then tend the wounded.*

"When we break contact," Thjostolf called, "I want Erik and the machine-gun crew to go first! Peel right and cover our retreat!"

"IHO, cap!"

The ground began to shake. The clunkers were getting close. Ahead, Erik heard elven voices shouting. Wendyll and Kolskegg appeared out of nowhere, just ahead of Brutus' line, and flashed some quick hand signals. *Infantry dispersing. Clunkers driving up the main road.*

Erik sank lower into his hole and flipped his safety off.

For a moment, there was nothing. Then, several silhouettes appeared over the ridge. The Alnethar scouts moved forward cautiously, leap-frogging in teams of two, a few yards off the trail. They advanced about a hundred yards and disappeared behind the rise. Then, the sound of the engines erupted loudly in their ears, and the first of the clunkers emerged.

Chapter Twenty-Two

The Clunkers, 7 July 1160

Erik could only see the turret and the main gun before it stopped. It was a massive machine, larger than the clunkers Erik had seen in Haelhan. Atop the turret, the commander peered through a pair of binoculars, hidden slightly behind a machine gun on a pintle mount. They were staying as concealed as they could; the commander was being cautious. He clearly recognized the disadvantage of the terrain.

A whole minute passed by. Then the Alnethar scouts appeared over the rise, just a few yards from the bomb. They stayed low, and scanned the brush. Erik saw one of them looking at his position, and took a long, slow breath, willing himself to be still.

The Alnethar looked away.

One of them turned, and waved the clunker forward.

There was a grinding of gears, and the steel beast lurched onto the trail. A row of infantry followed close behind, using the clunker as cover.

Asvald's mouth was open, his eyes wide. Dimitri was trembling, and beside him, Pavel had his eyes shut, muttering prayers under his breath. Erik couldn't judge them. He was apprehensive, too, though he knew he wasn't showing it. It wasn't safe to show fear in combat, especially with such inexperienced men at his side. They were watching him, he knew it. They were looking to see if he was afraid. Fear was poison. Fear was a guest that, if entertained for even a moment, would tear a man apart.

He glanced at them. "Psst!"

They all looked at him, and he grinned.

"Time to get murderous!"

They grinned weakly in return, and Erik turned his attention back to the matter at hand. He looked at the scouts. They were past the bomb now, completely unaware of what they had just walked over, and getting closer to the firing lines. They were only a hundred yards off now.

He counted them, there was eight, bounding over each other. A small enough element to handle. That was Khalan's job. He was setting up a rear security position, circling around behind the rest of the Jomsskari to watch their backs. The scouts would be past the firing line before the clunker was attacked.

The clunker disappeared behind the rise, less than four hundred yards off. Another clunker emerged over the lip of the plateau, followed by more infantry. For a few moments, Erik could only hear the first clunker, the sound of its growling engine was growing louder by the second. The earth was shaking, trembling under the advance of the steel brutes.

The enemy scouts passed by the Jomsskari positions. They looked around fruitlessly, and continued bounding forward. They were wearing the same khaki uniforms as their predecessors, but had cloaks, cloaks that shimmered ever so slightly as they went...cloaks like the Jomsskari carried. They kept moving, down the trail, and Erik hoped that Khalan's team had gotten into position to cover their backs.

The clunker crested the rise. Out of the corner of his eye, Erik saw a small fire light at Brutus' position.

One.

The clunker's treads reached up into the sky, and the whole thing crashed down over the edge of the rise.

Two.

The scouts were almost fifty yards past the Jomsskari' firing line, but Erik couldn't think about them. There was a clunker.

Three.

The clunker's treads crushed everything in its path, snapping branches, the sound of it like a throbbing headache, rattling and roaring.

Four.

The clunker was on the bomb, and the clunker commander was out of the hatch again, binoculars raised to his eyes.

Five.

It needed to go off, it needed to go off *right now.* The clunker was still rolling and there was no explosion.

Si—

There was a flash of light, smoke, dust, and the clunker was lifted several feet into the air. It was so loud that Erik felt the impact in his gut and his helmet jumped from his head –

"Fire!" Thjostolf had already started shooting, and then Dimitri began to shoot, his tracers arcing through the brush and into the kill zone. From the other side of the trail, Brutus' team was shooting, too. The tracers crisscrossed into the infantry behind the clunker, and Erik saw them fall en masse, shivering with each strike. In a matter of seconds, he saw no less than fifteen souls depart. It was surreal.

The Alnethar infantry dispersed into the brush on the sides of the trail, just as Rhys' mortar began to fire. Erik shot an elf over two hundred yards away, and shouted corrections to Dimitri. "Bring it right! Right! Okay, good, get those guys! Watch your tracers, you're shooting high! Feck yeah, bust 'em up, right there!"

A blast from a mortar round landing among the Alnethar

sounded on the left side of the road. Erik heard Khalan's gun opening up behind him, and then Erik felt a sharp pain in his shoulder, like a burning knife had stabbed right through him. Crying out, he ducked down and tried to get a look at it. He had been hit, an Alnethar bullet had found him. Blood was running down into his armor, hot and sticky.

"Feck! Arse, Thjostolf, I'm hit!" he shouted.

There was another mortar blast. Thjostolf shouted above the din, "How bad?"

Erik struggled to keep his head in the fight. "I'm okay!" he shouted back. "Flesh, no artery!"

There was blood on her scarf; he untied it hurriedly and stuffed it into his pocket.

Edwin appeared beside him, and laid a paw on his back. "Let me see, master."

Erik swore profusely. "Check for an exit wound," he said between clenched teeth as he pulled gauze from his kit. "What's it look like?"

"Bright red blood, master," Edwin said. "There's an exit wound directly behind, about the size of an acorn."

"Is it spurting?" Erik asked.

"No, master."

The Alnethar were reacting aggressively, and pressing the attack. In the center of the trail, the clunker had ground to a halt, the treads gone on the left side. Smoke billowed from the rear of the vehicle, and the frame had bent upwards. The turret began to traverse towards them. Someone was still alive in there.

"Displace!" shouted Thjostolf. "Dimitri, get your arse outta there!"

The main cannon fired.

To his right, Erik only saw dust. His ears popped, a tree splintered, he felt the heat across his back, Edwin yelped, and sharp pangs spread across his legs. He looked over at Dimitri's position.

They were gone.

His ears were ringing, and he noticed that the sound of battle had grown strangely dim. He couldn't see any part of them, they were just *gone*. Dimitri and Pavel, their machine-gun, they were all gone. In their place, he saw a shallow crater.

Erik snapped into action and shouted, "Asvald, feckin' move!" He leapt to his feet. The pain in his legs intensified and he stumbled. Edwin yelled at him, "Master, they've gone, they've fallen back!"

Erik glanced back and saw them running into the brush, all three of them. They had displaced in time. *Thank God.*

"Cap, machine-gun's falling back!" he shouted.

"Go!" Thjostolf yelled.

Erik fired another burst and turned. Dimitri and Pavel were setting up their machine-gun, fumbling with the ammo belt. Erik saw Asvald, kneeling behind a tree, loading another stripper clip into his rifle. Thjostolf and Gabryl had jumped up, too, and they all fell back. Behind them, another mortar round detonated.

Erik saw bodies in the trail, and realized that it was the scout element. Khalan's gun had stopped firing, they were clear to the east. As they reached the line, Erik threw himself into a ditch and began to check his legs. There was no blood, only bruises. He was okay.

"Asvald, get over here!" he shouted.

Asvald arrived a moment later, and stared at his wound. "What happened?" he asked.

Erik thought it was a stupid question. "Here," he said, shoving a wad of gauze from his medical pouch into the boy's hands, "Pack this in the hole in my back. Get in in deep."

Asvald did as he was told, and they quickly it bandaged. "Make it tight," said Erik. "Are you hit?"

"No, I'm okay."

"Dimitri and Pavel?" Erik picked up his carbine and began firing.

Asvald glanced back. "They got knocked over but I think they're all right."

"Break contact!" shouted Thjostolf. "You three, go! Circle to the other side of the feckin' trail, we'll consolidate and hit 'em again!"

"Go!" shouted Erik. "Get out of here!"

The Alnethar infantry were forming a perimeter around the clunker. Erik could see the crew leaping from the wreckage. One of them emerged screaming, his body in flames, and fell to the ground. Then, with a sudden *whoosh*, a pillar of flame erupted from the top of the turret before dying down. Like a funeral pyre, the clunker burned.

They circled around the bend, crossed the trail about five hundred yards up, and linked up with the rest of the team. Rhys and Hirsch arrived a moment later, carrying the mortar tube and base plate. Erik checked everyone for injuries. Dimitri and Pavel had both taken shrapnel all over their bodies, but only a few shards had broken the skin. Khalan had twisted his ankle running up the hill, and Yolf had been grazed by a bullet. He was thinking that they had done quite well until he checked on Brutus' team.

Vladamir was dead. He had been shot in the top of the shoulder and the bullet had torn through his subclavian artery and his lung, and had come out the hip. He had bled to death while they tried to get him to the rally point. Erik saw Asvald leaning against a tree, tears streaming down his face.

He came over to him, and knelt beside him. Asvald refused to look at him. For a moment they were silent, and then Erik said softly, "Don't dwell on it."

Asvald didn't reply. Erik saw the young goatherd's rifle leaned against the tree. Taking it, he pressed it into Asvald's hands. Asvald looked up at him.

"Get your head right. We can mourn later but now we have to fight. Can you do that?"

Asvald nodded.

"Good." Erik slapped him on the shoulder. "You did well today, you know."

He turned to check on the others. Yuri was covered in blood, but it was Vladamir's. He was crying, too, but he managed to speak. "Can we return him to the village?"

Gabryl looked at Thjostolf. "I can send Edwin to fetch two litter bearers, and they can bring him home."

Thjostolf nodded. "We're going to relocate to the patrol base," he said. "Meet us there."

Edwin bounded off into the brush, and the rest of them picked themselves up and headed south, finding refuge in the dense forest.

They located their patrol base and began to refit on ammunition. Thjostolf sent Wendyll, Khalan, Peter, Yolf, and Ansel to scout the enemy positions along the trail. The rest of them ate quickly, cleaned their weapons, sent a few men to refill everybody's canteens, and waited.

Wendyll's team returned in less than an hour. "They're trying to clear the clunker out of the trail," he reported. "They've established a narrow perimeter, but the trees are closing in around their positions and breaking down their communications between positions." He drew a simple map in the dirt. "These were our position here, when we sprang the ambush, and here is where their positions were. At our first contact, I shot and killed one of the drivers as they advanced up the draw, and we killed the one clunker with the bomb. I only see two other clunkers on the trail. I do not know where the last clunker is."

"How many men?"

"On the trail, captain? Fifty, give or take a few. I believe that we killed or wounded about twenty." Wendyll took a drink from his canteen and tapped the ground. "They're sending out scouts to try to locate us. Ten to twelve man elements, each with two machine-gun teams."

Thjostolf nodded. "A dead driver isn't going to stop the clunker, and I bet they'll use their periscopes from now on. If I had to feckin' guess, I'd say they split forces and have two clunkers and their remaining infantry looking for another way in. They're probably going to establish a base of operations and try to goad us into a straight fight. How many mortar rounds do we have?"

Rhys checked his notes. "I have another thirty-three rounds of high explosive, and ten rounds of white phosphorous, cap."

"We need to send a couple of mortar rounds into their positions every hour or to make sure they don't sleep. We take two teams out and try to isolate and kill their scouts. They'll break contact when they see us, so we need to feckin' anticipate their movements and start whittling them down."

He looked around at the rest of them. "My team and Khalan's team will start off," he said. "Khalan, you and your guys need to hang back and maneuver as necessary. We will move in a traveling overwatch. When we get back, my team will rest while Khalan's team takes point and Brutus' team provides overwatch. We keep rotating, two shifts on and one shift off. Rhys, Wendyll, and Kolskegg, figure out a rest plan to put a spotter out there and drop rounds on them. And if you get the opportunity to put some effective fire on their infantry, feckin' do it, but don't waste a round."

He turned to Erik. "You're going to be pulling double duty, okay?"

"I got it, cap."

"Remember," he said, to all of them, "If anyone is taking significant contact, or getting overrun, pop one of your red flares. Rhys, when you see a flare, you need to drop rounds on that position. Our rally point is South Pitch. Anyone left at this position needs to gather as much ammunition as they can carry, destroy the rest, and feckin' beat feet to the rally point. Any questions?"

Nobody said anything.

"First leg, get your gear together and be ready to leave in five minutes."

Edwin arrived a few minutes later, with two of the villagers. They took Vladamir's body and headed back into the brush. There was no time to mourn their loss, but Erik was pleased to see the change in Asvald. Asvald didn't look frightened anymore. His face was set.

They formed up and Brutus counted them out of the patrol base. With Edwin leading the way, they set out.

They moved slowly. Edwin sniffed the air frequently, his was tail low and his ears pricked up. They pushed north, towards the clunker trail. Once they were about three-hundred yards from the clunker trail, they turned west, moving parallel to the enemy's avenue of approach. Erik noticed that there were no birds anymore, they all seemed to have realized that this part of forest was no longer hospitable.

They hadn't gone more than a hundred yards when Edwin froze and sank into the ground. Then, he turned, pawed his nose, and pointed to the southwest, off to their left.

Thjostolf slipped up and they whispered quietly. Then the half-elf returned to his place in the center of the formation and signaled to Khalan. *Contact left. Flank left.*

Khalan's team picked up and vanished into the brush to the south. Thjostolf waved his team forward and they continued, stalking through the brush, to the west for about fifty yards before turning sharply to the south. They were boxing the enemy into a close ambush.

Erik heard a voice, then, Alnethar rifles, and machine-guns, dead ahead. A moment later, Khalan's team returned fire.

"Move up! Push right, Edwin!" called Thjostolf quietly.

Erik could see muzzle flashes ahead, and saw that the Alnethar were forming a firing line. They would break contact at any moment.

"Get on line!" hissed Thjostolf. "Hurry the feck up!"

They were less than seventy-five yards from the Alnethar. Erik took cover behind a tree and saw one of the Alnethar machine-gun teams ahead. They were packing up their weapon and preparing to pull back.

The Jomsskari opened fire. To their left, Khalan's team was laying down heavy fire, and Erik saw that one Alnethar had already been killed. Tracers crisscrossed the forest like angry bees.

"Get 'em, boys!" shouted Thjostolf. His voice had a bizarre, childish quality, as if he were enjoying himself immensely.

The Alnethar reacted quickly. Seeing that they were being flanked, they began to return fire against Thjostolf's team, bounding back into the concealment of the forest. Bullets snapped and hissed past Erik's head and the trees above showered them with bark and leaves from the onslaught. Then a single flare shot up into the air, bring orange, burning above the treetops.

"They're calling for fire! Break contact, break contact!" shouted Thjostolf. "Peel left, peel left!"

The fire fight was already over. In a matter of seconds, the Alnethar had fled west, and the Jomsskari were running back to the east. They linked up with Khalan's team and got a quick headcount. "No wounded, plenty of ammunition left over," Khalan reported.

"How many did we get?" asked Thjostolf. "Could anyone tell?"

Khalan said, "They had at least two dead and another wounded. We saw the litter-bearers picking up their casualties." He nodded to Sergei and smiled. "This one here shot their machine-gunner in the eye. He should spend some time with the snipers."

There was a whistle, and an explosion some distance behind them. Thjostolf glanced over his shoulder. "They're mortaring where the flare landed," he said, and began counting explosions. "That has to be at least a three-tube battery," he concluded. "And they're firing accurately, too. These guys are good."

Erik smiled. "Not good enough."

"Well, now we know we can't feckin' occupy any position they held," Thjostolf said.

"Where to, cap?" asked Khalan.

"Feckin', let's cut south and pull back east," Thjostolf said. "Asvald, do you know the game trails around here?"

"Yes, captain."

"Take point with Edwin. Get us on one and take us back towards the village for a couple hundred yards. Then we push north again and see if we can't engage another patrol."

They circled the area for another couple of hours, doubling back every so often to ambush anyone trying to follow them. Finding nothing, they pushed up towards the clunker trail and found some high ground where they could see what was going on without exposing themselves.

The Alnethar were deployed about fifty yards off the road to the left and right, and had a pair of machine-guns set up on the trail, a hundred-fifty yards ahead of the disabled clunker. The Alnethar were trying to push the burned wreckage from the road with the undamaged clunker, but it was proving difficult. Some of them were trying to hack down trees to circumvent the obstacle, but it seemed that Gabryl's incantations had been effective.

"Why did it catch fire?" Erik wondered out loud. "Brutus didn't think eighty-five pounds would do the job."

"I guess the belly is weak," Thjostolf replied. He was watching the enemy through his binoculars; they were nearly seven-hundred yards from the clunker. The rest of the team had formed a perimeter around them. "It looks to me like we set off their fuel tank and that cooked off their incendiary ammunition. That's the only thing I can think of that would make that fecker burn like that."

Erik was beginning to feel the weight of fatigue on his body. As they lay in position, he checked his wound, and found that the bleeding had stopped. He changed the bandage, assisted by Gabryl, who murmured a few words in a strange tongue. "It will aid in the healing," he explained. "And ward off disease."

There was a whistle, and a mortar round landed in the clunker trail, off to the left of the disabled clunker. The Alnethar began shouting to each other, and then another round landed in the forest to the right side of the trail. Rhys had begun his harassing fire routine.

There was a long silence, and Erik heard the Alnethar shouting. He noted characteristic stress in their voices: a high-pitched timbre, and a fear that was audible, even from so far away. Someone was calling for a medic.

"Let's pull back, circle to the southwest, and try to get eyes on those other clunkers," said Thjostolf.

The sun had set, and darkness was growing fast. The Jomsskari were set in at the edge of the forest overlooking the plateau, almost a mile south of the clunker trail.

Below them, three hundred yards off, an Alnethar clunker struggled with the terrain. It was stuck in a ditch where the stone had crumbled away beneath it, leaning at almost a forty-five degree angle. One side was completely off the ground. A second clunker had hooked up a tow bar to the back of it and the two of machines strained against the force that held it in. Thjostolf had been right, they were looking for another way in, and had discovered how treacherous the path up the mountain really was.

The infantry had dug in, there were about twenty men in two man foxholes in a half-circle facing the mountain. Erik couldn't see as well as Thjostolf could in the failing light, but he could tell the Alnethar were tired. They were in a rest plan – one man awake while the other slept.

Thjostolf gathered everyone together and said, "It's going to be a dark night – waning crescent moon with cloud cover. Peter, you're in charge of overwatch. Edwin, Erik, Khalan, you're coming with me."

They waited for another two hours. Then Peter and his team moved into position, setting up on the edge of the wood line. Gabryl took Dimitri and Pavel and set up to the north, covering against a counterattack from the clunker trail.

Erik and Thjostolf blackened their faces and hands with mud. Khalan's face was already dark. Then, the assault team slipped out of the woods and slowly crept to the south. They had brought twenty pounds of high-explosive, and Thjostolf had built a satchel charge with a slow fuse. They had spotted a weakness in the enemy perimeter. On the southern edge, there was nearly a hundred yards of space without a foxhole. That was their opening.

They slipped down the mountain, keeping a wide berth around the enemy perimeter, until they were even with the gap. Then they watched. Erik couldn't see a thing. The sky was dark, and he was relying on Khalan and Thjostolf's ability to see at night to keep his bearings. Edwin sniffed the air, and murmured to Thjostolf, "The men on watch are eating and drinking."

They got close to the ground and crawled forward through the grass. They were only two-hundred yards from the enemy perimeter, but it took them over an hour to cross the distance. Every movement sounded loudly in Erik's ears, but the enemy was silent.

Just like stalking a spider.

Ahead, the clunkers had given up for the night, and had turned off their engines. Erik knew that meant that the Alnethar were different from the Iaelians…if they could see as well in the dark as their southern relatives, then they would have used this time to get the clunker unstuck.

They passed undetected through the hole in the enemy perimeter, and Khalan patted Erik's shoulder and pointed. Erik went in the direction that his friend had indicated. He could only see a few meters ahead, and he smelled them before he saw them. It was a slightly nauseating smell, like sweaty fruit. He guessed it was their deodorant.

Each movement was slow and deliberate, as he cleared bits of grass out of his way. His heart pounded. And there they were, dead ahead, Erik saw two helmets facing away. A gentle snoring sound came from the one of the right, but the one on the left shifted uncomfortably. He saw a hand, pale against the starlight, lift a small biscuit to his mouth. A moment later he heard gentle chewing.

He drew his kukri and, every so carefully, crept forward.

The Alnethar burped, and his sleeping comrade rolled over.

Erik froze.

The sleeper lay still, and resumed snoring.

Erik was at the lip of the foxhole now. He didn't dare breath. Then, in a single, deft movement, he covered the Alnethar's mouth and drew the knife's edge across the dark-elf's throat.

The sensation both horrified and thrilled him. He knew instantly that he would never forget it. To hold another person and feel their life draining from their body, to hear the bizarre, unearthly whistle that issued from the neck, was a feeling never forgotten. Erik felt his heart pound, and his own breath hung in his chest...

The elf struggled for only a second before laying still. Beside him, the sleeper slept on, oblivious.

Steeling himself, Erik moved past the foxhole and on to the next one. There was no time to dwell on what they were doing. Thjostolf had ordered them to kill every other man when possible. The psychological effect was more valuable to the fight than the actual casualties.

Fear is poison.

Erik came up on the next foxhole and killed another elf in the same manner. It was somewhat easier the second time around. Perhaps that was because this time the sleeper stirred, and Erik killed him too. Then he took a grenade from the dead elf's gear, pulled the pin, and rested the elf on top of it, so that the weight of the body kept the spoon from flying off. When they picked up their dead, it would detonate.

They would kill all of us, given the chance – Jomsskari, greenhorns, men, women, and children. And Shayna... This was no time to be squeamish.

Khalan appeared out of the dark and pressed his mouth against Erik's ear. "We got the east half of the perimeter," he murmured. "Thjostolf is setting the charge on the clunker now."

Erik nodded, and followed Khalan to the western edge. He watched as Khalan disappeared into the night, and returned a moment later, wiping his kukri on his pant leg. "We haven't got time to get all of these guys," he whispered.

"Can you see Thjostolf?"

"Yes." Khalan looked around, his eyes glinting in the darkness. "He's about to light the fuse."

"What about the officers?"

"All dead. Come now, let's get out of here."

They slipped back out of the perimeter. Erik saw a match flare by the clunkers, and then disappear again. A few moments later, Thjostolf and Edwin appeared at their side, and they slipped up the hill to the cover of the woods.

They pulled in Gabryl's security element and waited. Thjostolf kept an eye on his watch, and told the teams to get down.

There was another few moments of agonized silence. Then came the blast. Fire leapt up from the clunker, and Erik heard shouts, followed by screams of surprise. In the light of the flames, Erik could finally see the whole scene clearly. The stranded clunker was still leaning in the ditch, but the other burned brightly. The back end of it was a raging inferno. On the ground around them, there were several foxholes, and the bodies inside them did not stir. Around the perimeter, voices cried out in despair. Then he heard a grenade detonate.

The Jomsskari slipped back into the forest and disappeared into the night.

*   *   *

Erik slept dreamlessly for his four hours, and when he awoke he saw that the sun had already started to rise. He heard the *thunk* of the mortar being fired, but there was no other sound.

He looked around. Thjostolf was talking to Gabryl off to his left, speaking in a low voice. Pavel and Dimitri were asleep, and Asvald had the machine-gun. Edwin sat in the center, next to the sacks of ammunition, sniffing the air.

Erik got something to eat and checked his wound. Gabryl's words had done something, though he wasn't sure what. The wound looked like it had been healing for a day or two, not twelve hours. The tissue inside the wound channel was suturing itself together, too. He no longer needed to pack the entire wound. After he replaced his bandage, he woke up the machine-gunners and they adjusted their tiny perimeter.

"How long have the others been out?" he asked Thjostolf.

"Five hours," said the captain. "There was sporadic fire to the northeast about two hours ago, but we haven't heard anything since then. They should be due back soon."

In fact, it was almost another hour before the patrol came back. Yolf, Ansel, Sergei, and Sacha collapsed almost immediately and went to sleep, while Khalan, Peter, and Brutus' team pulled the first guard. Brutus slipped up to Thjostolf and briefed him.

"We encountered a patrol on the main trail and ambushed them, why not," he said. "Another one of their patrols hit us from the left flank, from the west, you see? And then, we broke contact. They carried their wounded, to the main base I believe. We took no casualties at that time. I believe they have started to patrol in larger elements, perhaps eighteen or twenty men. I do not think they suspect that we are so few, but any of their patrols are now large enough to pin down our entire company, if we cannot break contact, yes?"

Thjostolf nodded. "They're probably trying to clear the woods north of the clunker trail, and then begin pushing us southeast.

413

I guess they figure if we were a larger element then we'd have set up a less fluid defense. Feck!"

"They outnumber us, six to one or more, captain. But I digress. We then circled to the west, and got eyes on the stranded clunkers you attacked in the night." He whistled in reverence. "That unit is broken, captain. They have abandoned the clunker they lost in the ditch, blown it up, no less. They fled down the mountain. We saw them, only twelve of them left, all carrying the bodies of their comrades."

"Excellent," Thjostolf said with a nod. "That means they have, what, two clunkers left, and between fifty and sixty infantry, with a small mortar battery? Is that about right?"

"By my estimation, it is, captain. It does not account for the wounded that can still fight."

Thjostolf thought for a moment. "Wendyll, Kolskegg?"

"Wendyll's spotting for Rhys, cap," said Kolskegg.

"That's fine. We need you to start picking off officers and NCOs. Take Sergei, and teach him to lay still and chose his targets. We need to feckin' deprive them of their leadership and heavy-weapons crews as soon as possible."

He looked up to the north and spat. "We have to try to draw them into the forest and isolate smaller elements. Maximize on their limited communications and fatigue. Soon enough they'll run low on water, and when they do, they'll have to send a patrol to the river to gather water. We kill that patrol or prevent them from reaching their objective, and they'll have to withdraw."

There was a moment of silence, and then he said, "Of course, if we run out of ammo before they run out of water, we're fecked."

Chapter Twenty-Three

The Counterattack, 8 July 1160

Kolskegg led Sergei into the forest, and they darkened their skin and camouflaged their weapons. Sergei, Kolskegg learned, was an expert hunter, and an experienced stalker. He had the patience to be a sharpshooter. They talked briefly about their plan of action, and then moved out, heading north.

About twenty-five minutes into their journey they heard movement off to their left, and sank into the foliage. They listened for over an hour, and heard Alnethar voices chattering. Kolskegg knew that Thjostolf and Brutus would be leading their teams out shortly, but he didn't want to get involved with this Alnethar patrol if he could help it.

They laid low, and presently the enemy picked up from their position and moved past them. One of their flank men passed within fifteen feet of Kolskegg, but they remained oblivious. It was clear, however, that they were even more vigilant now than they had been before. No doubt, the word of what had happened in the night had spread. To kill every man would have been bad enough, but killing every other man was almost playful. It demonstrated absolute control, and that was what they needed. They needed the enemy to fear them as more than mere mortals.

Kolskegg waited until the sound of their movements had faded to the south, and then they moved out again. By his estimation, they were four hundred yards south of the clunker trail, and seven hundred yards southeast of the enemy base around the crippled clunker.

They cut to the northwest, and found themselves a bit of high ground overlooking the clunker trail. Kolskegg nestled into a clutch of stones, and Sergei laid down in some ferns just a yard or two to his right. Kolskegg handed Sergei his binoculars and they watched.

Two hundred yards to their right, the Alnethar had set up a pair of machine-guns covering the main avenue of approach down the trail. Behind them about another two hundred yards, the clunker, now charred and hollow, lay dejected to the side of the trail. The other two clunkers were deployed behind them. On the north edge of the trail, a team of Alnethar soldiers hacked at the trees, making a path for the armor to get around.

Kolskegg whispered, "We'll engage the machine-gunners first. If we don't, they'll spot us and open up on us."

Sergei nodded.

"Which one do you want to shoot first?"

Sergei thought for a moment. "The one on the right, closest to us," he whispered.

"All right. We wait for a mortar blast before we shoot, so they won't hear the shots. Rhys will be firing a few rounds in a little while, so we just wait until then. Then we kill the gunners and wait for a chance to get us an officer or two."

Sergei nodded.

They lay quietly for another forty-five minutes. Kolskegg kept listening for any sounds around him, but the forest was deathly quiet. He could hear the Alnethar talking among themselves. Sergei was struggling to stay awake. He had just got off of a shift, and had been awake for almost thirty hours continuously. While they waited, Kolskegg made a sketch of the area and estimated the ranges to his targets.

Sergei pointed suddenly. "They're almost done with the detour."

Kolskegg nodded. "They'll be rolling down the trail pretty

soon. We need to take our shots and then alert the rest of our guys."

A few minutes later, there was a whistle, and Kolskegg brought his rifle up. A moment later, a mortar round detonated in the trees near the detour. Kolskegg waited, his crosshairs hovering over the heads of the gunners. They had sunk low into their holes, but Kolskegg still had a shot.

"Take the one without the helmet. Can you see him?" Kolskegg asked.

"Yes."

"Next explosion, okay? Two hundred yards."

"Got it," Sergei replied.

Kolskegg heard the whistle, and let out his breath. The next instant, a blast sounded from the west, and Kolskegg fired. He didn't even hear Sergei fire, but both of their targets fell.

He worked the action and lined up on the next target. "Take the one on the right," he ordered. There was another blast, and the report of the rifles was lost in the explosion. The machine-gunners went down.

He turned his attention to the northwest, and watched the enemy's movements through his scope. They were huddled down now, taking cover from the incoming rounds. Nobody had heard them.

Something rustled behind him, and he turned and looked.

Someone was crouched, not fifty feet away.

He couldn't see if it was friend or foe. The figure was low in the brush. He must have known the snipers were there, but couldn't see them yet. Kolskegg saw Sergei looking back, too, and put his finger to his lips.

Kolskegg brought his rifle around, very slowly, until it was aimed at the figure. The figure looked back and forth, and then slowly, raised up above the leaves.

It was Erik.

Kolskegg let his breath out, and Erik heard him. They looked at each other for a moment, grinned, and each turned away. Kolskegg heard Erik moving off to the south, but only for a moment. He knew that their entire patrol had just passed their position, and was impressed by how little he heard from them.

He looked back toward the enemy, and saw them beginning to emerge, looking distrustfully at the sky. He started to look for officers. Beside him, Sergei lifted the binoculars to his eyes and began to scan.

They watched for another ten minutes before choosing their targets. Kolskegg saw two officers in a foxhole, going over a map. They were both older, and had the grizzled look of veterans. But Kolskegg had noticed something else as well. There were several Alnethar in the brush on either side of the trail, binoculars in hand, scanning the forest. They weren't too far from the mortar battery, which he could barely see. They were in defilade, dug in near the center of the enemy positions.

"We need to fire simultaneously," Kolskegg said softly. "And then slide back down this rise and displace. If those spotters see us, they'll call down a barrage on our heads."

Sergei nodded. He looked exhausted, but he adjusted his iron sights and took aim.

Kolskegg called his target and put his cross-hairs on the back of the officer's head. They breathed in deeply, released their breaths together, and fired.

Even as his finger pressed the trigger he knew he had made a mistake. Something was wrong. He felt eyes on him, someone could see him, though he couldn't say how he knew. Before he had finished cycling his weapon, Kolskegg heard the *thunks* of the mortars firing, and then all hell broke out around him.

The trees overhead splintered with each blast, dust and flames and flashes of light. The earth was shaking. *They saw us; they must have seen the muzzle-flashes or a fecking optic glint!* He grabbed Sergei and pulled him back, and they were slithering like frenzied snakes through the firestorm and then –

Searing, excruciating pain. And silence.

He felt, for a moment, that he was airborne, before the ground struck him in the face. He felt warmth across his pants and he didn't know if he had been hit or if he had just urinated on himself. Sergei was gone, he didn't know where, and suddenly he heard a high-pitched squeal. He realized it was just his ears ringing from the sounds. But it was quiet now. The earth stopped shaking, the lights stopped flaring.

Thoughout his whole body he felt nothing but pain.

He lay still, panting, and looked down. For a moment, he didn't understand what he was seeing. Then the realization struck him, and he felt panic beginning to rise in his stomach. His right leg was gone. It had been severed at the knee. He could see the pale blood, the white, trembling flesh, and his pants were smoking as if they had been on fire.

My leg's gone.

His mind struggled frantically. *My leg's gone.* He couldn't organize his thoughts any further than that. He felt his whole body shaking, and tears streaming down his face.

"Oh man, I gotta get up," he whimpered, "I gotta get up, I gotta move, I gotta move..." He felt strangely absent from his own mind, and only the most basic instinct of a wounded animal remained. They would be coming any minute now, he had to go, he had to go now.

"I need my weapon." He looked for it. It was off to his left, just out of arm's reach. He struggled against his body, his fingertips barely reaching the sling, then it was in his hand. He had it, he had his weapon.

"I gotta get up," he kept saying, but he couldn't take his eyes off the bleeding stump. He was beginning to feel incredibly dizzy, and his thoughts were jumbled. He couldn't believe it. *Feck, my leg's gone!* Then, he heard a noise to his left.

Sergei was gasping for breath. He was laying a few feet away, blood streaming from a wound above his eye. The young man was clutching his thigh, and Kolskegg could see that his left leg had been torn. His foot hung on by a few strands of flesh.

Something about seeing Sergei woke him up. His mind began to focus. He had to do something, and quickly. *Tourniquet.* The word hung in his mind for a second before it made sense. Kolskegg always carried two tourniquets, all the Jomsskari did.

He forced himself to sit upright, and reached into his first aid pouch. "Hang on, Sergei," he said, his teeth clamped shut, "Hang on, we're gunna get through this."

His sanity began to come back, and he worked as quickly as his shaking hands would allow. He slid the tourniquet over his stump and tightened it high on his thigh. At first it felt better, but then the pain grew even worse. As he tightened it, he felt the blood pressing against the band, pounding with the rhythm of his heart, fast and tremulous. He felt very cold.

I gotta get up, I gotta get up...

He couldn't see his wound to tell if he had stopped the bleeding, so he kept tightening it until his fingers were white. Then he tied off the windlass and dragged himself over to Sergei. "Come on," he said, setting his face as bravely as he could, "We need to fix that."

Sergei had his mouth open to speak, but nothing came out but strange, animal gasps. The panic was killing him faster than the wound would. Kolskegg grabbed him and growled, "Hey! Pull yourself together, you're fine, you just got cut up a little, nothing we can't fix. Hey! Hey!"

Sergei laid back down heavily, his hand in his mouth. "It hurts, it hurts..."

Kolskegg's head was swimming. It took every ounce of resolve to keep from just laying down and waiting to die. "Come on, man, you're going to be okay." He was trying to get the tourniquet around Sergei's leg but his fingers had turned to rubber. Finally, he got it in place and began to twist. Sergei cried out, and let out his breaths in short, gasping sobs.

Kolskegg heard voices shouting behind them, and movement. He looked back and saw a flash of a brown tunic. The Alnethar were moving towards them.

Feck!

He tied off the windlass, grabbed his weapon in one hand and Sergei with the other, and began struggling into the brush. He had no plan, no idea where he was going or what he was doing. Only one thought entered his mind. *Get away.*

There were voices behind him, breaking twigs and brush. He couldn't see anything; there was sweat and blood stinging his eyes and his head was spinning. The pain in his body was waning from the fear.

An Alnethar screamed behind him, and he rolled onto his back, trying to raise his weapon but the sling was caught on something. The enemy was descending on him, weapons pointed at his face, screaming and shouting. He saw their furious faces, saw the glint of their bayonets, heard the bushes around him shaking and the heavy footfalls of running. *God, don't let me die on my back!*

Machine-gun fire erupted; there were shots on all sides, and he fell back to the ground, engulfed in chaos and shrapnel. He felt Sergei struggling beside him. He tried to reach him but...

Hands gripped his vest and he felt himself sliding, dragged with incredible force into the foliage. Pain raked his body. There were explosions, hand grenades were detonating. Tiny pieces of steel cut into his hands, burning hot –

"Kolskegg! Kolskegg!"

He looked up, and through the dust and bedlam he saw Erik.

"I got you, man, hang on!"

He couldn't muster a reply.

He saw someone firing a machine-gun, and heard Thjostolf shout, "Break contact!"

Brutus yelled, "Left flank! They're moving on the left flank!"

Someone shouted, "Asvald, get Sergei!"

"Get them the feck outta here!" Thjostolf yelled.

"Peel right!"

"Peel right!"

"Peel! Peel! Go, now!"

"Feckin' move!"

Kolskegg saw Thjostolf pop a flare, and felt himself hoisted up. The world was upside down, and he heard Erik grunting. Branches whipped him in the face. Bullets snapped, passing close by.

Whistles, explosions. White smoke, acrid and thick, filled his nostrils. He felt around for his weapon but he couldn't find it, as he bounced, trying to raise his head to see where they were going.

The sound of gunfire began to slack off. Kolskegg saw the Jomsskari falling back around him, and saw Asvald carrying Sergei. Brutus ran up and put his hand on his back. "You will be okay, my friend, we are moving to the rally point."

They pressed on, and the pain returned, so intense that he vomited. Erik finally set Kolskegg on the ground. When he looked around, he realized they were at the rally point. Kolskegg was shaking uncontrollably, but managed to crack a grin. "Sergei okay?" he asked, his voice trembling.

Erik didn't answer. His face was grim, intense with concentration. He gave him a shot of khem-khat and Kolskegg felt the drug wash through his body like ice water.

What followed was a strange, alien sensation. His mind felt fogged, but in a good way now. He was oddly happy. The pain seemed to melt away to a dull throbbing. The colors of the world seemed to fade to grey and white, and he actually felt his heartbeat descending. It was very pleasant. Erik was doing something to his leg, but Kolskegg felt inexplicably sure that everything was fine. After a few seconds – or hours, he wasn't sure which – Edwin was panting in his ear, and he felt himself lifted into the air on a litter. Then the forest wafted past over his head. The rays from the sunlight winked through the trees and reminded him of a ballet. He wanted to dance, but that would be difficult now. He saw a villager at his feet, and tried to wave cheerfully at him, but his hands didn't want to move. It was okay, though. He didn't know the villager's name but they were probably friends.

Then the barley brushed his face, and the sun warmed his freezing skin. The smell of the central hall enveloped him, he felt his body armor pulled off, and he was overcome by a strong desire to go to sleep.

*   *   *

Erik was struggling to hold himself together.

They had been patrolling near the enemy positions when they spotted Kolskegg's position and headed southwest to give him space. When they heard mortar fire they took a security halt and listened for movement. Kolskegg had fired a volley some time later, and then Erik had seen explosions where they had left him. His mouth was still dry from the scene. It kept playing over and over again in his head. He remembered rushing back, seeing the Alnethar closing on them, seeing Kolskegg struggling in the dirt, a trail of blood behind him, an Alnethar raising his weapon to bayonet him where he lay... and then Erik had fired, and everybody else had, too. But this time the Alnethar had sent twenty-five men at least, and they were aggressive, angry, and eager to kill one of these feckin' jai-khu's that had slaughtered their brothers in the night...

The entire Alnethar unit had joined the attack with mortars, infantry, machine-guns, and clunkers that had finally found a way around their charred wreckage from the day before. On the verge of being overrun, Thjostolf had ordered a full retreat, and Erik had scooped up his friend and ran like an animal fleeing a forest fire.

Almost everybody had taken shrapnel wounds. Most were superficial, but Yuri had taken a long splinter in his shoulder. Erik was digging it out and his fingers were slick with blood. Edwin had dashed off to fetch litter-bearers for Kolskegg and Sergei. After Erik had patched them as best he could, he had sent them back to the village.

Yuri had a large stick in his mouth, and Lenka was holding his hands. Every time Erik tried to move the splinter, Yuri would tense, his teeth digging deeper into the wood. Erik had given him a small dose of khem-khat but it hadn't taken effect yet.

"Okay, hold still," he said. "Almost got it." He got the tip of his knife underneath it and got a grip. Then, in a quick motion, he jerked it out. Yuri cried out, caught his breath, and looked back. "Is it out?"

"Yeah, here you go. Keep it as a souvenir. Show your kids." Erik put the chunk in Yuri's hand and bandaged the wound. "We still need you on the line," he said. "I know it hurts, but you need to suck it up."

Yuri nodded. "I'm okay. Just so long as it's out." He picked up his rifle and asked, "Is there any more ammunition?"

Erik pointed to Sergei's discarded weapon. "He had some left."

He got up and went over to Thjostolf. Wendyll had just returned after a quick reconnaissance and was giving his report. Erik drew close and listened.

"They have moved up the trail and are conducting a wide sweep of both sides of the main avenue of approach," Wendyll was saying. "They are taking their time and conducting reconnaissance by fire." Even now, Erik could hear sporadic shots to their west. "They have plenty of ammunition, but as you said, they appear to be running low on water. I saw several soldiers offering canteens to each other, and redistributing water. I believe they intend to reach the lake to refill their water supply. They have made no attempts to cut south towards the river, and at the rate they are going, they will be at the village by evening."

"Did you see if they brought up reinforcements?" asked Thjostolf.

"I was unable to reach the plateau," Wendyll said. "And consequently, I could not tell if they brought reinforcements."

Thjostolf nodded. "I don't know if we can feckin' dig a clunker pit in time," he said, "But we might be able to bring down some feckin' trees or something. Feckin', anything we can do to delay them and force them to make a break for water, that's what we feckin' need to do. So, let's start there. Head north-by-northeast; feckin' set up security on the trail and feckin' pile some logs up so they have to dedicate their resources to clearing the road. And feckin', we keep hitting 'em, keep slowin' 'em down...”

“We could make booby-traps,” Erik suggested. “In the forest, ahead of their advance: trip-wire hand-grenades and spike pits.”

“We're running low on manpower,” said Thjostolf. “Feckin, with Kolskegg and Sergei out of the game we've only got fifteen guys on the line, with Wendyll, Rhys, and Hirsch running the mortar and spotter team. We don't have a feckin' reserve.”

He sighed, and glanced up at Erik sharply. “How's Kolskegg?”

Erik shrugged and said, “He's alive.”

“Will he stay alive much longer?”

Erik didn't have an answer. “It depends,” he said slowly, “On if I live long enough to get back to him. That leg needs to be amputated, and there's a severe risk of infection that I have to address.”

“Do you need to go perform surgery and get back here?”

“Sometime in the next six hour, yes.”

Thjostolf shook his head and looked away. “Kolskegg's been with me since the Belvade,” he muttered. “Feck! Okay, run your happy arse back there and feckin' fix 'em both up, and then feckin' get back here. We have exactly no time to waste.”

“I hear and obey, cap.”

“Everyone else, we move out in three minutes. Distribute the last of the ammo and grenades.”

As he turned to go, Thjostolf shouted after Erik, “Hey! And bring up some axes!”

*   *   *

Erik ran down the game trail, gasping for air, his feet aching inside his boots. It was almost 1000, and the Alnethar were closing fast. His hands were tingling from the exertion, but he kept pressing on. His body was exhausted, but he refused its pleas for him to stop.

He passed the place where he had first met Shayna. He ran through the rocky ground, past the rhododendrons, and came bursting out into the open barley fields. The sight that greeted him was shocking.

Great stones had risen up in the lake, and the goatherds were driving their flocks over the water and into the mouth of the cave. The fields were deserted, the young barley abandoned. There was no movement inside the village. He ran across the fields and crossed the square, his breath came out in ragged gasps as he burst into the central hall.

Yolf's father, Oleg was there, and four other men. Ulrich stood at the edge of the hall, inspecting his fingernails. He looked up at Erik as if bored. Kolskegg and Sergei were lying on the tables.

"I need to operate," Erik gasped. "Boil me some water. Oleg." He realized he didn't know anyone else's name. "I'll need you to assist." He threw his weapon and helmet on the table beside them and began to roll up his sleeves. "Tell me they're still alive."

"They're alive," said Oleg, "Sergei has calmed down, and Kolskegg is delirious." He glanced back at the troll, and said in a low voice, "The magician has evacuated the rest of us. He was about to lead us through the cave."

"We gotta do this first," said Erik. "You, hold his arms, and you, hold his good leg. Kolskegg, can you hear me?"

Kolskegg looked up at him and smiled weakly. "Hey, man. Did we win?"

"We sure did," Erik said, with a best smile he could muster. "Listen, this is going to hurt like hell, but it'll save your life."

Kolskegg nodded. "Khem-khat?"

"I'm sorry, if I give you any more it'll kill you." He pulled out his tools, washed his hands, and braced himself. "Okay," he said. "Here goes."

Peeling the flesh off of a friend's body was the least pleasant experience of his life, excepting, perhaps, listening to the sounds of his screams. The blast had torn the leg off, leaving jagged, filthy scraps of tissue and bone behind. It was a massive infection waiting to happen. He cut off the torn tissue, sawing the bone, and sewed the wound up. It didn't take long, but to Kolskegg, it must have been a lifetime. Mercifully, he passed out half-way through, and Erik finished the job and bandaged it.

He wiped Kolskegg's blood off of his hands, and tried to mop it from his uniform. He was still panting heavily from the run, but he didn't have time to wait.

He washed his hands again, took a deep breath, and turned to Sergei. "You ready?"

*   *   *

They carried the wounded across the lake, and Erik gathered as many axes as he could find. As he was preparing to leave, he heard a voice behind him, and turned.

"You don't tire much, do you?" The troll looked at him, his eyes empty.

"Just doing the job." Erik replied. He didn't want to talk to him.

Ulrich laughed coldly. "'The job.' Such a noble thing to do, you know. Tell me, how far are the pests? I can smell them already, and it annoys me."

"Less than a day," said Erik shortly. "I have to go."

"Ah, yes, so you do," said Ulrich. He yawned, and stretched, and meandered towards him. "I like you," said Ulrich lazily. "You and your friends, your Jomsskari, are slightly less pathetic than the rest of the mortals in this dump you call a world. 'Skari'… isn't that old Haellic for 'a pack of mongrels'?"

Erik glanced at him, tying the axes into a bundle. "You could come help us, you know."

"I could, couldn't I?" said the troll, and laughed coldly. "I have seen many civilizations rise and fall, and I have never taken part. This is your war and your concern. I have already done more than I like by letting your little friends pass through my realm. Do not press your luck." He walked away, and called over his shoulder, "Good hunting, young one."

Erik shook his head and didn't reply. Slinging his carbine, he picked up the axes and began to run back.

He wished she had stayed behind. He didn't expect to see her again, and he would have cherished another kiss. As he ran, his thoughts strayed to her – the curve of her back, the smell of her hair. He didn't want her to see his corpse. She must have been terrified that would happen after seeing Vladamir's body and the two wounded. There would be more bodies before this was over...

He took the clunker trail and had only followed it about a mile when he saw the Jomsskari ahead. They had set up security further up the trail. Brutus was preparing two more satchel charges. One was from the last sack of improvised explosives he had made and the other was from the last of the high explosives they'd brought with them.

Thjostolf and Gabryl came to meet him. "Distribute the axes," Thjostolf ordered Erik. "They're about two hours out from this position."

"IHO, cap." Erik felt as if he could barely stand, but he summoned his resolve. As he turned to go, Thjostolf grabbed him by the shoulder. "Is Kolskegg okay?" he asked quietly.

Erik glanced around. "I can't say, cap," he replied. "He's got a better chance now but he's all torn up. He needs a hospital."

Thjostolf nodded, and Erik caught a glimpse of something in the half-elf's eye; grief, perhaps, or despair. It lingered for only an instant before Thjostolf steeled his gaze and said, "Go on, get these trees down."

They worked feverishly, and in less than an hour they had felled six trees on the trail. Brutus put a hand-grenade in the branches, and tied a wire to the pin, so that when they tried to move the trunk, it would go off. They could hear the clunkers advancing; the sound of their engines was getting closer. They pulled in their security element and headed south. Thjostolf wanted to hit their flanks as they moved up to the blockade. He hoped that the infantry on the flanks would pursue them and become isolated when the main body couldn't follow.

They circled up and took stock of their position. They were getting low on ammunition. Erik only had four magazines left, and most of the greenhorns were down to fifty rounds for their rifles. The machine-guns were down to a thousand rounds each, except for Khalan, who only had seven hundred rounds left. Rhys reported that he was down to four high-explosive rounds and six phosphorous, and Thjostolf wanted him to target the clunkers with the phosphorous as they stopped at the blockade. If they got lucky, they might set off another fuel tank and kill another clunker.

They settled in about five hundred yards from the blockade and waited. They didn't have to wait long. Soon, they spotted infantry moving slowly through the forest to their left.

Thjostolf moved up alone, about a hundred yards ahead of the Jomsskari' firing line. Erik saw him settle in behind a log, and wait. The enemy was a long ways off still, but they moved steadily. Occasionally one or two of them would fire a couple of shots into the brush, hoping to elicit a response, but the Jomsskari were silent, and the militiamen followed suit, staying low in their positions.

Thjostolf waited until they got within fifty yards, and then he popped off a shot at their point man and took off running. The Alnethar fired a few shots at him, and six or seven of them gave chase. Thjostolf was dodging and weaving, and Erik heard bullets from the Alnethar passing overhead.

Thjostolf leapt over the firing line and kept running, ducking out of sight. The Alnethar were nearly on top of them when the Jomsskari opened fire, throwing grenades and shooting them as they ran. All of the Alnethar went down hard. Behind them, Erik could hear their comrades screaming in frustration. Then Thjostolf shouted for them to break contact.

They fell back, trading sporadic gunfire with the Alnethar who had been sensible enough to stay back. Erik could see the clunkers through the trees, trying to get an angle on the Jomsskari. They were moving carefully, and Erik felt sure that they knew the Jomsskari were short of men and equipment. At least they had time on their side, as long as the water held out.

A group of infantrymen assaulted the Jomsskari' position and the Jomsskari responded with a withering fusillade of bullets, and pulled back, deeper into the forest. Then the elves started mortaring them, but they couldn't see the Jomsskaris' positions. All of the rounds landed almost a hundred yards too short. The Jomsskari slipped off to the east and then moved north, until they could see the blockade. There, they waited.

The clunkers hit the blockade about half an hour later. The tangled mess of limbs and boughs would jam their treads, and they spent some time trying to find a way around. After a few moments of silence, they heard an explosion, and Erik guessed that someone had found the grenade Brutus had hid. Then Rhys started dropping mortar rounds, and Erik watched from a distance as the phosphorous exploded, sending white sparks and smoke into the air. They were not so lucky this time. Neither of the clunkers exploded, despite scoring a direct hit.

The clunkers had had enough. They backed up about fifty yards and shot several rounds into the blockade. The blasts splintered the wood and cut them a path. The infantry circled around the north, and secured the northern side of the trail. Erik knew that the Alnethar only had another mile to the village and the Jomsskari were rapidly running out of space to maneuver. As they neared the valley, the landscape narrowed, and the distance from north to south decreased steadily. The Jomsskari only had about a thousand yards before they hit the river.

The enemy seemed to know it, too. The infantry began to sweep southeast, clearing the forest. Erik knew they were trying to push the Jomsskari into the fields, where they would have to either fight to the death in the wood line or risk the run across the barley. The barley would put them out in the open, with machine-guns, mortars, and clunkers at their heels. Now, at least, the Alnethar knew the land. The Jomsskari were losing their initiative.

Thjostolf ordered them to fall back east. They reached the tree line and bounded over the barley fields quickly. Ahead, Erik saw that Ulrich had left the stones in place, leading over the lake to the cave.

They formed a firing line in the outskirts of the village, and took to the hard structures. They dispersed, redistributed their ammunition, and waited. Erik set up in the tannery, on the south-west corner of the square, fortifying it as best he could. Beside him, Gabryl and Asvald established their firing positions and settled in.

On the top floor of the building, Georgi and Lenka had set up their machine-gun.

Erik's fatigue was taking a toll on him, his eyes struggled to focus, and he felt nauseated. He took out his canteen and took a drink. The water was warm, and the canteen almost empty, but it woke him up a little. The constant rush of adrenalin was beginning to be insufficient. He could have slept through just about anything.

He thought of her piercing, blue eyes shining with hope and youth. He thought of her lips, and the taste of her. Every precious sensation was so foreign to him now, like a vivid dream he had once had. His shoulder ached under the bandage, his stomach churned, and his mouth was dry.

Asvald was looking at him, but Erik didn't have any jovial quips this time. He looked back at him, and then at Gabryl, and Edwin. Thjostolf, Dimitri, and Pavel were in Josef's house to the north, and Khalan was in the barn. Wendyll had holed up in a raised position somewhere to the northeast, and the rest of them were taking up positions in whatever cover they could find.

Erik took a breath, and let it out slowly. He saw movement in the wood line. The infantry were dispersing and taking stock of the situation before they moved in. He took out his binoculars and watched. The enemy was taking cover in the wood line. Erik imagined the trepidation that must have filled their hearts as the enemy looked out over the vast barley fields and knew that this was the ground they had to cross. Their need for water was palpable.

"Watch where they drop down," he said to Asvald. "They'll only be up for a couple seconds before they drop to a crawl, and then they'll jump up again. It will be long enough to be seen and get some distance, but too long to be accurately engaged. Wait for them to pop up again, and then shoot them."

"Right." Asvald was still looking at him. "Are you afraid?" he asked suddenly. His voice was trembling a little.

Erik looked at him. "Of course, I am," he said. "Courage has nothing to do with being fearless. It has to do with looking fear in the eye and telling it to go feck itself."

Asvald swallowed, and looked out towards the fields. "What are they doing?"

"Regrouping and preparing for the final assault," Erik said simply. "They'll start mortaring us in a minute."

Asvald nodded, his breath short and shallow.

"Just watch your sector," Erik said. "Keep your head and kill them as they come."

The clunkers appeared over the rise. The first began to cross the field to the north, and the other turned south and began to cross the field through the center. The infantry fell in behind. Almost immediately, Erik heard the *thunks* of the mortars, and then the barley field ahead erupted.

Chapter Twenty-Four

The Fight, 8 July 1160

There is great relief in combat.

In the midst of battle, there is little time for reflection. The problem of eternity is both distant and immediate, but there is no time to worry. For that, he was grateful.

He was grateful to simply be silent. No philosophy, no noise, no questions.

As the world shattered before him, and the visceral instinct to survive precluded the lesser concerns of living a happy life - here, in this moment, there is great relief.

Nothing. Nothing. Nothing, nothing, no thing, no one, nowhere, no why.

But today - "nothing" is comforting.

Nothing to be upset about - only the maw of death.

It's nice to deal in absolutes.

They were walking the mortars in, using them to clear the field ahead of the infantry. Erik could see the clunker to the north staying close to the cliff wall. They were flanking towards the barn.

"We gotta move!" he shouted. "Georgi, Lenka, displace! We're moving north!"

The mortars were getting closer, about two hundred yards ahead of the enemy infantry. He couldn't see where the mortars were, but he was sure Wendyll could. It was over fifteen-hundred yards to the wood line from Wendyll's position. Erik wasn't sure if Wendyll could accurately engage the mortar crews, even if he could see them.

Georgi and Lenka came running down the stairs, and Erik led the way. Running at a dead sprint, they crossed the square. The blasts were getting closer and the earth was shaking beneath his feet. His heart pounding in his throat.

The clunker to the north was almost halfway across the field by the time they reached the barn. Erik stuck his head in the door and saw Khalan and Peter glance back at him, hunkered low behind their meager cover. "We're reinforcing this flank!" he shouted. "Let's try to kill that clunker!"

Khalan shouted, "Brutus!" and the dwarf appeared out of the ground, with satchel charges in his hands. "Come on, there's a farm house to your right!"

They rushed inside and the machine-gunners set up their weapon in the window. Erik, Asvald, Gabryl, and Brutus gathered quickly.

"Once it gets within a hundred yards, we cut off infantry on the right side of that clunker," Erik ordered, "Then, we four flank right while Khalan holds down the infantry on the left. Isolate that clunker, plant the charges, and go. Khalan, you guys make sure to displace or that clunker will hammer you!"

Brutus shook his head. "We cannot kill the clunker with so little explosives," he said. "We'll have to blow off the treads, why not, and kill the crew ourselves."

"Okay," Erik yelled. The sound of thundering blasts was almost too much to be heard over. "Asvald, get on my arse and cover us! You got that?"

Asvald nodded.

The window frames shook, and Erik heard machine-gun fire from the west. He couldn't tell if it was friendly or not, but it picked up rapidly.

Alnethar infantry appeared in their sector of fire, they were flanking the barn. "Georgi, hold fire, wait for them to commit!" Erik shouted.

Georgi didn't hear him. He was already firing. The Alnethar began to return fire. Bullets struck the walls, tearing out chunks of wood around them. Erik swore and turned to his team. "Okay, let's go!"

Everything in his being told Erik not to leave the shelter of the house, but he did anyway. Rushing out to the right and using the rise as cover, they circled around the hilltop where Erik and Shayna had their first, awkward talk. Then, they hooked left and formed a firing line in the defilade of the slope leading down to the lake.

There it was; the clunker was turning towards the barn with its gun traversing. Then, with a thunderous boom, it fired. The farmhouse exploded, splinters of wood flew almost calmly through the air as black smoke billowed from the wreckage. The machine-gun inside was silenced; Georgi and Lenka were certainly dead. Khalan's gun continued to fire; he would be the next target. The Alnethar were less than fifty yards from Erik's position, as they wheeled towards the village, moving to envelop the Jomsskari and finish them off once and for all.

Erik and those with him opened fire. There were nearly twenty Alnethar infantry on this flank alone. As the Alnethar moved forward, their commander shouted instructions.

The Jomsskari were accurate. One by one, the Alnethar fell, their attention focused on the barn and the burning farmhouse. Erik shot their commander and watched him fall to the earth. He saw Khalan's tracers arcing to the far side of the clunker, and the clunker's turret start to traverse.

"Go, go, go!" Erik shouted.

They were up already, dashing through the knee-high grass. Erik was loading as he ran, his empty magazine falling where it may. There were only three Alnethar still up, and they saw them coming but too late. Erik struck one with the butt of his carbine, and drawing his kukri, he fell upon the elf. The cuts came hard and fast until his foe lay twisted and twitching at his feet. When he stood again, he saw Asvald beating an Alnethar with his rifle, and Edwin dragging a screaming elf across the turf by his throat with a trail of blood following.

The clunker fired its main gun – devastatingly loud, the whole machine rocking on its chassis, and the side of the barn collapsed. For a moment, Erik feared the worst… then, he heard Khalan's gun again. The orc had displaced to the other side of the barn. He would not be killed easily.

There was no one between them and the clunker. Brutus rushed up, lighting the fuses on the satchel charges as he went, and tossed them in the path of the clunker. Then, his short legs pumping, he rushed back, and they all found themselves huddled in a ditch. The fuses were not long. The charges went off mere seconds later, sending stones and dirt into the air. Erik looked up. The clunker was grinding to a halt, the treads were slipping off the wheels.

"Take that *jai-khu* out!"

They rushed forward. Erik shouted, "Asvald, cover right!" and pointed to the rear of the clunker. Asvald took cover behind the heavy armor, and began to fire at the Alnethar on the other side.

Erik put the barrel of his carbine into the driver's view port and emptied his magazine. Inside, he heard ricochets and screams. The sound of the reports echoed back and forth inside the steel confines. Brutus and Gabryl had already started to climb on top, and pry the hatch open. Erik leaped up after them and pulled out his revolver and his last grenade. "Open it and duck," he shouted.

Brutus had a grenade out, too. As the hatch opened, Erik jammed his revolver inside and squeezed off his shots. The tension

on the hatch released immediately, and blood spurted from inside –
an arterial hit on some poor bastard within. The grenades went in and
they all ducked low. The turret shook with the paired blasts. Erik
heard rounds snapping overhead, and Asvald shouting, "They see us!
They see us!"

"Keep shooting!" Erik shouted, loading his revolver. Brutus
flung the hatch open and reached in, yanking out the lifeless body of
the Alnethar clunker commander. Erik jumped inside, headfirst, and
shot the first body he saw.

It was cramped, sweltering hot, and sticky with blood. The
acrid smoke of the grenades had not cleared, and he gasped for air.
"Brutus, help me aim this thing!" he shouted.

There was no room inside. He couldn't sit behind the gun, he
knew that much, it would crush him when it fired. With great effort
and some clever contortion, he straddled the corpse in the gunner's
seat, his head pressed against the roof, and tried to figure out where
everything was.

There. Erik saw the main gun, the ammunition behind it, and
a view port for the commander. He opened the breech and jerked out
the empty shell casing. It was blazing to the touch, and he smelled his
flesh burning, but it was out and he grabbed another shell. Brutus slid
down inside, his small stature perfect for the tiny space he was
working in, and began calling directions. "We've got a shot on the
other clunker," he shouted, "Traverse right!"

Erik spun the handle, and the turret began to rotate. He had a
small sight in front on him, and he looked through it. There, almost to
the outskirts of the village, the second clunker was stopped. It was
targeting Thjostolf's position.

"I got him!" Erik shouted.

"Fire!"

Erik couldn't find the trigger. "Where's the feckin' trigger?"

he screamed.

"There, the red button, on the floor, try that!"

Erik mashed it. The gun fired, recoiling back into the confined space, and Erik couldn't hear anything. Brutus was shouting something, but everything was quiet. He looked through the sights and saw that he had missed. The shell had landed short.

Vertical, he thought. There it was, marked by up and down arrows in white paint. He spun the handle, and the gun angled higher. He checked the sight and Brutus ejected a round and began to feed another round in. The shot looked good, if he was reading the sights correctly. Brutus slapped him on the shoulder and Erik plugged his ears and stomped the trigger again.

The clunker rocked and the gun recoiled. He heard the explosion this time, the massive blast, and he looked through the sight and saw that the target was burning with the turret completely gone.

For a second, he couldn't believe it. They had actually killed both clunkers. *They had killed both clunkers.* Suddenly he dared hope, if only for a moment, that he might make it through the day. He was starting to hear again. He heard rounds pinging off the sides of the clunker, and he began to traverse the turret. Then Brutus grabbed him and shook his head, climbing up. Erik took his word for it and followed.

The air outside the clunker was by no means cool; it was midday in the summer heat, but after being in the clunker, Erik felt as if he had jumped into cold water. The bright sun made him squint, and he saw Asvald loading a clip into his weapon. Gabryl was on the other side, firing, shouting something he still couldn't hear.

Then something struck him squarely in the back. It felt like someone had punched him, only it was so much stronger, and the force of it threw Erik off the turret and onto the ground. For a few moments the world spun senselessly, and he tasted grass and blood.

He struggled to pick himself up. "Eshé-ma!"

A hand grasped his shirt and rolled him over, and he looked up to see Brutus standing over him. He patted Erik's chest, and laughed. "That's why we wear armor!" he shouted above the din. "You're okay, my friend. Come now, let's go!"

Erik took his hand and the dwarf pulled him unsteadily to his feet and handed him his carbine. Erik took it and checked the magazine. It was empty. He reached into his pouches.

"Brutus, last mag!" he shouted.

Brutus nodded. "Mine, too!" he shouted. Then, "They're charging!"

Erik looked over Asvald's shoulder and felt his mouth run dry. There they were, twenty of them at least, with their bayonets fixed. From the approaching line, he heard a rising battle-cry, and there was no fire from Khalan's gun now. The machine-guns were silent; they had either run out of ammunition or had been killed.

He began to fire, and the rest joined him, but the enemy was too close. He stepped out and met them as they came, swinging his carbine. His stock connected with an Alnethar's face, he felt the jaw break and the Alnethar fell. And then, there was another, the enemy's bayonet slicing through the air and passing his hip by an inch as he dodged. Erik thrust his weapon into the elf's throat, and he heard a shot and another one fell by his side. An Alnethar raised his weapon to shoot and Erik felt the bullet strike his carbine as it was snatched from his hands. Erik drew his revolver in his right hand and his kukri in his left, as the Alnethar was lunging – *bang!* – Erik shot him in the eye, and Gabryl screamed in pain. He recognized the voice, and then Edwin flew past him and he saw another elf get dragged to the ground. Erik fired again, and cut, and hacked, and then -

It was quiet.

He spun around, looking for another elf to kill, but they were all down, some dead, some dying. Asvald was off to the right, clubbing an Alnethar on the ground to death with his rifle, and Brutus had one in a choke hold. Erik rushed over to the dwarf and grabbed the elf's head, snapping his neck.

He looked around. Gabryl was standing, leaning against the clunker, his helmet off and his left arm bloody. Erik's carbine was on the ground, the wood around the bolt splintered. Edwin growled and said, "Masters, the rest are fleeing!"

Erik looked. Across the field, a few elves were almost to the wood line. The mortars had stopped firing, and Erik saw Khalan and Peter emerging from the barn.

"Gabryl, let me see it," Erik said. "Where are you hit?"

Gabryl shook his head. "I'll be fine, doctor. Check on Georgi and Lenka, see if they're alive."

Erik ran down to the farmhouse and looked inside. He saw Lenka's body, punctured by hundreds of splinters and pieces of shrapnel. the boy's face was grey and hollow. He couldn't find Georgi for a few minutes. Then he found an arm, and then a leg. That was all he could find.

He stepped out of the wreckage, gagging, and rushed over to the barn. Khalan, Peter, and Sacha were fine. Ansel had a bullet wound to the hand. It had severed his little finger and ring finger. They hung on by a few shreds of flesh. Erik wrapped it up quickly, and then he saw Yolf.

Yolf was dying. He lay gasping for breath, a chunk of shrapnel was in his throat and there were two bullets in his torso. Erik gave him two doses of khem-khat and moved on. He had to prioritize, to find someone he could really help. Yolf was just too far gone. Behind him, Sacha cradled Yolf in his arms, sobbing.

Rhys was wounded as well. Erik found him lying in the floor of Josef's house, keeping pressure on a bullet wound to his thigh. He was gritting his teeth and looked like he was in a lot of pain. Erik knelt beside him. "Let me see it," he said.

Rhys opened his hands, and Erik stared. White foam was billowing out of the wound, mixing with the blood and the pale skin beneath. It looked entirely foreign; Erik had never seen a wound like this before. *Some kind of Alnethar weapon?* Glancing up at Rhys, he touched the foam and smelled it.

It smelled...minty.

"What is it?" asked Rhys. He sounded worried, and Erik didn't blame him.

Minty? Erik racked his brain, trying to think of what it could be. He smelled it again, and then, he began to laugh uncontrollably.

Rhys stared at him. "What is it?"

Erik couldn't stop laughing. "It's toothpaste, man." He reached into Rhys' cargo pocket and sure enough, there was a toothbrush and a tube of toothpaste. "It's just feckin' toothpaste. They feckin' shot your hygiene kit!"

Rhys stared at him, and then leaned back and began laughing as well. "That is...so very good to hear, doctor."

Erik tried to control himself, but he couldn't stop laughing. He wiped away the foam and got a better look at the wound.

It had missed the artery and the femur. Erik could see the bullet underneath the skin in the back of Rhys' leg. It had entered through the pocket and penetrated less than an inch. It had probably already passed through the wall before it hit him.

He cleaned the wound and sliced open the skin above the bullet, popping it out like a big pimple. Then he bandaged it up, both of them laughing until tears streamed down their faces. As Erik got up and moved to the next building he said, "Man, your nickname is 'Minty-Fresh' now."

He found Thjostolf in the square, with Hirsch, Yuri, Dimitri, and Pavel. Thjostolf saw him coming and rushed over. "Rhys is hit," he said, "You better – what the feck are you laughing about?"

Erik told him, and Thjostolf shook his head in wonderment. "Man, he had me feckin' worried sick," he said. Then, suddenly serious, he asked, "Who else?"

Erik told him. Yolf, Georgi, Lenka...

The greenhorns stared at him somberly. Hirsch sat down and stared at the ground. Thjostolf ran a hand through his hair. "What about ammo?"

"I don't know about anybody else, but I'm out and Brutus is out. I think Gabryl's out, too."

"Yeah, we're all feckin' out." Thjostolf looked at him. "Where's you weapon?"

"Destroyed." Erik looked around. "Guess I'll snag one of these Alnethar rifles."

"Well, you've got your pick. There's plenty of 'em lying around." Thjostolf lit his pipe and took a long draw. "We need to start gathering weapons and ammo. Set up an observation post at the edge of the plateau and get ready to do it again."

Erik nodded, and reached into his belt, pulling out his tobacco pouch. He had saved the last few scraps for such a time, and he carefully and lovingly rolled one final cigarette.

He found Khalan, and the two of them wordlessly made their way to a shady spot near the bridge. It was quiet there, and the brook babbled quietly, as if the sound of battle had never even happened.

They sat down, and Erik struck a match, lighting the cigarette. After a few draws, he passed it to Khalan. They didn't speak. They just savored the taste and the calm, as the smoke billowed from their nostrils.

Finally, Erik spoke. "That was..." He trailed off.

Khalan nodded. "Yup."

"I mean damn."

Khalan passed the last stub to him. "Here, finish it." Then he asked, "Are all the Jomsskari alive?"

Erik nodded. He took the last drag and flicked the ember into the water. "Yeah," he said. "Well, assuming Kolskegg didn't die since I last saw him."

Khalan looked at him. "Do you think we will be able to live through another?" he asked.

Erik didn't answer. Then, with some effort, he stood. "Let's get to work."

*   *   *

They piled the dead enemy by the destroyed clunker, and began to consolidate whatever resources they could salvage or scrounge. As much as they wanted to rest, there was a singular task to be done: prepare for the next assault. For over two days now, they hadn't been able to reach the plateau, and hence, they had no idea if the Alnethar were moving reinforcements up. Finding out would be the first priority.

It turned out that Wendyll had started shooting at the mortar team almost as soon as they started firing. He had killed two gunners and their commander, and their observer as well. While the battle had raged on all sides, he had calmly and precisely calculated shot after shot. Erik recalled how his own hands were shaking with fatigue and adrenalin, and how cloudy his mind had been. He couldn't imagine the sort of discipline and focus Wendyll must have mustered to take those shots. As it was, only two mortar rounds had landed inside the village, and neither of them had been effective.

Wendyll and Brutus took Asvald and Sacha and headed up the clunker trail. They carried as many shells from the captured Alnethar clunker as they could. Brutus intended to daisy-chain them with det cord and bury them in the path near the plateau. They left as the sun began to set, and Erik watched them go.

He wondered if they would be back in a few hours, with news of another attack. If the Alnethar sent more men, they didn't stand a chance. They'd have to flee.

Erik tried not to think about it. For now, they had won, with four greenhorns dead, Kolskegg and Sergei maimed, and all the rest of them wounded in some way. It felt oddly pyrrhic. He expected to feel elated, or at least relieved, but he was so tired and all he could think of was the urge to sleep.

It had been so fast. Once the action picked up, it was quick and decisive... but Erik felt a strange guilt, as well. It was curiously like the guilt he had felt when he was told that his unit in the Belvade had been destroyed, that he alone had lived. He felt the guilt most poignantly as he covered Lenka's body with a blanket, and covered what was left of Georgi beside him. He resisted the urge to question what had happened. He knew he couldn't answer for why they had died, and not him. There was no reason to be given.

As the sky darkened, and they began their rest plan, he wanted nothing more than to lay his head down. It was not to be, not yet. Wendyll and Asvald returned and reported that there was no enemy activity on the mountain. The few Alnethar who had fled the field had been spotted halfway down the draw, heading north to safety. Erik, Peter, and Khalan went up to meet Brutus and Sacha, who has stayed behind at a hasty OP, and relieved them. For a few hours, they manned the post, which overlooked the edge of the plateau, and chatted idly about nothing in particular. Erik was glad the greenhorns weren't there for once. He had missed his time with

Peter and Khalan. And as much as he appreciated the greenhorns...well, that wasn't fair. They weren't greenhorns any more. They had proven themselves in combat. They were veterans now. In fact, all of the Jomsskari had started to refer to them as "the guerillas."

When they were relieved, they walked back down the clunker trail, each lost in their own thoughts. Erik's mind returned over and over again to Shayna. He hoped she was safe, hoped she was doing well. Maybe he'd get to see her soon. He needed to check on Kolskegg and Sergei as soon as they got a chance, perhaps that would give him the opportunity.

Thjostolf and Wendyll manned the observation post that night, and Brutus, Rhys, Gabryl, and Edwin relieved them in the morning. There was a new dynamic between the Jomsskari and the guerillas now. Even Erik and Asvald joked together. As they sat cleaning their weapons, Erik felt that, even if he was a little jai-khu, Asvald could be a nice guy to know. He had certainly proved himself courageous in combat. Erik may never learn to like him, but he could respect him.

The next morning, Thjostolf ordered them to begin carrying clunker shells up the trail. He planned to set up a much more extensive defense system of anti-personnel mines improvised from Alnethar hand grenades and anti-clunker mines from the shells. Rhys gathered the Alnethar mortars and began teaching a few more of the guerillas how to operate them, putting Hirsch in charge of his own battery.

"Once we've established security," Thjostolf said, "We'll go through Gob-Heshem and deliver the dead to their families. Erik," he added, "You need to go with that detail. I want you to check on the wounded." He was smiling, though, and Erik knew that he was being given a chance to see Shayna again.

They each took a pair of shells and began to walk across the field. Erik was talking to Sacha, who had asked him what Haelhan looked like. Erik was just beginning to describe Havenstead when Thjostolf said, "Oh, feck."

Erik looked up. Edwin was sprinting up the trail. "Master!" he cried. "Master Thjostolf!"

They all braced themselves. Edwin came skidding to a halt in front of Thjostolf. "Master, we've spotted a column coming up the mountain. They are a day's journey from the top."

"How many?" demanded Thjostolf.

"More than two hundred infantrymen, master Thjostolf, with trucks and clunkers and artillery in plenty."

Erik closed his eyes. *Two hundred?*

And then Edwin spoke again, and Erik caught a hint of excitement in the wolf's voice, "They're ours, captain!"

They left the explosives where they lay and ran up to the edge of the plateau. It was exactly as Edwin had described, a long column of men and clunkers were snaking up the mountain. Their scouts were pushing up the mountain, only a few thousand yards off, and Thjostolf flopped down beside the observation post and began to laugh.

The scouts spotted them, and all of the Jomsskari waved to them. In a few minutes, they were shaking hands with their relief. Erik was struck by how clean their uniforms were, and how rested they appeared. "You guys are a sight for sore eyes," he said.

They bantered for a moment as the convoy drew closer, and then a colonel came huffing up the hill. He looked around at the bedraggled and filthy Jomsskari, and sneered. "You guys been on vacation up here?"

Thjostolf laughed, but the colonel didn't. "Well, we're here now, so you fellows can take it back to Feldhall and clean yourselves up. You'll be interested to know that the rest of us have been fighting a war!"

Thjostolf raised an eyebrow, and Erik shook his head and turned away. He was sure the fight for Feldhall had been intense, but he felt insulted.

Thjostolf stayed calm. "Well, sir, I certainly appreciate your efforts. As to this mountain, I'm sure you want to be shown around. This here behind me is the only avenue of approach through the forest. And down there, just past the ridge," he pointed, "Is the first clunker we killed."

The colonel's attitude changed. "You met the enemy?"

"Yes, sir. We have repelled several attacks."

"And they brought clunkers up here?"

"Five, sir. The first two assaults were air-mobile, on the backs of their griffin allies."

"Five clunkers..." The colonel rubbed his chin incredulously. "But you didn't have artillery, did you?"

"We had a mortar tube, sir."

The colonel looked around at them as if they had all suddenly grown antlers.

Thjostolf went on. "There are two more killed clunkers about six hundred yards to the south, if you want to inspect them. The rest are further back. Come on, sir, I'll show you the area. This is your mountain now, after all."

The colonel looked at him, and then at the guerillas. "Who are these fellows?" he demanded.

"Local fighters," said Thjostolf. "Come with me, sir. I'll give you the tour."

They led the convoy down the trail and Thjostolf briefed the colonel as they went. "I'll write up a full report for you," he added. "But first, we have critical casualties that need to be evacuated, and we desperately need more ammunition."

"Of course, of course." The colonel seemed more reserved now then he had been previously. The sight of Alnethar bodies on the sides of the road had that effect.

They emerged into the barley fields and Thjostolf related to the colonel how Erik had led the assault on the flanking clunker. The colonel had lapsed into silence, and looked over the scene in wonder. The Alnethar bodies were still piled high, waiting to be buried, and Erik saw the newcomers covering their noses with their shirts. The colonel stared at the corpses for few moments before speaking. This time, his voice was somewhat more humble. "You held this position against impossible odds, captain. We had no idea you were in sustained contact. I shall be most interested to read your report, and I will be sure that Lord Hoskuld is aware of your efforts."

Thjostolf gave him an appreciative nod. "Thank you, sir," he said. "And please send Lord Hoskuld my regards, as well."

The relief element consisted of an entire battery of Haellic howitzers, a company of Iaelian clunkers numbering fourteen, a company of Dionysian engineers, and two Haellic infantry companies reinforced by an A'kayliian heavy-weapons company. They were equipped to hold the mountaintop for months without support. From their comrades, the Jomsskari learned that the Alliance had repelled the Alnethar attack on Feldhall and had built another fortress, called, "OP Hague," along the river.

The battle had been a bloodbath. OP Hague had been nearly overrun twice, and the Alliance forces had sustained numerous dead. But the Alnethar had underestimated the strength and resolve of their enemies, and had lost over half of their assault force. Now, as best as they could tell, the Alnethar were regrouping, licking their wounds, and reevaluating their tactics. In this interim, Lord Hoskuld had decided to push out another two fortresses, one of which was to be built on the plateau.

"What are you going to call it?" asked Thjostolf.

"We were thinking, 'Mount-Hall,'" said the colonel.

There was a moment of silence, and then Erik spoke up. "I've a better idea," he said. "Call it OP Vladamir, after the first of the locals to be killed out here. Feck, it's their land, they bled for it – they earned a little recognition."

The guerillas all looked at him, and Asvald cracked a grateful smile. The colonel looked over Erik appraisingly, and nodded. "OP Vladamir it is, then."

*   *   *

The relief moved back into the forest the following morning, and began to clear the trees from the edge of the plateau to make room for OP Vladamir. They had brought everything the Jomsskari needed – ammunition, replacement weapons, medical equipment – as well as the simple pleasures – tobacco, hard candies, and soap.

But best of all, they had brought the Jomsskari their mail. There was a great deal of whooping and hollering before they settled down to read their letters.

Peter's younger brother had gotten married to his grade-school sweetheart. "He writes, 'It is unfortunate that you were in training at the time, or else I'd have made you my best man.' Damn, guys, folks at home don't even know we're here yet."

Thjostolf held up a newspaper. "This is from a month ago," he said. "Feckin', says there are rumors of war in the north and an 'expeditionary force has been dispatched to investigate.' It's buried on the eighth page, next to celebrity news."

"'Investigate,'" murmured Khalan, and shook his head. He had only received one letter, and he opened it. "It's from my uncle," he said. His eyes scanned the page, and Erik saw his brow furrow.

"What is it?" Erik asked.

Khalan didn't answer for a moment. Then, "My father died."

Wendyll put a hand on his shoulder.

"Died in his sleep," Khalan went on. "Six weeks ago." He put the letter down. "Eshé-ma."

They read on silently. Erik hadn't gotten any mail; it didn't surprise him, all of his friends were here, but he felt the weight of Thassed's death as well. Thassed had been a father to him in A'kaylii.

Rhys suddenly crumpled his letter, threw it, and stalked off. They all looked up in surprise. After a moment, Brutus picked the balled paper up and smoothed it out, reading over it. "His girlfriend broke up with him. She writes that she does not wish to be married to a soldier, because she would become lonely."

"Did anybody get good news?" asked Wendyll.

Peter held up his hands. "What? My brother got married, right? Does that not count now?"

"Yeah, jackass," said Erik, with a wink. "Show some love to the little man."

"I love you too, you tattooed freak."

Thjostolf nodded. "Yeah, I got some good news."

They all looked at him. Thjostolf glanced up at them, smiled wistfully, and said, "Aud took her first steps, is saying 'love dada' over and over again, and sings her baby doll to sleep."

"Thank you," said Erik, standing up. "I needed that. I was getting depressed."

He walked over to Khalan and knelt down. "You okay?" he asked quietly.

Khalan nodded but didn't say anything.

Erik knew him well enough to know not to press the issue. Instead, he picked up the last letter. "This one's for Kolskegg," he said.

Thjostolf looked at him. "We should get over there," he said. "We need to deliver the dead, and I think the guerillas have fought their war. I'm sure they want to go home."

He turned around and called for Rhys. When the elf had returned, his expression was still taut. Thjostolf got a quick headcount. "All right, guys," he said. "It's time we revisit the issue of Gabryl and his little mission."

Erik had almost forgotten. He looked at Khalan, and Peter, and all the rest. They were all silent, thinking.

Thjostolf spoke again. "Remember what we agreed on. Feckin', we all go, or none of us go. We'll probably get a replacement for Kolskegg. They say they've got some guys who passed Jomsskari Selection who are shipping up here, so we might get one of them. Feckin', I could care less if that guy comes with, whoever he is. We'll ask him when he gets here. But the rest of us need to decide together, whether we report back to Lord Hoskuld at Feldhall, or go with Gabryl."

There was a long silence.

Wendyll said, "I wish to go."

Khalan nodded. "Me, too."

Rhys added, "I wish to go as well."

Thjostolf looked at Peter. The halfling smiled at him, and winked. "I've always wanted to kill a dragon."

Brutus nodded. "Why not?"

Thjostolf nodded, and looked at Erik.

Erik nodded, weighing his words. "I could not live," he said slowly, "Knowing that so great a task was set before me, and I refused it."

Thjostolf looked over his company, and Erik saw a little smile forming on the edge of his mouth. "Now you know why I chose to lead you, and no others." He looked at each other their faces, approvingly. "Then I guess I'll go tell Gabryl that he won't fight alone."

Chapter Twenty-Five

The Settlement, 9 July 1160

Thjostolf told the colonel that they had preexisting orders that Lord Hoskuld was already clear on. No further details were required. Then they picked up their dead and crossed the stone pathway across the lake.

The cave had been opened up, and torches now lit the way. They hung in the air, unsupported, their golden light filling the path ahead. Erik was surprised at how long the path was, in the darkness it had seemed somehow shorter.

Ulrich met them, glanced at the bodies, but didn't say anything. He lead them to the edge of the chasm, muttered a guttural incantation, and a bridge appeared before them. It was clear, like glass, but in the light of the thousands of torches in Gob-Heshem, it gleamed like sunlight.

The guerillas were awestruck, and looked around at the vast city with their jaws hanging open. Erik noticed that Ulrich led them in a circuitous path, making a wide berth around the nest they had seen on their last visit to the dragon-city. He didn't speak the whole time.

They walked for over an hour, crossing great squares, circumventing massive palaces long bereft of their ancient occupants. Edwin trotted along at Gabryl's side, his tail wagging slightly.

"Ulrich," Thjostolf said abruptly, "What is this?"

They all turned and looked. Thjostolf was stopped, looking at a mural painted painstakingly on the side of a wall. It showed mountains, rivers, valleys, and plains, with runes in various places. The mural was huge, over two hundred feet tall and equally wide.

Thjostolf stared at it for several minutes before Ulrich finally came back to him.

"That's the Ahaern River," Thjostolf said. "And this is where Havenstead is."

Ulrich glanced up at it, and returned his gaze to the captain. "This is a map of the old empire," he said. "It covers the better part of the globe. Come now, I will not permit you to linger."

Thjostolf looked at him. "If we're going to help each other, we're going to need to know as much as we can."

Ulrich smiled, and this time, his smile seemed a little less forced, almost polite. "You shall know more," he said, "When we prepare to leave. But until then it is none of your concern."

Thjostolf took another long look at the map, and then turned to go. Erik saw that Gabryl was smiling. Why, he could not guess.

They kept moving. They passed through a row of pillars with comparatively small rooms carved into the stone, and then they found themselves in a long, wide corridor. Ahead, Erik saw daylight that was whiter and purer than the torch light that had led them thus far. After another hour of travel, they had reached the gates of Gob-Heshem.

The gates towered over a thousand feet above them. The doors, wide open now, were carved of stone, with gleaming bronze bands supporting them. From the center of the gates, Erik could barely see the hinges, but the locks were visible as they passed through – immense, gleaming, and thick. Erik could not imagine opening them, much less breaching them.

They emerged into the sunlight, and for a moment Erik was blinded. As his eyes adjusted, he saw a vision so beautiful it stopped his breath. To the left, the snow-capped peaks shone, hundreds or thousands of feet above. The mountain had once sloped gradually, but it had been carved into a series of shelves, each shelf hundreds of feet deep. They were reinforced by boulders, precisely fitted to each other, fifty feet high. The shelves were covered in flowers, trees, fruit vines, and fountains of water. A river flowed through the center with a waterfall at every shelf. Through the center of each shelf, a great bridge stood over the river.

To the right, the mountain sloped gently downwards. Erik could see for miles. He saw the river snaking down, its water glinting in the midday sun, and watched as it broke into a delta in the lowlands. The ground in between was cleared of trees; it was a vast, uninterrupted steppe that fell gracefully into the Wilderness below.

In the center, dead ahead, Erik saw the missionaries. They were several miles off, on the far side of the gardens, but from what he could see, their land was more than satisfactory. It was easily four times the size of the valley they had left behind, with vast stretches of coniferous forest behind them traveling up to the peaks above, immense fields, and gentle hills and rises.

They had all stopped, and none of them realized how long they had been staring until Ulrich became impatient. "Is it not enough that I have given them this bounty, without you wasting my time?" he snarled. "One would think you simpletons had never seen a tree before."

"What is this place?" asked Asvald breathlessly.

Ulrich rolled his eyes and stalked off. Gabryl answered him. "These," he said quietly, "Are the Hanging Gardens of Gob-Heshem."

They made their way across the gardens. Ulrich picked an apple as they walked, and Erik followed suit. It was the best apple he had ever tasted. Words failed to capture the taste that flooded his mouth. Soon they were all eating as they walked, chatting animatedly amongst themselves.

Ulrich looked back at them and shook his head derisively, but a moment later he said, "Throw the cores into the gardens. They will bloom in the spring." His voice betrayed his pride in the place, and Erik guessed that Ulrich had gone to great lengths to maintain the gardens since the fall of the Dragons.

As they drew closer, Erik saw that the missionaries were felling trees and building homes. The goatherds had moved their flocks to pasture, and the farmers were marking their fields. When they saw the warriors coming, they shouted out in joy and rushed forward.

They reached the outskirts of the new village, and Erik, who was at the head of the column behind Ulrich, saw the missionaries dropping their tools and come running to meet them. He looked around, and finally spotted her. She was running up the slope, her face illuminated, and a moment later she had her arms wrapped around his neck and her face buried in his neck. All around them, the villagers embraced their sons and the Jomsskari alike. Their chatter rose to a roar of voices.

She was crying, and he heard her voice in his ear. "I was so scared, when they brought Vlad, and then Sergei and Kolskegg...I'm so glad you're okay, I've been praying this whole time..." Her words became incomprehensible through the tears.

He kissed her forehead, and she looked up at him. Rachel and Hindelle were coming towards him, and the old lady, leaning painfully on a cane, grasped his hand and thanked him for returning. He was truly glad to see her, and that she was doing well.

He saw Thjostolf stride to the edge of the encampment. There, standing with the aid of a pair of rough crutches, was Kolskegg, and beside him Sergei. Both of them were pale, their legs conspicuously absent, but their faces relieved and smiling. All the Jomsskari embraced the two of them.

It took a moment for Erik to realize that there was a cloud hanging over the joyous reunion of families. The chatter was beginning to die down. Erik knew that there would be families searching for their sons, and that every one of them feared the worst.

He saw Oleg standing a few yards off, staring at the litters covered in blankets. Erik glanced back at Thjostolf, who was awkwardly disengaging himself from several small children. Erik let her go, and turned to him, taking off his helmet. "Oleg," he said quietly.

Oleg shook his head. "My son...my Yolf..." he began, but he couldn't finish. Beside him, his wife buried her face in her hands and turned away.

The atmosphere had changed. Everyone was silent. The elders had come forward, and spoke to Thjostolf for a moment. Then Abraham turned and addressed the assembly.

He hesitated, and when he spoke his voice trembled. "Yolf, Georgi, and Lenka have given their lives."

*   *   *

They buried the dead. The entire village stood in silence before the open graves. There was no sound but the quiet sobbing of the families and friends as four wooden boxes were lowered into the earth.

Josef turned to Oleg and asked, "Would you like us to say a few words?"

Oleg shook his head. "There are no words."

There was a long silence. Every person present looked on but nobody moved.

And then Khalan stepped forward. In that rigid and precise manner that only the military could invent, he marched slowly in front of the first grave, Vladamir's, and stood at attention. Then, almost mechanically, he drew his kukri and cut open his hand, held it over the grave, and let a few drops of blood fall down into the earth. He repeated this for every grave. Then, taking a step back, he offered a slow, methodical salute, turned, and returned to his place.

Each of the Jomsskari followed suit, each of them burying a part of themselves with their fallen comrades. Sergei and Kolskegg joined them, struggling across the field on crutches. The guerillas did as well. When they had finished, they fell in behind Khalan, until the entire force stood at attention to the side of the graves.

Thjostolf was the last to go. He saluted, and when his hand had dropped, he called, "Detail, post!"

Erik, Khalan, Brutus, and Peter had Alnethar rifles with bayonets fixed. They fell out of formation and each stood behind one of the graves. Then, as one, they planted the rifles, stabbing the bayonets into the ground behind the gravestones.

As they returned to their positions, Erik caught a glimpse of the troll watching from a distance. As the gathering began to disperse, and undertakers began to fill in the graves, Ulrich turned and disappeared into the gardens.

*   *   *

There was a feast that night, though somewhat sparser than it had been before. The missionaries had only been able to bring their barley reserves with them, leaving the young barley in the fields behind. They had to ration their food now, until they had a couple of good harvests. Ulrich had told them not to "pillage his gardens," and the elders, together with Gabryl, thought it was best not to press the issue. In any event, they had enough to give thanks for. And while they ate in the open field, as none of the buildings were complete, Erik felt that the village was in a veritable paradise. They had everything they would ever need here, as well as security from the war on the other side of the mountains.

They ate under the stars, by the light of a bonfire, and as they finished their meal, a few of the missionaries picked up fiddles and lutes and started to play dancing music. Erik and Shayna sat together and watched the proceedings for a while, until she insisted that he join her and he found himself in the chaotic, spinning jig that the missionaries enjoyed so much.

It was only in such a faithful community, he thought as he listened to the laughing and foot-stomping around him, that such joy could follow a funeral. It was strange, but in a good way, and Erik decided that he liked it. This little village, in stark contrast to the Appollonian church in Haelhan, seemed to have a spirit of life in it that he had never experienced before. He never wanted to let go.

Death had been averted. Once more, God had spared him and not others. Eternity would have to wait – the "now," once more primary.

Faith as despair. It seemed wrong, but it made sense to him. There was no other way he could make sense of the events of his life, or the lives of others. Certainly there was no other way he could reconcile the deaths around him with the terrible thought of eternity. The sacred geometry of chance – the gamble of who got hit and who didn't – only despair presented itself when he demanded an answer, and all he could do was embrace that despair and rest.

I'll wait.

Now, in my despair, I will believe.

He had been so sure he would die, so sure that his tumultuous fall into the black was coming to a close, that he was unsure of what to do with his survival.

The Absurd persisted, and it demanded more than mere faith. Belief in any old thing would not do. The failure of his reason left him with only one path to take. Every moment, he had to reaffirm it.

Every second, he fought to hold onto it. Constant, active resting. For it was only in rest that he could begin to see, if only in a shadow, the reality of God as more than a trickster. It was in surrender that God would allow him to see the faintest glimmer of hope.

Constant, active resting. The struggle to remain oriented to that person he was beginning to see – the "who" he had searched out for so long. But the "who" was not himself. He was beginning to understand that who he was didn't matter. What mattered was who God was.

Who, where, why, what the hell. *Rest.*

Death had been averted – he had been spared, for the moment. His despairing faith in a "who" he did not understand, extended, for the time being. But there was peace in that – a peace he could not explain to one who did not know it, so foreign and yet so familiar.

There was nothing left to hold onto.

*　　*　　*

The following morning, Erik and Khalan helped Josef build the walls on his new home, and they began forming the roof. Gabryl and Ulrich strolled through the gardens, discussing the coming mission, but Erik tried to put it out of his mind. He didn't want to think about leaving this place, for although he knew the day would come, he wanted nothing more than to settle himself amongst these people. For once he had a place he wanted to stay. Even A'kaylii had been foreign to him, despite the lengths he had gone to for his status in that country.

Kolskegg and Sergei were doing well, but both were still weak. Erik peeled off the bandages and cleaned the wounds again. Thankfully, there was very little evidence of infection. As Erik swabbed the stump with a solution of antibiotics, Kolskegg read his letter.

"My baby boy is here!" he exclaimed. "Helene says he came a few weeks early, but he's healthy and gaining weight quickly."

"Congratulations, man!" Erik shouted to Thjostolf, "Hey, Kolskegg's a father!"

The Jomsskari gathered around and slapped his shoulders. Peter said, "If you hadn't cheated and got that little nick on your leg we'd chuck you in the river to celebrate."

"Yeah, 'little nick,'" said Kolskegg, laughing. "I'll put a 'little nick' between your legs, see how you like that."

"That kind of makes me upset," said Erik, crossing his legs. "Let's talk about something else."

"What name did she give him?" asked Brutus.

Kolskegg scanned the page, and grinned. "Gunnar," he said, "For my father."

Erik sighed melodramatically and shook his head. "Well, it's too bad you're going to die from this wound and never see him. Poor little orphan Gunnar."

"Feck you. In a few weeks I'll be home in bed doing fantastic and unspeakable things with my wife and you guys will be wandering around looking to suck some dragon bollocks."

Thjostolf laughed. "Ah...feck, he's right."

Kolskegg pointed at him. "You see? The trick is to get your leg blown off. I'm a very clever fellow, you know."

They had to deliver him to OP Vladamir to get him back to Feldhall. As they were putting him on the litter, Wendyll came up carrying a long package. "I have something to give you," he said.

Kolskegg stared at him. "You got my rifle?" he said. "Damn, I thought it was lost in the firefight!"

Wendyll nodded. "I thought you would want it," he said with a smile. "And when you get home, if you like, contact my cousin, Aldrydd. He runs a shooting school north of El Commulbalbro, and he'll give you a job if you want one."

Kolskegg nodded. Then a curious look crossed his face, and he looked over to Sergei. Sergei was on crutches, standing a few yards off. He beckoned to him, and Sergei came closer.

"You're a good shot," Kolskegg said, "And I doubt if I'll see you again, in this life at least." He passed his sniper rifle to the boy, who took it and held it with wide eyes. "My parting gift to you," he said, "As thanks for standing at my side."

"Thank you." Sergei had a wide grin spreading across his face that he couldn't seem to contain.

Kolskegg nodded. "Well," he said, a little gruffly, "You've earned it."

They all said their good-byes, and then Brutus and Wendyll carried Kolskegg back through Gob-Heshem. As they disappeared into the gates, Erik looked back at Sergei, and smiled. The boy was beaming, and kept looking over the rifle, running his hands up and down the polished stock.

⚹   *   *

That evening, Shayna found Erik as he sat on a pile of felled trees. She sat down next to him and leaned her head on his shoulder. He looked over at her, and nuzzled her head. "Hey, there."

She smiled at him, and took his hand. They sat in silence for a few moments, and he took in the smell of her hair.

"How's your shoulder?" she asked.

Erik glanced down at the bandage. "It's almost healed," he said. "Turns out, Gabryl's a better doctor than I am."

She kissed his cheek gently. "Did you lose my scarf?" she asked. "I'll give you another."

Erik laughed. "No, I didn't want it to get soiled," he said, reaching into his pocket and pulling it out. It had dried blood on it, and looked faded and ragged on the edges. "It could use a scrubbing, sure, but I like this one."

She took it. "I'll wash it," she offered.

"No, I can do it, it's no big deal."

"I want to wear it," she said. "You don't need it unless you leave, and I want it to smell like me, for when you do have to go."

She lapsed into silence. Over the gates of Gob-Heshem, the sun was setting and the mountainside was alight with golden fire. It looked like a dragon's city, in every way.

"They're different," she said suddenly.

Erik glanced at her. "Who?"

"The boys who came back," she answered. "Asvald, Sacha, Yuri...they've all changed."

Erik nodded. "It changes you."

"How so?"

Erik sighed. "When you've been in combat," he said softly, "There's a psychological switch that you have to flip. You have to stop thinking about killing as...well, as sin. Killing has to become something you're skilled at, the same way you get skilled at carpentry, or cobbling, or any other trade. It's just your job, it's how you make your way in the world. You can always tell a veteran from a greenhorn that way. They change in how they view killing. A greenhorn might look forward to taking another man's life. He might think it'll be some great adventure, or he might think it's a grave moral wrong. But a veteran does it out of practical necessity. And when you flip that switch, the first time you realize that it isn't fun, that it isn't...you know, glorious in any sense..." He fell silent for a moment, and then said, "...You never forget making peace with death."

She looked at him, her eyebrows furrowed. "What happened out there?" she asked.

Erik looked at her and smiled. "I'll tell you someday," he said. "But not today." *How could you explain something like war?*

"What were you like?" she said after a moment. "Before, I mean?"

Erik laughed. "I was a whiny little kid," he said, "Who thought that God had cheated him." He glanced at her, and winked. "You wouldn't have liked me at all."

After a moment, they set off walking and the conversation changed to lighter matters. He picked her another flower, and this time she put it up in her hair directly. As they circled around the village, he had a sudden thought, and stopped.

They were standing on a grassy knoll, a little ways from the outskirts of New Stadfesta, south of the barley fields and overlooking the rest of the village. It was a little secluded, but not by too much. They were still only a few minutes walk to the square. He looked around, and she watched him, an amused smile on her face. "What are you looking at?" she asked.

He grinned. "I was just thinking this would be a great place to build our house."

She looked around, and nodded. "Yes," she said softly. "Yes, it would."

"We'll dig into the hill to lay the foundation," he said, "And put a porch on this side, so we can sit and see the rest of the village. We'll put a window here so we can see the sunset every night, and we'll put our bedroom facing the east, so that every morning we can see the sunrise together."

She smiled, but didn't say anything.

He talked on for a few minutes, pacing back and forth and pointing to where they would put rooms, and she began to laugh. "You're going to build me a house big enough for three families," she said.

"Well," he said, "I don't want you to live in a lousy little shack, now do I?"

She embraced him, and they stood for a few moments, rocking gently. The sun had set completely now, and in the gathering darkness he heard an owl hoot. For a time, he felt as if everything was right in the world, and he thought that he could dare to hope for a quiet life, after the war was over, after he had served his time, when the world no longer needed the skills he had learned in the crucible of war. As he listened to her quiet breathing and felt her heart beating against him, he closed his eyes and prayed that he would see this place again, and that, if there was any way, he could live the last of his days here, with her, in peace.

They returned to the village and Shayna joined her family around the bonfire. Erik spotted Ulrich again. The troll had been absent for the most part, but every so often he would appear and watch the missionaries with his arms folded, alone in the darkness. Feeling bold, Erik walked over to him and stood beside him, taking in the view.

"You've found yourself a lovely one," the troll observed.

"Yes, I have."

Ulrich's eyes were as dark as ever, but Erik thought he saw a glint in them. What it was, he could not tell.

"How long before we move out?" he asked.

"A week, perhaps, or a month. I cannot say." The troll was uncharacteristically polite, and Erik thought he caught of hint of preoccupation in his voice.

"Why so long? Not that I'm complaining," he added.

Ulrich glanced at him. "You saw the egg." It was a statement.

"Yes, I did."

"The flame is lit. Soon the young one will come into the world, and I must ensure its safe arrival. There are a great many things to consider, and not one of them may be dealt with quickly."

Erik glanced at him. For a moment, he was unsure if he should ask, but curiosity got the better of him. "Why do you care about the egg so much?"

Ulrich turned towards him, and smiled politely, but coldly. "Good night, doctor." And he stalked off into the night.

Erik stood in the darkness for a few minutes, then shrugged, and went back to the fire. They were all there, his brothers the Jomsskari, as well as the missionaries. Sisel stuck her tongue out at him, but this time she smiled afterwards.

Shayna sat beside him, entwining her fingers in his, and they sat listening to the banter around them. Soon her head was resting on him, and she fell asleep. He put his cloak around her, and kissed her sleeping nose. Khalan came over and handed him a mug of ale, and they chatted in low voices. Khalan didn't bring up his father, and Erik didn't force the topic on him. Whatever the cause, Khalan was more reserved now than he had been in the past. Before long, they lapsed into a friendly silence.

As they watched the flames, talking together, sharing mugs of ale, Erik looked at each of their faces. This would not last. Whenever the time came, he would have to leave this paradise. They would return to the war, to find this demon-dragon. The time would come that all of this would be left behind, and he would have to leave Heaven and return to Hell.

But until that time, until duty called him away, he could not have been happier.

ABOUT THE AUTHOR

Ike Barnett is a veteran of the Global War on Terror and served over a decade in law enforcement. He lives in Tennessee with his wife.

www.ingramcontent.com/pod-product-compliance
Lightning Source LLC
Chambersburg PA
CBHW022203030726
47494CB00019B/119